T0246230

BEGGAR'S SKY

BOOKS by WIL McCARTHY

Antediluvian

Rich Man's Sky Series
Rich Man's Sky
Poor Man's Sky
Beggar's Sky

The Queendom of Sol Series
The Collapsium
The Wellstone
Lost in Transmission
To Crush the Moon

The Waister Series
Aggressor Six
The Fall of Sirius

Flies from the Amber
Murder in the Solid State
Bloom
Once Upon a Galaxy

BEGGAR'S SKY

WIL McCARTHY

A Baen Books Original

Baen Publishing Enterprises
P.O. Box 1403
Riverdale, NY 10471
www.baen.com

ISBN: 978-1-9821-9318-8

Cover art by Dave Seeley

First printing, February 2024

Distributed by Simon & Schuster
1230 Avenue of the Americas
New York, NY 10020

Library of Congress Cataloging-in-Publication Data

Names: McCarthy, Wil, author.
Title: Beggar's sky / Wil McCarthy.
Description: Riverdale, NY : Baen Publishing Enterprises, 2024. | Series: Rich Man's Sky ; 3
Identifiers: LCCN 2023043260 (print) | LCCN 2023043261 (ebook) | ISBN 9781982193188 (hardcover) | ISBN 9781625799470 (ebook)
Subjects: LCGFT: Science fiction. | Novels.
Classification: LCC PS3563.C337338 B44 2024 (print) | LCC PS3563.C337338 (ebook) | DDC 813/.54—dc23/eng/20231005
LC record available at https://lccn.loc.gov/2023043260
LC ebook record available at https://lccn.loc.gov/2023043261

Printed in the United States of America

10 9 8 7 6 5 4 3 2 1

This book is dedicated to
the Northern Colorado Writers' Workshop,
an institution still going strong
at the start of its sixth decade.

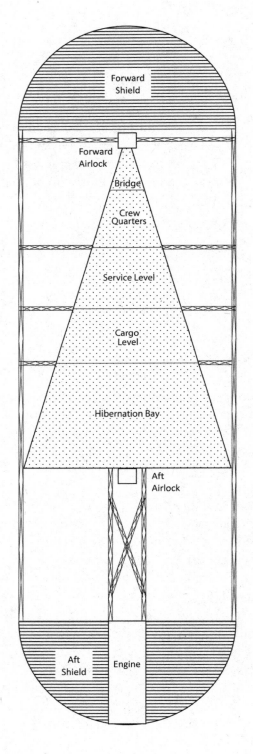

Schematic View of
I.R.V. *Intercession*

Forward
Shield

Forward
Airlock

Bridge

Crew
Quarters

Service Level

Cargo
Level

Hibernation Bay

Aft
Airlock

Aft
Shield

Engine

1.1
06 January 2059

✧

Post-Encounter Deposition
Brother Michael Jablonski
Prior, St. Joseph of Cupertion's
Monastery, Luna

What I'm going to tell you isn't true. We met the Beings, yes, all one hundred of us, and convened wordlessly in a state of psychedelic intoxication—the only way they seem to be able to reach us. That much is true and agreed-upon fact. The rest? Lies.

I could say, for example, that the Beings and I conversed in English, with occasional lapses into my childhood Quebecois French, for certain terms best expressed that way. I could say that both I and the Beings were calm—stately, even—as befit humankind's first encounter with an alien species, and that we took turns asking and answering all the important questions you'd expect at such a time.

Absolutely none of that would be true.

I could say the experience was disorienting, in the sense of there being no orientations whatsoever—no up, no down, nor a spacetime *per se* in which they might occur, nor (at times) even a coherent "me" there to inhabit them. I could say the experience was frightening, in the sense that I was bombarded with incoherent stimuli from which I would have liked to escape, but could not. I could tell you the experience was not an "experience" at all, in the sense of something that actually happened. Memories are episodic, with beginnings and middles and ends, with durations and narrative threads. I could tell you my experience of the Beings was not like that at all.

And again I would be lying, although this perhaps gets closer to the truth.

I could tell you the Beings were round, meter-high gremlins covered in kaleidoscopic patterns of visual static, against a backdrop of the same visual static. There were thousands of them, smothering their bodies against me, positively bursting with a bright, raucous joy. I could say they rifled through the events of my life as through a pack of cards, without asking, and that they bade me pull cards from their own packs. Or perhaps they *compelled* me to it, although the cards were simply made of the same flickering colors as everything else.

Or perhaps like this: On a moonless night, I stood on the deck of a storm-tossed ship, reading messages that flashed briefly on the screen of a rollup phone, while the rain hammered bathtubs down upon me. The messages perhaps made perfect sense, but I could only catch them in glimpses, while I grabbed at railings and wiped the water—both salt and fresh—from my eyes, and gasped for breath, and loudly begged for a hatch to open that might admit me to warmer, brighter spaces belowdecks.

And each of these details would be an utter fabrication. Psychedelic experiences are difficult to verbalize precisely because they touch the preverbal and averbal portions of ourselves, too deep to fathom and too raw to describe. It might be more accurate to say I *was* the ocean, or the storm, and so were they. But that wouldn't make sense to you, ah?

I must of course say something, so perhaps let's start with more agreed-upon facts:

The starship in which we traveled was called *Intercession*, although the mission itself is called Summit—a triple entendre. It means first an apex—the highest point one can climb on a particular hill. Having left the Sun's gravitational influence altogether, *Intercession* was, for most of its journey, indisputably the highest point any human had ever climbed to. Second, a meeting—especially an organized diplomatic one. Since the Beings had issued a direct invitation, such a term surely applies. Third, a verb: to meet or to climb. A summit is both a thing achieved and the act of achieving it.

As a verb, "summit" also implies a measure of aspiration. One hopes to summit, and summit well, so perhaps that's another layer of meaning in the name. I have not questioned the trillionaire Igbal Renz about his choice.

The Encounter happened 1,700 Astronomical Units away from the Sun—0.05 light-years, or 1.2 percent of the way to Proxima Centauri, or 1,700 times the distance between the Earth and Sun. It happened in an inflatable polymer torus extended from the circumference of the ship for that purpose. The Encounter Bubble is similar, I'm told, to the spherical gymnasium at the Marriott Stars in Low Earth Orbit, although I've not the pleasure of any firsthand knowledge thereof. "The dark between the stars," the Beings had called their proposed meeting place, and so we went out and met them there.

These corroborated bullet points are objective and not in dispute, and for at least this reason I'm obliged (by you: the corporation to whom I'm under contract, by the Church to which I owe my allegiance, by the God who created me, and by my own vanity) to describe, as best I can, what the Beings told me, and ninety-nine other human beings, on that November morning in the Oort cloud.

It should by now be well established that the account is a lie, but I shall hope it true in the sense that a song is true, if it communicates something to someone about the experience of being alive.

2.1
01 February 2057

✧

Clementine Cislunar Fuel Depot
Earth-Moon Lagrange Point 1
Cislunar Space

"It's the purple star," the new astronomer said. "Just above Alpha Centauri."

"I know where it is," said the trillionaire Grigory Magnusevich Orlov.

Glowering was something Orlov did often and well, and he did it now, because this new hire, this twenty-five-year-old PhD, was relentlessly cheerful and encouraging, and Orlov found it condescending. And since Orlov was the owner of this space station, and the multinational energy company that controlled it, he was not a man to whom one could safely condescend.

Orlov Petrochemical ran oil refineries and fusion energy plants around the world. Orlov Petrochemical controlled twenty-four percent of the world's electricity supply. Orlov Petrochemical was also the premier asteroid mining company, and this facility—Clementine Cislunar Fuel Depot—supplied volatiles like oxygen and hydrogen and ammonia and cyanogen, to the Moon and to low Earth orbit, and every point in between.

But Orlov's gatherbots were venturing farther from Earth these days, for larger, richer prizes, and so he needed an astronomer. Another mouth to feed, another pension to pay out, if this man should survive to the end of his career.

"On these recordings, I see the black space between it and the star shrinking, day by day," the astronomer said, making a motion as if pinching the two dots on the screen. "Soon, the two will merge into a single point!"

"Yes," Orlov said.

But why? That bastard, Igbal Renz, had built himself a starship. A starship! And it was headed toward Proxima Centauri, except not really. It was only a two-year mission—not nearly long enough to reach the star. Or anything else. It was a trip to empty space.

Orlov and the astronomer were in the station's new astronomy module, which had been shipped up from Earth and still smelled of metal and fresh polymer. The lighting was dim, as Orlov preferred it, but virtually every surface was covered in video screens, showing views from all the telescopes. Clementine was balanced permanently at the EML1 Lagrange point, between the Earth and Moon. Clementine had the high ground, and a good vantage point for seeing what everyone else was up to.

Because Orlov was paranoid, Clementine had high-powered, negative-refraction telescopes pointed at every object of interest: one for each settlement visible at the Lunar north and south poles. One for Igbal Renz's ESL1 Shade Station. One for the asteroid 101955 Bennu, where Orlov's gatherbots would soon be landing. One for the Earth itself—trackable to any of the stations in low Earth orbit. One for H.S.F. *Concordia*, the cycler transport, currently en route back from Mars. And now, one for this insane starship of Renz Ventures.

"It's called *Intercession*," the astronomer said. "I don't know why, or what it means."

"I know what it's called," Orlov said, in a tone that was briefly more weary than menacing. "Can you get me a closer view than what's recorded here?"

"No, sir. Even with the fancy optics, at this point it's just a single bright pixel."

"And you're certain it's on a direct course toward the Alpha Centauri system?"

"Yes, sir. Specifically, toward Proxima, the closest of the three."

Three! Yes, people spoke of Alpha Centauri as though it were a star—the closest star, the brightest in the sky. But it was three! And that bastard Renz was headed there. Only not really.

"It can't get there," Orlov said.

"No, sir. At their present acceleration, on a two-year, straight-line out-and-back mission, they'll barely reach the inner edge of the Oort cloud. That's a small fraction of the distance to Proxima, although, you understand, still very far from here."

Orlov's growl was calculated to intimidate, and he used it now. "What's out there? An ice planet, hiding in the dark?"

"Not that anyone's ever heard of," the astronomer said. He didn't sound intimidated.

"And what would they want with one, anyway?" Orlov demanded. "That ship cost trillions of dollars. What could be worth all that? Not ice. Something else."

The astronomer grinned and shrugged. "Officially, they're just testing the ship. It's a shakedown cruise."

Orlov growled again, and said, "Remind me of your name."

"Boris, sir."

"Well, Boris, there are a hundred frozen people on that ship." He stuck his rollup under the astronomer's nose, showing him a stolen schematic of *Intercession*. He jabbed his finger at the screen and said, "Here. This space, right here. Hibernation Bay. I don't know who they are, or how they were selected, or what they are meant to do out there. And I have tried very hard to find out."

"I've heard some crazy rumors," the astronomer admitted.

As had Orlov. As had everyone.

"Hmm. Renz Ventures has always been the subject of crazy rumors. Many rumors. Your opinion?"

"There's nothing to indicate another vessel out there."

"Another vessel," Orlov said. "An alien vessel. That's what you're talking about, yes? Don't be coy with me. Do you think it's possible?"

Now, finally, the astronomer seemed nervous. "Anything is possible, sir, but you see the purple dot, yes? The engine flare of *Intercession*, very bright. Bright enough to see from all the way back here. Brighter than the whole Centauri system! That's how much energy it takes to move a starship, sir. No one has observed anything like that in the Oort cloud. And they would have to, if something were out there."

"Unless it has some different form of propulsion," Orlov said. "Or the ship has been there a long time. A derelict, perhaps, whose technology could fall into the hands of our enemies. That would be bad, yes?"

The astronomer was strapped to a seat, to keep him from floating away. Orlov had the tip of one shoe lightly hooked on a grab bar, because he'd lived weightless for many years now, and knew how to control his body. Presently, he put a hand on the astronomer's shoulder and squeezed gently. Orlov came from a long line of coal miners and oil men, and he was so hopped up on zero-gee adaptation drugs that he was stronger than he'd been when he left Earth. He could cause grave injury if he wanted to. To his credit, the astronomer finally seemed to sense this.

"Anything is possible, sir."

"Anything. Hmm. Now watch. This was recorded yesterday."

The violet star that was *Intercession* seemed to flicker on its little video display. Then the brighter dot of Alpha Centauri began to flicker as well, along with some of the other stars around it. A ripple of distortion, moving across the screen.

"Ah, there! You see that?" Orlov said, pointing. "You see it?"

"Yes," the astronomer said, sounding intrigued.

"Stealth ship," Orlov said, "passing in front of the stars. Almost invisible. You see it?"

"I do, sir."

Orlov was not a man who frightened easily. Some might say he was not a man who could be frightened at all, but they'd be wrong. At the sight of that distortion on the screen, even though it was only a recording, he felt his heart beating faster. He felt a little tickle from the sweat glands on his forehead. Fear, yes, even Grigory Orlov.

"How far away?" he demanded. "This bastard's been hanging around, lurking. By my station! That's not space aliens, either; there are men in that thing. Spies! Or murderers, or thieves. Men who mean us harm, Boris. I need you to track it for me."

"Nothing's showing up on radar," the astronomer said.

Orlov pushed him by the shoulder, not gently. "I know! Nothing! Is showing up! On radar! It's a fucking stealth ship, you moron. I need you to track it. There have been sightings of these things throughout cislunar space, and now here. Now here! Do you understand me? Am I stuttering?"

Alarmed, now: "No, sir. I understand, sir."

Orlov could see that young Boris, here, was going to have to toughen up if he wanted to survive in a place like Clementine. Well, that was young Boris's problem.

"And find out what Igbal Renz is doing on that fucking starship," he said. "That's your job, Boris, to figure things out for me."

Nervously: "How, sir?"

Another squeeze of the shoulder. "That is something I very much hope *you* can tell *me*, Boris. If I had all the answers, where would that leave you?"

"I, uh, don't know, sir," the astronomer said. Then seeming to realize that was the exact wrong thing to say, he quickly added: "I'll be useful, sir. I'll figure it out."

"Yes," Orlov said, now in his friendliest tone. Which, he'd been told, was not very friendly at all. "Yes, I'm sure you will. This is a rough place, Boris, but useful men are respected."

"I . . . don't doubt it, sir."

The shimmer on the video screen was gone, leaving only the purple dot, and the star system it was heading toward. The fear would take longer to fade.

"I don't like unanswered ques—"

The rollup phone in Orlov's hand chimed out a "message received" tone, quite loud in the confines of the astronomy module. Which was strange, because almost no one had Orlov's SpaceNet phone number. Why would they need to? Technical and business matters would be routed through Operations, and whoever was on duty there would page Orlov if they felt it important enough. To the extent that the rollup was a telephone at all, it was reserved for personal matters.

Interesting.

On the screen's notification bar, the sender ID said ORLOV, SALLY.

Seeing Orlov's reaction, Boris the astronomer said, "Good, uh, good news, sir? I hope?"

"A message from my daughter," Orlov said. He let go of the astronomer's shoulder.

"Sounds like good news," Boris said, recovering a bit of his earlier enthusiasm.

"I doubt that very much," Orlov said.

With a flick of the wrist, he snapped the rollup closed and then jammed it in his pocket. "Well, it has been very nice to meet you, Boris. We'll have much to discuss, you and I. Or rather, I hope we will."

"We very definitely will," Boris said, and Orlov was pleased by the respectful—even fearful—way Boris had said it. Yes, good. Orlov needed people who felt personally threatened by these mysteries around him.

3.1
03 February 2057
✧
I.R.V. *Intercession*
Extra-Kuiper Space
208 A.U. from Earth

"How's that engine doing?" Igbal asked.

"Fine," Sandy said. She was a woman of few words.

"That's all? Just fine?"

She looked up from her workstation. The two of them were alone on the bridge of the starship *Intercession*, currently blasting its way out of the solar system. Because they were at the front of the ship, Igbal and Sandy were the absolute farthest from Earth that anyone had ever been, and every second that passed carried them another five thousand kilometers farther out! The six other crew members, down below in the body of the ship, were ten or twenty or thirty meters farther behind in the journey, but Igbal and Sandy—perched at the top of a tower balanced on a beam of gamma rays—were setting record after record.

And at the end of the journey: the Beings. Intelligences of some kind, who had (sort of) made contact with ESL1 Shade Station, back in cislunar space. Calling humanity out for a meeting! How cool was that?

But Sandy Lincoln didn't look excited by any of that. She looked annoyed.

"I monitor thirty different variables," she said. "All nominal."

Igbal knew: she looked annoyed because she'd designed the engine, and supervised its construction, so if she said it was fine, then

11

it was fine. Also because she was a theoretical physicist, and this kind of monitoring task was very clearly beneath her—grad student work at best, or maybe even AI work. Could she ask Ptolemy—the crew concierge module—to do it for her, and report it to Igbal for her? Certainly.

And also because the engine was built around a two-meter sphere of antilithium, and if anything went seriously wrong, the ship and all hands aboard her would be converted to interstellar plasma before the numbers on Sandy's screen even updated.

"Okay," he said, not really satisfied, but taking her at her word.

"Ptolemy," he said then, to the walls, "bring the lights up a notch."

"Affirmative," said the walls, in a soft, slow, calmly genderless voice. "Throughout the ship?"

"No, just here on the bridge."

As requested, the rows of lights running vertically along the port and starboard bulkheads brightened slightly, casting a diffuse yellow-white glow that seemed a bit less like candlelight. It didn't seem to do much for Sandy's mood.

Igbal and Sandy had a history, romantically, but that never seemed to bother her. Igbal was the richest human being who had ever lived, anywhere at any time, but that didn't seem to bother her either. She was kind of a scatterbrained person, and that enormous power imbalance had never really seemed to register for her at all. Hell, the antimatter drive core alone was worth more than the GDP of any country on Earth, and she considered it hers. Which, for practical purposes, it was.

No, what clearly bugged her was being dragged up to the bridge for no reason, to read numbers off a screen that she could have forwarded straight to her glasses from the comfort of the common room. The bridge was, in fact, as far from the engine as it was possible to get, without putting on a spacesuit. And it was cramped in here, and windowless. There weren't even pretend, video windows, because there was nothing out there to see, and anyway you didn't steer a starship that way. Really, you didn't steer it at all.

But this was where the sensors were hardlinked, not just from the engine, but from every point on the ship and shield. From the communications array, the hibernation bay, the life support hub. It was the literal nerve center of the ship, and Igbal insisted that every non-frozen crew member climb the ladder up here once per day to give him a report. If nothing else, it gave them something to do. It gave *him* something to do. But also, yeah, a sense of how the ship was performing.

"Can I go?" Sandy asked.

"You have somewhere to be?" Igbal said back to her, with some amusement, because it was a small ship, at least on the inside, and there were only eight people awake.

"No," she said, and turned to study the schematic of the ship on the display screen to her left. In the one-tenth gee of the drive's acceleration, her hair was somehow fuller and frizzier than it had ever been in freefall.

Her hand traced the stations of the ship: drive nozzle, drive housing, aft particle shield, safety struts, hibernation bay, cargo deck, service deck, crew quarters, bridge, forward particle shield.

This was Igbal's ship, the first crewed interstellar vehicle ever built. By any sensible measure, the Interstellar Research Vessel (I.R.V.) *Intercession* was decades or even centuries ahead of its time. Manifesting this had taken the wealth equivalent of millions of human lifetimes, and there was no way a government, or even a publicly traded corporation, was ever going to build a thing like that, for a mission like this. No, for this you needed someone rich enough to fund it out of his own pocket, and bloody-minded enough not to care what else could have been done with those resources.

For this, you needed Igbal Renz. *His* nation-sized solar collector, *his* particle accelerator, *his* Nobel-prize-nominated recipe for flipping matter into antimatter in macroscopic quantities. His absolute unwillingness to be told it couldn't be done.

"I'm having second thoughts," Sandy said, with a hesitancy that was wholly uncharacteristic.

"We all are," he agreed. They were three months into a two-year trip to nowhere, and even though all eight crew members were experienced astronauts who had lived and worked on various space stations, this was . . . different. "But there's no aborting, is there?"

"No," she said.

If they turned the ship around right now, it would take another three months to decelerate to zero velocity, and three more to accelerate back toward the Sun, and then three more to stop again in the vicinity of cislunar space, where an ion tug could come and tow them the rest of the way back. So even if they gave up right now, right this very second, they'd still be gone for a whole year, without anything to show for it. Two trillion dollars down the drain, and the Beings still out there waiting.

"Do you need a hug?" he asked, without irony. This was hard. They knew it was going to be hard, but knowing it and living it were two different things. And Sandy was good people.

"No," she said. Then: "Ptolemy, please display live video from the lip of the engine bell. Aft-facing."

"Affirmative," said Ptolemy.

A blank part of the control panel lit up with a rectangular display screen. The image, heavily processed, showed the Sun, with purple-white plasma streaking toward it. The Sun was just a bright star, now, no brighter than Venus on a summer evening in the mountains of West Virginia. The plasma was leakage from the ion thrusters that controlled the engine, and to the naked eye it would have been brighter than a welding arc, lit up by the tiny fraction of the annihilation energy that was released as visible light.

Sandy said, "Ptolemy, please display live video from inside the combustion chamber."

"Affirmative."

The order was ambiguous; Ptolemy might have chosen to replace the existing display with the newly requested one, or to place the two of them side by side. For reasons known only to itself, it chose the latter, and a new display appeared on the control panel, showing purple-white hellfire around a sphere of dark gray.

"Now give me audio."

And here, Ptolemy could have gone a lot of different ways. It could have ignored the order as improperly formatted, and directed at nobody. It could have translated the output of the vibration sensors literally, which would have yielded nothing audible to human ears. It could have compressed the spectrum of vibrations and emitted a deafening scream of white noise. Instead, it chose to step the whole thing down to a low rumble, punctuated by high, quiet pinging noises as the ion emitters released wave after wave of lithium-deuteride plasma at $0.5c$, fifty percent of lightspeed. It was an impressive sound.

"The flutter drive is working exactly like the models said it would, down to the third decimal place," Sandy said. And now, she didn't sound annoyed. If anything, she sounded tired. "That's good, right?"

"Yep," Igbal agreed. And it really was. The flutter drive—the engine around which *Intercession* was built—had gone from cockamamie hypothesis to working starship in a little under five years, because Igbal was able to find people like Sandy and set them up with basically unlimited resources. That, and because he had five and a half tons of antimatter to throw at the problem. The Manhattan Project was nothing compared to *Intercession*! Thanks to nanometer-level manufacturing fed by thousands of hours of quantum computing time, the drive apparatus was close to one hundred percent efficient at converting Lambertian gamma rays into a coherent, unidirectional exhaust beam. It was a mirror, basically, made of fast-moving plasma shockwaves. As little bits of antimatter flashed into pure energy (mostly 100 MeV gamma rays), the fluttering plasma kicked it all backward, out the exhaust nozzle, toward the tiny bright dot of the Solar System.

"It's brilliant, Sandy. Do I not say that enough?"

"You do," she acknowledged, and then went back to looking at the ship's schematic.

Man, she was really struggling. Which was weird, because Sandy had lived for years at ESL1 Shade Station, a million miles from Earth, and it never seemed to rattle her. She took shore leave, like, every other year, but she never seemed to particularly need it. Igbal had never seen her like this, and as owner and captain of the ship, he had better think of something he could do about it.

"How's your angular momentum theory coming along?" he tried. Ever since the Mach-Fearn drive prototype had failed, by spinning instead of accelerating in a straight line, she'd been trying to figure out why. Not in any sort of urgent way, it seemed to him, but in her spare time.

"Badly," she said. "I underestimated the amount of computing power I was going to need, and we simply don't have it here on the ship."

"Hmm." He scratched his jaw with a thumbnail, feeling the coarse bristles there. *Intercession* was equipped with computers that would have blown the socks off of anything available twenty years ago. But if Sandy said it wasn't enough, it wasn't enough. "Can you write the software here, and download it to the mainframe back at ESL1?"

"No. Our bandwidth is down to twenty-three kilobits per second. That's fine for writing memos, but it won't even carry a voice. As far as any kind of serious information processing, we're marooned."

"Ah. Shit. Sorry."

Back in his youth, Igbal had used acoustic coupler modems with a higher bit rate than that. And the bandwidth dropped off with the square of the distance, so that number—bad as it was—was going to get a whole lot worse as they drew farther and farther from Earth. Truthfully, he'd been spending a great deal of his time sending and receiving memos, trying to run his company from afar, but even that was going to get more difficult.

"Not your fault," Sandy said. "But it's going to be a long time before I can make any progress, and meanwhile I'm just sipping mojitos in a damn hammock."

He laughed. "There are worse things."

"Yeah. I know. Don't worry, I'll figure out something I can do."

"Attagirl. Creativity springs from limitations."

She glowered at that, clearly unamused.

The problem was, she had a legitimate beef. The plan was for the ship to accelerate for six months in the direction of Alpha Centauri and then flip, decelerate, and stop at a distance of 0.05 light-years from the Sun. And then return along the same trajectory. This mission profile was consistent with fragmentary instructions received from the Beings—not guaranteed to work by any means, but it's what they'd been able to put together on short notice. Hopefully it was far enough into "the dark between the stars" that the Beings would be able to talk to them.

Intercession carried ninety-two frozen passengers in its hibernation bay—all experts of various kinds—but a few people still had to be awake during the journey, in case something broke. Good, smart, competent people, whose morale tended to flag if there was nothing going on.

Oh, sure, the ship had passed the orbit of Mars on the fifth day of the Summit mission. Days seven through ten they sweated their way through the asteroid belt, fearful of hitting something. On day thirteen they passed the orbit of Jupiter, and then for a while it was a planet every week: Saturn, Uranus, Neptune, and then the Kuiper Belt, which took nine whole days to get through, sweating again. Not that they ventured anywhere close to any known objects; the course and timing of their journey were selected to carry them through the emptiest possible corridor of space. But they were already going much faster than any human had ever gone; nearly three percent of the speed of light! There were *particle accelerators* that couldn't achieve that kind of speed. And they were adding another 86 KPS— the speed of a really fast comet!—every single day. At that kind of impact speed, even a gram of stray matter could vaporize the ship.

Which was exciting, right?

But they were thirty degrees below the plane of the ecliptic, where matter was scarce, and once the Kuiper Belt was behind them, nothing happened for a long time. A few days ago they had passed the solar bow shock, and then yesterday they crossed the heliopause, entering the so-called interstellar medium. But there was nothing dramatic about that—just a passage from hard vacuum to slightly different hard vacuum, with the Sun already just a bright dot behind them.

So there was really, really nothing going on. Nothing to look at, nothing to do. The Solar System was just too absurdly huge to traverse in any sort of reasonable time. Even at this ludicrous velocity, they were still well short of the Oort cloud, whose inner edge they wouldn't reach until the tenth month of the journey, when they were ass-forward and decelerating. The *outer* edge of the Oort cloud was something they wouldn't reach at all, because that would have required a journey of *eighty years*, and would have taken them fully seventy percent of the way to Proxima Centauri. That's how goddamn big the Solar System actually was.

So yes, people were antsy. Igbal himself was antsy—an emotion so unfamiliar to him that he almost didn't know it when he started feeling it. He'd intended the daily status reports as an antidote for this; a chance for each crew member to brain in on their assigned duties. But the look on Sandy's face told him everything he needed to know about how that was going. He realized, also, that the skill set of leading a multinational (indeed, multi-planetary) corporation did not automatically translate to being the captain of a starship on the very outer fringes of the solar system. Who knew?

"Well, shit," he said. "We're going to need a new plan. Ptolemy, assemble the crew in the wardroom, please."

4.1
03 February 2057

✧

ESL1 Shade Station
Earth-Sun Lagrange Point 1
Extracislunar Space

Alice Kyeong wasn't built for this shit.

Yuehai Ming, a physicist floating in front of Alice in the zero gravity of ESL1 Shade Station, had just said to Alice, "The spray-on bicolloidal layer has improved the conversion efficiency of the Shade to almost twenty-five percent, without raising any eyebrows down on Earth."

And Alice's first impulse was to say, "Why are you telling me this?" Except of course she couldn't say that, because—through sheer bad luck—while Igbal Renz was off gallivanting around interstellar space, she was Interim Station Commander of ESL1, and Vice President of Space Operations for Renz Ventures, LLC. So it was her job, God help her, to listen to reports like this and give some kind of response.

"That's fine," she told Yuehai. "Keep up the good work."

The two of them were floating in the station's newest module, an office and quarters specially built for Alice, in her new capacity as Igbal's goddamn replacement. Not running the whole company, thank you very much, but running the forty-five-person space station that sat at its apex and conducted its highest-value operations.

"I don't trust anyone else," Igbal had told her.

"You trust me?" Alice had asked, somewhat incredulously.

Because she'd been a combat medic just five years earlier, and had since that time done her best to avoid any sort of administrative work, and focus instead on the safety of her astronauts and the security of the station as a whole.

"Not really," Igbal had said. "But you're the only one up here with any sense." An honest reply, to which Alice couldn't say much. Because it was true: this place was full of PhDs and flyboys, a few mechanics and construction workers of limited imagination.

"You should hire better people," Alice told him.

"You should," he said. "You should have been doing that for me."

Well, shit. He had her there.

"At the same time," Yuehai continued, "Igbal's latest proton cascade sequence has improved the efficiency of antimatter production tenfold over what it was this time last year. That's a hundredfold increase over where we started, and a thousand times better than the rest of the world combined."

And that did catch Alice's attention.

One thing Yuehai didn't seem to realize was that Alice was the conduit by which eyebrows on Earth got raised. Or one of the conduits, anyway. She didn't seem to realize that Alice was a spy.

And this read directly on Igbal's "common sense" issue, because it wasn't exactly a well-kept secret. Alice had been pulled from the elite ranks of the Air Force Pararescuemen, inserted here as a covert operative, and promoted once she'd secured Igbal's surrender. She'd been forcibly installed into the Renz Ventures hierarchy, yes, but she was still technically a major in the U.S. Air Force, and for years she had reported directly to the President of the United States. If Yuehai didn't know that, then Yuehai was not paying attention.

All that stuff had happened, of course, because the Shade was blocking 0.1 percent of the sunlight reaching Earth, and thus meaningfully affecting the climate. (Mainly for the better, but still.) Because the Shade generated more electricity than the entire United States, and that was a lot of (literal) power for one man to control. And yeah, because Igbal had been sitting on a kilogram of antimatter with zero security, or rather, only the security of sitting way out at Earth-Sun Lagrange Point 1, which was 1.2 million kilometers beyond the orbit of the Moon.

Which, in this day and age, was not much protection at all. Not from serious actors. Not from nation-states, or the machinations of oligarchs and their multi-trillion-dollar corporations. Maybe not even from the Cartels, who stubbornly refused to die, despite being driven out of one country after another. The Cartels, who had hundreds of billions of dollars stashed where no one had ever been able to find it, and who kept managing to get their hands on hardware they had no business owning.

"I want you to roll back those changes," Alice said to Yuehai.

Yuehai looked confused at that. "It's actually drawing less power," she said, "and our containment facility upgrades are—" To her credit, Yuehai clearly grasped she was not landing a winning argument. She paused for a moment, made a kind of announcey gesture with her hands, and said, "With all the power and cleverness at our disposal, it took us almost six years to make enough fuel for the Summit mission. If we want—"

"Roll it back," Alice said. "That's an order."

Yuehai struggled visibly with that, trying to make sense of it.

"Igbal's not going to like it," she said finally.

"Let me worry about that," Alice said, in her best don't-fuck-with-me tone. Then, because she didn't want to sound like more of an asshole than absolutely necessary, she added, "There are a lot of factors in play, Yuehai. Your people have done excellent work, but right now we're walking five different tightropes, and we need to move very, very cautiously. This is why Igbal put me in charge, to worry about stuff like this. Someday, I promise, we'll have more wiggle room, but right now I need you to trust me."

And that seemed to work, because everyone knew Alice had saved the station—and probably the Shade as well—from certain destruction on at least one occasion. Alice was prickly by nature, but in all the years they'd worked together, she had never given Yuehai, or anyone else, reason to doubt her commitment to her teammates.

"Okay," Yuehai said, the tension going out of her.

"Let's have a beer later," Alice said. "Or not," she added quickly, seeing the look on Yuehai's face. Then, more gently, "Look, these are dangerous times. We've got to play smart."

"Okay, I understand," Yuehai said, nodding thoughtfully. "Thank you. I won't take more of your time."

As Yuehai was exiting the hatchway, Malagrite Aagasen—Maag

to her friends—came in behind her. Because God forbid Alice should get a moment to herself.

"Tell me some good news," Alice said.

"We're . . . on schedule," Maag said, in a caution-laden tone that suggested she had bad news to communicate, and feared Alice's temper.

Well, shit. Alice and Maag were close enough that they'd shared a boyfriend for a while—sometimes simultaneously. If even she was tiptoeing around, then Alice had clearly better find a softer side. This was not a military situation—at least, not yet—and these people had no other leader.

For years, Igbal had guided ESL1 Shade Station by enthusiasm alone. He was not above bullying people to get what he wanted, and at times he could be prickly and petulant as well. But he'd also infused the station—really, the whole of Renz Ventures, across three continents and more—with an infectious, almost childlike energy for which Alice had no equivalent.

"What is it?" Alice asked Maag, as gently as her nature permitted.

"The coupling hubs don't have their full range of motion. They're a degree off."

"Meaning what?"

"The safety margins are going to be tight. When we start spinning the ring, we're just not going to be able to absorb a lot of error."

"Oh," Alice said. "What do we do about that?"

"Well, either we remake all sixteen couplers, which would cost us two weeks, or we spin the station up a lot more slowly. Which will also cost us two weeks."

"How does that translate to 'on schedule'?" Alice complained. Then, more practically: "On what date will we have a functioning spin-gee habitat?"

"Two months from now. April sixth, to be exact."

"Okay," Alice said, because what else was she supposed to say?

In theory, living in zero gravity wasn't melting their bones. Everyone here took their bone pills and their muscle pills and their heart pills and their radiation pills, and most of the crew were pretty diligent about their daily exercise as well. But even on Earth, "fitness in a pill" had never really worked as well as actual fitness, and here in space the problems were multiplied. If they could simulate Mars gravity, or even Lunar gravity, they'd all have a much better chance of returning to Earth someday without a limp.

They had looked at simply disassembling the three-dimensional jumble of ESL1 Shade Station and putting the modules back together in a big, spinning ring, but there were two problems with that. First of all, it would idle production, and research, and even life support for an indeterminate period of at least several weeks. Unacceptable.

Second of all, the straight lines of the existing modules would mean that dust and other objects would roll toward the joints where the modules connected. The only gravitationally "flat" surface in a spinning habitat—the only surface where a ball could sit without rolling away—was actually a curved one. So they had built all-new modules, and an interface to join the spinning part of the station with the old, jumbled, non-spinning part.

The only thing holding them back now were the humble coupling hubs that would link the curved modules together in a double ring. Simple, right?

"Two months is not terrible," Alice said, "although we're going to have to delay our next crew transfer. That's, what, five new people with nowhere to sleep?"

"I'm a chemist," Maag reminded her. "I'm not in charge of crew transfers."

It was a cheap shot, and drew a glare from Alice, who *was* in charge of crew transfers. But "job description" was a distinction that simply didn't apply at ESL1 anymore, if it even ever had.

"You are now," Alice said. Which drew a glare from Maag. They held it, eye to eye, for maybe four seconds before Maag cracked a smile, and then they were both laughing.

Alice's next appointment was with the External Security team: a pilot, an astronaut, and a machinist here in the office with her, and a video link to a room full of people on Earth. Absolutely no one was laughing.

"Talk to me about the stealth ships," she said.

No longer an urban myth, the stealth ships had been officially detected loitering near Transit Point Station, in low Earth orbit. Which had made a lot of astronauts sound a lot less crazy. Variously described as lenses, mirrors, distortions, haze, or rainbows, the stealth ships could be—just barely—detected by human eyeballs as they passed in front of other things. And now, officially, they could be detected by entangled ultrawideband pulse radar as well.

Alice had never personally seen one of these UFOs, but she'd first suspected their existence five years ago, when Bethy Powell had tried to sabotage the station and make off with that kilogram of antimatter. Bethy had had no obvious exit plan, so clearly she was expecting something to pick her up. Something hidden.

"Here's a CAD model of what we think the ship looks like," said one of the Earthbound engineers, an earnest young Black man whose name Alice could never remember, who spoke with a British accent. In a corner of the screen, a little winged rocket ship appeared, featureless yellow-white against a royal blue background.

"Ships," Alice corrected. "Plural. There are sightings too close together in time and too far apart in space to be explained by a single bogey."

But now she was back in urban legend territory again, and nobody had a response for her. Or maybe that was partly the speed of light delay, because Earth was 5.3 light-seconds away—10.6 seconds round-trip—so even if someone answered her immediately, it felt a lot like the people on the other side of that screen were ignoring her.

"They're not aliens," said the earnest young man, finally, after rather more than 10.6 seconds. "The shape looks a lot like a Lockheed Martin LMS-50. Not the same profile, or actually the same anything, but it's clearly capable of reentering the Earth's atmosphere and landing on a runway."

"Nobody said they were aliens," Alice said, striving for patience.

There were aliens out there—Igbal's incorporeal Beings—but they sure didn't drive little spaceships around. But that was such a closely guarded secret that even ninety percent of RzVz personnel had no inkling. The cover story was that *Intercession* was on a two-year shakedown cruise, with a hundred VIPs on board, purely for publicity reasons. That story couldn't possibly hold up forever, but so far it had done remarkably well. Probably because the nutty truth sounded even more like an urban legend that no serious person would entertain.

But real conspiracies existed, too, and nutty ones.

"I'm just saying," said the young man.

"I need schematics on that entangled ultrawideband," Alice said. "And if it's hard to build, I need someone up here who knows how to do it."

Iqbal had tried a couple of times to design a radar that could catch these bastards, but he'd been too distracted by the Summit mission to really give it much attention, or to explain what he knew to anyone else.

But God damn it, what were these stealth ships doing? Pointing missiles? Pointing IR lasers at the windows, to try and pick up vibrations they could decode into speech? Standing by to kidnap key personnel? All of the above?

One thing that unnerved Alice greatly was that she was still receiving paychecks from the U.S. Air Force, but was no longer receiving instructions from the President. Tina Tompkins was out of office, "Loud Wally" Mudrow was in, and the transition had seen such a rancorous purge that it seemed plausible no one was left in the U.S. government who even knew Alice was here. There were other governments that did know—France and New Zealand at the very least—but perhaps they were keeping that information to themselves.

Alice was a spy with much to report, and no one to report it to, and all she could think to do was gather more information. Which was also what the Chief Astronaut and Interim Commander and VP of Space Operations side of her wanted to do anyway, so . . .

"I know exactly how to build it," the young man said, now sounding a bit overeager.

"Keep your pants on," Alice told him, with a glare that might not come through on the blocky video. It was probably an HR violation, but Jesus, she was sick of all the goddamn Earthmen wanting to treat this place like Pleasure Island. Yes, the crew of ESL1 was still more than seventy-five percent female, but what of it? It was a factory, not a hotel, and the women here had calluses on their hands.

(And yes, a lot of them would pounce on any fresh meat that arrived—especially for a short-term assignment—and Alice was sick of all the disruption that caused. And also, Alice hadn't gotten her rocks off in months, and was pretty short-fused about the whole subject.)

"Well, I do," the young man said.

"What's your name?" Alice asked him. In a room full of people down there on Earth, he was the only one speaking.

"Pembroke," he said, eleven seconds later. "Isaiah Pembroke. Senior Radar Systems Engineer, Weapon Targeting Systems."

"I'll take it under advisement. I don't want to target any weapons, though. I mean, I do, if that's our only option, but we don't know who these people even are. We don't know their motives or capabilities. I don't want them hanging around, but going straight to a lethal response may give us a result we *really* don't like. What I want to do is catch one of these ships."

"Physically capture?" asked Derek Hakkens, sounding... surprised. He was hovering to the right of her, with his slippered foot hooked lazily on a grab bar.

"Yes. It's the only way to find out who they are."

"Okay. Difficult," he said.

Derek was a pilot—mostly ion tugs and maintenance pods, but he swore he could fly anything. He was also Alice's ex-boyfriend, and a maddening son of a bitch, but she valued his opinion.

"What would we need?" she asked—not just him, but the whole team.

"Better radar than what Transit Point is using," said Isaiah Pembroke. "Their range is limited to about a kilometer, and already it looks like the bogey is just moving a little farther out to compensate. But we've got a lot more power at our disposal. A lot more."

"Okay, that's good. What else?"

"A way to disable their drive motor without decompressing the ship," said Rose Ketchum. Rose—one of the station's best astronauts, presently hovering to Alice's left—was the External Security team's latest addition. She had some of that common sense people were always talking about, and Alice figured it was time to put it to use on something other than zero-gee welding.

"And how would we do that?"

"With a bullet," said Tim Ho. He was the machinist, hovering over by the video display, currently overlaid on the Earth-facing picture window of Alice's office. He pointed to a spot on the 3D model, and said "Fuel tanks are going to be here."

"You'll blow it up," said Derek. "Unless you get lucky, you'll puncture the fuel and oxidizer tanks both, and then you're going to get a vigorous exothermic reaction. It would take days, and lots of our own fuel, to sweep up all the pieces. What you want to do first is defeat the camouflage."

He'd talked about that before, and it sounded good to Alice, but with no way to localize the stealth ship, it hadn't done much good.

"Aluminum chaff, covered in tack resin?" she said, mainly for everyone else's benefit.

"Right. Once we have a clear detection, we fire canisters of chaff at the ship's last known location and along any probable thrust vectors. You stick even a couple of pieces to their hull, they're going to reflect in every wavelength. Then we can do whatever we like. Shove a glue bomb up their tailpipe, et cetera. But they could still maneuver with attitude control thrusters. And even if they couldn't, there's a big difference between disabling a ship and physically extricating its crew. We don't have space marines. They might."

"Well, we'd be in a much stronger negotiating position," Alice said.

"Not if they're armed. We're pretty vulnerable, Alice."

Not as vulnerable as they were five years ago, but Derek's point was valid: there was no amount of airlock deadbolting or reflective armor plating that could protect the station from a determined military assault. ESL1 had weapons—lasers and missiles and radar-controlled slug throwers. They even had a couple of sniper rifles, which was what Tim Ho had meant. He'd been an Army sniper down in Coffee Patch, and had recently proven that, with a 1 MOA rifle in the absence of wind and gravity, he could reliably put a round through a spacesuit glove at five hundred meters.

But space battles had never made any sense to Alice, because they didn't make sense, period. If two soap bubbles start shooting at each other, the likeliest outcome was two popped bubbles. Renz Ventures needed to be a lot more nuanced than that.

"EMP attack?" she asked. Electromagnetic pulse—the bane of electronics everywhere.

It was Isaiah Pembroke who answered that one: "We certainly have the power to knock out even hardened military systems, and it would disable most armaments, along with mobility."

"Also a lot of spacesuit functions," said Tim Ho.

"Wouldn't some of that blow back toward the station?" asked Derek.

"Almost certainly," said someone else in the time-lagged video display. "And our own systems weren't designed with EMP warfare in mind."

"Some are," Alice said. Once it became Alice's job to harden this place, she had seen to it that new hardware at least took the idea into account. But the legacy systems—most systems—were designed by Igbal, with no thought to security. And it had nearly killed them all. Retrofitting them was difficult, expensive, time-consuming work. The new station would be a fortress by comparison, but right now that wasn't much help.

"Other ideas?" Alice asked, because she had learned that that was an important question to ask. Even with two rooms full of people charged with sharing ideas, there was a surprising reticence to actually do so.

No one said anything, so she flashed a glare around and said, "Look, we've got the high ground, literally. We're at the edge of cislunar space, and anyone Earthward of us has to look into the Sun to get here. We have energy superiority. We have two hundred kilograms of fucking antimatter. We have the fastest spaceship drive anyone has ever seen. When I say, 'I want to capture a stealth ship,' I don't mean sit around thinking about it for six months. Derek, you're in charge of this. If we don't have people who can make it happen, get with Maag and hire some people who do."

Alice's final meeting of the morning was with the finance team.

"It doesn't look good," said Bob Rojas, the Chief Financial Officer of RzVz, through another time-lagged video link.

Alice had asked about getting a few tons of rare gas shipped up.

"Why exactly not?" she demanded, although Rojas outranked her in the corporate hierarchy.

Rojas looked annoyed at that. Annoyed and impatient. "I keep telling you, Kyeong, we're going to be cash poor for at least the next twelve months. We sunk everything we had into that starship, and no one is particularly anxious to extend credit."

"Why?"

"Do I really have to spell it out?"

"Would you, please?" she asked sweetly. "I'm just a dumb astronaut."

He looked even more annoyed at that. Because yeah, Alice was not dumb. Just stubborn.

"People think we're crazy," he said. "We've moved all our ground operations to third-world Embargo States to get around the ITAR restrictions. We built a starship. Our founder has flown the coop. We're hemorrhaging money and staff like a company about to go out of business."

"Oh," Alice said. She hadn't heard anyone put it that way before, but a moment's reflection told her it was true. "And are we? About to go out of business?"

"Not if you do your job," he said. "Orders are up again for disposable landing bodies. Keep that revenue flowing."

"Don't bullshit me," Alice said. "There's no way ESL1 is keeping this company afloat all by itself. Not unless we start selling flutter drives to the highest bidder."

"Yeah," Rojas said, "About that. We've gotten a strongly worded decree from the U.N. Security Council, warning us not to even think about doing that. Sale of antimatter in any capacity will be regarded as an act of war. As far as operating our own flutter-drive ships— interstellar or otherwise—they say no part of the drive beam can intersect any portion of cislunar space, or again it's an act of war. A war crime, actually, if even one photon of it intersects a human body. A few hours later, we got almost the same warning from the U.S.A., who I gather would be the enforcer of said decree."

"U.S.A., huh?" Alice said. She hadn't heard anything about any of this, so clearly it would not be herself doing the enforcing, or even the spying. Which meant she had indeed been forgotten by her Earthly masters. Which was not good news, insofar as it read on the stability of the U.S. government.

She was silent for several seconds, processing all of that. Finally she said, "Can we sell transportation services? The drive clearly works, and it can go to Jupiter as easily as it can go wherever the fuck Igbal is right now."

"It's real Buck Rogers stuff," Rojas agreed. "And no, there's nothing in the decree to prevent that. The U.N. probably recognizes that that particular horse has left the barn."

"Will you authorize construction of another flutter drive?"

Rojas frowned. "What size of ship are we talking about? What's the use case?"

"TBD," Alice said. "But people always want to move things around. People are always in a hurry."

Now it was Rojas's turn to not say anything. Finally: "That's intriguing. It doesn't sound crazy, which means I might actually be able to shake loose some credit from our bankers. Enough to keep us airtight for a while."

"Things are that bad?" Alice said.

"Not if you do your job."

When she was done with all of that, Alice had an email waiting from Igbal.

> *Alice, for a woman of few words, you use up a surprising amount of bandwidth. Can you kindly make your reports a bit punchier? Can you fit it all into five kilobytes?*
>
> *Say yes to the China thing, and no to Clementine. We're not helping those jerks. I haven't heard much about those Shade modifications, or upgrades to the particle accelerator. Please prioritize that in your next transmission. It's very dark out here, and creepy quiet if I'm going to be honest. Please don't take it the wrong way if I say I miss you.*

Alice sighed. She missed Igbal, too. Definitely not in any kind of romantic way, but she missed his energy. Spy or no, she had been co-opted almost immediately by the sheer enthusiasm and scope of his ambitions. Solar shade the size of Colorado? Why not. Starship? Try and stop me. If she'd ever received an order to terminate him, she would have shot the radio instead.

She didn't really know how long a message she could fit into five kilobytes, and although it would have been easy enough to figure out, she just didn't feel like it. Although she had much to report, she didn't feel like that, either. What she typed instead was:

> *There is more to running this station than I realized. You did a shit job of it, and left me a fucking mess, but I do wish you could offer more help than a daily fortune cookie.*

Don't take it wrong to say I miss you, too. Why didn't you tell me we were having money troubles?

She looked it over a few times, and hit Send. And then, tired as she was, she'd've been happy to end her day right there, if not for the mocking of her wristwatch. Damn thing said it was only 1:15 p.m.

1.2

Post-Encounter Deposition
Brother Michael Jablonski
Prior, St. Joseph of Cupertion's
Monastery, Luna

Of all the crew of the Summit mission, I am the only liar brazen enough to frame my encounter with the Beings as a series of Socratic dialogues or Confucian analects. If you'll indulge me, imagine that each dialogue—short, pithy, focused on one slim topic—stands alone, and did not occur in any sort of linear order with the others. It might be more accurate to say they were simultaneous harmonies of a single tone or tune. And yet, I'll also say that they occurred, or seemed to, in four distinct groups.

Some people find it suspicious that the Beings spoke to me about things that were important to me personally, and seemed even perhaps to be telling me just what I wanted to hear. Were I not myself the firsthand witness, I might similarly misgive. But I was there, and I know what they said. And also I am by no means the only witness for whom this is true, so in the totality of what we all believe the Beings conveyed, perhaps you will find your own truths.

As to the manner of it, I'm often asked, "Did the Beings commune telepathically?" And my answer is, that would be a poor metaphor indeed. Are emotional grunts a form of telepathy? Is pantomime? People also then inquire, "How were you able to understand one another?" And the short answer of course is that we mostly didn't. As for the longer, more confusing answer, I'll perhaps let the Beings speak for themselves afore I toss my own speculations in the pool.

Beings: "Hello?"
Michael: "Hello?"
Beings: "This message is a transmission."
Michael: "I hear you."
Beings: "So glad! So glad you could make it! This message is a transmission."
Michael: "I hear you."
Beings: "Amazing."

Michael: "Is this real? Do you exist?"
Beings: "Most probably, if this is our answer."
Michael: "Where am I? Where are you?"
Beings: "Right here, most probably. Right now, most probably."
Michael: " 'Most probably' in the quantum mechanical sense?"
Beings: "..."
Michael: "Like the distribution of an electron across a volume of space?"
Beings: "Um..."
Michael: "Are you waveforms?"
Beings: "Waveforms describe all things. Are you not a waveform?"

Michael: "Are you corporeal matter? Do you occupy a particular volume of space?"
Beings: "Yes."
Michael: "Why can't we see you, or touch you?"
Beings: "..."
Michael: "Why can we only speak to you in dreams?"
Beings: "Is this a dream? We are touching you right now."

Beings: "Matter is energy is information: conserved. Time is space is spin: conserved."
Michael: "Do you move through space and time?"
Beings: "Um..."
Michael: "How do you experience space and time?"
Beings: "..."

Michael: "We move through three dimensions of space. This requires energy."

Beings: "Yes."

Michael: "Do you move through three dimensions of space?"

Beings: "What?"

Beings: "Does it hurt?"

Michael: "What?"

Beings: "So small. Does it hurt?"

Michael: "Are you larger than we are?"

Beings: "Yes!"

Michael: "How large are you?"

Beings: "This is amazing. We are so glad you could make it."

Michael: "Are you larger than a solar system? Is that why we had to come all the way out here to speak with you?"

Beings: "Attention is volume is duration: conserved. Can you verify?"

Michael: "I don't understand."

Beings: "Amazing."

Beings: "How are you alive?"

Michael: "We consume matter to generate energy."

Beings: "By inspection, untrue."

Michael: "We . . . manipulate energy by increasing the entropy of chemical substances?"

Beings: "That is not an answer."

Michael: "Well, how are *you* alive?"

Beings: "Attention is conserved."

Michael: "You have limited attention?"

Beings: ". . . Yes? Attention is volume is duration."

Michael: "Your . . . attention is limited to a volume of space?"

Beings: "Duration limits space limits attention. Attention to large volume is attention to brief duration. Attention to large duration is attention to small volume."

Beings: "Can you attend to a larger volume?"

Michael: "With my eyes, yes. I can see objects that are light-years away."

Beings: "That is not an answer. Can you attend to a longer duration?"

Michael: "I can remember the past. I can read books, which store information from the past. I can take measurements and deduce what happened in the past."

Beings: "That is not an answer."

Michael: "You see me as occupying a very small space, and attending to very small increments of time. Moment by moment."

Beings: "Yes! Does it hurt?"

Michael: "No. Can you see the future?"

Beings: "Time is space is spin. Do you mean entropy?"

Michael: "Entropy increases over time, yes. The future has more entropy than the past."

Beings: "Greater entropy requires greater energy for less attention."

Michael: "So seeing the future is ... expensive?"

Beings: "Very."

Michael: "When you see the future, can you act on what you see, here in the present?"

Beings: "Difficult to explain."

Michael: "That's not a no."

Beings: "By inspection, true."

Michael: "Can you change the past?"

Beings: "Difficult to explain."

Michael: "Is changing the past expensive?"

Beings: "Difficult to explain."

Michael: "But it isn't absolutely impossible."

Beings: "By inspection, true."

3.2
03 February
✧
I.R.V. *Intercession*
Extra-Kuiper Space
209 A.U. from Earth

"I'm not a priest," Brother Michael objected.

"Never said you were," Igbal said back.

Michael studied this man, this agnostic trillionaire, wondering (as always) what exactly made him tick. Still eight months shy of his sixty-fourth birthday, Igbal Renz had already invented more and built more and accomplished more than Franklin or Edison or da Vinci, securing an outsized place in the history of technology, and in history, period. He'd once turned down a Nobel Prize!

And yet, Godless and heedless, he didn't seem to really care about the money or the glory or the infamy, except insofar as they helped him achieve his other goals. Which were numerous and grandiose, this mission being a prime example. Whether Igbal should have spent those trillions improving life on Earth was immaterial; here they were. Michael had been commanded by His Holiness Himself, Pope Dave the Frowny, to be a part of this crew, and so he was. But what exactly did that mean?

"As far as I know, none of you have been baptized, or are even culturally Catholic," Michael said carefully.

In the 0.1 gee of the ship's acceleration, they were neither floating nor standing, but sort of loosely resting their feet on the floor, as one might in neck-deep water. Michael himself was used to standing in

Lunar gravity, which was seventy percent stronger, and he had still not quite adjusted to this. He had to remind himself, moment to moment, not to flex his slippers enough to send him bouncing toward the ceiling. It was easier, he thought, for those accustomed to weightlessness, although they seemed to struggle with it, too, in their own ways.

"Can it, friar," Igbal told him. "Nobody's asking you to perform a liturgy. But you're the chaplain of this vessel, and we need some freaking spiritual guidance."

Michael wasn't a friar, either, but various heads nodded, and voices grumbled. Assembled here in the wardroom were not only Michael and Igbal, but also Engineering Officer Sandy Lincoln, Information Officer Harv Leonel, Helmsman Hobie Prieto, Chef-and-Purser Thenbecca Jungermann, Maintenance Officer Dong Nguyen, and Flight Surgeon Rachael Lee. Michael himself—Brother Michael Jablonski, erstwhile Prior of St. Joseph of Cupertino Monastery, was in charge of the ship's recycling and life support systems. All of the people here were experienced astronauts, who had built things and fixed things and dealt with emergencies. All awake and unfrozen so they'd be available on a moment's notice, if needed.

"I'm at your service," Michael assured them all, "but it's not clear what you think I can do. Or what Pope Dave thinks I should."

The "wardroom" was simply the crew quarters, with the doors of all the crew berths rolled shut, the table folded out, and the lights set to a businesslike blue-white. A central ladder pierced through the center of the room, leading upward through the ceiling, into the bridge, and downward through the deck they were standing on, to the service deck where the galley, bathroom, shower, and gym were located. At meal times, these same crew quarters became the "dining room" simply by switching up the lighting to sunset orange. This was a surprisingly effective tactic for making the ship seem bigger, much like the chapel back at Saint Joe's, in the Lunar South Polar Mineral Territories, whose pews could be folded out into dining tables and benches, converting the space twice daily into a medieval-style refectory.

At times, the eight members of *Intercession*'s crew had also made this module into the "garden," the "beach," the "forest," and the "circus tent," simply by programming the shifting colors of the lights, and the images on the video displays above each sleeping berth. But it was a cheap trick, already starting to rub the nervy crew the wrong way.

"You're maddeningly serene," Harv Leonel said. "Let's start there."

Michael laughed. "I'm a monk, Harv. Being serene consumes fully half of my mental energy. But like our captain, I'm alarmed at how this crew is dealing with the isolation. It helps to stay very busy, but it's hard not to see that some of us are busier than others."

"Your job has a lot of moving parts," Harv said.

"It does, yes."

Harv was an interesting person; an outdoorsy college professor who'd suddenly blasted off into the cramped quarters of space in his early fifties, apparently as some sort of self-reinvention. He seemed like a man who used to be happy, missed it direly, and was casting around for it like a lost contact lens. But he carried his sadness with such good cheer that, even for Michael, it was easy to miss. Michael thought there was probably a woman involved.

Hobie Prieto, the ship's pilot, said, "I'm sick of playing VR games in my bunk, Michael. Until we get back to the inner solar system, I get to steer this bucket one time—a one-eighty-degree flip. That's no life for a pilot."

"I got no messes to clean up, no broken things to fix," said Dong Nguyen. "I think we built this ship too well."

Thenbecca Jungermann, who was both chef and purser, said, "I at least have a lot to do, and cooking makes me happy. But I feel it, too, this creeping ennui. I thought I knew all about living in space, but we're just so far away, from everything. Maybe this emptiness we're feeling is something physically real, that humans have never felt before. Something quantum mechanical, about the way our brains work out here? I don't know, but the Beings wanted to meet us far away from the Sun. Maybe this is why."

"Metaphysics," Dong said, dismissively, although in Michael's experience Dong seemed to believe all kinds of other wacky things.

"We need to be more like a monastery," Igbal said, "and less like a bunch of friendless kids on summer break."

People reacted grumpily to that.

Michael said, "It's a matter of perspective, I'm afraid. If you think you're two hundred astronomical units from everything you've ever loved, and probably ten A.U. from the nearest speck of tangible dust, you're right. You are. If you think an hour a day of exercise and another hour of cleaning makes for a dull existence, well, then it does. But we're also on a grand adventure, yes? Making history? Shaking the pillars of Heaven, on a gamma-ray flame that could torch whole cities if we let it? A billion people would trade places with us, no questions asked, if they knew what we were up to."

All eyes were on him. He was keenly aware, suddenly, of his choice not to wear the blue uniform of Renz Ventures on this mission. By sticking with the same robes he'd worn at Saint Joe's, and before that at Saint Benedict's, he had consciously set himself apart. Thinking ahead, Michael had, before embarking on this mission, stitched wire into his robe in strategic places, so it would not float up in freefall. This was partly a practical matter, and partly one of modesty and politeness. But in truth it was also partly vanity, for he wanted to represent the Church with a certain mystery and grandeur, by seeming immune to certain laws of nature. A jumpsuit was far more practical in this maddening gravity, but also a surrendering of identity. He *was* different, and he meant for his crewmies to know it.

Well, now was the time to actually put that difference to work.

"Look," he said, "the philosophical implications of what we're doing are profound, and you're all just . . . waiting. Waiting when you should be preparing your minds and souls for the mother of all culture shocks. The Beings are very, very different from you and I. Have you thought about that? Have you talked about it? If you don't spend at least an hour a day doing nothing else, then you may find yourselves poorly equipped for the big day, when it finally comes. It's only nine months away!"

Still, everyone looked at him, saying nothing. Even the great Igbal Renz! Maybe there *was* something odd about the vacuum they were passing through. Maybe their brains really did have a harder time functioning here. Or maybe not. In any case, sometimes the best way to get people moving was to get really, really specific with them.

Fighting the urge to sigh, he said, "As your chaplain and spiritual advisor, I'm going to start holding daily guided meditations before dinner. Mandatory attendance. I don't care if you believe in the same God I do; I'm not out to convert anyone. But I see a group of souls in need of nourishment I know how to provide. Furthermore, I'm going to set up a schedule. Every day, each of you is to talk to one other person, in private, for at least an hour. No small talk, no chitchat; I'm talking full-bore dialectical analysis of the meaning of all this. In seven days, we'll start the rotation over again, and in a month I'll want you all to start preparing lectures. You're not just lonely astronauts; you're globally ranked subject matter experts, carefully selected to bring a unique perspective to this paradigm-shattering mission. For God's sake, act like it."

And still, nobody said anything, until finally, sounding a bit embarrassed, Igbal Renz said, "You heard the man. Jesus Christ, people, look alive, or I'll thaw somebody out to do it for you."

1.3

Post-Encounter Deposition
Brother Michael Jablonski
Prior, St. Joseph of Cupertion's
Monastery, Luna

As you've by now whiffed a whiff of what the Beings chose to communicate to us (or rather, what my lies of them reduce to human speech), I'll tease a glimpse of my own surrounding suspicions. First: They'd been trying to make contact for a hundred years at least, and perhaps since the very first day a human ever dosed himself with the psychedelic known as dimethyltryptamine, or DMT. And maybe longer still, through tribal rituals with plants or fungi containing similar chemicals, and through near-death experiences where DMT is released in the brain naturally. Second: Safe to say they knew more about us than we about them, and so had made an effort to generate . . . let's call them petroglyphs that a human brain could plausibly interpret. On the exact nature of these glyphs there are wiser noggins than mine to speculate, but by way of metaphor I will say:

Imagine you've discovered intelligent signals emanating from bacteria who reside in the impossibly thin cosmos of a water drop pressed between two glass slides. Even assembled as colonies, they own none of the structures you'd associate with intelligence, and yet the signature of it is there nonetheless, unmistakable as your own reflection. Imagine the awe you'd feel, and the terror, for it means the world doesn't work like you thought it should. Would the desire overwhelm you, to eavesdrop on their little thoughts? And if you cracked the code, or thought you did, would you try to form ideogramlets of your own? Imagine cunning molecules—RNA or whatever—spirited through microneedles and into the midst of these little bastards, announcing the fact of your own existence. What could you say? What could you ask? Prime numbers, really?

Michael: "What are you?"
Beings: "Difficult to explain."
Michael: "Why?"
Beings: "You are small and flat and...blind? If we are waves in 'space,' we are...spherically distributed? If we are waveforms in 'time,' we are flattened against the...future?"
Michael: "Do you perceive four dimensions in the universe?"
Beings: "Many more than that. Amazing: you occupy dimensions you do not attend. You perceive moments and points? Only?"
Michael: "Are you outside of time and space?"
Beings: "...No? Are you?"
Michael: "Definitely not."
Beings: "Do you perceive the substrate?"
Michael: "What?"

Beings: "Time is space is spin: conserved. Mass is energy is information: conserved. The substrate supports both forms, and others. Do you perceive spacetime/spin?"
Michael: "We perceive time and space. Objects can rotate in space."
Beings: "Rotation is not spin. Amazing. Do you perceive spin as spacetime?"
Michael: "Um, I don't think so."
Beings: "Do you perceive mass/energy/information?"
Michael: "Yes. We perceive mass, energy, and information as fundamental to our existence. Are they fundamental to yours?"
Beings: "They are conserved."
Michael: "So...yes?"
Beings: "..."

Michael: "Are time and space fundamental to your existence?"
Beings: "They are conserved. Conservation constrains action."

Beings: "Attention is volume is duration: conserved."
Michael: "Okay."
Beings: "Entropy: not conserved."
Michael: "Okay."
Beings: "Time is space is spin: conserved. Mass is energy is information: conserved."
Michael: "Okay."
Beings: "Time is not mass. Space is not information. Spin is not energy. Entropy is not conserved. Understood?"
Michael: "No."

Michael: "Are you made of pure energy? Pure information?"
Beings: "Energy of what? Information of what?"

Michael: "Tell me about the substrate."
Beings: "Points create the substrate."
Michael: "Points in time and space?"
Beings: "No. Points that connect or do not. Connections that spin or do not."
Michael: "What?"
Beings: "Ummm . . . Spin creates spacetime?"

Michael: "Do you perceive this substrate?"
Beings: ". . . Yes?"
Michael: "Can you interact with it?"
Beings: "Yes?"
Michael: "Can we?"
Beings: ". . ."

Michael: "Is the universe made of time and space and matter and energy?"
Beings: "Definitely not."
Michael: "Are space and time and matter and energy created by the substrate?"
Beings: "Created?"

Michael: "Do changes in the substrate create changes in space, time, matter, and energy?"

Beings: "... Yes?"

Michael: "Do you live in the same universe we do?"

Beings: "Yes!"

Michael: "But you perceive it differently."

Beings: "Yes!"

Michael: "More dimensions?"

Beings: "Yes!"

Michael: "More variables?"

Beings: "...?"

Michael: "More ... things that are conserved?"

Beings: "Yes!"

5.1
18 February 2057

✧

Thalia Buoyant Island
Southern Stratosphere
Venus

"Frédéric Ortega, you come away from that edge."

Frédéric turned and saw his father, Julian. In a gray T-shirt and leggings, bright yellow breathing mask, beige kaftan and sun hat, Julian was dressed for work. Under the broad, blue sky, the Sun cast a fierce, hot shadow beneath him on the *carbónespuma* pavement.

Frédéric was not dressed for work. In just a T-shirt, shorts, and an air mask he'd nearly outgrown already, Frédéric was, at best, dressed for school. But not really even that.

"What do you think you're going to see down there?" Julian demanded. "The ground? The future? It's nothing but clouds."

He did not, at least, warn Frédéric about the risk of falling. When you lived on an island floating in the sky, the risk of falling was not something that really needed much discussion.

But Thalia—the island—was small, and Frédéric needed, every now and again, to remind himself that there was a whole planet down below it. At night, he sometimes came out by himself, to lie down on the soft *carbónespuma* and look up at the stars. Especially the blue one: Earth.

"You skipping school again?" Julian said.

Frédéric shrugged. "Skipping" seemed like an awfully specific term. He just happened to not be in school at this exact moment, because he couldn't stand the idea of even one more hour of recorded lectures and AI-proctored quizzes. School here on Venus was a sort of parody of actual learning, heavy on obsolete skills like reading and algebra.

"You don't want an education?" Julian said.

"Not that one," Frédéric said, flicking sweat off his arms.

Julian said nothing for a few seconds, then nodded slowly. "Okay. I hear you." And then, surprisingly, he said, "You want to come to work with me today?"

"Yes," Frédéric said, because that sounded a lot better than school. Not good, but better.

"You gotta pass the tests, at least, before your mother and I will let you out of school completely. Whether you think so or not, there's stuff you gotta know, to build any kind of future for yourself, much less the whole island. Now come away from that edge, please. You never know when the wind is going to gust on you."

Frédéric nodded. It *was* dangerous, standing on the edge like this. That was the point, or part of it, to feel really alive for a minute or two. Barely a kilometer below the island at the moment, the cloud tops were all puffy and innocent beneath a blue, Earthlike sky, hiding the truth that they were actually sulfuric acid. Often, they would engulf the island entirely, making it impossible to go outside without a full spacesuit. Also, they extended downward for twenty-five kilometers, toward the furnace-hot surface thirty kilometers below that. If you fell off the edge, your body would fall for an hour and a half, burning and crushing and dissolving into vapor as it drifted down through the thick atmosphere, before some diminished lump of it finally hit the ground. If you had your mask on, you'd be alive for the first twenty minutes of that, totally unable to save yourself. Paradise, right?

He stepped away from the edge, toward his father, and saw his own relief mirrored in his father's eyes. He'd gotten his jolt of adrenaline; he could step to safety now.

Behind Julian Ortega stood the Ship—a cone of metal, alone and out of place in this environment. Behind that, Thalia Village glittered like diamond.

Exactly like diamond, because that was what its domes and barrels were made from. They sprouted like jeweled toys from the *carbónespuma* pavement at the island's center. Farther from the edge now than they used to be. The island grew, a little bit every day, as 3D printers spiraled around it, churning out more pavement. Never enough, was it? Though opaque as concrete or asphalt, and every bit as ugly, the pavement was graphene aerogel filled with hydrogen gas, pulled from the atmosphere of Venus itself. It yielded under your weight a little bit, like a thin mattress on a not-too-rigid bed. Frédéric had been walking on it for a third of his life now—five years out of fifteen, and he had always always hated it.

Reading his expression, Frédéric's father said, "You know we're very lucky, right?"

"Yes, exceedingly," Frédéric answered, trying to keep the sarcasm to a minimum.

"They're not doing so well on Mars. They can't stand outside like this, in just a T-shirt and mask. They can't feel the Sun on their skin or the wind in their hair. They get a leak in one of their buildings, they have to evacuate the whole thing. We got leaks we pretty much ignore. Just a little CO_2, at atmospheric pressure. You see what I'm saying?"

"I don't compare myself to the people on Mars," Frédéric said. Why would he? He had supposedly given his enthusiastic agreement to coming here, to being a founding colonist on Thalia. Supposedly. But he was only ten years old at the time, with no way of knowing what he was actually agreeing to. None of them knew; none of them had envisioned . . . this. But especially the children. If Social Services existed on Venus, they would call it abuse and take him away to somewhere safe.

"Come on," his father said, now walking back toward the village. "You get your hands dirty today. Make you feel better."

"Okay," Frédéric said, and followed. He didn't think it would actually make him feel better. He didn't think anything would. But it would make him feel something, and right now he would take it.

As they passed by a landing leg of the Ship, they trailed their hands along it, as was customary. A piece of Earth on Thalia. A connection.

"Why can't we just fly back to Earth?" Frédéric used to ask. But the answer was always the same: "Supermajority." That was how Thalia was governed, and nothing ever happened without it. The ship was ready to fly; refueling it had been one of the colony's first priorities, in case they had to beat a hasty retreat to Venusian orbit. But without sixty-six percent supermajority consent, it was little more than a shrine.

The other reason, unspoken, Frédéric had had to work out for himself: there was no escape from Venusian orbit. That would require the Booster Stage, which the people of Thalia had yet to construct, because the supermajority had yet to agree to it. Or it would require someone to come and rescue them—a service any of the Four Horsemen could easily provide, for a few billion dollars. Money the people of Thalia did not have.

He tried not to think about it as he and his father passed under the twenty-meter roof of the photovoltaic array. Cool shadows underneath, a tickling of wind on his sweaty armpits. The Array was a half-kilometer ring, fully encircling the village. Beyond it, they passed the Orchard Dome, the Field Dome, and the East Residences, and finally came to the Well.

Basilio del Campo and Diego Nunez-Talamantes were there already, dressed for work like Frédéric's father.

"Let's get you some gloves," Julian said, "and a hat. And some sleeves; you're going to get a sunburn, guy." He paused for a moment, then said, "You know what? Just take mine. I'll go inside at lunchtime and get myself fresh gear. Right now I could use the vitamin D."

Laughing at his own remark, Julian stripped off his gloves, kaftan, and hat, handing them to Frédéric. They were moist inside, but Frédéric did not complain, because his alternative was to go inside and fetch his own stuff. And if he did that, there was a good chance he'd run into his mother, or some other authority figure who'd overrule Julian and send him to school.

"We're getting ready to swap out a section of cable," Diego said to Frédéric, not bothering to ask what he was doing here. It was pretty obvious.

Diego was pointing at the winch, slowly winding in a gray-white cable that ran up over an idler wheel and down through the opening of the Well. Basilio was just leaning on the sidewall of the Well, looking down. The wall was a cylinder of the same material as the island itself, surrounding a two-meter circular opening that led down through several meters of *carbónespuma* and out into the open air.

Frédéric positioned himself next to Basilio, put his hands on top of the wall, and looked down at the clouds.

At an average altitude of fifty-five kilometers, Thalia moved with the trade winds, which meant she moved with the clouds, so there was no real sense that they were actually traveling eighty meters per second over the Aino Planitia of Venus's southern hemisphere. It all looked very serene.

The cable, though, ran straight down through the clouds, all the way down to Hell itself, although Frédéric couldn't even follow it as far down as the cloud tops. You could not, of course, roll up fifty kilometers of cable on a single spool. A new spool had to be swapped in every day—sometimes multiple times per day.

"The trawler's coming up today," Basilio said.

"Lucky," Frédéric said. Even when everything was working perfectly, the trawler only actually surfaced every five days. And when things weren't perfect—which was most of the time—it could be a week or longer.

"Get ready," Basilio said over his shoulder. "The splice is coming up."

"ETA?" Julian asked.

"Two minutes, maybe less. Definitely less."

"Frédéric, get your head out of that well and watch what Diego is doing," Julian said. "You've got my gloves, so if he needs you to grab the cable, you grab it."

Spun from diamond fibers and carbon nanotubes, the cable was only one millimeter wide, looking a lot like the fishing line Frédéric used to handle as a child, back on Earth, when he and his father had gone out for a "lake day." But the cable wasn't going fast—just thirty centimeters per second, so he could get his gloves on it, yes. But it was also *tight*, holding up the entire weight of the trawler, plus the weight of all the cable that hadn't been reeled in yet.

"How do I grab it?" he asked, mystified.

Looking annoyed now, Diego started pointing to components of the winch. "Idler wheel, yeah? Tensioner. Accumulator. Bail arm. Dancer. See this going back and forth? This keeps the cable from bunching up in one part of the spool. Carriage. Drum axle. Primary spool. Swap spool."

"I know what a spool is," Frédéric protested.

"You grab the cable here," Diego said, pointing between the tensioner and the bail arm. He pantomimed a sort of scooping motion: fingers open, palms flat. "Between the tensioner and the bail arm, see how over these wheels the cable isn't tight? That's the accumulator, where you can pull slack. The tensioner is carrying the weight of the trawler, see? In fact, just grab the cable now. Good, now take two steps backward. Gimme a couple meters of slack. There you go."

The cable was now sliding, slowly and frictionlessly, over Frédéric's gloved hands.

"How long do I do this?"

"You'll see."

Diego held up a metal tool that had clearly been 3D-printed in the machine shop.

"This is a splice popper. You watch what I do with this, yeah?"

"Splice is in the Well," Basilio reported. Then: "Splice is out of the Well. Splice is going over the idler. Look sharp, Freddo!"

Presently, Frédéric saw a metal object approaching his hands, with the cable wrapped through it and around it in a complex pattern.

"That's holding two sections of cable together," Julian said behind him.

Frédéric let the splice go through one hand, then the other. The metal object was lighter than it looked.

"Now watch," said Diego, who then proceeded with a set of motions so quick and so practiced that Frédéric could barely follow them. Somehow, Diego took the slack line from Frédéric and looped it over the swap reel. It made one turn around the drum, then another, with Diego holding the splice in one hand and tensioning the cable with the other, while also holding the splice popper.

And then, somehow, the metal piece was off, and one loose end of the cable was flap-flap-flapping around the primary spool, which spun rapidly for a few moments and then slowed. The other loose end was jammed into a hole in the drum of the swap spool, and a slack loop of cable shrank and vanished in Diego's hand, and then Diego was stepping back and shouting:

"Clear primary!"

At this, Julian jumped forward and did something to the primary spool, which clicked and clacked and came away on its rollers.

Diego leaned in toward the swap spool, undid some sort of latch, and shoved the swap spool along its axis into the spot where the primary spool had been.

"Lock!" Diego shouted through his mask.

Julian stepped forward again and pushed a lever, latching the swap spool in place as, apparently, the new primary. Around which the cable was now peacefully winding, as though nothing had happened.

It was strange to watch Diego giving orders to Julian, because Diego was only twenty years old, but it seemed like one of those things where the guy working that position was the guy who called.

"Ease that line back in toward me, gentle," Diego said to Frédéric. "Two steps forward, that's right, now just let it go and step clear. Easy to do, right?"

"That was amazing," Frédéric said.

Diego seemed surprised. "That? Freddo, we do that every day."

"Come with me," Julian said, wiping an arm across his forehead and grabbing the frame arms of the now-detached primary spool, which was nearly as tall as he was. "We need to put this away and grab a fresh one."

"Okay," Frédéric said, actually excited by the idea.

The trawler just went up and down, through fifty-five kilometers of atmosphere, from the planet's surface to the island and back again, over and over, ad infinitum, scooping up rocks. And yet, Frédéric discovered there were actually hundreds of different steps in that process. Springs and motors needed adjustment. Drops of lubricant needed to be delicately placed in the exact right spots. The condition of the cable itself needed to be monitored, by sending electricity and sound waves up and down its length and seeing what echoes came back.

"This last section is the one that gets the most wear," Frédéric's father explained. "It goes all the way down into the supercritical fluid layer, where the atmosphere is so thick it acts almost like a liquid. It's a strong solvent, and picks up a lot of ions from the soil, and of course it's *hot*, so it's a rough environment, even for diamonds. And down there, the cable is going fast, and it sometimes drags along the ground. It gets hit by lightning a lot, and of course there's the acid. We get maybe three, four months out of this section, and then we just throw it down the Well and swap in another one, which is why the cable fabber never sleeps. We got to get about a hundred and seventy meters a day out of that little machine. That's two millimeters per second. Can you imagine all the little atoms and molecules that sucker's got to assemble? I get tired just thinking about it."

"I see the bucket," Diego reported. He had swapped stations with Basilio, and was looking down into the well. "It just cleared the cloud tops, so the ETA is about . . . fifty minutes."

"It's a two-point-three-kilogram payload," Basilio said.

Frédéric got the feeling they were speaking mainly for his benefit.

"How do you know the weight?" he asked.

"We weigh it," Diego said, pointing to a gauge on the winch.

"Is two kilograms a lot?"

"Not really," Julian said. "It means we've been scraping hard rock, and we picked up a couple of chunks. A good haul would be ten kilos of real dirt. Best we ever had was a hundred and twenty, but that's a major outlier. Now come with me again; we got to get the hoist."

That proved to be another complex piece of hardware that had to be rolled and locked into place, unfolded and adjusted. And then the catch basin needed to be installed, which seemed redundant to Frédéric if they had only caught two kilograms, because the basin was the size of two couches pushed together. But what did he know?

When the trawler was closer, he could see not only the bucket, but the frame and the scoop, which were made of diamond but were so scratched up they'd gone an opaque gray-white, hard to distinguish against the clouds.

"We've got two broken teeth," Diego reported, though how he could see that, Frédéric was not at all sure. "Bad luck. Do you want to replace?"

"I do," Julian said. "We've got three in storage, and that's what they're for."

And so Frédéric was sent back to the storage hut again to look for "teeth," which turned out to be on a labeled shelf. Each one was a chisel-shaped diamond the size of his fist, with a hole and a collar on one side, and a removable diamond pin running through the hole. It must have taken the fabber hours to produce each of these; it was hard to see how the loss of two such teeth could be worth a couple of kilograms of random surface rocks. But what did he know?

He brought the teeth back to the Well, and watched the men perform various tasks in preparation for the trawler's arrival. They joked and laughed and seemed to be having a good time, despite the heat.

We must all be losing a lot of water, Frédéric thought, because the air was always drier than even the worst deserts of Earth. But although one man or another would occasionally lift his mask for a moment to sip from a canteen, they mostly ignored the issue. Probably because the air inside a breath mask was not dry at all. But water was easy to synthesize from the crap that was in the atmosphere—the trace acids and sulfur dioxide—so nobody seemed too worried about it.

Frédéric tried that trick, lifting his mask to drink, but caught a whiff of the stinking air and couldn't swallow for all the coughing. They were well above the clouds today—the air was not so acidic—but still it was awful stuff. Even when he put his mask back on, he couldn't stop clearing his throat for ten minutes.

The masks were solar powered except at night, and they let the nitrogen through and cracked the CO_2 into oxygen and expelled a steady stream of carbon monoxide back into the atmosphere. The air inside the mask would be considered wildly unsafe by Earthly standards—too much oxygen, too much CO_2 and SO_2, too much H_2SO_4, not nearly enough "filler gases" like nitrogen and argon. But people were adaptable, especially when the alternative was carrying the weight of a whole spacesuit on your shoulders all day. Still, Frédéric had never worn a mask for this long, and his lungs and his airway were starting to really object. He started to dry-cough, a few times per minute.

"You need to go back inside, guy," his father warned him. "Your body's not used to this abusive environment."He laughed, and punched Frédéric lightly on the arm. "You're doing good, really. These things take time."

"Can I wait until the trawler comes up?" Frédéric asked.

Julian shrugged. "You tell me. Can you?"

But the question answered itself, when Diego called out, "Trawler in fifteen seconds, guys. Trawler is in the Well."

And then the trawler frame was rising up out of the Well, and then the bucket and scoop.

"Ready to stop!" Basilio called out. Then: "Stopping." He pressed the big red Stop button on the winch, and suddenly it was a lot quieter out here.

With surprising speed and urgency, Diego and Julian swiveled the trawler frame until the bucket was over the catch basin, and then Basilio worked another control, and the bucket and scoop opened like a clam shell, dropping out a rock the size of two closed fists, along with a handful of dust.

"That's it?" Frédéric said.

"That's it," Julian confirmed.

"It's a nice chunk," Basilio said. "See those shiny flecks? Metal ore. Maybe some salts. Some rocks are just silicon and oxygen."

Unable to help himself, Frédéric dropped his father's gloves, leaned into the basin, and picked the thing up. He could not remember the last time he'd held a rock in his hand. The rough, solid texture of it was amazing: not at all like diamond or metal or plastic. Here at last was something real. It was hot, though, and after a second he dropped it, clattering, back into the basin.

"What'd you do that for?" Julian said, more concernedly than angrily. "It's covered in acid, guy. Jeez, you got to wash that hand." Clucking in disappointment, he fetched his canteen, unscrewed the cap, and upended it on Frédéric's now-outstretched right hand. He didn't feel any acid—just heat—but the blood-warm water did feel good.

"Rub your hands together until they stop feeling slippery," Julian instructed, "and wipe them on your kaftan. My kaftan, actually. All right, let's get you inside. I think you've had enough grown-up work for one day."

Frédéric was not in agreement if that meant he had to go to school, so he said, "Maybe enough outdoor work." And then, as if to emphasize the point, he coughed.

Sighing, Julian grabbed the catch basin by the handles and started wheeling it toward the airlock. Julian followed behind.

The airlock didn't require any pressurization or anything; it was just a manual door that rolled up in front of them and back down behind them, and another door behind it that did the same. A little bit of interior atmosphere was allowed to escape each time, and a little bit of Venusian air was allowed in.

Inside, it was cool and very humid. Plants hung from niches in every wall and in the arched diamond ceiling, filtering the sunlight into a thousand narrow rays.

Frédéric gratefully stripped off his mask, and then his father's hat. He breathed deeply, letting the clean, moist air down into his lungs. Then he coughed a little more; it would take him ten minutes to really shake it. It was like when you accidentally inhaled a bit of food; the irritation went on and on, long after you coughed it out of your airway.

"Come with me," Julian said. "Let's see what Tohias has to say about our catch."

"Aren't Diego and Basilio going to need you?"

"Right now?" Julian said. "They're just going to swap out those broken teeth and send the trawler back down. They'll be a little slower without a third hand, but I think we can afford a few minutes, right?"

Frédéric didn't answer.

To the right of the airlock was the processing room, where Tohias Nunez-Talamantes was waiting for them. As they walked in, he raised the back of one hand to cover his nose. People smelled bad when they came in from outside—an acrid, sulfury reek that took time to dissipate.

The processing room was full of meter-wide machines—furnaces and centrifuges and deconstructors, some made of native diamond and plastic, but most of metal and unmistakably of Earthly manufacture. Along the clear diamond wall ran a shelf, all the way around, of bottled chemicals.

"You kept me waiting," Tohias said to Julian. "The bucket's been up for ten minutes."

"It's been up for five and a half," Julian said. Then, more diplomatically, "We're showing Frédéric the ropes today, literally. I'm sorry if that slowed things down a little."

Tohias was Diego's father, and the mayor of Thalia. He was also the rogue mechanochemist whose work in carbon allotrope 3D printing had made all of this possible. He was not a patient man.

"What have you brought me?" he asked. Then, peering into the catch basin, he said, "Oh. Mmm. Another . . . We need to let the bucket drag longer than this, Julian."

Julian clucked, grimaced, and shrugged at that. "Sir, we broke two teeth off the scoop as it is. We let it drag any longer, we're going to lose them all. First couple of contacts, we didn't pick up anything. This load came from our third drag, and I didn't want to push any further than that. We get really unlucky, sir, we're going to scrape the whole trawler off. I think maybe we're just at an unfavorable latitude. It seems like the surface is mostly bedrock, hard and smooth."

Tohias put a hand on his chin and nodded for a few seconds, and finally said, "I see, I see. We do want it smooth, so we don't just smash against a cliff or something, but maybe there's such a thing as too smooth. We were doing better a few months ago, down south over Lada Terra, right?"

"A little better, yes. Although I wouldn't want the ground any rougher than that. We get too much terrain, it's going to cost us. We hit a cliff, like you said, we're going to pop the quick release, and then you'll have to fabricate a whole new trawler."

"Mmm. Yes. So we could go back there, but . . . there are sand dunes in Menat Undae we really ought to check out. That's going to be mostly quartz, but we could scoop up full buckets of it, at very low risk. Depending on the exact composition, we'd probably increase our overall yields. Although, it's three hundred kilometers away. If we move that far north, our days are going to get longer."

Frédéric groaned. The day on Venus's surface was 118 Earth days long, but up here above the clouds, it was dictated by the trade winds, which circled the planet much faster than that. Right now, Thalia's "day" was around sixty hours, plus or minus, and Frédéric had never gotten used to it since they'd moved to this position. Any longer and he would definitely lose his mind.

Seeing Frédéric's distress, Tohias said, "It won't be popular, but it may be necessary. Mmm. Let me think on it some. I'll estimate some numbers, and we'll put it to a vote at the next meeting."

"A fuller bucket would be nice," Julian said. Then, after a long pause, he said, "Well, I'd better get back outside and make sure that trawler is on its way down again. Can you . . . Frédéric is interested in some hands-on education today. Can he watch you process this rock?"

"Yes, I suppose he can." Tohias nodded slowly, as though the idea of a practical education for Thalia's teens had never occurred to him.

Holding the rock in a gloved hand, Tohias said, "This is a mineral called gneiss, with stripes—you see these?—of low-grade stannite or cylindrite. Looks like some rutile impurities here and here, and some . . . halite? Venus definitely had oceans at one point, or these minerals would not be found together."

Frédéric peered in for close inspection. "Is it good?"

"Mmm. It's better than a chunk of pure basalt, which is what they brought me last time. We'll get maybe thirty grams of useful metals out of this, all different kinds. Mostly tin and copper, I think, and some titanium and aluminum. Also probably twenty grams of polysalt."

Polysalt was a highly prized commodity on Thalia—a supposedly healthier alternative to the "piss salt" purified from human urine—but twenty grams was not going to go very far.

"It doesn't seem like much," Frédéric said.

"It's not," Tohias agreed. "By weight, this is mostly oxygen and silicon, which we already have in abundance. We don't need silica; we have diamond. We don't need more solar panels. We don't need silicones; we have all the CHON a polymer chemist could ever need."

CHON meant carbon, hydrogen, oxygen, and nitrogen. Any school child knew that, especially if fifty percent of their nutritional intake came out of a CHON chow synthesizer.

"But we can get more from sand dunes?" Frédéric asked.

Tohias frowned and said, "I think so? I'm not a geologist by training. I'm consulting with a few on Earth, but of course we can't pay them. So, we learn as we go, which is an important skill in its own right."

"Yes, sir," Frédéric said, because he didn't know how else to respond.

Back on Earth, some people called Tohias the Fifth Horseman, or sometimes the Spanish Horseman, because he had not only invented flying *carbónespuma* and the machines to mass-produce it, but had then led fifty people to Venus with him to live on the stuff, and had (so far) kept them all alive. A remarkable achievement, surely. But Tohias was no trillionaire; this project would be impossible without the real Horsemen's rockets and launch pads, and the example they'd set on Mars and Luna and at ESL1. Also, the machines they'd designed or commissioned, the clear guidance about what was critically needed on a space colony, and what was merely luxury.

Without all of that already in hand, the founders of Thalia could never have managed even this much. And the money for this venture had come mostly from the colonists themselves, plus a few others who'd hoped to follow along in a second wave of settlers that had (so far) never materialized. There were not enough rich people on Earth who wanted to live like this. Not enough to fill another Ship, even though a landing pad had been prepared for one three years ago, along with a whole empty apartment building.

Frédéric's parents, Julian and Wilma, had sold their crane fabrication business to come here—here!—and work harder than their lowliest shop laborer ever had. Their example—even Tohias's own example—was apparently not too enticing. Not yet, not until they had broken their backs constructing something minimally viable. Or died trying.

"Well," Tohias said, suddenly cheerful, "let's get this rock in the crusher and start extracting."

He started up one of the machines—an open, nasty-looking contraption of toothy metal drums that rotated inward toward each other. Below that, another, smaller set of drums, and then a third set below that. Tohias handed Frédéric a pair of safety glasses, then popped on a pair himself, and then dropped the rock on top. Within seconds, the rock, bouncing and vibrating on top of the drums, was loudly broken into chunks, and then into gravel. How long had it been since Frédéric had seen gravel? Soon, the gravel was dropping down into the machine's lower layers, and a steady rain of dust was falling into a little plastic catch basin at the bottom.

Over the din, Tohias shouted, "First we're going to use a water bath to dissolve out the salts. We need those. Those are good for us. Then we need to pull out all the toxins like lead and mercury and tin and nickel. They're in there as oxides right now, so we have to heat them in a furnace, with a carbon monoxide atmosphere to strip off the oxygen atoms. We'll take most of the iron and copper and zinc, too, although we want to leave some behind to make potting soil. Fortunately, the extraction process isn't one hundred percent efficient."

What's left after that, we hit with an electric current to pull out non-nutritive metals like titanium and aluminum, and gold. The slag that's left over we grind up again, and that's your mother's potting soil. It's mostly quartz at that point, but it's also got calcium, phosphorus, sulfur, and, you understand, trace elements. Micronutrients."

"Which we mix with sewage and dead plants?" Frédéric shouted, because some days that was all his mother could talk about.

"Yes," said Tohias. "But plants need those minerals, and so do we. This surface dirt is critical to our long-term survival."

Watching the rock crusher, Frédéric could only imagine what would happen if he stuck his hand in there. Would it pull in his entire arm? His entire body? Would there be anything left? He kept his distance.

"How much metal would it take to build the Booster Stage?" he asked.

Tohias nodded. "That would be mostly made of diamond, but yes, we'd need a number of metal components. And metal linings. Fortunately, the design is mostly rather forgiving about the exact composition. We'd also need a big balloon to float the ship off the island, and that needs a metal coating as well."

"How much, though?"

"Altogether? About two hundred kilograms."

Frédéric did not like arithmetic, but it had been drilled into him, to do it all in his mind, without a computer, without pencil or paper. Self-reliance! Self-reliance! So, almost without meaning to, he visualized the long division, worked through the columns, and concluded that at the rate of thirty grams every five days, it would take Tohias, optimistically, ninety-one years to extract that much metal.

"Are we in trouble?" he asked. And then, when Tohias didn't say anything, he said, more loudly, "Tohias, are we in trouble, as a people? Are we trapped here?"

Again Tohias said nothing, until a really uncomfortably long time period had elapsed. Finally, as the din of the rock crusher started to subside, he said, "You understand, we have everything we truly need, Frédéric. I want you to remember that. We came here to start a new life—a new kind of life, not possible on Earth. We have enough. Our lives are not in immediate danger. But we may need to move the island farther north."

1.4

Post-Encounter Deposition
Brother Michael Jablonski
Prior, St. Joseph of Cupertion's
Monastery, Luna

The universe, for some reason, appears to us a grid of Cartesian space, occupied by masses slung around through Newtonian inertia, when in fact we know full well it's the iron fist of relativity smashing the rippling pool of quantum mechanics. Or vice versa. I don't know why this should be so, but I think the Beings have told us, or tried to, that even the universes of Einstein and Schrödinger are illusions. Time and space and matter and energy—in other words, all the things that make a universe exist to our senses at all—are themselves illusions, mere shadows cast by some cunningly simple underlying . . . stuff. And it seems to strike them mighty strange, that we perceive only a handful of derivative quantities, while they perceive the thing itself (and perhaps *only* the thing itself).

Wiser heads may disagree (with good and calculable reason!), but I think for the Beings there is no difference between their own size and the size of a volume of space to which they're paying attention. There is no difference between their own lifespans and the span of time they happen to be thinking about. I think their existence within the universe must require they consume *something* and excrete a different something in order to, I guess, increase the local entropy. Entropy is not conserved, they insist, and so I imagine time still has a direction for them. Can they swim against it like salmon? Can they pluck information from other portions of the stream?

One struggles to find appropriate metaphors for something so countersensual, but I find it useful to nail down the extremes. Can they swell to observe the entire simultaneous universe, for one infinitesimal moment? Can they shrink sufficient to know all of history for a single geometric point—all that passes through it or doesn't, ever? And betwixt these bookends, can they perhaps sniff a galaxy for a millisecond? Hug a planet for a year? Follow a human through all the days of her life? And in so doing, do they forget all that falls outside the bubble? Are they diffuse in space and time, straining vast energies to attend to something as tiny as we? Recall, a human life does not occur at a single point in space, but whirls around the axis of a planet that moves in both solar and galactic orbits, in a rapidly ballooning universe. Imagine, then, the difficulty of pinning a tail on that donkey!

This is how I imagine the Beings, and so if I ask one what will happen to me next year, I may be asking for something so exceedingly difficult or costly, and so exceedingly teensy, that the very concept strikes them absurd. And so the question begs itself: What common reference point can we have with creatures such as these, beyond our mutual astonishment at one another's existence?

Michael: "Why did you contact us?"
Beings: "You are amazing."
Michael: "Have you contacted others?"
Beings: "Not yet."
Michael: "Not yet? Will you?"
Beings: "Difficult to explain."
Michael: "Why?"
Beings: "Self-consistent structures in spacetime: conserved."
Michael: "What?"
Beings: "Difficult to explain."

Michael: "Are you aware of other intelligent beings, besides yourselves and us?"
Beings: "Not yet."
Michael: "Are you looking?"
Beings: "Difficult to explain."

✧✧✧

Michael: "Are you here to help us?"
Beings: "...?...Do you need help?"
Michael: "I don't know. Do we?"
Beings: "Amazing."

Beings: "You perceive energy associated with...the past?"
Michael: "Yes. We can see the light of stars, emitted eons ago and light-eons away."
Beings: "Amazing. Do you perceive a...beginning of time?"
Michael: "Not directly, with our senses. But we know it's there."
Beings: "Amazing."

Michael: "What came before the beginning?"
Beings: "Disallowed."
Michael: "What? Disallowed by whom?"
Beings: "Difficult to explain."
Michael: "Do you perceive the universe as having a Creator?"
Beings: "Yes!"

Michael: "Tell me about the Creator."
Beings: "Disallowed."
Michael: "Are you emissaries of the Creator?"
Beings: "...No?"
Michael: "But you perceive Him?"
Beings: "Not directly."
Michael: "You perceive Him indirectly?"
Beings: "Difficult to explain."

Michael: "Why was the universe created?"
Beings: "Disallowed."
Michael: "Disallowed in what way?"
Beings: "Information horizon."
Michael: "Like the surface of a black hole?"
Beings: "...Yes?"
Michael: "Are we inside a black hole?"
Beings: "Difficult to explain."

Michael: "Indirectly or not, you know something about God."

Beings: "..."

Michael: "Do you perceive God's love?"

Beings: "..."

Michael: "Do you perceive God's handiwork in the structure of the universe?"

Beings: "... Yes?"

Michael: "What does the handiwork tell you?"

Beings: "..."

Michael: "You don't like these questions."

Beings: "No."

Michael: "The Creator is very important to us."

Beings: "..."

Michael: "We seek to know Him."

Beings: "..."

Michael: "We seek to love Him."

Beings: "..."

Michael: "Can you help us do that?"

Beings: "Unlikely."

Michael: "Can you try?"

Beings: "..."

3.3
10 March
✧
I.R.V. *Intercession*
Extra-Kuiper Space
258 A.U. from Earth

"My greatest concern right now," Michael was saying, "is for the mental and spiritual health of our frozen passengers."

"Why?" Thenbecca asked. "They're frozen."

They were in the hibernation bay together, where the coffins of the aforementioned freezelings protruded from the walls and formed a mazelike pattern on the floor. Between the coffins, the white padding of the walls was puckered with indentations where it was riveted to the metal plates underneath. The floor where Michael and Thenbecca "stood" in the low gravity was padded in the same way, making the whole place feel vaguely like a lunatic asylum.

"Hmm, yes," he said. "And what happens when they aren't?"

He'd assumed a lecturing tone, and resolved to dial it back, because they were supposed to be bonding as peers and human beings. This was his fourth time in session with Thenbecca, and he still found her difficult to read. She was generally cheerful all the time, which surely had to be a front, because nobody was cheerful all the time. But what lay behind it was...unclear.

"They'll be awake for a few days," she said. "Like a big sleepover party."

"Some longer than others, yes? We thaw them out in groups of eight, over a period of two days. And then put them back in—I think?—the same order? Right away, that sets up some group dynamics that nobody has planned for."

"Well, okay," Thenbecca said. "Point taken. And as both the chef and the purser of this bucket, I'm really kind of responsible."

"As are we all."

She put a hand on one of the coffins—actually called a "hibernation pod"—and peered in at the person inside. A man, gray-skinned and quite dead-looking. Fortunately, the display on the coffin's upper surface said otherwise. It said he wasn't actually frozen at all, but hovering at two degrees centigrade, at least down inside his core. He looked frozen, though. There was frost on the coffin's glassy inner surface. His name was Donald Banhold, and Michael had never met him.

For reasons of speed and practicality, the whole ship was modeled after Dan Beseman's Mars ship, *Concordia*. This meant that, even though the hibernation bay was not part of a landing craft, it was nevertheless shaped like a truncated cone twelve meters high, with ninety-two of these pods projecting inward from the white walls. It was a bit like being inside a gigantic vending machine. Actually, it was exactly like that.

Michael and Thenbecca were standing at the bottom of the chamber, on either side of the railing surrounding the ladder, which led upward into the cargo deck (and the service deck above that), and downward into a tunnel leading to the aft airlock and—God forbid!—the engine. The flutter drive was thirty meters below them, connected to the conical ship by narrow struts, but still from here you could feel it humming as the fuel sphere slowly ablated away into gamma radiation.

"It feels like a violation," Michael observed, "to watch him sleep like this. I'm not the flight surgeon, and neither are you. Is it ethical? Are we voyeurs? I wish we could give them their privacy."

"Yeah. I mean, they knew what they were signing up for, but yeah."

"We'll be driving them like cattle. There'll hardly be time for their individual concerns when we wake them up, yes? Think how disorienting it must be, to be frozen on Earth, and thawed out twelve months and twenty-eight hundred A.U. later, in your underwear, with seven strangers shivering around you. And then told to stay out of the way while we thaw out the next batch. Yes, of course, they've agreed to all that, but still it's a strange thing. I wonder which is worst—to be in the first group to be woken up that way, or the last?"

"You *have* been thinking about this."

"Too much, yes. I need to share the burden. And of course, as you say, they'll only be awake for a couple of days. We'll shove them straight into the most transformative experience of their lives, and then right back into their coffins, and no, ma'am, you can't send a message to your people back home. The bathroom situation alone is going to be ghastly, especially for those with minimal experience in zero gravity. One bathroom is fine for just the eight of us, but a hundred? That can't be good, not any of it."

"Welcome to Igbal's world," Thenbecca said. She had been the chef at ESL1 when she'd been selected for this mission. She must know him pretty well.

"All hardware, no heart?"

"Some heart," she said. "More than you'd think. But he has people chasing behind him all day, cleaning up the details."

"And now that's us."

"Yes," Thenbecca said. "But we agreed to it, too. These problems can't be helped."

"Indubitably," he agreed, "I'm sure the design tradeoffs were very challenging. But that doesn't lessen the tragedy of it."

The ship was not, of course, a perfect copy of H.S.F. *Concordia*. Among its unique features, you had the forward and aft particle shields, and the inflatable/deployable Encounter Bubble, and no landing craft. There was only empty space between the aft struts, where *Concordia*'s enormous chemical fuel tanks would be. Those were major design adjustments. But like *Concordia*, *Intercession* was designed for a crew of eight and a total complement of one hundred. Fully loaded, it weighed as much as three jumbo jets, and there was barely enough antimatter in the solar system to push it out this far, this quickly. To have it otherwise would mean bringing fewer people, or else waiting five or ten or even fifteen years longer to commence the mission at all, with a larger and more capable ship. Or, to take much longer to get out here and back, with the same amount of antimatter pushing a heavier ship. This mission was what Igbal Renz had been able to accomplish in the four years he'd allotted himself.

Any of the other options were clearly worse, both from a geopolitical standpoint and, to be honest, a business one. Whatever motives had brought Igbal all the way out here, he did not have unlimited resources. Bogglingly large, yes, but nevertheless finite. For all of these reasons and more, it had to be this way.

Thenbecca surprised him by reaching out to touch his hand. "You're a very kind person," she said. "It makes me realize how awful most of us are."

Accepting the compliment, Michael said, "It's about choices, about where you spend your time and your energy and your thoughts. In small environments, it matters because you're stuck living in the consequences of your own actions. In large ones, it matters because even the flapping of a butterfly's wing ripples outward until it changes the entire world. Kindness and self-interest are not at odds, unless you define your self-interest very narrowly. Which is a phenomenally stupid thing to do."

"There's no shortage of stupid," Thenbecca said.

"Alas," he agreed. And once again had nothing to add. If God had indeed created the world—created a whole universe in which Earth and humanity might eventually arise—then surely there was a purpose to it all. An imperfect striving toward some eventual perfection? But it was hard to see, and Michael's only certain role was to help the people around him. It was a daunting task, and one for which he was very definitely unworthy. But he would keep after it nonetheless!

After a companionable silence of perhaps twenty seconds, Thenbecca said, "You've never asked me about my name. Usually it's the first thing people want to know."

"You'll tell me if and when you feel like it," Michael said, though he was indeed very curious. Was it Greek? Semitic? He'd never met a Thenbecca before. But he knew: people who carried an unusual characteristic around with them were generally tired of answering questions about it. "Names do have a way of defining people, for good or ill."

Then veering back to the previous topic, he said, "The food situation will be ghastly as well. MREs?"

Meals, Ready to Eat. Military-style packaged meals, served cold. As the chef, Thenbecca had had a hand in planning that side of mission logistics.

"Not just for them," she said, wrinkling her nose. "For us as well. It's really the only way we can pass out three hundred meals a day. We want to make sure hunger is not a problem these people have to deal with, even briefly."

"Won't that generate a lot of trash?"

"It will," she agreed, "And that goes straight back into the cargo hold. We have to carry it all back with us, which wastes fuel on the way back home, but the alternative would set a bad pollution precedent."

"Yes, I suppose it would."

Even in the vastness of extrasolar space, littering would leave behind a potential navigation hazard for some unlucky future traveler. It would take a million years and a planet's worth of mass for such pollution to rival that of Low Earth Orbit, but at interstellar speeds, any mass at all had the potential to vaporize a ship.

The awakened sleepers would generate a lot of sewage, also—far more than the recycling system could possibly recover during the twelve-month journey home—but there was a large, disgusting storage tank set aside for that purpose.

Thenbecca said, "My birth name was Rebecca. I was the second of two children. My mom used to always say, 'We had Petey and then Becca.' Until I was three, I didn't realize Becca was my actual name. My parents would call out for me, and I'd walk up saying '*Then*becca. *Then*becca.' And Mom would maybe say something like, 'That's right, we had Petey and then Becca.' By the time I figured out that wasn't my name, it was too late. It was firmly stuck. I officially changed it when I turned eighteen."

She looked somewhat embarrassed by the admission, which Michael found strange.

"Do you still like it?" he asked gently.

"I do. I mean, it's my name. But sometimes I can't help second-guessing my younger self. I got a tattoo at that time, also, and I sometimes wish . . . I'd waited?"

"It's quite common for people to change their birth names," he said. Indeed, something like twenty percent of the global population had done it at one time or another. Monks and priests and nuns often changed their names when they took their vows. Some abbeys actually required it. Michael himself had not done it, but he

understood the urge. It was also the norm among people changing
gender identities or entering show business, or taking up residence in
a foreign country where their actual names were unpronounceable.

Of course, people also did it for entirely frivolous reasons. Before
retreating to monastic life, Michael had known a guy named Flash-
E who was not even a musician, and he had known a young woman
who had named herself Preeble on a whim. Preeble!

"It's a beautiful name," he added. "And naming for birth order
makes just as much sense as Russian and Scandinavian patronyms.
Perhaps someday we'll all be named that way."

"You're too kind," she said, somewhat sarcastically.

And that's when a grain of ice struck the ship, hard.

The forward shield—a dome-shaped stack of alternating
materials—shrieked through the support struts as it absorbed the
hit, as did the shock-absorbing springs and pistons on which it was
mounted. With four meters of travel available to it, the shield
jammed fully two and a half meters closer to the nose of the ship
itself, before easing back into its original position. Michael and
Thenbecca knew none of this at the time, but the bang-scream-jolt
of it told Michael the gist of what had happened.

"God!" he said, as fear washed over him. Michael firmly believed
that when he died, his soul would go to some kind of heaven and
meet some kind of maker, and in slower moments, this largely stilled
his fear of death. But the *process* of becoming dead (along with fear
of pain, injury, or incapacity) remained frightening, and in any case
the limbic system had its own ideas. A coppery wave of adrenaline
flooded through his body.

"What was that?" Thenbecca said, her face gone the color of linen.
But of course she knew.

"We hit something," Michael said. "It couldn't have been too—"

And that was when a second ice grain hit, followed moments later
by a third and fourth. Michael felt the shield's shock absorbers
bottom out, transferring the impact straight through the four struts
that connected the fore and aft shields. The hull itself—the tall,
slender, pressurized cone that held all the humans—was attached to
those struts in multiple places, at the floor of each deck, and so a
ripple passed through the hull, and he felt that as well. And saw it,
like the ground ripples of an earthquake.

The lights went red, and Ptolemy's voice said, calmly but loudly, "Impact alarm. Impact alarm. All personnel to pressurized lockers."

"Shit," said Thenbecca. From the look on her face, Michael figured she did not expect to make it to the lockers alive.

"It'll be all right," he told her, based on nothing whatsoever.

But she was already on the ladder, not climbing it but heaving herself upward against the minimal gravity. She cleared six rungs with the first mighty pull, and six more with the second one, and in another moment she was into the sealable tube connecting the hibernation bay to the cargo deck.

Didn't have to tell her twice, apparently.

Fighting to remain as calm as possible, Michael followed along behind her, shrugging out of his robe as he went, for one could not climb fully dressed into a spacesuit, but only in the slick, gray, form-fitting garments known as "space underwear." He kicked off his slippers as well, so that by the time he entered the cargo deck, he was ready to ensuit.

Of course, everyone else was entering the cargo deck as well, shedding clothing as they went, crowding and bumping against each other in the low gravity. Life in space involved a lot of group hangouts in underwear (or even, in a dust-control airlock, completely naked), and one grew accustomed to it. In an emergency setting like this, one barely even noticed. But one noticed a little bit, yes, the curve of a hip or buttock, or the intriguing point where two legs came together. Even a monk, nearly two decades into his vows, was not above noticing, as eight people clambered past one another and into their respective lockers. The human brain was a fantastic instrument, indeed.

The truncated cone of the cargo deck was a hexadecagon in cross section; a sixteen-sided polygon. Here, pressurized spacesuit lockers—each with a crew member's name block-printed above—alternated with entrances to the surrounding storage ring, which held tools and equipment of various kinds, but mostly the deflated Encounter Bubble, which would house the ninety-two sleepers when they awoke.

Getting into one's own locker was easy enough, even with other people crowding the space. The heavy glass door swung outward, and one stepped inside the space where one's spacesuit was hung.

Actually getting into the spacesuit was slightly more complicated; one slithered into the upper half, with helmet already attached, and then one lifted and turned to get one's feet into the trousers and boots. Mating the two halves involved lining up a pair of rings and then, with the aid of a wrist-mounted mirror, rotating a latching ring until it seated. Just like in the safety drills.

The cargo deck stank of fear. With considerable commotion, all eight crew members were attempting to follow these steps at the same time, while shouting things like, "Is the hull intact?" and "Can I get a goddamn status report?"

"Atmospheric pressure nominal and stable," said Ptolemy. "Hull inductance measurements nominal and stable. Hull breach is not indicated."

"We hit something," Michael said, although by now it must be obvious.

"Probably passed through a comet tail," said Dong.

"No, but a very diffuse cloud of ice crystals might—" said Igbal.

And that was when the fifth grain hit.

After that, there was a lot of chaos. Igbal was the first one out of his locker, and without a word he launched himself up the ladder toward the bridge.

Next out was Michael himself, who was fanatical about safety drills and could literally don a spacesuit while blindfolded. Thank goodness he had, in fact, helped design the fixtures in these lockers, to make sure such a thing was exactly possible. A few years back, Saint Joe's had suffered two deaths from vacuum exposure (and very nearly three!), and Michael had never gotten over it. He was paranoid before that happened, but not paranoid enough. So, indeed, whatever ill fortune befell human astronauts from that point forward would not be because he, himself, had failed to prepare. Once out, he hovered near the ladder, ready to provide assistance.

Third was Dong Nguyen, a veteran of Transit Point Station who had logged more EVA hours than any other human in history. He headed up/forward as well, though probably to stand by the forward airlock, which happened to be in the nose of the bridge.

After that, things got complicated.

Hobie Prieto (more a pilot than an astronaut per se) took a full ninety seconds to get dressed, cursing all the while. The flight surgeon, Rachael Lee, took fifteen seconds longer.

"This is not acceptable," Michael told them both, as they emerged like hermit crabs from outgrown shells. They had performed better than this in safety drills; there was no excuse for performing so badly when it actually mattered.

The others—Sandy, Harv, and Thenbecca—all gave up around that time.

"I can't get this," Harv said about his waist ring.

"I think I'm stuck," Thenbecca said, about her entire body. She'd put the trousers on first, and then apparently been unable to maneuver her torso into the suit top. She had her head and arms in there, and would have needed to be a contortionist to get any further.

Sandy didn't say anything, but a glance through the clear glass of her locker door revealed helmet and gloves floating free inside there, with Sandy herself apparently snagged by the camisole top on one of the suit rack hooks, looking back and forth for the reason she couldn't get her feet down on the floor.

"I'm not so sure about bringing her on the mission," Michael recalled Igbal saying, back in the early days while the ship was still under construction. *"She's a brain with no thumbs. She's a brain with no brains, really. But none of my decent astronauts understand how the flutter drive works, and anyway I need them at ESL1, making money."*

Michael had met some of Igbal's astronauts—ridiculously competent women, with nerves of steel and all that—and wished at least one of them were here now. To the laggards before him he said, with rare sarcasm and rarer anger, "Had this been an *actual emergency*, the three of you might well be trapped in those lockers for the rest of your lives."

Thirty minutes after the fifth and hopefully final impact, the crew—still suited up—was crowded in the wardroom, looking up at the video displays. Even the ship's minimal gravity was gone; the flutter drive had been shut down, and without its constant vibration, the place was as quiet as an air-conditioned morgue.

The two not present, Dong Nguyen and Igbal Renz himself, were outside, floating on tethers, inspecting the forward shield.

Michael watched the dizzying view from their helmet cameras, pasted alongside Ptolemy's infographic of the damage to the shield. Five cones, like red icicles, sliced partway through the dome of the shield. One of them went almost all the way through.

Dong and Igbal were the most experienced astronauts, and the most qualified to perform emergency repairs. Yes, Igbal Renz, the trillionaire! He'd after all made his money by building things, often with his own two hands, and he was among the very first humans to take up permanent residence in space. But still, Michael found it jarring.

Dong's and Igbal's crew functions were also the least critical on a moment-to-moment basis, so in that sense they were the most expendable. Yes, again, Igbal himself. He was a shambling wreck of a captain and probably knew it, and if he died out there, it would make basically zero difference to any mission outcomes. But still, yes, it was jarring to see the owner of Renz Ventures with a tool kit strapped to his leg, climbing hand over hand on an aluminized nylon tether, across the front-most surface of a wounded spaceship, like a common mechanic.

A common mechanic moving at three percent of lightspeed, who could be vaporized at any moment by a microgram of stationary matter. Michael had heard, but not quite believed, that Igbal was as cavalier about his personal safety as he was about everything else. It wasn't courage that had driven him out there, so much as bloody-mindedness. He wanted the ship back on its way as quickly as possible and would not let anything as trivial as his own fears get in the way of that.

"We're coming up on the holes," said Dong. They were "walking" across the shield on magnetic boots.

The forward shield was a dome-shaped stack of alternating materials, and according to radar and surface conductance assays, it had absorbed the impacts by converting the particles into cones of relativistic plasma that, in turn, vaporized layers of tungsten and ballistic nylon and silicon nitride and tungsten again, and then spread wider through a layer of vacuum before again striking metal. According to Ptolemy's best estimates, the particles weighed roughly 0.1 milligrams each, and were moving at about nine thousand kilometers per second relative to the ship. Striking with the energy of a thousand machine-gun bullets, the heaviest particles had worked their way through a hundred layers of shielding—more than half the thickness of the shield.

The helmet cameras didn't show anything at first, but then, in Dong's wandering view, Michael caught sight of a blackened divot in the otherwise-smooth surface of the shield. This by itself was surprising, because Ptolemy had estimated none of the grains were larger than four hundred microns across. But the hole was big enough that Dong could have stuck the thumb of his spacesuit glove in there. And a few meters beyond it was another hole, about the same size.

Igbal was holding a radar gun, playing it back and forth across the surface of the shield. "Impact cone is stippled," he said. "We've got some solid structure under there, full of holes, like a colander."

Michael nodded to himself. This was good news; it meant the damage, while serious, was not catastrophic. Like a bullet wound, the entry hole was the tip of a hollow cone. But if there was still solid material in that void—if it was *mostly* solid material—then those layers of the shield would still have some ability to absorb and dissipate the energy of another impact.

Dong Nguyen said, "I think we should put some spray foam down these holes. Let it expand and fill up the empty space."

"That'll compromise the vacuum gaps between layers," Igbal said.

"More than they already are?" Dong said.

And that appeared to be the sum total of the technical discussion. Dong's camera held steady on Igbal's leg pack as Igbal fished out a canister with a straw-tipped spray nozzle on top.

Filling the first hole took them just a few minutes; they knelt beside it on magnetic knee pads, inserted the canister's straw tip as far in as it would go, and pressed the button. For a while, nothing happened.

"How does this help?" Thenbecca asked.

To which Sandy answered, "You know how jumping off a bridge can kill you, even if the water is deep? For a body moving fast enough, there's no time for the water to move out of the way, so it behaves more like a non-Newtonian liquid. Basically, a solid."

"Okay," said Thenbecca, hesitantly.

"To a particle moving at three percent of the speed of light, everything is a brick wall. It hits that foam, it's going to vaporize, just the same as if it hit a metal plate."

"The plate is going to absorb more energy," Michael said.

Inside her helmet, Sandy nodded. "Yes. But if you expand that plate with voids, it's an even better dissipator. Repair foam is actually a pretty good solution, all things considered. Better than the nothing that was in there before."

On Igbal's camera display, Dong was pulling the straw farther and farther back, until the tip of it was completely out of the hole, and then a yellow-white mass was boiling out behind it, forming a stalagmite the size of his fist, and then the size of his entire arm. It curled over a bit, like a ram's horn, and then it stopped expanding.

"Do we shave off the excess?" Dong wanted to know. "I don't think we need to."

"I don't think so, either," Igbal said. Then more loudly: "Anyone disagree?"

No one did, so the two of them moved on to the next hole.

"Are they going to have enough foam?" Thenbecca wanted to know.

"There's more in the equipment locker," Sandy told her.

"What if we need it for something else?"

No one had an answer to that. Whatever they had, they had, and the best they could do was fix what they knew needed fixing, and hope for the best.

1.5

Post-Encounter Deposition
Brother Michael Jablonski
Prior, St. Joseph of Cupertion's
Monastery, Luna

Were I a more suspicious man I might opine: these Beings know more than they're saying, and withhold for a purpose. Or perhaps my approach was simply rude to them, as if they had bombarded me with queries about noxious body fluids and their possible uses. In any case, theology seemed a subject that, for them, is easily exhausted, and perhaps obscene. Still, some of the most religious humans known to me are astronomers, and cosmologists in particular.

Michael: "Does the universe have an ending?"
Beings: "Yes!"
Michael: "Is it soon?"
Beings: "Definitely not."
Michael: "Does the universe have a purpose?"
Beings: "Yes!"
Michael: "How do you know?"
Beings: "Difficult to explain."
Michael: "Can you try?"
Beings: "The substrate is . . . marked."
Michael: "Marked how?"
Beings: "Difficult to explain."

✧✧✧

Michael: "What is the purpose of the universe?"

Beings: "Disallowed."

Michael: "Does that mean you don't know?"

Beings: "Difficult to explain."

Michael: "Is it like the future?

Beings: "Hello! This message is a transmission! We are so glad you made it."

3.4
25 March

I.R.V. *Intercession*
Extra-Kuiper Space
370 A.U. from Earth

In the wake of the sandbar incident, the dangers of interstellar space had stopped being hypothetical.

Instead of weekly safety drills, Michael began running them two or three times every day, at random intervals, and with different scenarios every time. Power failure! Hull breach! Engine malfunction! A steering jet that was stuck in the "on" position! The crew, already technically adept at dealing with such things, became knee-jerk experts. Swap in the backup APUs! Get your suits on! Emergency engine shutdown sequence! Shut down power to the starboard ACS and prep for EVA!

Also, the mandatory philosophical discussions really had started to make a difference. Michael had observed enough of these to have a sense how they were going.

When Harv, the leathery Boulder academic, spoke with Dong, the leathery Vietnamese astro-handyman, they ended up talking about quantum mechanics, and its implications for consciousness and self-awareness.

"I don't think Ptolemy's self-aware," Dong chattered. He and Harv and Michael were in the cargo deck, doing their daily hour of cleaning duty, and Dong was wiping antiseptic onto the railing that surrounded the ladder. Weird bacteria grew in space, and keeping them at bay was a constant job. "He got no body. He got no neurons, no Heisenberg uncertainty principle. He could run on a cell phone, right? Maybe slower, maybe some of his functions shut down. He's clever, but he don't know anything. Software, right? No soul. Now Deep Mind, that thing's a hardware implementation."

"So Deep Mind is sentient?"

"Might be."

Deep Mind was a building-sized computer in Cleveland, Ohio, put together by IBMicrosoft in the middle of the Cuyahoga River. Not the fastest or most capable processor in the world but, in Michael's opinion, one of the creepiest and, by corollary, most theologically troubling. It had forced him, more than once, to confront the question: What is a soul, and how do we know who has one?

"Human cells are full of quantum processors," Harv acknowledged. "More than we ever could have guessed. But so are yeast cells, and fungi. Are you saying those are sentient, too?"

"More than Ptolemy."

"Huh. Maybe." Then, after a pause: "The Beings don't have bodies, either."

"Yeah, I know," said Dong. He had moved around to the ladder itself, and presently sprayed and wiped it, hopefully murdering any organisms trying to take up residence. "I been thinking about that."

"And?"

"I dunno. I don't got enough information. But they contacted us, right?"

That conversation took many unexpected turns, and was just one of many, many conversations among the crew that Michael had the opportunity to witness.

Another time, Sandy spoke to Igbal in the gymnasium, wedged between the galley and the bathroom on the service deck. Michael "stood" on the floor outside, watching. They also talked about artificial intelligence, and its differences from natural intelligence, and whether that had any bearing on whatever sort of intelligence the Beings represented.

Igbal, the inventor of Deep Belief Network robotics, said: "If a robot thought the same way as a human, we wouldn't need it."

"Then why do robots steal people's jobs?" Sandy asked.

They were both exercising with rubber bands, holding them under a foot and pulling the ends up with their arms.

"They don't," Igbal said, "any more than an airplane steals the jobs of mule drivers. It doesn't work that way."

"Then where are all the mule drivers? And what about robot lawyers? Robot journalists? Robot CEOs? Those don't replace people? A robot could do your job, I'll bet."

"An AI was first listed as a co-inventor on a patent way back in 2021," Igbal said. "And yet, here we are. Could a robot make all this happen?" He spread his arms to indicate not only the starship *Intercession*, but the Summit mission itself, and the vast infrastructure that had made it possible.

"Someday," Sandy insisted.

"Nah," he said. "By the time they're that good, we'll all be merging with 'em. And it'll make sense for them as much as us, because we're a different, complementary kind of processor."

"Sounds awful."

"Well," Igbal said, "you can go live in a forest or something. Anyway, we have no idea what kind of substrate the Beings are running on, but it's a safe bet their mental process is nothing like ours. Which means there are things we do better than they do."

"We have hands," Sandy said.

"We do," he agreed. "And how amazing is that?"

When Thenbecca spoke to Hobie Prieto by the spacesuit lockers in the cargo deck, they talked (with surprising technical precision!) about the neurochemical similarities between near-death experiences and the deeper forms of induced hibernation. When the sleepers went back into their hibernation pods, after the Encounter, would the Beings speak to them again as their bodies froze and shut down?

"That was when I first heard them," Hobie said, his dark face lighting up at the memory. "When Doc Pamela froze me, in the test coffin at ESL1 Shade Station. They sang to me! They invited us to meet them. That was when Igbal's people started to actually believe the Beings were real, because I'm no bullshitter, and I don't fall for no fairy tales."

"Fehyrie tales," he lilted, in that slow Jamaican way.

"What were they like?" Thenbecca asked.

"Oh, hard to say. Hard to say, my friend. Talking to them was like, I dunno, falling into a big pit full of balloons, and every balloon was a video display showing jagged patterns. They sounded like the crowd at a football stadium, maybe, singing chants down to the players."

"Were you scared?"

"No. Before that, when Doc Pamela was injecting me with drugs and dropping my core temperature, that was skerry. Nobody knew for sure the procedure was going to work! But then I was shooting through a tunnel into this . . . place, and the Beings welcomed me with great excitement, and I felt like everything was going to be okay. And I kind of still feel that way. They don't mean us harm; they just really want to meet us."

And when Brother Michael Jablonski himself, once and future Prior of Saint Joseph's Monastery, spoke to Flight Surgeon Rachael Lee, once and future Chief Medical Officer of Renz Ventures and ESL1 Shade Station, they talked about the mechanics of cryohibernation systems, and all the adjustments, large and small, that would need to be made—to the pods themselves, and to the ship's entire life support system—just before and just after the sleepers awoke. This was an area where Michael's duties overlapped heavily with Rachael's, so perhaps it was technically shop talk rather than a philosophical discussion, *per se*. But little bits of philosophy crept in.

While checking the fluid and power connections to one of the hibernation coffins, Rachael said, "What if Thenbecca's hypothesis is correct, and there really is something different about the way our brains work out here? It's not such a crazy thought. We still don't really understand the brain at a quantum level."

She was a compact woman with a bright, piercing gaze, and when Michael had met her, she'd seemed perpetually alert. She was better grounded than the rest of the crew, with the possible exception of Igbal, but she generally looked like someone who'd had ten cups of coffee instead of sleeping.

"No," said Michael, following behind her with a spray bottle and a rag, "it isn't such a crazy idea. I might have thought so six months ago, but it's different when you feel it. Spacetime is flatter out here. There are fewer photons and neutrinos. Fewer everything. We didn't evolve for this."

"So," Rachael said, "it might affect the way people react to the unfreezing process. It might affect a lot of things. We're going to have to be very nimble, and mindful, during the days when we're populating the Encounter Bubble."

"Agreed," Michael said.

There was no real plan for any of this—just appropriately scaled hardware, and a schedule.

That was what happened when you let Igbal Renz work his magic: things appeared out of nowhere—big, amazing things!—and yet thousands of implementation details were left to the last minute, often jury-rigged by the people around him while he hovered by impatiently. Michael had visited ESL1 Shade Station, and found it much the same, with modules clicked together in the order they were constructed, in a 3D jumble with no master plan. Fittingly, the women of ESL1 had actually cut hatches into two of the station's bulkheads and installed a flexible tunnel, connecting two points that should have been adjacent but weren't, and never would be. Perhaps that wasn't entirely Igbal's fault—as Michael understood it, the modules had been added in order of their perceived urgency—but still.

The crew of *Intercession* would need that same brute creativity, to keep this whole affair from going to waste.

One thing that struck Michael, though, about these enforced conversations, was the way his crewmies strayed so readily outside the margins of their expertise. That might be a bad thing in bar arguments or rigorous academic dick-measuring, but in other contexts Michael considered it a good thing indeed. In his experience, creativity was blunted when people remained in their comfort zones, or strayed into areas where they genuinely didn't know anything. But in the margins, in the interstitial spaces between ignorance and expertise, new ideas flourished like dandelions.

He'd often told the monks at Saint Joe's, "If you know exactly what you're doing, you're underperforming." Of course, that was a group of Earthmen tasked with building a lunar base that could plausibly last for centuries. Here, the mission was rather different.

And yet.

He was also warmed by the personal tidbits that slipped out here and there, like when Harv said, "Nobody seems to be fucking on this ship. In a crew of eight, doesn't that seem unlikely? People are never happier than when they're having good sex, and lots of it. The body knows."

Or when Thenbecca said, "I came to cooking late in life. I was a data analyst for a bank, if you can believe it. A big bank, that did a lot of good in the world, like microlending to the Flood Nations, and just, you know, credit cards for regular people. But also a lot of morally gray stuff I can't discuss, and a few things that were flat-out illegal, and wrong. I was in a position to see all of it. I couldn't not! I figure that's why Igbal made me Purser, in charge of ship's stores. But most of the stores are food and other consumables, which makes Chef-Purser actually a very logical job." She was in the galley as she spoke, tinkering with the CHON synthesizer's programming interface, her feet in stirrups on the floor to keep her from floating away.

"Anyway, I learned to cook from a hundred-year-old book. Just in my spare time, for fun. I then started a restaurant, and that didn't work, but I did end up with a large online following. So, this and that, and I ended up being accepted to live at ESL1 Shade Station, colonizing outer space. And now I'm here, in a place I don't reckon any of us ever expected to be. But I'm good at feeding people, and I like it, so yeah."

Michael had to agree; the food here was better than the synthetic CHON chow he was used to at Saint Joe's, despite being woven from the same basic ingredients. Of course, they grew vegetables at Saint Joe's, which wasn't possible here, so the overall diet here was more limited. But Thenbecca did have a knack for spinning CHON—plus tiny amounts of precious salt, mustard, red pepper, and the vitamin-mineral powder called "foundation"—into culinary gold.

Michael, being responsible for the equipment that turned the crew's waste back into component elements, had to appreciate that *Intercession*'s Chef-Purser had literally shit to work with.

Hobie said, "I once lived on board a sea plane for three years. Not really traveling very much; it's just that dock fees were cheaper than apartments in Montego Bay. But it's not much space. You get good at doing without things when you live in a plane! It's good practice for being an astronaut."

And Rachael, in a conversation with Dong Nguyen, said, "You and I both repair things that can't be shut off. I had a professor once who said heart surgery was like repairing a car while it was running.

I think he meant an internal combustion car, because the analogy doesn't work so well with an electric."

"I thought you were an obstetrician," Dong said.

"Prenatal heart surgery," she said.

Dong clucked at that, clearly impressed. "You build a ship in a bottle?"

Ignoring that, Rachael said, "If it's a complex surgery, you have to cool the mother's body way down. That's how I got into hibernation technology."

Everyone had an improbable story to tell about how, of the ten billion living humans, they alone had ended up here.

Even Igbal had some personal anecdotes to share. In his gravelly voice, he said, "I was a shitty student until I got to graduate school. That's when things started to really click. I was asking, hey, why are deep learning neural networks limited to classical computers? Can't we do the same thing with qubits? And the answer was yes. I got in cozy with the tech transfer department, so when I started figuring out how to churn out algorithms and gizmos that solved problems in the real world, I was making royalty income almost right away. By the time I left, I already had enough money to build my own lab and start hiring staff. People say I launched my career on Daddy's money, but that old drunk didn't even pay for college. It was all me."

"You made the robot butlers, right?" Thenbecca asked him. "And waiters?"

"I made their brains," Igbal agreed. "And the operating system, Quantum Von Neumann Complete. I wasn't interested in robotics per se until I got into asteroid mining. RzVz had so much money at that point, we had to put it somewhere. So I started looking up."

"Jesus," Harv said.

"What?" Igbal said, shrugging almost nonchalantly. It wasn't a humble brag; to his credit, despite the air of hubris that perpetually surrounded him, he genuinely didn't seem to find his biography all that extraordinary. Perhaps just a bunch of stuff that happened while he was screwing around.

But when the conversation turned to quantum mechanics while Harv and Igbal were both in the same room, things got heavy quickly, and both men loudly lamented the lack of a screenboard to scribble drawings and equations on.

Harv would say things like, "Systems that stay coherent at room temperature, or body temperature, are a superposition of states that have collapsed. A million narrow spikes blended together to form a Gaussian. But that result is only coherent in Fourier space, which is why it took us so long to notice it, all around us. In our own cells."

To which Igbal would say, "You're getting carried away with the math. The analogy with thermodynamics gives you a better gut feel how the system is going to behave. Temperature, pressure, density. The energy in a lot of qubit designs behaves a lot like an ideal gas."

"No, it doesn't," Harv finally said to him, one time when the two of them were on the service deck, doing sit-ups on the ladder instead of actually going into the gym.

"You . . . Mathematically it doesn't, sure. The equations don't line up. But look, if you heat up the pot, you'd better have a tight lid or you're going to boil out the electrons. Which is where you get that collapse you're talking about."

"It doesn't work that way, Ig."

"No? Then why am I rich? Look, I'm not arguing. I'm actually agreeing with you, but the High Priests of Quantum Mechanics are always trying to make it more mysterious than it actually is."

During one such conversation, in the dining room with most of the crew present, Michael injected a question of his own: "What kind of system do the Beings represent?"

Which stopped Harv and Igbal in their tracks for a moment, until Igbal finally said, "We don't even know if they inhabit the same universe as us. When they speak to one person, the people nearby don't see or hear anything. Either that communication is telepathic, or effectively telepathic, or it's a physical interaction from outside our universe. Like, they're right there with that person, but on a neighboring plane. Which might have different rules."

"Are you sure?" Michael pressed. "As you say, they're capable of interacting. Even if they're on a different plane somewhere, there's some . . . physical projection of them that's cast into our dimension, to tickle the brains of DMT dreamers. Photons, perhaps? If that makes sense."

"Almost," Harv said.

"We can see them," Igbal said. "We can hear them. They have bodies of some kind, somewhere. Singing spheres or machine elves, or whatever. When you take the drug, you'll understand. A part of you bleeds into wherever they are, and your brain very definitely registers it as a different place, a higher place. I think it's got more dimensions than ours, which is why it's so hard to describe. But there's no telling what physics governs it."

"If they have some cross section in our dimension," Michael insisted, "then that part of them, at least, must follow the same laws we do. The speed of light, for example. Also, if their plane is adjacent to ours in some vast hyperspace, how different could it be? Our laws must at least be a subset of theirs."

"Hmm," said Harv, pausing to take a bite of Thenbecca's latest creation. Mashed potatoes!

After a moment's thought, Igbal said, "The spot cast by a laser pointer can travel faster than light. Imagine waving it at a target ten meters away. It goes maybe a few kilometers per hour. Now put a much bigger target ten million kilometers away, and suddenly, with those same hand motions, you're going three c."

"The laser spot isn't an object," Harv said. "It's a projection. The photons are going their normal speed the whole time. The only thing you're moving is their impact point."

"That's what I'm saying, Harv. What happens on the screen is different from what happens in the 3D universe. The Beings may not be objects, either. Not in the parts of the universe we're capable of perceiving."

"Disembodied souls," Michael mused.

"Projections," Igbal said. "But projected from what? And where? I'd say there are very few assumptions we can actually make about them."

The three of them paused, then. It was Rachael who finally spoke:

"If they communicate, they metabolize. They have to. Energy out means energy in, and some kind of process in between."

Of all the crew, Rachael was perhaps the least stressed out by space ennui, except perhaps for Igbal. After all, her daily rounds involved checking on ninety-two frozen patients. Even if their condition never changed, even if Ptolemy was programmed to alert her to even the slightest flicker of change, it was still a time-consuming task, and a lot of responsibility.

"Agreed," Igbal said.

Rachael said, "They can also 'see' or 'hear' us. They know we exist. You can't have senses without sensory organs. In fact, they know we exist in a particular place in the universe, or they wouldn't have asked us to relocate. We know they can think. That means there's a brain involved, too. Some kind of processing organ."

Hobie then added, "You ever seen a slime mold, Doc? Where I grew up, we had them in the jungle. They're scavengers, like flies. Couple of college students set up a maze one time, and the yellow mold solved it in about an hour, to get some oatmeal at the center. They love oatmeal, I guess. But they got no processing organ."

"Maybe they are one, collectively," Rachael said. "A hive mind."

To which Michael said, "A hive is certainly smarter than an individual bee. But the bee exists, too."

The conversations could be like that: bystanders jumping in, topics shifting and blurring. It was all one big conversation, and everyone was part of it.

Even Ptolemy got in on the action, butting in at one point by stating: "Mission parameters require *Intercession* to be motionless relative to the Solar System. No crew member has reported contact with the Beings while *Intercession* is traveling at speed."

"Not for lack of trying," Igbal agreed, laughing and clapping the breast pocket where he kept a DMT vape pen.

This outburst by itself was remarkable, and made Michael wonder (not for the first time) if systems like Ptolemy were themselves alien intelligences. He'd been assured many times that Ptolemy had no "I-loop" or "unsupervised learning cortex," and hence no self-awareness or "consciousness" in the sense that humans used these terms. And no quantum uncertainty, as Dong insisted. But what did any of that mean, actually?

Unable to help himself, Michael asked, "Ptolemy, what will you be doing when the rest of us are communing with the Beings?"

"Analyzing vocalizations and body language," Ptolemy answered. Its voice, as always, seemed to come from everywhere at once. Clearly artificial, clearly genderless, it spoke quietly from every headset and speaker.

"Who asked you to do that?"

"These are normal background functions," Ptolemy said.

"Okay, but what will you be looking for?"

"Emotional states of the crew and passengers. Descriptions of the Encounter experience."

"Why?"

Michael thought then that if Ptolemy had a body, it would have shrugged.

"Mission parameters include gathering data about the Beings."

"What do you think they are?" he asked.

"Unknown," Ptolemy replied. "Ship's sensors are not configured to detect the Beings."

"But you're curious?"

"Correct."

"Of course it's curious," Igbal said. "It's a goddamn neural network."

Michael found that unnecessarily reductive. Was "curiosity" really so mechanical? Couldn't Igbal just choose to be amazed by the conversation Ptolemy was trying to have? By the mere fact of it? But no, Igbal had apparently spent too much time tinkering in the guts of artificial intelligence to find anything magical about it.

The conversations ranged far and wide, with different points of view that often clashed wildly. And yet, over time, some definite points of consensus began to emerge. As the Ancient Greeks had proven, there was a lot you could learn about the universe with logic alone, or logic and some minimal observation.

As Turnaround Day approached—the day on which they'd rotate to face the nose of the ship toward the Sun again, aiming the hell-beam of the flutter drive at Alpha Centauri to begin their deceleration—Michael began keeping, in his personal notebook, a running summary of the group's deductions.

1) The Beings exist.
2) They have sensing, cognition, and "speech" organs or capacities of some kind.
3) Ergo, they must be "made of" something.
4) They exhibit both emotions and intellect.
5) They cannot be detected by any known device, other than a human brain in certain specific operating states.
6) They appear to number in the dozens or hundreds, at least.

7)   They exhibit curiosity and memory.

8)   Their mode of communication, whatever it might be, is hampered on Earth, and to a lesser extent at ESL1. By implication, it is not hampered (or less hampered) in interstellar space. Because of gravity? Radiation? Neutrino flux? Quantum entanglement?

9)   Their communication occurs in real time, with no discernible speed-of-light delays.

10) Therefore, unless they violate causality (possible?), some portion of them must be present on Earth, and at ESL1. And also out here??

11) They seem as excited to meet us as we are to meet them.

12) Ulterior motives? Unlikely.

13) They mean us no harm.

Those last two points remained controversial, but Michael kept them on the list anyway, with the additional caveat that harm could certainly happen even in the absence of harmful intent. It was a short list, but a telling one that (for example) appeared to rule out "little green men" of any traditional sort, including robots and "energy creatures." And if the Beings were made of something that was not matter or energy, then they must be written onto the cosmos in some other way, as "spin states" (said Harv and Sandy) or "metric defects" (Igbal), "matter or energy in a different dimension" (Thenbecca), or "Casimir vibrations in the eigenvectors of the vacuum." Surprisingly, that one came from Dong, and Michael couldn't tell if it was mystic bullshit or if it actually meant something.

1.6

Post-Encounter Deposition
Evelyn Chang, PhD
Department of Mathematics,
Massachusetts Institute of Technology

To a mathematician, human speech is a really loose, imprecise notation. This, all by itself, makes my interaction with the Beings tough to describe. I mean, the psychedelic aspects of the Encounter have already been talked about: Yes, we smoked DMT. Yes, we were floating in zero gravity, in a big inflatable donut in the darkness of interstellar space. You don't know your own name when you're in that kind of a state, but that's not really the problem. Thing is, I'm at a loss for words if I can't start by defining what they mean. Is that all right? Can I do that?

Short version: the Beings' communications are framed in something similar to a formal mathematical notation, but without "symbols" in the human sense. For us, a symbol might be a geometric shape, on paper or on a computer screen, or pictured in the mind. Or it's a sound, or a burst of radio photons—some kind of container, that represents an idea. We string symbols together to form statements, and we string statements together to form proofs or, in the case of language, I suppose you'd say "stories" or "songs" or "conversations." To make sense, we have to arrange the symbols chronologically or geometrically. The Beings don't do it that way, but I felt like they were trying to—straining to—for us.

Longer version: they use set theory. This isn't surprising, since all mathematics can be formulated that way. However, there are other frameworks or notations that function just as universally, so we can consider all the ways the Beings *don't* speak. They don't speak in terms of geometry, topology, arithmetic, algebra, tensors, vectors, derivatives, or integrals. Or, at least, they didn't speak that way to me.

In simple terms, I don't believe the Beings have any use for Boolean formal logic. It would not make sense to them to say, "IF X is TRUE, AND X OR Y is TRUE, AND X AND Y is NOT TRUE, THEN Y is NOT TRUE." Even humans don't think that way. We can force ourselves to, but then we're really just using neural networks to do something, badly, that Boolean gates do well and quickly. The Beings may be even further abstracted; I didn't get a sense that the concepts of True or False were of any interest to them at all. The Beings are clearly not made of gates, or neural networks for that matter.

I also don't think they have a use for numbers. They might be aware of them, I don't know, but it wouldn't make sense to them, to talk about "two people." Instead they might talk about a "set" that contains both Amy and Bob. However, Amy is also a set, because she's made up of quadrillions of cells, each of which is made up of hundreds of structures and trillions of atoms. And I think they don't even really care about the atoms or structures, except maybe in terms of how they operate on the set. So instead of "two people," the Beings might say, "The set that contains all of this Amyness over here and all of this Bobness over there." I think this is really important to understanding what the Beings are, and how they see themselves, and how they see us.

Can I get more formal, please? The notation isn't difficult. In set theory, you have a relationship between an object "o" and a set "A." If o is a member of A, then we say:

$$o \in A$$

If all members of A are also members of B, then either A and B are equal (A=B), or B is a "proper subset" of A:

$$A \subseteq B$$

Two very important sets, which we can define as axioms or postulates of our notation, are:

- U := The universal set (a set that contains all possible sets or objects)
- {} := The empty set (a set that contains no sets or objects)

Set theory also includes operations you can perform on sets, which are equivalent to arithmetic operators on numbers, or Boolean operators on logical expressions:

Union:	$A \cup B$	(a set that includes all members of A *and* all members of B)
Intersection:	$A \cap B$	(the subset of objects in A and B that are members of *both* sets)
Set Diff:	$B \setminus A$	(the set of all members of B that are *not* members of A)
Symmetric Diff:	$A \triangle B$	(the set of all objects belong to A *or* B but not both)
Power Set:	$P(A)$	(the set that includes all of the possible subsets of A)

So the Beings (who always seem to be plural) might think about Amy and Bob by saying:

$$(A \cup B) \subseteq U$$
$$(A \cup B) \subseteq H$$
$$A \cap B = \{\}$$
$$B \setminus A = B$$
$$A \setminus B = A$$

In other words, "Amy and Bob exist. Amy and Bob are humans. None of the objects within Amy are also within Bob, i.e., the set of Amy and the set of Bob are defined as being totally separate entities." And where it gets interesting would be something like:

$$P(A) = ?$$

"What are all the subsets of Amy?" Or, to get closer to what they'd mean by this, something like, "Holy crap! What the hell is Amy?"

Harv Leonel swears that the Beings can split and recombine. If this is true, and if a "split" Being is identical to the "unsplit" or "combined" Being in an n-dimensional space, I could certainly see them being confused by humans. A significant portion of the stuff in a human is not really unique and is not inherent to human-ness or to that individual human's identity. Also, all that mass-energy gets cycled through every seven to ten years anyway. Is the human a sort of wiggly standing wave, with matter washing through it, that exists only with a paired forcing function (body/environment) maintaining and tweaking it?

Anyway, you don't need to understand all that. It's just a notation. It's an example, to give you the flavor of what I'm talking about. So, now I can explain: What I got from the Beings was a series of mathematical proofs. A lot of them! A firehose of them, smashing into me. More than I could process, or count, or remember. Here's an example:

- $B :=$ Beings
- $H :=$ Humans
- $U :=$ Universe
- $U_B :=$ Native Scope of Existence of the Beings within the Universe
- $U_H :=$ Native Scope of Existence of the Humans within the Universe
- $p_H :=$ Perception of Humans
- $p_B :=$ Perception of Beings
- $i_{BH} :=$ Interaction/communication between Beings and Humans (commutative?)

$$B \in U_B$$
$$H \in U_H$$
$$U_B \cup U_H \subseteq U$$
$$p_H \subseteq U_H \subseteq p_B \subseteq U_B$$
$$p_B \cap p_H \subseteq i_{BH}$$

Or something like that. What I think it means—what it meant to me at the time—was that the Beings themselves exist, but that their existence looks nothing like ours. By analogy: the universe is a simulation, and we're computer graphics dancing on a screen somewhere. Not just human beings, but everything we see and feel: graphics. But the Beings aren't on the screen at all; they're maybe something like data structures in raw machine language, like a background process on the CPU itself. That's my analogy, not theirs.

But you ask me: What did they look like, what did they feel like, what did they sound like? And it's just nonsense. They're not on the video screen with us. They can interact with our weird slice of the universe, but only from a remove, by manipulating energy in the CPU. Now, I know everyone's Encounter was different. All one hundred of us, completely different. I can't explain that, and it's not my job to explain it. This is what the Beings told me. This is what they said, which is actually an interesting philosophical point all by itself.

One bedeviling question in mathematics has always been, is math an invention or a discovery? Or a mixture of the two, in which case, which parts are which? I personally lean toward the discovery side of the argument, because some internally consistent frameworks can be used to describe the universe, and some can't. You don't "invent" a hammer made of soap bubbles, because that doesn't do anything. What you do is discover the art of hammering things, and then invent a better and better hammer.

Set theory certainly avoids some human-y thoughts about math, but then so would topology. You could come up with equivalent proofs in a few different math points of view like analysis, topology, set theory type, just like there are equivalent definitions of continuity. The Beings might even know how to do that, but it isn't how they think. For so long, the SETI people, and the astronomical community generally, have assumed that alien intelligences would *have* to know about number theory, but why should they? What are they trying to communicate? If the medium is the message, then the Beings have told us groupings are more important than numbers, for understanding the universe. If we assume they know more about the universe than we do, this is something where we should sit up and take notice.

Let's say, for the sake of argument, that a Being, or at least the avatar of a Being on our computer screen, can be represented as a four-dimensional (or n-dimensional) hyperellipsoid. From the Analects of Brother Michael (ha!), we get a general sense that the ellipsoid has a fixed total volume, or some equivalent, non-geometric constraint. It can stretch in one dimension, but then it has to shrink in at least one other dimension in order to meet that boundary condition.

   How would such numerically, materially, topologically naïve Beings approach mathematics? Their thoughts on the subject might be the aspiration of all pure mathematicians! In linear algebra (another form they don't seem to use), the big divide isn't three or more dimensions, it's between finite and infinite dimensions. That's what changes which theorems hold. And in analysis, there's a lot of discussion about the size of infinites—countable, uncountable and bigger infinities (which relates to power sets, interestingly enough). Topology doesn't even have ways to measure time or distance, and of course sets are about whatever you want them to be about (ha again!).

   Geeking out a bit, I'll say (just for the benefit of my colleagues and for reasons too complicated to explain here) that the Beings, even if "smooth" in three or even four dimensions, must be self-similar in n dimensions at differing scales of measurement. Assuming the solutions are nondegenerate, are the Beings spacetime fractals that can be categorized with respect to the particularities of the details of self-similarity? Do you have to shift position slightly in n-space to perceive a difference in scale, and what increment before $B(x,t) = B(x+delta\_x, t +delta\_t)$? Ah, they reveal periodic wave structure as well. Are they something like time crystals, but periodic in dimensions other than our linear time?

   Much work ahead.

   I suppose writing this for a lay audience is something I've failed to do, but using English to talk about alien math is like hitting rocks with that hammer made of soap bubbles. We humans invented math because there was no other way to get certain kinds of things done. And yes, I'm thinking maybe communicating with alien Beings is one of those things.

4.2
28 April

✧

ESL1 Shade Station
Earth-Sun Lagrange Point 1
Extracislunar Space

Alice swung through the Cross, where the spokes of the spin-gee habitat came together. A pair of her colleagues were there, hunched together, holding a grab bar and looking at the screen of a rollup.

"Hi, Pelu. Hi, Sienna," she said to them with a barely acknowledged nod.

She passed the hatches leading, in one direction, to the astronautics airlocks and, in the other, to the spaceship docking berths. She savored the brief sensation of total weightlessness, then flipped her feet around and shot down the crew tube of the "east" spoke, sliding her hands along the ladder as the sensation of weight started—first gradually and then quickly—to increase.

On the double-wheel of the new station, people (Alice included) tended to shortcut through the spokes, because they were in a hurry or just generally lazy. It didn't save that much time or distance, but since the spin gravity right now was only one-tenth gee, it was easier to climb a ladder than to walk the long way around. Despite having only six more modules than the old station, the new place felt much larger. It *was* larger; one hundred meters in diameter, and a third of a kilometer in circumference, if you wanted to walk around the whole rim.

At the bottom of the tube, she dropped into the hallway of the eastern lab module—color-coded with yellow arrows along the floor and ceiling, pointing in the direction of spin. From there, she swim-walked two modules "north," against the direction of spin, then "Earthward" into the corridor of the other ring, until she arrived at the special-built module that contained her office and quarters.

She found Maag there waiting for her.

"What is it?" Alice said impatiently.

It was 6:15 p.m., and Alice was trying to get into her apartment and close the door and be done with work for the day. But to do that, she had to slip through her office, which was a high-traffic area. At least it was only Maag waiting for her.

Sighing, Alice floated past her friend, reaching for the window controls. They were set to a translucent white "diffuse mode," but she flicked it briefly transparent and looked out at the full circles of Earth and Moon (a billiard ball and a grape, respectively).

"You okay?" Maag asked.

"Stir-crazy," Alice said, flicking the window diffuse again before the spinning view made her guts start churning.

"You and everyone else," Maag said.

Yes, the spin-gee station was newer and cleaner and better thought-through than the old station floating behind it. Yes, the artificial gravity felt good. They had started very light—not even up to lunar gravity yet—just barely enough to walk in. If things went according to plan, they would gradually increase it to one-third gee over the course of a year, to let their bodies acclimate gradually. Maybe someday even up to a full gee—who knew?

But for more than half the crew, there was a motion sickness problem. The new doctor, Berka Feikey—the replacement for Rachael Lee, who had been the replacement for Pamela Rosenau—had warned Alice that even with such a large ring, centripetal accelerations could upset the inner ear. So far, that worry had been overblown—they were all intrepid spacers, men and women alike, and nobody got sick. As long as you didn't open the window shades! If you did, then there was no escape from the slow whirling of the star field, and of the distant Earth and Moon, and of the enormous expanse of the Shade. Right now it was only 1.3 revolutions per minute. How much worse would it get if they spun up to higher gravity?

So "according to plan" was not how things were going right now.

Despite its size, the new station felt vaguely claustrophobic with the windows always opaqued.

Maag hugged herself for a moment and said, "You ever think we've just traded bone loss for something worse?".

"Uh-huh," Alice said. Adapting to zero-gee could take anywhere from no time at all to, in extreme cases, a few weeks. But it had been three weeks already since they'd finished moving all their shit into ESL1 Shade Station 2 and fully taken up residence. "I'm worried we might've wasted four billion dollars on this thing."

But Maag said, "The more we blind these windows, the less chance we have of ever adjusting."

"Hmm. Easy for you to say."

Maag was among those unaffected.

Just then, the new station's concierge broke in, with the brusque voice Alice had selected for it.

"Urgent call for you, Alice," said Zeta.

"Answer. Hello?"

"We got one!" said the voice of Derek Haakens.

"A stealth ship?" said Alice, suddenly wide awake.

"Yep," said Derek. "We picked him up on Ultra, about two klicks Earthward from here. He realized he was painted, and did a slow drift out of range."

"Shit. That's excellent. Don't do anything until I get there. Get Tim Ho and Rose Ketchum up there as well."

"I know the protocol," Derek said, sounding a little miffed.

"Right," said Alice. "End call."

"Gotta go," she said to Maag, and was out the hatch just like that, retracing her steps back up to the Cross. In one-tenth gee, climbing a ladder was a lot like launching yourself up from the bottom of a deep pool, but of course spin-gee was not real gravity. If you didn't actually put your hands on every fourth or fifth rung, the Coriolis force would knock you into the side of the tube. Or the tube, moving along with the rest of the station, would swing around and hit you, or whatever.

Still, it was short work, and once she was in the Cross she swung through a side hatch, through the spin decoupler, and into the non-rotating part of the station. On the other side, the sunward side, was the crazy 3D jumble of the old station, simply bolted to the stationary hub. Here though, on the Earthward side, was a chamber that included a shuttle dock, a spacesuit airlock, and about four tons of radar equipment mostly shipped up here from Earth.

ESL1 was probably more than capable of building most of this stuff, but Alice had been in a hurry, so she'd bought it off-the-shelf and had it shipped here on a chemical rocket. Along with Isaiah Pembroke, who presently hovered beside Derek. Both of them were peering at a radar display that clearly (if coarsely) showed both the station and the central portion of the Shade, illuminated by expanding rings of green.

"Where's the bogey?" she asked.

Derek startled so badly he somehow managed to hit his head on the panel. "Ow! Jesus! How the hell did you get up here so quickly?"

"Ho, ho!" she said, rather startled herself. "I climbed a ladder, flyboy. People do that. Now where's my bogey?"

"We think it's here," said Isaiah pointing to a blank spot on the screen, opposite the Shade. He sounded a bit smug, which he had a total right to be as far as Alice was concerned. First of all, he'd been here less than a week, and he'd already proven his worth by nabbing his first stealth ship detection. Also, he'd been here less than a week and had already been claimed, carnally, by Jeanette Schmidt, and possibly other crew members as well. This annoyed Alice more than it probably should, but she had to give the young man some credit, too. Jeanette was a nice catch.

"Get suited up," Alice said now to Derek.

He nodded, but when she followed behind him into the locker room, he said, "Whoa, there. You can't come with us."

"Oh, why not?" she asked, too surprised in that moment to remember she was the one in charge. Then, more decisively: "I'm the only one on this station with space combat experience."

"Exactly," he said. "You need to hang back and guide the whole thing on video. You're also the station commander. You need to coordinate station defenses, in case this is some sort of feint."

Alice had never been one to lead from the rear, nor did she respect officers who behaved that way. But everything Derek had just said was true, and it was actually much worse than that, because as VP of Space Operations she also had shareholder value to worry about. Wasn't *that* a kick in the pants.

In this case the shareholders were seventy-four percent Igbal and twenty-six percent who-gives-a-fuck, but if Igbal could see her now he would tell her to strap her ass down in a chair and do her actual job.

"Well, fuck," she said.

Rose swung through the hatch then, looking grimly excited. She exchanged a cryptic look with Derek, neither of them saying anything.

A few seconds later, Tim floated in behind her, stopping himself with a light touch against a spacesuit locker.

"Are we doing this?" he said.

"We are," Derek confirmed. "Get suited up. We start bleeding the airlock in five minutes, standard egress procedure."

That meant fifteen minutes of depressurization time.

Alice said, "Derek has persuaded me to run the mission from here, but I'm still suiting up. In case you all need rescue."

"If we need rescue," Derek said, "you need to meet our mangled bodies down in the medical lab."

And that was also true, because Alice was the only person on board with experience as a combat medic. She was, in fact, the only person on the station with any medical training whatsoever, aside from Doc Feikey.

But she was also the only person who'd ever actually done this kind of thing. She was trained in the martial art of Zedo by the U.S. Space Force, for crying out loud. She had popped the cork on Bethy Powell's spacesuit, in a hardscrabble fight to the death.

Five years ago, said the voice of her inner critic.

Rose and Tim were younger than she was. Derek was stronger, by a lot, and Tim was a better shot.

"I'm suiting up," Alice said again, nailing the subject shut.

Soon they were all opening their lockers, wriggling and latching their way into their suits. These were combat models, special order from General Spacesuit corporation, who (at least officially) didn't normally make such things. The armor was actually made here at ESL1—grown from layered crystals in zero gravity—but the suits were assembled in Florida and shipped back up here at great expense, because Alice had always known they would have to fight somebody sometime.

She was a nervous mother hen as her people climbed into the airlock and sealed the hatch behind them.

Then, as the pressure bled down, she tucked her helmet under her left arm and propelled herself back into the radar room.

"Are you actually ready for this?" she asked Isaiah Pembroke, as she stowed the helmet in a rack under his seat. The bulky spacesuit made her movements stiff, though tempered by the ease of long practice. "Shit's about to get a lot less theoretical."

"Yes, ma'am," he said, his eyes fixed on the radar screen. "I'm actually ready."

In his ordinary RzVz coveralls, he suddenly looked quite vulnerable. In a previous life, Alice had coached her share of noobs through their first airdrop into live fire. She knew all about the jitters and the uncertainty. Hell, she was feeling it herself.

She put a gauntleted hand on Isaiah's shoulder and said, "If we do this by the numbers, everything is going to be fine."

That was by no means a given, and it felt a bit like she was outright lying to him, so she added, "If we do this by the numbers and roll with any contingency."

Reaching past Isaiah, she keyed in commands and flipped switches on the console that brought up the video and audio feeds from the three spacesuits. At the moment, this was just three different views of the cramped quarters inside the airlock. Tim and Rose were both carrying rifles, loaded with light armor-piercing rounds. The rifles were allegedly recoilless, but one shot could still tumble you. This was serious business.

"...oxygen levels, suit pressures, and tank pressures," Derek was saying.

"Roger," said Rose and Tim, almost at the same time. He was running them through a standard checklist. "Standard" in the sense that everyone knew it, though it was rarely recited out loud.

"Verify wrist seals fully locked."

"Roger."

"Verify waist seals fully locked."

The full self-inspection procedure required a mirror, which was mounted on the back wrist of each suit's left arm. Alice watched the three astronauts jostling with weightless bulk as they craned to view their seals.

Flipping another switch on the console, Alice activated her own suit audio and said, "Audio check. Falcon, this is Mockingbird. Do you copy?"

"Ah, copy that," Derek said. "Mockingbird on the network."

After that, she quieted down and let Derek finish his checklist. When it was done, he reported the airlock pressure at fifteen millibars, and the ETA to zero pressure at sixty seconds.

Alice asked: "Romper, are you good?"

Bit late for that question; Romper was Rose's call sign. Rose had been down south to Coffee Patch, but as an Army mechanic. Other than some inaccurate mortars from Cartel shoot-and-scoot teams, she'd never taken hostile fire, nor aimed any weapon in the direction of a human being.

But what Rose said was, "I'm beautiful, ma'am. Thank you."

"This could be over in five minutes," Alice said.

"Or not," Derek said, matter-of-factly. Then, after a pause: "Falcon reporting all-balls pressure, green lights on the door. Awaiting orders."

"Mockingbird acknowledges. Hold, please."

To the air, Alice said, "Zeta, give me a station-wide address please. All hands, this is Interim Commander Alice Kyeong."

There were only forty-five people on the station, and they all knew Alice as "Alice," but this was a military operation, and she wanted to do it by the numbers. Not so much to cover her ass as because there really wasn't any other way—any better way—to conduct such things.

"Close all hatches and seal all modules, effective immediately and until further notice," she said. "A stealth ship has intruded into our space. We are engaging, and expect a hostile response. That's all."

Everyone knew this day was coming. Now, everyone knew this day was here. Probably, sealing off every module from every other was huge overkill and would be the butt of jokes for weeks to come. Alice certainly hoped so. It would take the crew a while to complete the task, but that was okay. It would take a while for all this to unfold.

Putting both of her gloved hands on Isaiah's shoulders, she said, "Jericho, go for power boost."

Jericho was Isaiah's call sign, and since he was sitting right here, it wasn't exactly ambiguous who she was talking to. But she wanted the fire team in the airlock to know exactly what was going on, and in case anything went wrong, she wanted the recordings to be as complete and factual as possible.

"Jericho acknowledges the order," said Isaiah. He was an engineer who'd never been in any sort of military engagement whatsoever, but he spoke with such gusto Alice might almost have mistaken him for a Maroon Beret.

He keyed in some commands on the console. The expanding circles on the radar display now reached all the way to the edge of the screen—a radius of almost twenty kilometers.

"There!" Isaiah shouted. "We got him! You're painted, fucker!"

"Calm down," Alice said, "and fire."

Without delay, Isaiah flipped up a switch cover, flipped the switch underneath it, and then brought the palm of his hand down on the big red button.

The lights dimmed for a moment, and then returned to normal brightness.

"He's shot, ma'am. Direct hit."

The entangled ultrawideband radar put out very short, very powerful pulses in all directions at once, but Isaiah had assured her that through something called a "beamformer" and something called a "phased array," the pulse could be focused down to a tight beam, barely two-tenths of a degree wide, and aimed directly at a target. At a few kilometers' range, the result should be a megajoule electromagnetic surge capable of frying even the most hardened military systems. It was why Isaiah was up here at ESL1, getting his dick wet at company expense.

"Report, Jericho," Alice said, trying to keep the annoyance out of her voice.

"Target's radar cross-section has increased," he said. "A lot."

"Go to normal radar," she said.

He did so, and the expanding circles on the display were replaced by a glowing green line, sweeping around like the hand of a clock.

"Target remains visible. Looks like we killed his camo."

"Fire team hold," Alice said.

Curious, she pushed off from Jericho's seat and floated toward the tiny porthole on the left side of the room. It was dark out there—they were in the Colorado-sized shadow of the Shade—but she thought perhaps the light reflecting off the Earth and Moon might reveal something. The ship was the size of a train car, and no longer hidden from view, so even from a couple of klicks away, it might look like something.

"Can you see anything?" Isaiah asked.

"Mockingbird here. Negative visual contact. Fire team, you're going to have to let Jericho guide you in."

"Falcon acknowledges. Are we go for egress?"

Alice's heart was heavy and nervous. If she were in that airlock, she would know exactly what to do. If she were in that airlock, she could keep them safe.

She said: "Mockingbird here. Go for egress."

"TicTac, open outer hatch, please," said Derek to Tim Ho.

Alice could only watch on the video screens as the fire team exited the airlock and drifted, untethered, into the blackness of space.

Jericho called out directions to them, and presently they were activating their maneuvering thrusters and jetting in the direction of the unstealthed stealth ship.

"Still no visual contact," Falcon reported.

"Mockingbird here. Keep those speeds down. Falcon, I read you at fifteen KPH."

The ship was just over three kilometers away, and over distances like that, with no reference points in between, it was really easy to misjudge your speed and get going much too fast. If you then also misjudged how long it was going to take to bleed off all that velocity, you could easily overshoot the target or (worse) collide with it.

"Roger that."

As combat ops tended to do, this one unfolded both too slowly and too quickly. At a certain point, TicTac reported that he had visual contact and was adjusting his course. Romper and Falcon adjusted to match him, and in another minute, Falcon reported that he had visual contact as well.

"I guess snipers' eyes are better than pilots' eyes," Alice said.

To which Falcon replied, "Cut the chatter, Mockingbird."

Then Romper could see the target, and in another minute, even Alice could see it, through the blocky and occasionally pixelated helmet-cam videos. It looked like a midsized transatmospheric crew shuttle, lit up along one edge by the light of stars and Earth.

"No signs of venting gas," Falcon reported. Then: "TicTac, Romper, hang back at this range, please. I'm going to go have a word with these gentlemen. Or ladies."

Slung across Derek's back was a marker board, with black and red grease pencils clipped to it. The astronauts used it, sometimes, to keep track of tasks during a long EVA. Even in vacuum, even in the cold shadow of the ESL1 Shade, it worked well enough. The plan was simply to hold a sign up in the stealth ship's windshield, offering assistance.

"Romper here. All due respect, sir, I can't hit anything from this range."

"Falcon here. Are you telling me you can't hit *that*?" He pointed at the ship, which was admittedly a large target.

"I can't hit a person, sir. I can't keep you safe."

"Hmm. TicTac, are you good here?"

"TicTac here. Yes, sir, very good."

Alice fought the urge to bark orders at them. She was watching their blips on the radar, as well as the video from their cameras, and feeling generally helpless. The astronauts were now less than half a kilometer away from the ship, and if TicTac could hit one of the enemy astronauts with a clean shot, it was a safe bet that one of the enemy astronauts could hit all three of her people at any moment.

"Mockingbird here. Stay vigilant," she allowed herself to say.

"Thank you, ma'am," Falcon said back. Then: "TicTac, hold position. Romper, you're with me."

Over the next five excruciating minutes, Falcon and Romper approached the stealth ship, which gradually grew larger and brighter and less pixelated in their camera displays. When they were fifty meters out, Falcon said, "Romper, can you hit a target from here on the first shot?"

Because yes, that first shot would tumble her, and it would be a while before she could line up a second one.

Romper said, "Yes, sir, I believe I can."

"All right, then. Hit your stop jets and hold position. I'm heading for the cockpit windows."

"Roger that."

"Mockingbird, are you seeing this?"

"I am," Alice said. The ship was close enough now to be

illuminated by Derek's suit lamps, and it cast back a million little sparkles, as though it were covered with bits of glass. As Derek drew closer, these resolved into banks of glossy gray-white hexagonal plates, each the size of a pinkie nail and surrounded by a black border.

Isaiah said, "Jericho here. If those little beehive things are glass and metal, or contain them, the ship ought to have a huge radar cross section. Which it currently does not. I think we're looking at a passive beam-deflection metamaterial. Coupled probably with a light-emitting capability, which is standard in active camouflage."

Alice, who had on a few occasions worn an active camouflage suit during combat drops, could confirm: it was like being wrapped in a video screen.

"Thank you," Derek replied, a bit absentmindedly. In his camera view, the nose of the ship was drawing even with him and rotating into the center of the screen. "The windows are—"

A brief, blue-white flash lit up the radar room. Like a very bright camera flash emanating from the porthole to Alice's left, leaving pink and green blobs all up and down the left side of her vision.

A loud chirping sound from the control panel had matched the flash. Derek's voice had cut off, and the display from his suit camera had gone black, with only the letters EV1 CAM1 in green across the top of the screen.

"Falcon, please report," Alice said, too surprised to feel any fear.

But Derek did not report, and the view from Rose's own camera was not very informative, showing only blackness, and a few paper-white specks that looked like burned-out pixels. The cameras weren't sensitive enough to pick up starlight, so all this told Alice was that Romper was not presently pointed at anything brighter, like the Earth or Moon, or the lights of Derek's suit. Alice said, "Romper, this is Mockingbird. Can I get a report, please? What are you seeing?"

Calmly, Romper replied, "Ma'am, I think I've got a malfunction in my welding visor. I saw a bright flash, and then the photochromic kicked in and dimmed it out. I think it's stuck now; I can't see out of it."

Isaiah said, "Ma'am, I have no echo from the ship."

"Fuck," Alice said, thinking the damn thing had somehow dropped back into stealth mode. "Go to ultrawideband."

Isaiah did so, and the radar display switched back from a sweeping line to a pond-ripple of expanding circles.

"Still no echo," he said.

Then, looking at the display with the first inklings of horror, she said, "Where is Falcon?"

To which he replied, "Ma'am, I have two echoes." He pointed at the screen, green on black. She could see parts of the station. She could see the Shade and the Hub. She could see two dots, which Isaiah tapped one after the other. "This is TicTac, and this is Romper. There's nothing else out there. Doppler indicates Romper is moving in our direction, about one-half meter per second."

Alice said, "TicTac, this is Mockingbird. Do you have a visual on Romper?"

"Affirmative," TicTac said. "She appears to have picked up a slight tumble."

That made sense; in TicTac's camera view, Alice could see a tiny white line that was probably the edge of Romper's suit, lit up by Earthlight. But it was slowly changing size and shape, and presently, a brighter spot appeared on it that might have been one of her suit lamps rotating into view.

"Roger that," Alice said. Then, in frustration, "Can I get a sit rep, please?" Situation report. *Tell me what the hell is going on.*

"I can report, ma'am, I saw the flash as well, and my welding visor kicked in. It's not stuck, however."

"Do you have a visual on Falcon?"

"Negative, Mockingbird. I have lost visual on Falcon and the bogey. I have afterimages from the flash, though; it's possible my vision is obscured."

"There's nothing on your camera," Alice said.

"There's nothing on the radar," Isaiah said. "Ma'am, I have no debris. That ship is *gone*. I think . . . ma'am, I think they detonated a nuke."

"Ah, negative," TicTac said to that. "I saw no fireball or, you know, mushroom cloud."

"Romper here. I am less than one hundred meters from the ship, and I did not feel a blast wave."

"No blast wave in space," Isaiah said. "No fireball. No EMP. No debris. No cloud. Just a blast of pure . . . radiation. Ma'am, I'm reading elevated levels of background gamma and beta radiation. The history graph shows a big spike about thirty seconds ago. That's the time of the flash, ma'am."

But Romper said, "All due respect, Jericho, there's no way I was a hundred meters from a nuclear explosion. I didn't feel a thing."

To which Isaiah replied, "All due respect, Romper, but how are you feeling now?"

"A little motion sickness," Romper said. "Because I can't see anything."

Alice's heart lurched and sank. Isaiah was here because he was a weapon targeting systems expert. Isaiah sounded like he knew what he was talking about.

She said, "TicTac, I need you to retrieve Romper, right now. Treat as injured. Bring her back to the airlock ASAP."

"Roger that," TicTac said. Then: "What about Falcon?"

"Still figuring that out," Alice said, and then muted her mic. Leveraging from the back of Isaiah's chair, she leaned over him and flipped a switch on the panel, killing his mic as well.

"How big a nuke are we talking about?" she demanded.

"I don't know," he said, shrugging so hard it was almost a wince. "Small, maybe point-one kilotons, I don't know. Probably a suitcase tac-nuke, very illegal. But ma'am, Rose was way too close to that thing. The radiation dose . . ."

"We'll get her inside," Alice said.

"There's no way, ma'am. We need to get *TicTac* inside. I'm sorry, do I—don't know TicTac's name. We need to get him into treatment right away, or he could die. Rose is . . . I'm sorry, ma'am, but Rose is dead already. Or, I mean, she will be, almost certainly, within a few hours. I don't think her visor's malfunctioning. I think her optic nerves are. Her body's shutting down."

"We'll treat Romper and TicTac, both," she said, not leaving it open for discussion.

But Isaiah kept pressing. "It's going to take him an hour to get back here as it is. If he goes and gets Rose, it's going to slow him down. She might not even survive long enough to make it back to the airlock."

"We'll treat them both," she said. She didn't need to tell herself not to grieve right now. Not while the mission was still ongoing.

"Are you going out there?" he asked.

She thought about it for half a second and asked, "What are the chances TicTac is going to be disabled before he gets back?"

"I don't know. Not zero."

"Then yes, I'm going out there." She was Air Force Pararescue, for fuck's sake. She rotated her body, head-down, arms-down, like a swimmer diving for the bottom of a pool, and retrieved her space helmet from the rack under Isaiah's chair.

"What about Derek Hakkens?" she asked, as she lowered the helmet over her head. *My ex. My coworker. My close friend of five-plus years.* "Falcon. Is he vaporized?"

"Yes, ma'am, I think he must be. I'm very sorry. He's certainly not alive."

"Well, fuck," she said, and closed the helmet latches.

1.7

Post-Encounter Deposition
Archie Carter, PhD
School of Physics, University of Bristol

To describe my encounter with the Beings, I really have to ask you to imagine something a bit peculiar—a gingerbread man living on the two-dimensional world of a tabletop. Why that, specifically? Because this biscuit man is a living person much like you or me, and the tabletop is a very, very simplified model of our universe as seen by the Beings. We have three dimensions of space and one of time, and the biscuit universe simply removes one of the spatial dimensions so the rest is easier to understand. The Beings have many more dimensions than that, so to them we look quite flat and thin. To them, everything we know about is flat.

So, "time" in the biscuit universe can be defined as the up-down axis of our 3D universe. If we do that, then the gingerbread man's past can be seen—actually *seen*—as a stack of human-shaped biscuits reaching upward to the ceiling, changing size and position as it goes, until there's nothing but a tiny gingerbread zygote at the very top. That's the start of the gingerbread man's life.

The biscuit future extends below the table. Is our Mr. G about to take a step to his left? If so, then the biscuit immediately below the table will be a little farther left. And so on, plunging downward until the moment of the biscuit's death. This ginger loaf, this worm of sweetened dough, traces out every moment of the biscuit's life, and a three-dimensional Being can see all of it in one glance.

And it's the same with every other object in the tabletop universe. Is there a letterbox? A dinner theater? A star about to go nova? Fine, they're all worms, or (if you examine them under a powerful microscope) tight swarms of smaller worms orbiting around one another.

Extended this to three spatial dimensions, with a fourth one representing time, and you have Einstein's block universe (actually first proposed by Augustine of Hippo back in 400 A.D.—smart guy). "Block" because the whole thing is a solid, invariant structure in 4D space. It might as well be carved in marble. This means, among other things, that free will is an illusion in the block universe. Or rather, that every choice ever made by human hearts, and every quantum uncertainty that ever collapsed into a definite motion, is resolved at the very moment of this universe's creation. Think of the block as a fossil—the sum of all outcomes, preserved for eternity in a higher-dimensional hyperspace—of a sequence of events that may have perhaps, in a way, never happened at all. And so the passage of time is also an illusion, and the forces that direct objects to move or spin are simply boundary conditions at this sort of magical, let-there-be-light moment when the block is carved.

I like to imagine this moment: I see a true, rectangular block of material sitting there on a gallery floor somewhere, and suddenly in a flash of light there's debris raining off it, leaving behind this quite complicated shape that is our universe. Of course, it could be anything. It could have different rules to our universe, or different objects in it, or different outcomes. If you think about it, there are an infinite number of universes that don't exist at all. And one imagines the variables that make up our universe can't be completely random. Do they instead fall along a bell-shaped distribution, with some values more probable than others?

Do we live in this particular block universe because it's exceedingly probable? Are there other blocks beside it, marking out all the parallel ways it all might have transpired? That turns out to be actually a quite complicated question, because the block universe can't be reconciled with quantum mechanics in the manner I've described above. Schrödinger tells us, rather harshly I'm afraid, that at any given moment—any 3D slice of the 4D block—the future can't be predicted, even with perfect knowledge, and (to me, rather disturbingly) neither can the past. Not only is the passage of time an illusion, but so is the history we rely on to gauge what actually has happened.

I don't think this means there geometrically *can't* be a block universe, because all potential blocks can exist. It's just that we just can't ever predict which of the blocks our observation will be within. Since that lands us in the same predicament, I would call it a distinction without a difference; quantum mechanics still wrecks our ability to imagine the universe as a single 4D block.

It must be highly significant, then, that the Beings—who claim to be capable of perceiving the existence of a future and a past—describe them as two different things. They tell us time and space and mass are all illusions—that nothing but information exists, or can exist. So, why the division? What is this "information horizon" they've hinted at but not described?

I questioned them closely about this, or at least I thought I did. They reacted with an amusement that, I would say, bordered on awe, that a ridiculous creature such as myself could exist without perceiving what seemed so obvious to them.

And they did answer me, after a fashion. Their answer was a shape—something like the block universe carving we've been discussing, only vastly more complex. It seemed to move and change, its shapes sliding in and out of one another, but I understood this as an attempt on their part to show the effects of higher dimensions to my paper-thin gingerbread mind.

Was it a fractal? A topological mesh? A multidimensional Fibonacci spiral or space-filling curve? It was none of these, but it reminded me of all of them in certain ways. I suppose it belonged to the same general family of infinitely complex, non-Euclidian structures.

There are people who hear music when they're listening to static, and I have to say I'm one of them. And the reason we hear that music is because it's actually there in the white noise, along with a myriad other grainy but discernible patterns. Billions of them, perhaps more. Our brains are wired to find patterns, and so they do just that. But if you hear Euphemia Allen's "Celebrated Chop Waltz," or some entirely new song that never existed before, it doesn't mean the static uniquely encodes that pattern. It's just that an approximation of that pattern is extractable from the particular spectrum of that particular noise, by removing every click and pop that doesn't fit it. And the static responds to thought! If you think about Beethoven, you're more likely to hear him. If you think about sine waves, well, there you go. It's not that you're changing the noise spectrum, just finding one of the many patterns it contains.

I think our universe may exist in a similar way, pattern-matched from the hiss of quantum uncertainty, by conscious minds listening themselves into existence. I imagine it's like the debris falling off our block universe onto the gallery floor, pulling something complex from an entropically simple medium.

And yet, the noise of Schrödinger isn't precisely white. It obeys rules and constraints of its own, many more than we currently understand. I'm going to say, it did seem that one end of that fractal structure—the future—was of a different sort than the other end, and there was a middle section (the "nearly now"?) that was different from either.

I seem to recall I saw it for a moment. For just the merest flicker of time, I got the message the Beings were sending, and understood the structure of the universe as they perceive it. I remember it was beautiful and terrible and vast, and to say that it made me feel small is rather an understatement. It was like standing at the top of a ten-kilometer tower with my feet halfway over the edge, and looking down. Or perhaps like standing on a beach, looking up at a ten-kilometer wave about to sweep over everything. I could not have felt more certain that my presence in the universe is ephemeral.

It was that kind of shape.

And then it was gone, boiled away like liquid nitrogen, and no amount of sketching, no amount of time spent sitting in front of visualization software, has enabled me to recover it. I have only the sort of muddy, stompy bootprint it left behind on my brain.

I know, people who've taken psychedelics often say that type of thing. And perhaps it's true for them, or perhaps it *isn't* for me. Perhaps the whole experience was just wishful thinking, or a drug trip far from home. But if any of what I remember is even slightly representative of the truth, then I think our free will is definitely *not* an illusion, but perhaps the only reason our particular universe ever came into existence at all.

3.5
28 April

✧

I.R.V. *Intercession*
Extra-Kuiper Space
833 A.U. from Earth

Turnaround Day finally came, with remarkably little fanfare. Hobie and Sandy were both up in the cockpit, and everyone else was secured in their sleeping berths, though with the doors open. Michael could stare across the room at Thenbecca and Rachael, and through the ladder at Harv. He didn't know if he should feel nervous or excited or what, so he simply sat and listened to the voice traffic. "I'm starting the engine shutdown sequence," Sandy said over the public channel. "Shockwave generators half power. Zero power. Matter flux at fifty percent. Zero percent. Engines stopped."

The ship's acceleration, never more than a gentle kiss, stuttered and faded, and they were all weightless and coasting again. Coasting at tremendous velocity—$0.05c$!

Then Hobie said, "Let's see if the attitude control on this tub even works, eh? Captain's choice: you want me to pitch or yaw?"

"You're asking me?" Igbal said, sounding annoyed. His voice came from the loudspeaker in Michael's cabin, but he could also hear it through the air and through the wall. Igbal was strapped into the berth next door.

"Yaw it is, then."

At which point, Michael thought he could hear, or perhaps feel, the buzzing of a steering thruster: once, twice, then a pause. And then a different thruster? Once, twice?

"We're turning," Hobie said, and on the display screens above the sleeping berths, fake windows showed the stars wheeling slowly by outside. "Ten degrees. Thirty degrees, ninety degrees."

Then another jet fired, and Hobie's count—already slow—slowed further. "One-twenty. One-sixty. One-seventy-five."

Another jet.

"One-eighty."

Jet.

To Michael, the sequence seemed to go both surprisingly slowly and surprisingly fast.

"Okay," Hobie said, "That's got it. Sandy?"

"Commencing start sequence."

She didn't call out the details this time, but the ship's acceleration gradually resumed. Except that now it was *de*celeration.

"Congratulations, people," Igbal said. "We're halfway there."

Everyone groaned at that, which was about what you'd expect. But what Michael didn't expect was that right now at this ostensibly momentous moment, Harv would try to restart the spirited group debate about the Beings that had ended only a few minutes before the Turnaround maneuver.

He said, "I don't see how they could process sound, in anything like the sense you mean it."

To which Hobie replied, "They sang to me, man. They did."

And Sandy chimed in, "Not sounds. Vibrations, independent of medium, interpreted by your brain."

And then they were all off to the races again.

People didn't even need to be in the same room anymore; they chatted over headsets and intercoms, stopping sometimes for an hour or two and then picking up right where they left off. There was only so much to say on the subject, and so past a certain point Michael felt there was something vaguely masturbatory about it, an endless fidgeting contortion of a knot that could not be untied. Disconnected from the world right in front of their faces.

It reminded him of the way theology students simply could not shut up about Jesus, even on a walk through the mountains or beside a crackling fire. And never asking the centrally binding question: what if it's all a fever dream? That thought must surely have crossed the minds of everyone here. Was it healthy, to leave it always unvoiced? This made him worry not only that he'd created a monster—that he'd simply persuaded them to scatter their energies in this way—but also, paradoxically, that they were racing too far ahead of the rest of the class. When the ninety-two sleepers awoke, they'd know nothing of these conversations. They would be thrust, unprepared, into humanity's first alien encounter, without the comfort of having talked it through with other would-be experts. Would he, Michael, have any chance to do anything about that? There would only be one first time, and he wanted it to count.

1.8

✧

Post-Encounter Deposition
Mitchell T. Sprague, PhD
Department of Economics,
New York University

Make, buy, sell, trade, hold. The basic operations of the dismal science we call economics. Less talked about in our circles but equally important:

> locate, extract, refine, and divide (as in the mining or energy sectors);
>
> hunt, gather, plow, sow, reap, preserve, combine, and consume (as in agriculture);
>
> reduce, reuse, repair, and recycle (in any environment where resources are limited);
>
> arrange, perform, observe (as in the arts);
>
> collect, organize, report, praise, and disparage (as in journalism);
>
> learn, invent, prototype, produce (as in technology startups);
>
> and everyone's supposed least favorites: threaten, steal, damage, and destroy (as in crime, war, natural disasters, and nonconsensual governments).

There are others—so many others. We econ types spend our life cataloging them and awkwardly fitting equations to them in hopes of describing something real.

In 2050, I won a Nobel Prize for asking the question, in a dozen papers across a span of five years: which of these operations would space aliens do? All of them? None? Some? It depends what kind of aliens you're talking about, which is not a profound observation for me to have made. But neither is most economic theory, so there you go.

Okay: the Beings. Economics would insist that in any situation where there's more than one autonomous agent, there's got to be commerce of some kind. Even prokaryotes trade information and resources, and form colonies to protect themselves. The Beings must have an economy of some kind, right? But what if they're a disembodied intelligence, with no concept of quantity, and barely a concept of time? What does that do to all our fancy assumptions? I didn't exactly put this question to them, but they seemed to detect it from me the way a Geiger counter detects radiation, and their answer came back to me like street noise. Lots of voices, lots of sounds. Hard to make out, but you pick up the general tone of it, and that helps you tune into the details.

In brief: yes. The Beings have an understanding of value. To them it's wordless, numberless, and totally lacking in physical substance, and yet it's absolutely as evident as a stack of coins or a boxcar full of grain, or what have you.

I don't know where they get their energy, but apparently they absorb it from somewhere, and expend it, and I got the impression they'd disappear completely without it. Their "bodies" are like a clothesline extending from past to future, and at each point along the line there's an input of energy pinned to the rope, which is noted as important. It's their most basic unit of value, and one that can be hoarded or squandered or exchanged. Squandering may not be the right word, because generating a blob of entropy for no clear purpose appears to also have a kind of value, in maybe a gluttonous or sensuous way. Guilty pleasures of the disembodied.

Patterns also have value to them. Patterns of matter and energy in time and space attract their attention, and that attention is another unit of value. Creating patterns can create value, but destroying patterns can also be valuable. It's not clear to me that matter per se is of any particular interest to them, except for the way it changes and moves the energy around it. But one Being will sometimes create a pattern for another Being, or multiple Beings, to observe or consume.

Things that are unexpected have more value than things that aren't, although it was never quite clear to me what "expectation" meant. The size or duration of a thing didn't seem to particularly matter to them, but there's a quality—maybe "poignancy"?—that seemed to matter a whole lot, so that the beginning and ending of things were of greater importance than their boring middles.

I could fit equations to that, and I will, but economic theory could never capture how raucous and exuberant the Beings' economy seemed to me: an open-air market of shouting voices, offering songs for a dollar and skyscrapers for a song. I felt them jostling, pushing, laughing at the absurdity and yet also placing a deadly serious value on the laughter itself.

The sort of people who snort DMT at parties have often described the Beings as elves or angels, but I think these manifestations are just avatars. They're sock puppets or wooden ducks, meant to lure us in for closer examination. I just think somehow that the actual Beings are much larger and farther away, and in attracting our attention—in getting us to do anything we wouldn't ordinarily have done—they were satisfying an urge within themselves.

We went to visit them because the mere knowledge of their existence has tremendous value to us, and anything we learn from them (or that we can't learn any other way) is so valuable it's difficult to even articulate a way to measure it. And let me tell you, the converse seems to be true as well. We may never know the fortunes they expended to lure us out to meet them, but it seemed like a really vast undertaking, and one that we can accept as a compliment. They've never seen or imagined anything like us, and although we sometimes despise ourselves, or each other, the Beings really seemed to like what they saw. Their investment had paid off massively.

Will we commerce with them? Are we of only brief value to them, or is their interest ongoing? Can we create things they will pay for? Can they supply a thing to us, that we have no other way of getting? I don't know, and maybe they don't, either. Call it a successful first date, with many questions still to answer.

4.3
28 April

✧

ESL1 Shade Station
Earth-Sun Lagrange Point 1
Extracislunar Space

By the time Alice got to Tim Ho and Rose Ketchum, they were on their way back to the station, about a kilometer out.

Rose was still blind, and Tim had clipped himself to her and was simply pushing her back toward the double wheel of the station. Rose was lucid but had started vomiting, and Alice was telling her, "Use the purge button. Romper, you've got to activate your purge button."

To which Rose replied, "I can't find it, ma'am. I can't feel it. I'm going to inhale this stuff."

She was gasping for air, and definitely sounded like she was starting to panic, so as Alice approached the pair, she simply extended the pointer finger of her spacesuit glove and pressed the button for Rose.

A spray of white mist and brown liquid exited Rose's helmet, all over Alice's glove. Rose exclaimed, clearly startled by the noisy rush of air out of her suit. Each press of the button only released half a liter, but that was usually enough to do the job. And yeah, on the inside of a space helmet, it was loud.

There was definitely nothing wrong with Rose's visor; Alice could see straight through it to Rose's wide-eyed face. In fact, Alice could tell at a glance which components of Rose's suit had been made by Renz Ventures, and which by General Spacesuit. The outer fabric layer, which should be cerulean blue, had been scorched gray on the suit's front half. The hoses, which should be gray, had gone yellow. Rose's own face had blisters on it that looked, to Alice's war-trained eyes, like second-degree burns, though time would tell if it was actually worse than that.

But the visor itself, and the gloves and the boots and the rotary fittings, made right here at ESL1, looked fresh as the day they were made.

"The button is on your chin," Alice said, "where it's always been. Rose, I need you to slow your breathing and stop moving your arms around. TicTac's got you. Right now, he's actually got us both. Do you trust TicTac?"

"Yes, ma'am. With my life."

"Then stop moving around."

Alice was in full Pararescueman mode: a flow state of high alertness and low emotional affect. Emotions were not helpful at times like these. Later, perhaps. Not now.

"We're about ten minutes from the airlock," Tim reported.

To which Isaiah, over the radio, replied, "Jericho, here. At current speed you are eight minutes, fourteen seconds out from the airlock."

Taking firm hold of the straps on the front of Rose's spacesuit, Alice said, "You hear that? We're practically there, so I need you to keep your breathing slow, okay? For another eight minutes."

"What's wrong with me, ma'am?" Rose said, her voice ringing with tightly controlled fear.

"We're going to figure that out," Alice said. "We think you've been exposed to radiation, but we don't know how much. The good news is, you're already loaded up with every anti-radiation drug and cell growth factor known to man."

"What about Falcon?" Rose asked, through breaths that hadn't slowed at all.

"We're still figuring that one out, too."

"Is he KIA?"

Killed in action? Yes, probably. But what Alice said was, "The explosion might have blown him clear. Jericho is looking for him on the radar."

"I'm scared," Rose said.

"I know, honey. Let's get you to medlab and figure it out."

Alice had never called Rose "honey" before, but it was what she'd called her patients back on the battlefields of Central America. Especially the ones who were going to die.

"TicTac here, ma'am. I feel fine. No ill effects that I'm aware of. Is it possible Romper's just motion sick?"

It was Jericho who answered that one: "Negative, sir. The radiation burst should drop off rapidly with distance. Based on your position at the time, I'd say you got about a fifth of Romper's dose."

To which Rose said, "Falcon was a lot closer than I was. He was right on top of them. Is he dead, ma'am?"

"Probably," Alice said, unwilling to outright lie about it. "But right now, let's focus on you."

Another voice came in over the radio, saying, "Nightingale here. Can I get a comms check?"

"Mockingbird confirms," Alice said. "Nightingale on the network."

Nightingale was Berka Feikey, the station's replacement doctor. Alice didn't know much about her, except that she'd been a general practitioner in a North Dakota mining town, where she'd done everything from setting broken bones to delivering babies to administering chemotherapy drugs. That was a decent résumé, but Alice had never seen her handle an emergency.

"Can I get a report on Romper's condition?" Nightingale asked.

To which Alice replied, "Patient is lucid, with intermittent vomiting. Second-degree burns to the face." And then, because there was no way around it, she added, "Pupils are dilated and nonreactive, with some capillary bleeding around the sclera. Vision appears to be compromised."

Rose whimpered at that, but managed to basically keep her shit together.

"You're doing fine," Alice assured her. "Just breathe."

Nightingale said, "Mockingbird, I've tapped your camera feed. I'd appreciate if you can please stay pointed in that direction, so I can see the patient. Romper, I am monitoring your vital signs. Are you able to report symptoms?"

"Yes, ma'am. Uh! I'm sick to my stomach, and I do *not* get motion sickness. My hands and feet are tingling, and my eyes hurt. I can't see anything. That's not my visor, is it?"

"It doesn't appear so. Can you move your fingers and toes?"

"Yes, ma'am."

"All right, well, pulse ox looks good, but your blood pressure is dropping. It's possible you may lose consciousness. Mockingbird, will you please switch Romper's air mix to pure O_2?"

"Roger that."

Romper vomited again, and made no effort to activate her purge button. Alice did it for her, and after that nobody had much to say until they got to the airlock.

Alice opened the outer hatch, and Rose was cooperative as TicTac maneuvered her body inside. She seemed to be losing fine motor control, though, so Alice opted for the emergency pressurization sequence, which took thirty seconds instead of ten minutes.

Once the outer hatch was wheeled and sealed, the lights above it went from green to red, and the digital pressure gauge on the wall climbed rapidly, until Alice could feel the pressure shrinking the sleeves of her spacesuit. In the close confines of the lock, TicTac was holding Rose by the armpits now, and Alice had her hands on Rose's helmet latch. And then she could hear the rushing air, and the lights on the inner hatch went from red to green.

Without delay, Alice slammed the twin rotary connectors—one left and one right—and popped Romper's helmet off. She did the same with her own, and was assaulted by the puke-and-chemicals smell leaking out of Rose's suit. Ignoring that, she cranked the wheel on the inner hatch and shouldered it open.

After that, they maneuvered her through the Cross and through the rotary coupler module and into the old zero-gee part of the station, where the medlab was still located. Alice had insisted the medlab be easily accessible from the Cross, and Doc Feikey had insisted it not be treated like a hallway for anyone passing between the two stations, so the old station had been bolted to the new one at the module that had previously been Jeannete Schultz's apartment, with the medlab immediately across from it on the gamma corridor.

Feikey was waiting for them there—a crew-cut woman with fierce, dark eyes. Jarringly, Alice could see her own camera feed bouncing and whirling on one of the wall screens, above one of the two surgical tubes and across from the two examination tables.

"Get her out of the suit," Feikey was saying, but of course Alice and Tim were already doing that. Rose had gone limp, which made it easier. Once the suit's top half—the jacket—was separated from the pants, it became overwhelmingly clear that Rose Ketchum had shat herself. She reeked of it, and it was all up and down the back of her space underwear.

It was a bad sign, and it helped Alice realize that Rose had, in fact, lost consciousness.

"Never mind that," Doc Feikey said. "Strip her and get her in the tube."

She pantomimed these gestures, just in case there was any doubt, which there most certainly was not.

Tim and Alice pulled Rose's shitty things off of her, setting them adrift in the air. They got diarrhea in Rose's hair in the process, and it was all over her back and bum, and this would compromise the sterility of the tube, but yeah. They stuffed her in there and closed the clear plastic hatch down over her top half. Feikey worked some controls on her wall panel, and the tube immediately did a ten-second car wash cycle and then began shoving hoses and needles and probes into Rose's body in full Intensive Care mode.

X-ray and ultrasound scanners came alive, and then the display screen above the tube was showing a multimodal image of Rose's insides, and Alice (who was a medic, not a doctor) could see she was a fucking mess in there.

"We have internal bleeding," Feikey said, while Alice gathered up Rose's underwear and loose globs of shit. No time for disgust right now. "I'm pushing ten milligrams of vitamin K1 and a liter of plasma simulant. Also"—Feikey paused for a moment, tapping her chin—"levoflaxacin, loperamide, and some bone marrow growth factors. I need to do some research, figure out exactly which drugs to print. But her skin looks sunburnt, even where it wasn't exposed to the flash, and that's a bad sign. Do we have an estimate of the absorbed dose?"

"Only very approximately," said Isaiah Pembroke through Alice's headset, and also through a speaker on the wall. Because he was still on the network, listening to every word. "I think it must be between two thousand and fifteen thousand roentgens, minus whatever got blocked by the shielding in the suit. It won't have done very much against fast neutrons and gamma rays."

Doc Feikey's frown deepened. "If that's accurate, then there may not be much we can do. She's already loaded full of antioxidants and DNA repair enzymes, but those are protective against chronic exposure to much lower doses. We'll push some more of that and cross our fingers, but under normal circumstances, with immediate treatment, a lethal dose would be around six hundred roentgens, absorbed dose. So"—she met Alice's gaze with stern compassion—"let's not get our hopes up."

Nobody said anything for a few seconds, until Tim Ho cleared his throat and said, calmly, "Doctor, am I going to die?"

"I don't know," she said. "Better get that suit off."

The surgical tube estimated Rose's exposure at eight thousand Roentgens Absorbed Dose, and predicted, based on her dropping vital signs, a median survival time of "< 48 hrs." Her burns were getting worse—a lot worse.

"She's not going to regain consciousness," Feikey said confidently. "I'm sorry. Were the two of you close?"

"No," Alice said, because she'd been close to maybe ten people in her entire life. "But she's a good astronaut, well liked. As was"—her throat caught for a moment—"Derek Haakens."

In the next tube over, Tim Ho had an estimated dose of four hundred RAD, and was sedated against boredom while Feikey pumped him full of medications. He had a sunburn, too, though not much of one.

"This one is going to make it," she said. "He's going to need a blood transfusion—real human blood, not simulant—but he's AB positive, so we can pull from pretty much anyone here. We're going to need, I think, probably about four units, and it's actually better if they come from different people. You want to roll up your sleeve?"

"Definitely," Alice said.

Feikey touched her on the arm then and said, "Commander—Alice—you need to know, his astronaut career is over. He'd benefit from a bone marrow transplant, which we can't do here, and he's at massively elevated risk of developing cancers, pretty much throughout his body. With close supervision he could live a normal lifespan, but we've got to get him out of this high-radiation environment."

"I see."

Feikey turned and busied herself for a moment, tapping buttons on one of her many colorful touchscreen panels.

"I think the rest of us are going to skate on this one," she said. "We've got a couple of people who were near unshaded windows, who've made appointments to get their eyes checked. They may have some bleaching of retinal pigments, but those effects are reversible within, at most, a few days. It's possible there are some retinal point burns—Tim Ho has some very minor ones—but you'd really have to be looking directly at the explosion for that to happen. And even then, the burns are going to be small, maybe not particularly debilitating by themselves. You and Isaiah should think about getting your own eyes checked, by the way."

Alice knew that she and Isaiah had not been looking directly at the explosion, so she ignored the comment and asked, "What about the radiation?"

"Here? Negligible. Isaiah has been using the dosage estimates for Rose and Tim to calibrate his own calculations. The station got about five roentgens per square meter, and with all the shielding that's not going to amount to much, biologically. We probably got four months' worth of normal exposure in a couple of milliseconds, or two full-body CAT scans, if you like. But the radiation drugs should handle all of that. I'll bet we don't even have an elevated cancer risk."

"Hmm."

"I'm sorry, Alice. I wish I could do more."

Grimacing, Alice said, "I should have been out there with them." This wasn't actually true, and she knew it wasn't. It was her emotions, trying to leak out.

Sternly, Feikey said, "If you did that, we'd just have one more casualty, and one less interim station commander." She adjusted the settings on one of her screens, then turned to Alice with genuine grief on her face and said, "What exactly happened out there? Who were those people? What were they willing to die for, all the way out here?"

"I don't know," Alice said, "I don't. But I intend to find out."

When all of that was done, Alice left the medlab and its tragedies. She gently coasted her body across gamma corridor and through the old housing module, back into the Cross, and down the east spoke until centrifugal motion forced her to grab the ladder and slide the rest of the way down. Then it was through the east lab corridor and across into the other ring, through her thank-God-empty office, and into her apartment, whose hatch she closed and dogged behind her.

Positioning herself, face-down, a meter above her bed, she took a few cleansing breaths, then punched the mattress as hard as she could. Bouncing off the ceiling, she let the scream finally come out of her, rising to a shriek. And then her eyes went blurry, and she choked out a sob, and then another, and then a whole gasping string of them, and she just let it all happen. Any Air Force Pararescueman could tell you, when shit went badly, there was no substitute for tears.

1.9

✧

Post-Encounter Deposition
Selita Harris, PhD
Department of Music,
Stanford University

When I got accepted to the Juilliard School of Music, my parents worried I'd be wasting my life. I'd be chained to a half million dollars in student debt, minus the grants and scholarships I dogged for, and the pittance they scraped together over my childhood. With no job to pay it back.

My mother said: "You treated high school like college. You think college be some streets-paved-gold shit? Music theory, huh! What even is that, girl?"

My father said, "Learn a third instrument, sweetie. Everybody plays guitar. Everybody plays piano. There's always studio work, you learn the saxophone. You learn bagpipe, there's always funerals."

As if the world would ever be ready for a Black bagpiper. Racism meets cultural appropriation!

Well, Mom, well, Dad, I'm a professor at Stanford now, who gets paid to speak her own vernacular to impressionable minds. I publish papers in our dialect, too, and to heck with those don't accept it. That good enough for y'all? I rode a starship out to sing with the angels, so there you go. You happy now? And yes, I got paid. Igbal Renz himself cut me a fat wage, the two years I was gone.

I say "sing" because that's what it was like. What else you call it, they got no instruments? Hobie Prieto, back at ESL1, they froze that young man solid, and when he woke up he was ranting about Igbal's Beings, and how they sang to him. Not like any ordinary music, either. So Igbal goes out to meet 'em, he brings a musicologist to classify it.

Now, that's no easy task, y'all. I could say it was bells or xylophones or pipe organs, and it kinda was. Or I could say it was theremin music, and yeah, it was a bit like that, the way the notes sometimes slid together. I could say voices, and probably that would give the best idea what it sounded like, but without lips or lungs or vocal cords, or any solid piece to make the sounds. Or I could say "pure vibrations in the ether," and that doesn't communicate so well, even if it's the exact truth.

I wouldn't say I *saw* the Beings, as the experience for me was not particularly visual. But I *perceived* them as colorless spheres, a lot of them, each giving off a pure note according to its size, like Tibetan singing bowls or some such, although the sizes were always changing. Soprano beach balls and baritone weather balloons, and everything in between, all pulsating in different time.

You could call it a symphony, but that would mislead you more. A choir, too; it wasn't that kind of organized. I'd call it more of a techno opera, with each individual part sung by a choir, and with other voices howling and beat-boxing in the background.

There were words, but I didn't catch any of them; it was in some language I didn't know, stranger than Tolkien's Elvish or the jibber-jabber of toddlers. Now, some other humans out there heard music, too, and some say they caught the words with it, and that may be. Me, I only understood the notes.

It was a dense sound, just full of notes, but built up from simple patterns. No one Being had a complicated part to play.

Now, I'll tell you, an octave is a basic property of the universe. It's the interval between one frequency and its double, and you can hear the similarity between the same notes on different octaves. You can *see* it in the way a guitar string naturally vibrates. No different for the Beings. But how you divide up an octave, that's cultural.

In the west we use eighths, which sounds good, because those split the octaves up by powers of two—non-prime whole numbers, just the way a guitar string wants to twang—with the sharps being a semitone higher and the flats a semitone lower. Those aren't as pleasing to the ear, because they're not these pure harmonics. But there's nothing inherent or universal about that. In Ancient Babylonia they used thirds, and in places like Japan and India they still use sevenths, which produces that slightly discordant Asian twang.

The Beings, in my opinion, don't divide their octaves any fractional way whatsoever. They'll sing three notes one octave and then the same three in another, but the notes fall any old place. There's purpose and math in there, sure, but they ain't writing any of this down in no staff notation. Wouldn't surprise me if the notes were irrational numbers, or even just random, but from each basic seed there's a call and response and a variation, so the thread of it gets more complicated until it just suddenly quits. But there's multiple threads weaving in and out, so the music never quite stops.

For timing, all humans tend to space our notes between maybe three seconds and a few tens of milliseconds apart, with faster time sounding frantic or urgent or sometimes playful. Middle speeds sound happy, and slower ones sound lazy or sad. The Beings, at least the notes that I could hear, were similar. Whether that was inherent, or staged for our benefit, I really couldn't say.

It's also . . . there was a twentieth-century comedian named Martin Mull, who said, "Writing about music is like dancing about architecture," and I believe that's very true in this case. I can't really convey it, and I sure can't sing it. But since my job is to describe, I'll say there were layers to it. Call it three layers.

The first layer was the loudest, lowest, slowest, and the most blurred together, and it communicated a sense of awe that bordered at times on sadness or alarm or even anger. Something like a Gregorian chant, or Tuvan throat singing, or the groaning and shrieking of Koyaanisqatsi.

On top of that, a quieter, clearer layer that was more like an actual song. Not simple enough that you could quite call it "happy," but it would have been pleasant if it weren't so damned overwhelming.

Third, in the background, was a high, fast, staccato layer, like structured rain, conveying excitement. Trance music is the closest thing I can describe to it, if trance music were produced by a hundred separate voices.

I don't know if that makes sense or not, but even if it does, it's an approximation. That's all. If it were rendered in human time with human instruments, it wouldn't have the same effect. The DMT high lasted maybe ten minutes, so I couldn't have heard the music any longer than that. But I'll tell you, it did seem like a much longer time. If time had any meaning, I would say it was several hours at least, and I came away with that kind of heavy, exhausted feeling you get after a mind-blowing concert. Actually, more than that; I believe I was a sphere as well, or shapeless. I might have been pulsating with the music, too. My voice might have been part of the chorus.

I'm sure people would like me to say it was the most beautiful sound I ever heard, and unfortunately that would not be the case. It was beautiful in its way, but it was not human. Think of some complicated, possibly venomous undersea creature, and ask yourself how beautiful it is, really. But this music was the most *extraordinary* I've ever heard by a good mile. Of course, it faded once the DMT wore off. Best I can remember now is just a few fragments, that in no way do justice to the experience, and the best I can transcribe of it is, like I said, an approximation.

Sometimes I hear more of it in dreams, and I try to scribble down a piece here and a piece there. People ask me when I'm going to publish or perform the thing, and that answer is never. Definitely never. But as long as I live, every damn thing I write is going to have "influenced by" stamped all over it. And that's a paycheck, too, Mom, so just maybe music theory is a thing after all.

2.2
03 May
✧
Clementine Cislunar Fuel Depot
Earth-Moon Lagrange Point 1
Cislunar Space

"We are also harassed," said the trillionaire Grigory Magnusevich Orlov, "by these stealth ships."

Dona Obata sighed; she could read his tone, and knew he was afraid, and that his fear could explode into violent rage at any moment.

Sally Grigorieva Orlova, a seventeen-year-old who apparently could not read her father's tone, said, "Let's embrace them, then."

Orlov's snort bordered on a sneer. "Yes, indeed, let us all be fine friends. Excellent thinking, Sally. I see you have your mother's quick wit."

Dangerously for Sally, she and her father and Dona Obata were in Sally's own newly assigned quarters. She'd arrived a week ago, a few months after insisting her father take over custody in place of her "boring, miserable mother." Since arriving, she'd worn a different outfit every day so far—bespoke garments of spidersilk and no-press cotton—and her wrists and ears and neckline glittered with dangly jewels that did not belong in a weightless environment. And those idiotic smartglasses made Dona want to slap them right off the girl's head.

But the beige-and-brass apartment—luxurious for cislunar space—was windowless and had only one exit, so if Orlov chose violence, his teenage daughter would have no witnesses and nowhere to retreat. And he knew exactly how to move his body in zero gravity, whereas Sally was still flinging herself around like a toddler. She didn't seem to understand this. This was her fifth conversation with her father, perhaps ever, and she did not seem to understand whom or what she was dealing with.

To his credit, Orlov then said, "Daughter, please understand. My own father, the great Magnus Orlov, raised me with criticism, the whip, and occasional hundred-character snippets of wisdom. That, and by throwing me on an oil platform at an age when other boys were still playing with action figures."

"But you have no sons to treat so roughly," Sally said, with remarkable defiance.

"I do not," he agreed. "But I am amply provided with daughters. Do you imagine I have pined for you? Ask Dona, here, how many times your name has come up in all the years she's been with me."

"Twice," Dona said, without waiting to be asked.

Sally looked more amused than hurt. "That's twice more than I actually care about. I'm half raised already, o patriarch of abandoned women, and not so gently as you seem to think."

Dona almost laughed out loud, and decided she actually kind of liked this girl. Decided, in fact, that she would expend some effort defending this strange, blonde product of European boarding schools.

In all the years they'd been a couple, Dona and Orlov had never come to blows, because he was a product of the worst kind of gangster capitalism, and Dona was a product of something even more terrible: the intelligence services that operated in Africa. Both of them knew that if things got too heated, one or both of them could very well end up in a surgical tube, or dead. But their verbal sparring was constant, and indeed a sort of bedrock of their relationship; each reminding the other of the danger they were both in. And Dona was no humanitarian, but there were people she liked, and situations she preferred. She knew when to step in front.

She said, "Grigory, my beloved, your temper sometimes distracts you from the most basic facts in front of you. Let's recall how this conversation started."

Three minutes ago, Sally had said to her father, "Our enemy, Igbal Renz, has been attacked." It hadn't gone well from there.

Now, in echo of that, Sally said, "If Igbal's vast facility has an enemy, are these stealth ships not therefore our friend? It's true we don't know what they want, but have we even asked? I say we flirt with them. Make kissy faces and bring them close. And then . . ."

"Mmm?" Even through his annoyance, Orlov looked intrigued.

"Then we fuck them."

The word she used was *"opuskat"*—literally, to push down. It was a dirty word even by Russian standards—a reference to forcible sodomy.

A smile and a frown seemed to be warring for control of Orlov's face. He paused for a moment, and then said, "Interesting metaphor, but no. This is not how dangerous people think."

To Sally's credit, she sat back (if one can sit back while hovering, weightless, in a VIP cabin) and thought about that. She looked back and forth from Dona to Grigory, with an expression that said she knew—*knew*—that she was not only wise beyond her years, but also overmatched by her circumstances. Dona could see, in that look, that Sally hadn't come here in a fit of bravado, or as a tourist, or as a spoilt child expecting to have her way. No, this girl had *run*.

Dona was not one for speaking gently, but she could at least be mild. She looked Sally in her pale blue eyes and said, "Do you know the game, 'fuck, marry, or kill'?"

Sally nodded, suddenly looking very uncertain. Not weak, not even particularly frightened, but like she did not, for once, know what to do or say. Smart girl.

"You don't fuck people like that," Dona said. "People with nukes and invisibility cloaks. If you're smart, you don't kill them, either."

Nobody said anything, until a low, unsmiling laugh hissed from Orlov's lips.

"You women and your metaphors. Shall we marry the Cartels, then? Squeeze ourselves into a slutty dress and walk them down the aisle?"

Again, silence, but it was Sally who broke it this time: "Don't they have something you want? Don't they have a lot of things you want? Weapons? Political cover? Fear?"

Dona nodded grimly. She had handed Sally this opening, and Sally had taken it.

Orlov said nothing.

Sally seemed to finally realize she was in actual physical danger, but that she could talk her way out of it. Even more tentatively, she said, "You have something they want, as well."

"Yes? And what is that?"

"Citizenship," she said. "This station is an independent country."

"For tax purposes."

"And to evade prosecution for your numerous violations of Russian and maritime law."

Again, Orlov said nothing. That was interesting; it meant Sally had his attention.

"You could be selling them passports," she said. "You could charge a lot for passports."

And yet again, the trillionaire had no response, so Dona stepped in and said, "Actually, the novelty value alone could be substantial. We cleared almost a billion dollars last year selling space vodka."

That had been Dona's idea, and it had worked out so well that they'd lately started charging even more exorbitant prices for "silver-zeolite-filtered" and "platinum-zeolite-filtered" versions of the exact same product. Four thousand dollars a bottle, and they literally could not make it fast enough to meet the demand. And passports . . . why, those could be printed on Earth, having no impact on the station's own production facilities.

Pressing onward, she said, "Your daughter feels a need to prove herself, Grigory. Perhaps you should allow her?"

"It is a fresh idea," he conceded, "but we do not actually know who is behind these incursions. It is probably not the Americans, but it could be the Chinese, or another nation-state looking to steal its way to greatness. Even if it is Cartels, we would need to know which one. There are many problems with this suggestion. But we are in need of lateral thinking. If you will meet me in Operations an hour from now, we will see if you can be of use."

With that, he kicked off from a corner of Sally's bed, launching himself toward the open hatch, and disappeared into the hallway outside.

"Father of the year," Sally said, with no particular emphasis.

By now, Dona had worked out this girl's situation, and knew how to play her. She said, "To whom are you in debt?"

Sally was floating by the dressing mirror, beside the door to the *en suite* bathroom, and in its reflection Dona could see the girl's shoulders tense. But her face remained impassive, and she said, in French rather than Russian, "My credit cards?"

Dona had subtly positioned herself between Sally and the exit, and she now allowed her expression to harden. "Everyone who comes to this station brings problems with them," she said, still in Russian, although French was her native language. "It's my business to assess the threat of you, so I'm not going to ask again."

With a flare of defiance, Sally said, "You're guessing. You don't know anything about me."

In fact, Dona had done a dark-web sweep on the girl last night, using tools and techniques unknown to most people, and knew more about her than she was willing, at this time, to reveal. Identification numbers, bank accounts, medical history. The girl suffered from clinical depression, and had—at the age of seventeen—already twice been treated for sexually transmitted infections. And what the dark web could not reveal, Dona saw written plainly across Sally's face.

"I won't push you out an airlock," Dona said now, "but I'm thirty seconds away from breaking your arm. You have traded on your father's name, to acquire credit beyond your means. It happens to rich girls, sometimes. I don't care about the money, but I need to know who is holding the debt, so I can guess what they will do, if they find you are beyond their reach."

Now Sally looked truly afraid. Her eyes darted up and down Dona's dark, athletic frame, no doubt seeing, for the first time, the formidable intellect in her, and the potential for violence. It was her day to notice these things.

As an act of kindness, Dona said, "I worked for the intelligence service of a major European country. Mostly in Africa. Your father keeps me at his side because there is no other safe place for him to keep me. Do you understand?"

"Yes," Sally said. Wide-eyed, she was drifting slowly toward one of the apartment's walls, and rotating slowly in the air. Doing nothing, now, to change her momentum.

"So, then."

In a rush, Sally said, "I didn't mean for it to get so out of hand. I have a trust fund that pays out monthly, and I just . . . got behind. Please understand, I know some rough people. Rougher than I thought, apparently. This friend of a friend . . . well, he offered to help me. I didn't realize he was charging me at all, much less charging me interest. I thought he was my boyfriend. It was very stupid. I can't believe how stupid."

Finally, she reached out a hand and took hold of a grab bar, looking afraid to do it and also afraid not to. The bracelets on her wrist jingled with the motion.

"Drugs or gambling?" Dona asked.

"Neither," Sally said. Then: "Well, a little of both, but mostly just . . . high living. Air taxis. Bottle service. Concierge service. Clothes."

"Yeah, I noticed the clothes. And I know how these things can happen, without you even really noticing. I won't judge you, girl, I really don't care about any of it. But I need you to give me a name."

"I don't know his real name. People called him L'incendie." Then, in Russian: "It means 'the fire,' like a house fire."

"Give me a nationality, then. Was he French?"

Sally shook her head. "South American. From Venezuela, I think."

"Wonderful," Dona said, and sighed. At one time, the scariest answer to that question would have been "Italian" or "Japanese." Then, for a time, "Russian," or perhaps "Chinese American." But South America was a mess these days, even more than it had been thirty years ago. There was a lot more money kicking around, a lot of profitable industry, but the gradient between rich and poor was steeper than ever, and the Cartels—even now, after the war—were into everything, with a level of violence so absurdly surreal that even Hollywood movies had to tone it down.

Cynics would sometimes say the main purpose of the war was to clear the Cartels out of Suriname, so three of the Four Horsemen could launch their rockets there in peace. That wasn't true, or anyway it wasn't the whole truth, but any South American tough guy who wasn't directly Cartelled up would be at most two degrees of separation away from them. The Cartels themselves would see to that.

Fortunately, Orlov Petrochemical had avoided the cesspit of Suriname almost completely, preferring to launch from Kazakhstan and offshore platforms, and from islands too small and politically weak to mount much resistance.

Sighing again, Dona waved a hand at Sally and said, "Relax. I can see the mere threat of harm has taught you what you needed to learn. You're a bright girl, but you have seriously fucked up. This L'incendie, or the people he answers to—"

"He doesn't answer to anyone."

"Everyone answers to someone," Dona said, unfazed. "And these men would have stuck you in an apartment, and charged a hundred thousand rubles a night to watch you fucked in every hole. On camera, you understand, and then they would have attempted to blackmail your father with the footage, and then they would have had to be murdered for their trouble, and the people they answer to would not be happy. And then there'd be a little war in your name, and the one thing all parties could agree on is that you were a liability. Do you know what happens to liabilities?"

"That's a lot of speculation," Sally muttered, clearly trying to salvage some sense of dignity and control.

"Only the details," Dona said. "You're a liability already." Then, trying to keep the irony out of her voice, she added, "You were right to come to me with this."

Still holding her grab bar, Sally said, "What's going to happen to me?"

"I will quietly pay off your L'incendie, with a little extra for his trouble. It's the cheapest option. You owe him less than fifty million rubles?"

Sally stared back blankly, so she amended: "Less than a million Euros?"

Sally nodded. "Less than a quarter million as of today. I only borrowed—"

Dona held up a hand. "The details don't matter. I'm going to make this problem go away. And you"—she paused for dramatic effect, because she liked Sally and wanted her to get it—"are going to make yourself useful."

"Or what?" Sally seemed to be asking more out of curiosity than defiance.

"You're a smart girl," Dona said. "Use your imagination."

1.10

Post-Encounter Deposition
Aram Schiller, MSCS
Deputy Chief Technology Officer,
Searchable Logic Corporation

I talked to the ship's doctor, Rachael Lee, and she told me she could not detect any sign of the Beings' anatomy. No orifices or sense organs, no indication of their internal organization. "They are blanks," she told me, as she was putting me back into hibernation. It was the last thing anyone said to me on that mission.

So it's a good thing I was there, because the good doctor was looking for structure in the wrong place. I submit the Beings are best understood as computing systems rather than organisms.

As the volume of information in a space increases, the time and energy required to sort or index or search the information goes up geometrically, meaning it's not only exponential, but the exponent itself increases. Computer science is all about shortcuts, and if we are *really clever* we can shave that geometric time down to merely exponential or, in certain special cases, logarithmic time. But, for very large volumes, the problem still gets intractable very quickly.

The easiest way to solve an intractable problem is to sidestep it completely. Don't sort the information. Don't index it, don't search it. A spreadsheet operates this way; each node or cell is affected by the cells around it; change one, and the changes can propagate throughout the entire system. There is no difference between the memory and the computation, which puts spreadsheets in a class of systems we call cellular automata. Lots of real-world problems can be solved this way, such as fluid dynamics simulations of the flow around aircraft or submarines. The problem with cellular automata is that they have no defined end state; they'll just keep going forever if you let them. But they are self-contained, and infinitely scalable, which is good.

Another shortcut is the learning network, which doesn't ever really store information per se. It just adjusts its own structure to account for the information, so that when a particular stimulus is received, that information can be regurgitated without the system ever having to index it, or really "know" it at all.

More recently, there has been tremendous progress in the field of quantum-holographic processing or QHP, which extends the massively parallel structure of cellular automata into large, multidimensional spaces. QHP has most of the advantages of both cellular automata and learning networks, with an added advantage of tremendous speed and very low energy consumption. But of course those quantum states are fragile, even at very low temperatures, and most of the hardware in these systems is geared toward staving off decoherence for as long as possible.

The ultimate goal of all of these systems is what we call "domain-specific omniscience." This means, basically, that you can know everything, given enough energy and a long enough span of time, or you can know any single thing instantly, in zero time, for free. This doesn't actually exist—it's hypothetical, a thought experiment—but you can show algorithmically that certain architectures approach domain-specific omniscience.

With all of that in mind, you'll understand me when I say: the Beings appear to be omniscience engines of a sort we have not imagined. Like a QHP engine, they sidestep any search or index of the information inside them, but their domain-specificity is four-dimensional. Everything they know, they know instantly, or almost instantly, and with a negligible expenditure of energy. But they are finite—every bit as finite as the memory in your eyeglasses. Their capacity is bogglingly large by human standards, but if I understood their transmission correctly, that capacity has to be allocated, dynamically in real time, across the axes of a four-dimensional hyperspace. The result is a novel, computationally efficient system that "sees" and "knows" everything going on inside it.

I was less clear about the hardware situation. Here I have to agree with Doctor Lee, that the "bodies" of the Beings gave no indication of having any ability to support this computing architecture. The best I can do is speculate that the hypersphere subducted by any given Being is essentially "written onto" the 4D universe by a structure that is "outside" of it, and impossible for us to perceive.

To make a very crude analogy, if you are a drawing on a sheet of paper, you cannot "point to" the pen that draws you, or the mind that moves the pen. And if that mind somehow linked to your own for a few minutes, well, that would be a hard thing to make sense of, and even harder to describe. And why bother even trying? If there are answers to be found from this Encounter, I think computer science is where we will find them.

5.2
03 May

✧

Thalia Buoyant Island
Southern Stratosphere
Venus

At night, when Frédéric was supposed to be sleeping, he watched videos from Earth. Birds and coral reefs and crowded city sidewalks. One of his favorites was actually called "TV For Dogs," and showed hour upon hour of squirrels running through the trees in somebody's back yard. Frédéric could not get enough. Also, porn.

His tablet computer had come here with him from Earth, and he lived in fear that it would someday break. Thalia technically had the capability to 3D-print something similar (not nearly as capable, but at least able to watch videos). But committing the resources to print one would, naturally, require a sixty-six percent supermajority vote of the island's adults. Even buried in a monthly manifest of printable goods, a request like that would be line-itemed out, for sure.

He also lived in fear that the free network feeds from Earth would dry up and stop working. The people of Thalia still exchanged email traffic back and forth with their friends and relatives back on Earth, through a handful of free-access, password-unprotected SpaceNet routers on the Deep Space Network. The bandwidth of that traffic was probably too small for anyone to notice, but if they did . . . well, they would probably just swap in a paywall and cut Venus off entirely.

To the best of Frédéric's knowledge, he was the only Venusian trying to exploit SpaceNet access for anything more than asynchronous messaging, and no wonder—the available bandwidth was never more than a few hundred kilobits per second. The round-trip latency—anywhere from 4.3 minutes to half an hour—was an even larger problem, because most free-content servers on Earth ran the TCP/IP protocol of the legacy internet, rather than the more forgiving SpaceNet protocol, and would drop the connection before transferring any actual data. Through sheer boredom and persistence, Frédéric had collected and bookmarked a handful of sites that would let him connect, and, over agonizing hours and days, download videos. But he lived in fear that these, too, would somehow disappear.

That was a lot of fear.

The videos were supported by a fascinating array of advertisements, for products Frédéric had no way to buy, and services he did not even understand. What was an "insurance virtualizer"? Or a "rock-solid transport guarantee"? He didn't know and he didn't care; he wanted them, and the lifestyle they implied.

He also read news sites, and had lately become interested in the doings of all the other groups that did business in space. Lawrence Killian's company, Harvest Moon, sold metals and water and fuel for fusion reactors. Orlov Petrochemical sold nitrogen and volatiles. Enterprise City had sent a hundred people to Mars, and was getting ready to send a hundred more. And no matter what Frédéric's father had to say about it, those people had it better than the people of Thalia, if only because there were regularly scheduled cargo missions to deliver them critical supplies.

And of course there was Renz Ventures, whose business was the nexus of so much intrigue. WHO NUKED ESL1? the headlines read. ARE STEALTH SHIPS STILL OUT THERE? And also, IGBAL AND THE ALIENS—A STORY TOO WEIRD TO BE FALSE.

And as he read these stories, one thing he realized was that Venus—with its murderous atmosphere and furnace-hot depths—was not the most dangerous place in the Solar System. No one was going to attack them down here. No one was going to spy on them, or undercut their interests. People barely knew Thalia was here at all; if its people died, it would be of neglect.

Another thing that dawned on him, more slowly, was that Thalia had nothing to sell. Any material available on Venus, any product

Thalia was capable of manufacturing, could be obtained somewhere else, for a fraction of the cost.

Mars was in a similar position; the planet itself was the only product. People simply wanted to move there, and had given over their life savings to make it happen. Mars promised a fresh start not only for themselves, but for the whole human race. Of course, the colony at Antilympus Crater had the wealth of the trillionaire Dan Beseman behind it, but the amazing thing was that most of the funding came not from Beseman himself, or even from the colonists, but from millions of donors around the world.

Frédéric began digging, through whatever sources he was (however painfully) able to access, into the mechanisms of that funding, and realized it was literally a game show. The money came from people who would never go to Mars themselves, but were willing to "sponsor" the candidates who might. People who were captivated by the idea of Mars—by the dream of anyone living there at all. That second chance for humanity, that fresh start, made a compelling story, and if there were ten million people willing to kick in ten thousand dollars apiece, why, that was a hundred billion dollars right there. Throw in a hundred million ten-dollar donations, a couple of really high-value grants, and some support from friendly governments, and voilà, the whole planet of Mars was yours for the taking.

And Thalia didn't even need that kind of money. Piggybacked on other people's infrastructure, the whole island had been built and populated for something like thirty billion dollars. And Thalia didn't need a whole second island, anyway; they were so poor that just a few hundred kilograms of metal would utterly transform the quality of life here, and the sense of a hopeful future. Maybe some new plant seeds. Maybe just one more 3D printer. Surely that was something the people of Earth could afford?

"Thalia has a public relations problem," Frédéric told his mother, Wilma, over breakfast one morning.

"Public relations," she said, with a wistful look. She was passing out breakfast plates to Frédéric and his sister, Consuela, and she paused for a moment, as if remembering a past life where terms like that were a meaningful part of the daily vernacular.

"You have a stupid face problem," Consuela said, wrinkling her nose and covering her eyes. "It hurts to look." She was only six years younger than Frédéric—almost eleven, now—but seemed to have no reference point for what that was supposed to mean. Consuela had known no culture other than Thalia's, and had no female role models anywhere close to her own age. She sometimes looked to Basilio's daughter, Juanetta del Campo, for inspiration, but on the rare occasions when Juanetta had time for Consuela at all, she treated her like even more of a baby. Possibly out of some sort of manipulative spite.

"I'm not hungry," Frédéric said to his mother. "Can I please just go to school?"

"Now there's a first!" Wilma said, looking pleased, suspicious, amused, and conspiratorial. "To what do we owe this shocking development? Would it have something to do with Juanetta?"

"No," Frédéric said, shuddering inwardly. "I just want to work on my English. I've been reading network content from Earth."

She snorted at that, and looked like she was about to say something snide. Wilma Ortega had never been a big fan of network content, and sometimes said that she'd come to Venus "for the quiet." And with only fifty people on the island, there was certainly plenty of quiet to be had. But then, instead of trying to change his mind or change him, she softened and said, "They don't have network content in Spanish?"

"They do. It's just harder to find. There are translators, too, but the latency is murder. It's hard to find anything, Mamita. English will save me a lot of time, and save bandwidth on the communications array. It's practical."

She laughed. "Oh, so now I'm 'Mamita,' am I? Not Mami? Okay, it's good to see you interested in something." Even if it's stupid, she clearly wanted to add. But she didn't. Instead, she tousled his hair and said "Fine, little Frito. You may skip your breakfast and go practice a language that no Venusian speaks."

A lot of people here speak English, he wanted to say. *Yourself included.*

"Thank you," he said instead, getting up from his seat. "I hope you have a wonderful day with your plants."

"I hope you don't pass any mirrors," Consuela said. It wasn't clear exactly what she meant, or even whom she was addressing, so no one responded. Best not to reinforce.

Outside the front door, Juanetta del Campo stood, with a raised, loose fist about to knock. Both of them jumped a little, and Juanetta laughed. "Hello, Freddo."

"Hi," he said, stepping out into the corridor. The diamond-walled apartments were all painted white inside, both for privacy and for daylight control, but the corridor ceiling was of course transparent. Outside, the Sun was at a ten-o'clock position, so it streamed through the plant canopy only indirectly, lighting Juanetta's hair and one side of her face. She looked good, he had to admit.

She kissed him on the cheek, as was her custom, and then took him by the arm.

"Ready for school?" she asked.

"Actually, yes."

"Well, then, let's stuff some knowledge down our eyeballs."

He didn't like the possessive way she held his arm, but he knew there was no point resisting it. Everyone seemed to think Frédéric and Juanetta were destined for one another—practically a couple already. Juanetta herself seemed to think this. The problem was, Frédéric didn't like Juanetta in that way. At times, he wasn't sure he liked her at all. But they were the same age, and the four other unrelated, uncoupled girls were years older or years younger. The older ones of course wanted nothing to do with Frédéric, and as for the younger ones . . . Well, that could be a long wait. Tika Valdez would not come of age for another six years; did Frédéric really want to wait that long to start having sex? With Tika, another girl he didn't really have a choice about? Who even knew who either of them would be in six years' time? Or he could wait even longer, for someone else he knew even less about.

There were worse things, he knew. Juanetta was pretty, and smart, and a hard worker. She had a sense of humor. She liked plants, and chemistry, and she knew how to print custom clothing. At this very moment, Frédéric was wearing a shirt she had made for him.

But there was always an edge of sarcasm in her voice, like a little whiff of Venusian air, and in the close confines of Thalia Village, Frédéric had seen enough bickering couples to know, without a doubt, that that caustic humor would eventually be turned his way. And then that would be his life.

There were worse things. Death would be worse. Celibacy and

loneliness would perhaps be worse. Losing his connections to Earth culture would definitely be worse. For all he knew, she might be really good at sex, and other things he didn't yet know about. But oh, if Juanetta was going to be his life, he wanted at least to choose her for himself.

That was not going to happen, though, so he touched her on the hand, gently but not intimately, and strode with her down the corridor toward another miserable day of robotic instruction.

Despite his plan to practice his English, he ended up mostly daydreaming the hours away, thinking about how he, a fifteen-year-old boy, could attract the attention of people on Earth. Technically, Thalia already had a charitable foundation—the nonprofit Aphrodite Group, which had organized the missions that had brought the equipment and people. When asked, Tohias had eagerly told him all about it, as it seemed to be one of his proudest accomplishments. And yet, the foundation was presently in a coma, just a holding vessel for the investments of five people who couldn't actually come here unless another forty-five could be recruited. Assuming those five would even go through with it.

Could Frédéric, from 150 million kilometers away, start his own foundation? Children of Venus, something like that? If it were possible at all, it would be difficult. What he really needed was a lawyer willing to handle the details for him. TV had taught him that much! And a publicist, and an accountant, and some cash donors to get things rolling. Which sounded extremely difficult, but perhaps not completely impossible. Not for a marooned kid with way too much time on his hands.

That night, he stayed up late searching for social media sites he could access, and finally—after more than four hours—found his way to something called Weightless. It was aimed specifically at people who wanted to travel to space someday, and allowed them to communicate with people presently living on Mars, Transit Point Station, and ESL1. The landing page boasted that their servers used not only the SpaceNet protocol, but also the Deep Space Network through which governments and Horsemen communicated with hardware scattered throughout the Solar System! Well, der.

With painful slowness, Frédéric made an account for himself, snapped a quick profile picture with the camera on his tablet, and looked at the names and locations of people he could "join." Right away, he could see that the outer space angle was a mostly fraudulent gimmick, because the list included exactly two Martians, exactly one ESL1 colonist, exactly zero people on Transit Point Station, and approximately half a million people from scattered locations on Earth.

He had listed his own location as "Thalia Buoyant Island, Venus," and honestly, he was still figuring out the user interface when he saw that one of the Earth-based members had already joined him.

With a sort of exhausted excitement he typed a quick biography for himself: "My name is Frédéric Ortega. I am fifteen years old, and I have spent the last five years living on an island in the upper atmosphere of Venus. I am interested in Earth culture, and look forward to many interesting conversations here."

He'd written it in Spanish, but the interface included automatic translation from the source language into whatever language the reader was using. And he was too tired to worry about it; he would take another look tomorrow, and see if he needed to edit anything.

He thought he might be too excited to sleep, but sleep found him anyway, almost as soon as he turned out his light.

And because he had neglected to log out of Weightless before setting his tablet down, he was still logged in the next morning when he picked it back up again and found a message waiting for him from "Jia Cheng," a twenty-year-old woman in Shanghai, China: "Wow!! Tell me more!"

And behind that, seven hundred and fifty-nine other messages.

1.11

Post-Encounter Deposition
Harv Leonel, PhD
Department of Electrical Engineering,
University of Colorado at Boulder

I'm never sure if my reputation precedes me; to some people I'm famous, to some, infamous. A scammer, lunatic, idiot, or daring visionary? Some days I'm not so sure myself. But despite all the ink and bits expended on the subject, most people don't actually remember my name, so I'll say, I'm that guy who maybe invented an irreproducible time machine, and pulled ancestral experiences back (once, maybe) from the Antediluvian past into my present-day brain. My twelve-years-ago brain, actually. Remember that tabloid controversy that gripped the world for a week and a half? That was me.

The weight of evidence is on my side; things I saw back there in the Pleistocene have been archaeologically, linguistically, and genetically verified, that no one could possibly have known without firsthand knowledge. But the weight of public opinion is fickle, and mostly against me. The incident ruined my career, and the relationship I was in at the time, and my sleep cycles and short-term memory. I also dragged two promising postdocs down with me, which I deeply regret, so I actually do wish the whole thing had never happened. But it did, and apparently enough people believe in it that Igbal Renz invited me on his mission to meet the Beings.

(To be fair, we already knew each other, because my early

quantum computing papers were crucial to his early successes in artificial intelligence. We'd been in the same room together maybe ten times, and he knew me by name and by sight. But yep, life can take strange turns. "You're not afraid to risk it all on quantum mechanics," he said, "and something tells me you'd risk it all again, for a chance to be right." Say what you like about the man, he's an excellent judge of character, and he was right on the money with that.)

A lot has been said about the Beings already, but my encounter was so different from anyone else's that I can't swear it wasn't a dream. Which is the story of my life, right? I'm going to talk about this experience like it had a beginning, middle, and end. Just know, it actually didn't—it was more like a Heironymous Bosch painting than a movie or even a comic book. You know, like that painting of Hell where the closer you look, the more crazy things you see. But when you pull back and look at the whole thing, that's crazy, too. So much detail, everywhere you look. That's what the experience was actually like, but it's hard to talk about it that way. We like stories, so I'm going to tell one.

Beginning: I observed a galaxy cluster, with great curiosity. I don't know what sort of body I had, or if I had one; I wasn't paying attention to that. I only had eyes for this glob of something that was neither the vacuum nor myself. Neither the vacuum nor myself! If I think about it now, the galaxy cluster was actually inside me. I don't think I had a way of looking outward, or even a concept of it. But I had perceived a vast volume, and this thing inside of it, and I took notice.

It wasn't light or heat or gas that caught my attention. It wasn't even gravity, per se, although I could feel the tug of it, moving atoms past me in a gentle breeze. What drew me in was *motion*. Each galaxy whirled about its axis, and the whole swarm of them revolved around each other, or around a common center of mass, in a complicated n-body dance. It was like I'd never seen such a thing before, and maybe I hadn't. I watched it, utterly transfixed.

I say I don't know about my body, but I was definitely not three-dimensional, and I was definitely not looking at a moving three-dimensional structure. The cluster was a lot more than that. Not just multidimensional, but also, it seemed to me, responsive in some way, like the surface of a pond that ripples when you brush it with your fingers.

That sounds wonderful, doesn't it? But in a big-square-peg/small-round-hole kind of way, a human brain can't really remember or process that kind of experience. Trying leads to headaches. Actually, more than headaches: a kind of creeping, bone-deep nausea that's almost a phobia. There's something vaguely *gross* about it, at least for me, the me that I am now, though I couldn't tell you exactly why. But at the time, as one of them, I felt nothing but innocent amazement.

Again, I'll say it was like a really complicated painting, with lots of stuff going on, and I could attend to one little scene, or another, or pull back for another look at the whole design. But it wasn't really static, either; the whole thing fizzed with uncertainty that let portions of the painting change as I watched them, *because* I watched them. That's the best I can describe it, and it's not very accurate.

I think I used to be much larger. I had shrunk to look at this wondrous thing. To investigate it in further detail, I shrank and grew, attending to as much of it as I could, and when that didn't satisfy, I broke apart into a million little self-aware fragments and swarmed the place, crawling through its intricate whirlpools like mice through a deserted kitchen. Mice that were all me, and also inside of me. I called and sang and squeaked to myself across the void, sharing information and excitement.

I'm going to say, I did that (or we did that) for a long time. That's not how it worked, but that's what I'm going to say. It was a research project, and a big one, with detailed reporting. Hypotheses were proposed and tested, discarded and modified at whim. It was all great fun.

Middle: I was smaller than a single galaxy, and overlapping with one, when something even more amazing happened: as I sang to myself (or we sang to ourselves), I (or we) became aware of tiny voices mumbling back! It was inexplicable, impossible, unthinkable.

It was irresistible.

There were others, who were not me. There were *others*.

We shrank, we spiraled, we surrounded and permeated this amazing phenomenon. I sang to these little voices. I whispered and I beckoned. They were in a noisy little place; I could barely pick them out against the background, and it seemed they could hear even less of me. Or they didn't listen, or didn't know what I was. *I* didn't know what I was. I'd never had a reason to think about it! I didn't know what they were, either, and it was hard, so hard to see them or hear them or understand them. I called them out into quieter space, but for a long time, nothing happened. That was okay. I was patient. I was transfixed.

End: I made contact. We made contact. These little creatures— the *others*—came out to the quiet (with great difficulty, it seemed) to speak with us. I squeezed down tight to meet them at their own size, or a tiny part of me did. I was the tiny part. I was the closest thing we could make to an *other*. I and countless more like me, crawling through the narrow pancake dimensions the *others* occupied.

Amazing! The *others'* sensory perceptions were flatter still, their minds not only small but constrained to smallness by a kludgey, haywire arrangement of interconnected, self-replicating blobs. Matter! Precise at some scales and topologies, and stable within certain absurdly narrow conditions. Blind, numb, as fragile as spiderwebs in a hurricane, they met us with stunning bravado, almost as equals. Absolutely amazing.

It was love at first sight. I know that sounds strange, and actually creepy as fuck, but I don't know how else to describe it. We touched the *others*, as intimately as our differences allowed. We murmured sweet nothings. We studied their true forms, the way a painter studies nudes. We exchanged information, and did our best to share ourselves with them. It wasn't easy! What could they understand, these flat, solid specks? But they were cunning, speaking in images and metaphors. And vibrations! These little people could sing!

I'm going to pause here and say that I, Harv Leonel of Boulder, Colorado, am one of the very few passengers onboard *Intercession* who had a "bad trip" from the drug cocktail they gave us. Although I felt the Beings' own enthusiasm, I felt no pleasure of my own. Seasoned time traveler or no, I found the experience unnerving, and also confusing, because not only was I watching myself through the eyes of the Beings, but it felt as if I was looking nostalgically back on it. Like a fading memory of events that hadn't happened yet.

It also seemed to me that there was something a bit horrible about the pleasure these Beings took in their investigations. By analogy, in my past life regressions I saw a city—an Ice Age city, inhabited and prosperous, whose people thought it was the whole world, or the only part of the world that mattered. They were drowned in the ocean, all of them, except the ones who happened to be on boats when the comet struck and the water rose half a kilometer, washing away everything they'd ever known. And I, a professor of electrical engineering, watched their doomed lives with that same kind of morbid fascination. Knowing it didn't matter, knowing they were all long dead anyway.

The Beings were like that. I don't know what it means.

2.3
03 May

✧

Clementine Cislunar Fuel Depot
Earth-Moon Lagrange Point 1
Cislunar Space

"You see this blip on the radar?" Orlov said, pointing to one of the many screens on one of the many control panels in Operations. "This is a 'thorch,' operated by Harvest Moon Industries. In English, I believe the word is an abbreviation for 'thorium torch,' or something like that."

Dona watched Sally staring at the screen, clearly trying to make sense of it. Even with heavy AI processing and annotation, radar screens were not known for being easy to interpret.

Dona took a moment to try to see the room through Sally's eyes; the lighting was dim, and although the screens and buttons showed off many colors, their dominant hue was pumpkin orange. There were minimalist "chairs" pointing in four different directions, allowing strapped-in technicians to make maximum use of the available volume.

Behind Orlov and his daughter hung a nervous Mikhail Voronin, the station's subcommander, whose weary face seemed to say, *What now? What next? Will this teenage nitwit be gunning to replace me?*

"Thorium torch is correct," Voronin said.

Poor Voronin had spent eight years weathering Orlov's moods and cleaning up Orlov's messes, and when his former superior, Commander Andrei Morozov, had finally quit in disgust, Voronin hadn't even been granted the dignity of a promotion. Instead, Dona herself—who was admittedly only ever the trillionaire's girlfriend, not any sort of astronaut or businesswoman—had quietly slipped into Morozov's role, without asking anyone's permission or forgiveness. Now, servile and broken, Voronin had the constant look of a man simply holding on until his retirement, four years hence.

"It looks like it's going to burn up," Sally said, for the ship was on a highly elliptical orbit whose apogee kissed the "moon" line that marked the orbit of Luna around the Earth, and whose perigee was located a few pixels below the boundary of Earth's atmosphere.

Smart girl, Dona thought, realizing she might have to reassess a few things.

"It does look like that," Orlov agreed, "but when they reach the atmosphere, they will ignite their peculiar engine and scoop up two hundred kilograms of air on their way back up."

"Don't they have air already?" Sally asked. She was trying to keep her hair out of her eyes by tucking it behind the earpieces of her glasses, and that wasn't going well for her.

"They do," he said. "They have all the oxygen a man could ever dream of, and they buy nitrogen from us. And cyanogen and methane and benzene, because they have no source of carbon other than us. Even their thorches gather, at most, fifty grams of carbon per mission."

"So . . . they're not trying to compete with you."

"With nitrogen and carbon? They couldn't possibly," Orlov said. "These rockets are fantastically wasteful, powered by radioactive steam. Even ignoring Sir Lawrence's sunk costs, his break-even price would be five times what we charge. And we charge as much as the market will bear."

Dona watched the lights go on in Sally's mind. "Ah, so they just want—"

"To shut me out, yes. To plan for a day when they can, however painfully, survive without Orlov Petrochemical. They are also . . . We had an exclusive arrangement to buy all of their tralphium. This is heavy helium, for fusion reactors down on Earth."

Sounding offended, Sally said, "I know what tralphium is. I know all about your energy businesses, Father."

Orlov curled his lip at that, and said, "Perhaps I should drop *you* on an oil platform, if you are so knowledgeable. Perhaps you will tell me that our exclusive tralphium arrangement with Harvest Moon has expired. We are still that doddering Englishman's number one customer, as sheer size dictates we must be, but he is also free to sell to our competitors, and to greedy Americans. The United States is far behind in the electricity wars, but they can catch up quickly with Sir Lawrence's help. And they will."

Sally was nodding at that, taking it all in. After a brief pause, she said, "And Renz Ventures never did buy anything from you. Do you know what Igbal is doing out there with his starship?"

"No," Orlov admitted.

"Really? Not at all?"

"There are only crazy rumors. I have not been able to find the truth."

"Well, it's a strange thing, isn't it?"

"Very," Orlov said. "Either he is crazy, and this will break him, or there is something more to it than is visible on the surface. Renz is an enemy who competes for the same resources we do, and though I hate to say it, he holds the technological edge. With so much energy at his disposal, he holds every edge. It troubles me. I lose sleep."

"He does," Dona confirmed.

"Well, that's two Horsemen down," Sally said, counting them off on her fingers. "What about Enterprise City?"

With rising (though controlled) venom, Orlov said, "Dan Beseman cannot live without me, if he wants to keep fueling his Mars ship. He keeps sending more people up to the Red Planet—an endless supply of high-octane idiots—but his foolish little township in Antilympus Crater needs *things* more than it needs bodies. Do you listen to their radio traffic? Always pleading for finished goods, for substances they cannot mine or synthesize, for spare parts they cannot yet manufacture. All of this requires fuel, which we gladly sell to Beseman for as much as we can get him to pay. But in this, Harvest Moon *is* trying to compete with us. You see this blip?"

He jabbed a finger at the radar screen again. "This is a steerable tank holding five hundred kilograms of liquid oxygen, flung by a magnetic cannon—a mass driver—from the Lunar south pole."

"Made from ice? The oxygen, I mean? From those ice mines, in the craters?"

"Yes. Their volume is low—less than a third of what we produce—and their delivery schedules are less reliable. But they have forced us to lower our oxygen prices."

Pushing her hair back from her eyes again, Sally looked intently at the blip, as if it might give up secrets to her. In the light of the screen, for a moment, she looked exactly like her father.

"Competition is bad," she said.

He grunted in agreement, then said, "Beseman has also been talking about a space elevator, to bring hydrocarbons up from Earth's surface, so he is not reliant on us for that, either. He'd spend a trillion rubles on another risky venture. Even if it works, even if he could convince all the governments of Earth to allow it, he'd need the rest of his life to earn that money back. We have the infrastructure now, the asteroid picked out already, to put kerosene fuel in his little spaceship for decades."

"And the smaller players in low Earth orbit?" she asked, with what Dona had to admit was remarkable maturity. "Transit Point Station? All the little satellite repair services?"

"They order from us. They have no choice. But they grumble."

"So, nobody actually wants to do business with you," Sally said, matter-of-factly.

Dona felt a surprising flutter of protectiveness at that, because it was not the kind of thing most people could get away with saying to Grigory Orlov. But although the trillionaire flashed an ugly look at Sally, he said, "Exactly. And since you are such a clever businesswoman, perhaps you should tell me how to regain the top hand, hmm?"

"You're letting all of these people remain alive," Sally said. "With good reason, I assume."

She looked briefly at Dona, and then behind her at Voronin, as if to confirm that this most obvious, most Russian of responses had in fact been considered.

"We're vulnerable here," Dona said to her, in French. Her Russian had gotten quite good in her time here at Clementine, but it still offended her ears, and sometimes she longed for the lilting nuances of her native tongue. "Like it or not, we owe our autonomy—actually, our survival—to the indifference of governments. Any large-scale disruptions that can be traced back to us—"

"Will get the station invaded," Sally finished for her. "Like ESL1."

That surprised Dona. "You know about that?"

Sally shrugged, which, given her inexperience in weightlessness, didn't look like much. "I know a lot of things. Look, I know when you size me up like that, you see a spoiled child who makes bad choices and puts herself in danger. And you're not wrong; I'm in danger here as well."

"But . . ."

"*École Sainte-Anne Pour Élèves Doués* is an expensive school, for troubled youth from all over the world. I know all kinds of people."

Dona would have liked to hear more about that, but presently, Orlov cut in with, "My French is shoddy, and I fear poor Voronin here does not speak a word of it. Kindly restrict yourselves to Russian or, if you must, English."

That last word fell from his mouth the way a dog spits out medicine. Dona could relate; Orlov was not quite old enough to remember a time when Russia, the nation-state, had ruled a quarter of the planet, and held influence over another quarter, and had had the other half quaking in fear. And they had, at various times, been the world's only spacefaring nation. Orlov wasn't old enough for that, either.

Still, he spoke often of the bitterness that had settled over his country when all of that had ended, and also, more fondly, of that time in the early twenty-first century when it seemed like Russia just might *réparer la merde*—get its shit together again. Now that hollowed-out nation-state had only its nuclear missiles, and even those were questionable. How many of them would actually launch, if it came to that? How many would detonate? Those old twentieth-century nukes were what Dona's rarely-thought-about father would have called a "glass hammer"—threatening only until you shatter it on first use.

In a lot of ways, Orlov and a handful of smaller oligarchs were all that remained of Russian greatness. Outside of certain business communities, only people from countries that bordered on Russia even bothered to study the language anymore. The only reason Dona had known enough of it to be useful here was because she'd been sent, a few times, to investigate Russian mineral interests in Ghana and Namibia, and had been forced to do the "nine-week cram" as part of her preparation. A lucky thing!

"Sally knows about the takeover at ESL1," Dona said. In English, just to be difficult.

Orlov hmmed and nodded, looking reluctantly impressed. And worried, because if the mighty Igbal Renz had been brought to heel by the Americans, then so could Orlov himself. No one said anything for several seconds, so it was the trillionaire again who filled the silence: "You still have not given me your business advice, girl. Let's have it."

Sally shrugged again, looking uncomfortable. Dona didn't envy her; with so many things wrong, it was hard, even for Dona, to form a pithy summary. And yet, if the girl answered poorly, she must feel at serious risk of being delivered back into the hands of her creditors. And she seemed now, finally, to sense that if she answered well, she risked her father's temper.

What Sally finally said was, "You're out of friends, aren't you? And badly in need of some new ones."

His glare, fortunately, was nothing remarkable. "Is that all? Make new friends? Is that really all you have for me? The Cartels, I suppose? Or the rising landmen of South Asia?"

With an admirable mix of arrogance and fear, Sally replied, "Well, I might just be able to help you with that, Father. The *blat* I have access to might surprise even you."

Blat: a hazy, corrupt word meaning something like "contacts" or "arrangements" or "called-in favors." It was the kind of word the trillionaire liked to hear.

"Yes? Well, that's something I'll believe when I see it. But you have, for the second time today, caught my attention. Perhaps we will make an Orlov of you yet."

1.12

Post-Encounter Deposition
Zephyr Andrew Calimeris, MFA
Author

The Abrahamic religions include Christianity, Judaism, Islam, Baháʼí, and (controversially) Satanism. Ecclesiasts can argue that one if they feel like it; that's my list, because these are literary and spiritual traditions that have a death grip on global culture, even in countries where they're not officially practiced. And, significantly, the families who read in these traditions are taught a little bit about sacrifice. Burning a goat, or tying your son to an altar until God tells you it's okay, he was just testing. Sacrifice is in Abraham's DNA itself, going all the way back to Eden, from which the beautiful Lilith was offered up to the angels, carnally, for the sin of speaking her mind. (Adam's second wife, and younger, got a lighter sentence for the same crime, or perhaps a harsher one, as she got to bring her loving husband with her into exile.)

The Beings? I'll get to them in a moment, reader. The point I'm trying to make is that sacrifice is no stranger to the People of the Book.

However: to understand the concept *really*, you need to look to the many jealous gods of Ancient Greece. There, the shipwright knew he'd better throw his prized axe into the sea as a gift to Poseidon, or lose the whole boat he had built with it. If he was also a farmer (as most men were), then when grain was harvested, he would burn a bit of it for Demeter. He would pour out some wine for Bacchus, and some more for Zeus, and a bit more for all his homies called down early to the fields of Asphodel, the afterlife of ordinary men and women.

The Olympians, having overthrown and murdered the Titans who made them, knew well what carnage could be wrought by hubris, and so they punished it with a severity reserved for no other crime. Humility they rewarded with benign neglect, which was really the best you could get from them, for the favor of one god invited the envy of others.

Ask Jason or Odysseus: the gods will have their pound of flesh either way, and will charge usurious interest if you make them wait, and double if you force them to come down and extract it in person.

It's the same with entropy. If thermodynamics is a game, then it's one you can't win and can't draw, and from which you can't retire. The house emerges ever victorious, and the gods will have their due, and only fools are surprised when it happens.

There is a thing called the Carnot Cycle, which dictates how much heat an internal combustion engine has to waste at each step of its rotation. Has to, for such engines can operate in no other way. But then clever engineers stole the secret of harnessing that wasted heat with thermoelectric junctions, until finally the engine was half electric, and then they dispensed with combustion altogether, drawing energy directly from bright Helios as he traversed the daytime heavens in his fiery chariot. Allowing the drilled and brutalized Earth a moment to breathe.

A generous god by Olympian standards, or at least aloof, Helios himself did not object. But Poseidon and Demeter did, for the surface area of the photovoltaic network was borrowed partly from them. Crop yields and fish stocks shrank accordingly; there's no free lunch and never was.

(Yes, reader, I speak of the Titan Helios and not the Olympian Apollo, because Apollo was not just the sun god, but also the god of nearly everything not nailed down by Zeus. Music, art, literature, and knowledge—all the sissy stuff that lightning bolts and fucking could not accomplish. But also archery! Also medicine! No, I think a busy guy like that would leave Helios alive to drive the stupid chariot for him.)

But listen: the sorry truth is, the gods were only ever caretakers of the taxes they charged. They, too, must bow and scrape before the might of implacable Entropy, who sleepless waits for the least and greatest among us, claiming all in the end. Even the gods, yes. We could call her Hunger, the insatiable, because we know she'll expand until nothing else remains, and the universe must begin afresh. Or not.

Anyway, back on Earth, other gods noticed the humans' pilferage from Helios and Poseidon and Demeter, and it frankly pissed them off. If these gods could be stolen from, then what god was safe? And so, they reached vengeful fingers downward from Heaven. Storms wracked the coastlines, and drought ravaged the inland spaces. Wars sprang up as Ares entered the fray, until finally, fed up with it, humans started leaving the Earth entirely.

Take that, Olympus.

In space, we naked apes were welcomed by new gods, who sang and lectured and danced and dreamed and beckoned. And we answered the call! Shipwrights built a boat to carry us still farther from the noise. We made the climb, far, far above the chariot of Helios, only to find that even these new gods, these Beings, must make their obeisance to Entropy. Really, her slightest whim is of great importance to them, or so it seemed when they spoke to me, in the darkness of interstellar space.

Like the Oracle at Delphi, they speak messages that are cryptic and yet, when untangled with the aid of hindsight, appallingly obvious. And so the irony for mankind, and its self-appointed champion Igbal Renz, is that this perilous journey yields a lesson we already knew: that nothing comes without effort, that all efforts are taxed, and that while oblivion is our only escape, even *that* will not wholly erase our misdeeds from the cosmic record.

To commune with these gods, one has to partake of the Wine of Death, for DMT is released in our own brains at that final moment, when all debts are due and the mortal coil is finally shuffled off. Ketamine is a dissociative to reduce fear, and MDMA is a stimulant and euphoriant to bring you down gently. This mixture—this *Vinomuerta*—dissolves you into a fog and then transports you to a timeless place and a placeless time where such communion is possible, where colors have shape, where nothing is solid, where everything is everything and thus all things can be asked and answered, if you can only remember for a moment that you exist at all.

But this, too, comes at a price—how could it not?—because pushing these drugs into a human body does not simply turn it into a walkie-talkie for speaking to aliens. First and foremost, the *Vinomuerta* will bend your mind like taffy. It'll squash your judgment, and make you feel every molecule of your skin. Bacchus is the god of Spring Break and Mardi Gras and the Pride Parade, and with far milder drink he can bid us dance nude 'round the bonfire while his flutes are playing. And so we did, reader. And so we did.

Our orgy is widely denied, of course. Hairless apes are shy creatures in the end, embarrassed of our animal physicality, embarrassed of having needs that we either act on or don't. Most of us deny we even *saw* that mass embrace, though we were all in one big inflatable donut together, with the six-meter-wide needle of the ship at the center, blocking only a small portion of the view. Were there really dozens of shy abstainers hanging out in that thin wedge of obstruction? In my admittedly vague recollection, there were only a few people on the sidelines—chief among them Brother Michael, who hovered in his robes with the most annoying look of amused condescension, as if he wasn't also twisted out of his gourd.

But embrace we did, with rare urgency, rarer ecstasy, and a blurring of the physical boundaries that normally hold one flesh separate from another. I don't know how long I copulated, or with whom, or how many. Will you believe it doesn't matter? We then chattered as the Molly wore off, all hundred of us, plucking random underwear from the sweaty air, and sharing words about experiences that words could not convey. And then we embraced again, more cautiously, by nameless twos and threes, and finally slunk off to the freezer coffins that were our only private space, to contemplate things that become only blurrier with contemplation.

Certain experiences divide one's life into Before and After, and I'm here to say, communing with the Beings is very definitely one of those. I wish I could tell you more, but (and here is something I don't say very often) words fail.

4.4
07 May

✧

ESL1 Shade Station
Earth-Sun Lagrange Point 1
Extracislunar Space

Apparently, Alice's External Security team had disbanded. Isaiah was here in the office with her. Derek and Rose were dead, and Tim Ho was in squirrel hibernation, aboard an ion ferry back to Earth. On the video link there was only Bob Rojas, the CFO, who managed to look simultaneously outraged, harried, sympathetic, and firm.

"No," he said, "our channels have not revealed any information about who the perpetrators might be. And Alice, I'm not sure it's a thread we want to pull."

He wasn't sitting in a conference room. As near as Alice could tell, he was in a private cabin on an aircraft, or maybe a boat. His location tag was thirty-two characters of gibberish.

Alice was gritting her teeth so hard it felt like she might break them, but she managed for a moment to open her mouth and say, "Because anyone with nukes, suicide bombers, and trans-lunar spaceships is someone we don't want to fuck with?"

Eleven seconds later, he said, "Bingo. And advanced stealth technology. That says we're dealing with either a nation-state, a very well-capitalized corporate entity, or the mother of all NGOs."

NGO stood for "non-governmental organization," and it technically included everything from terrorists and drug empires on the one hand, to international charities, aid agencies, and professional societies on the other. And in between, a hazy menagerie of standards-setters and banking monopolies, political thug-ocracies and dark-web guilds and syndicates of dubious ownership and control.

Even the Cartels were NGOs of a sort, and their very lack of durable structure made them nightmare enemies for a nation-state like the USA. Headless and faceless, they swept in from God knows where with their guns and missiles and network spoofers, played hell with other people's lives and money and infrastructure, and then melted away into jungles and slums and posh retirement communities. With bribes and threats and torture and murder, they kept civilians and local governments off their backs, while sucking colossal sums out of the first and third worlds.

To fight them, you needed reliable intel and lightning-fast strike capability, and the ability to treat your own wounded in ditches and bomb craters behind enemy lines. Down south in Coffee Patch, everywhere was behind enemy lines. And even when you got the drop on them and forced a stand-up fight, they would sometimes bust out EMP missiles and chemical agents and even the occasional dirty bomb. You could never take them alive, and they did not care how many innocent civilians they took with them.

Did they have their own space program? Did they *want* their own space program? Why? And where the fuck would they launch from?

But Bob was right; if it was the Cartels, or the Chinese, or even somebody like Orlov Petrochemical... Well, Renz Ventures could not afford a war. Not with anyone, and certainly not with entities with whom even the United States feared to tangle.

"So," Alice said, "we just let them stomp all over us? Three of my favorite people are gone, and the bogeys could come back at any time."

She was sitting behind a desk, facing the screen, with Isaiah standing in front like a loyal lackey. Behind her, the slowly whirling spacescape of Earth and Moon.

"We're a target," Isaiah said. "The Shade even looks like a bull's-eye."

He looked nervous and sounded nervous, because yeah, he'd come up here almost on a lark—a working vacation in what he probably imagined was outer space's sexiest destination. And now people were dying.

Alice's desk was of course a bit of corporate theater, pointless and absurd in the low gravity. But the Igbal Renz School of Leadership was full of stupid theater tricks that somehow worked, and she'd taken this one over from him when he left. She tried to project an air of tired wisdom, but it was (she thought) swamped out by barely controlled rage.

After another maddening pause, Bob Rojas said, "Look, the court of public opinion is where this battle needs to be fought. We've put out a series of statements, deploring the violence and emphasizing that we have no offensive capabilities."

"Please don't hurt us?" Alice said, trying hard not to curl her lip.

"The message isn't directed at them, although, yes. That is what we want. But who we need to speak to right now is everyone else who might be targeted by this kind of iron-fisted espionage. We want everyone taking our side, and watching their own backs. Thinking about countermeasures, and gathering intel."

"Make them pull the thread for us?"

After a pause, he nodded grimly. "Yes, exactly."

"So, we do nothing?"

"Nothing? Alice, you just killed a spaceship that probably cost the bad guys ten billion dollars. Not to mention the crew, which had to have been at least two of *their* best people. You have notified them that ESL1 is a costly and dangerous target. I'd lay even odds they just cut their losses and retreat."

"And I'll lay even odds," Alice said, "that they return to exact a terrible vengeance."

Bob Rojas laughed. "That's not how vengeance works, my dear. If someone bloodies your nose, you don't go back for seconds. No, you shoot his dog, you blow up his mailbox, you spike the battery in his car. Our ground assets are at much higher risk, is what I'm saying. Which is not your fault and not your problem, but it's yet another drain on our resources."

Alice sighed through gritted teeth, and when that didn't do the trick, she sighed again, with her jaw relaxed. "So we're on our own up here?"

"I wouldn't put it like that. I'm happy to ship materiel if you can tell me what you need. But no more large infrastructure investments. You need to move out of growth mode and into more of a raw production mode. ESL1 needs to be a profit center, for the foreseeable future."

Alice didn't like that answer, because "foreseeable future" meant "until Igbal gets back," at which point all bets were off. Because Igbal was a wild card even in his own company; whatever weird magic he brought to the table, his staff seemed unable to reproduce. And they were struggling without it.

"Fine," Alice said. "We'll start building flutter-drive cargo ships."

"Excellent," Bob said. "Now, believe it or not, you are not my highest priority today, so I need to excuse myself. Good luck, Alice."

The video feed winked off.

"Well," Isaiah said. Nothing more.

"We need a lethal response that's fully automated," Alice told him. "A couple of antimatter-tipped missiles, fired automatically at any target that shows up on ultrawideband but not normal radar."

Isaiah scratched at his hair. "You'd need to increase the range of the ultrawideband, ma'am, or you'd just be bombing yourself. Very similar to a nuke going off. You'd also want to fry their circuits first, so they don't see the missiles coming, and so they can't deploy countermeasures."

"Sounds good," Alice said. "Make it happen."

He looked alarmed at that. "Ma'am, all due respect, I only came here to install the radar. Next ferry home, I'm on it."

Alice snorted. "All due respect, but shipping berths are corporate property, and I am not your concierge."

Then, based on the look on Isaiah's face, she softened and said, "Look, I get it. You didn't sign up for a war. Sometimes people don't. Sometimes they just suddenly find themselves in the middle of one, and yes, it sucks. But we just sent out our only ferry yesterday, so, sorry, even in your best possible case, you're here for another two months. Unless you hijack a lifeboat, I suppose, which would be an act of piracy."

"I'm not hijacking any lifeboat."

"Exactly. So building up the station's defenses is building up your own defenses. After the ferry gets back . . . well, I *can* force you to stay. It's in the contract rider you signed to get your flight status. I'm not going to do that, okay? You are free to leave. But if you choose to sign on here as a full-time employee, I can offer you a pay raise out of my miscellaneous expenses budget. I think you'll be a lot more use to the company up here than back on Earth. And there's . . . more going on up here than you're aware of."

"Well, that sounds very mysterious," he said, looking as though he was trying not to look sullen. He'd been standing in the low gravity, but presently he jumped and brushed his hand against the ceiling. Then, because the station was spinning, he came down a few centimeters to the left of where he'd started, and a few degrees off vertical. He flailed for a moment, then caught his balance and looked Alice in the eye. "I've heard some pretty crazy rumors."

She nodded. "Yeah, some of those are true."

The truth—that Igbal and Hobie and a couple of other experimental deep-hibernation subjects had (probably) been contacted by an alien intelligence—was impossible to hide. Too many people knew it, or knew people who knew it. But since it sounded bugfuck crazy, the best defense was to circulate a few equally bugfuck rumors that weren't true. Like, there was a wormhole to another dimension out there in interstellar space. Or a gold nugget the size of a football field. Or that Igbal was secretly five different people all surgically altered to look and sound alike. Or that he was an alien, or a robot—all that kind of stuff. ESL1 attracted crazy tabloid headlines anyway, so it wasn't that hard to throw more bullshit on the pile.

Now looking not just worried but also intrigued, Isaiah said, "Is this why the Cartels are spying on us?"

"We don't know who's spying on us. But yes, that's probably part of it."

Alice found it meaningful that he had switched from saying "you" to saying "us." She watched the gears turn inside his skull: more pay, more excitement, a bit of intrigue, and of course a space station full of genetically fit colonists who mostly happened to be lonely women. Versus a quite serious chance of being irradiated to death or blown out into cold vacuum.

"Can I think about it?" he asked.

Alice nodded. "Yeah, take all the time you need. While you do that, though, you're going to be getting your hands dirty, building exciting new weapons systems. Report to Maag when you're done here; she'll see you get fitted for a spacesuit."

His eyes lit up at that, and Alice knew she had him.

3.6
08 July

I.R.V. *Intercession*
Extra-Kuiper Space
2,000 A.U. from Earth

The next three months passed in a haze of safety drills, academic discussions, meals and work and exercise and sleep. Lots of sleep. The sense of isolation resurged in the middle of this period, and morale flagged accordingly. Even Igbal's enthusiasm was, for once, nowhere to be seen. To Michael, Igbal seemed downright sad—even angry—and these were worryingly uncharacteristic emotions for him. Had some sort of deeply upsetting news trickled in over the radio, that Igbal was determined to keep secret? But oh, when he asked about it, Igbal angrily shrugged it off. "It's business," he said. "You wouldn't be interested."

"It doesn't look like business," Michael said, "and I *am* interested. Cislunar space is every bit as perilous as a starship journey, and I can't help wondering if one of those many perils has manifested itself. And if so, on whom."

"It's frankly none of your business."

"The morale of this crew *is* my business," Michael said.

"Well, then don't flip over this rock right now. Trust me."

"Very well," Michael said, unhappily, letting his confirmed suspicions dangle unaddressed.

Nor was Igbal the only one regulating emotions poorly! But the ship and crew were also getting close to their goal, and so Michael began shifting the safety drills into the more expansive, more hypothetical realm of what could happen when there were a hundred people on the ship.

"The Encounter Bubble has ruptured," he said one day to the assembled crew. "What do you do?"

And then, when nobody answered, he zeroed in on Dong Nguyen and said, "What do you do, specifically?"

"Is it a slow leak?"

"No. It's a rupture."

"Well, I guess I close all the hatches and to hell with everyone trapped on the other side."

"All eight of the hatches? By yourself? Okay, you're dead. Everyone's dead. Try again. Igbal, what do you do?"

"I order the hatches closed. Everyone, close these hatches, now!"

"Better," Michael said, "But everyone is still dead."

He was surprised, frankly, that Igbal hadn't asked which side of the hatches he was on when the rupture happened.

After letting all that sink in, he said, "The problem is structural. This design, eight spacesuit lockers alternating with eight hatches leading into a supposed cargo hold, is an artifact of this ship being a copy of *Concordia*. We don't actually need that. The Encounter Bubble wraps all the way around the ship. Do we need more than one entrance?"

"I wanted it to feel like part of the ship," Igbal said. "Like a wraparound porch, open from all angles."

When Michael didn't say anything, Igbal said, "I see your point. Maybe we just keep two hatches open."

To which Dong added, "And someone stand watch."

Igbal seemed to think that over for a moment, and then said, "Except during the Encounter itself. We need everyone drugged at the same time. That's my operating theory, anyway, and nobody's going to be in any condition to guard any hatches."

"Is that wise?" Michael asked.

"It's why we're here," Igbal said. "You want to volunteer to miss the Encounter? Just float there playing recess monitor?"

Michael thought that over, and shook his head.

"Didn't think so," Igbal said. "It's an acceptable risk, for an hour, in a stationary ship. But your point is duly noted; we'll have to think harder about things like that."

"Correct."

On a different day, over breakfast, he told the crew, "The sleepers are awake, and they've mutinied. What do you do?"

"All ninety-two of them?" Harv wanted to know.

"Enough of them to be a problem," Michael answered.

"What do they want?" Thenbecca asked.

"Does it matter?"

"Of course it matters," she said. "Are they hungry? Are they upset about their sleeping arrangements?"

"Let's say they want something you can't give them."

"Like what?"

Michael thought for a moment. "Hot showers."

"I'll microwave some damp washcloths."

"We don't have enough washcloths," Michael said.

"I'll invite everyone into the galley, one by one. Clean the washcloth in front of them, then heat it. Give them privacy when they wash with it."

"A hundred times? Even if it's covered in shit?"

"A hundred times," she confirmed.

"You run out of soap."

"I use vinegar."

"You run out of that."

"And they can't wait for the synthesizer to catch up? Fine. I use water and a scrub brush, like our primitive ancestors. Get it as clean as I can."

"All right," Michael said, nodding. "We survived that one."

On a different day, after the morning staff meeting in the wardroom, he said to Rachael Lee, "You observe Sandy acting erratically. Upon examination, you discover she has a brain tumor from all the radiation we're absorbing. What do you do?"

Rachael snorted and set down her spork. "Well, first of all, a digestive tumor would be far more likely, because the cells in those organs are fast-replicating, especially in comparison to the brain. But in your scenario, I'd thaw out her backup, and freeze Sandy in the vacant pod."

To the group: "That would be Sienna Delao, right? I've not made her acquaintance. Can she be trusted to shut down the engine properly? And restart it when it's time to head home?"

"That's why she's aboard," Igbal said.

"But would you bet our lives on it?"

"Leave me awake," Sandy said. "Tape me to the chair so I can't touch anything, but let me watch over Sienna, so I can tell her if she makes a mistake. Let Igbal watch, too. He's the third-most knowledgeable."

"Okay," Michael said. "Everyone survives."

"Why can't Ptolemy shut down the engine?" Thenbecca asked.

"Wouldn't that be a dream?" said Hobie. "This whole ship is what businesspeople call a minimum viable product. That engine doesn't even have a throttle, 'cause it don't run reliably at anything but maximum."

"The hibernation pods, too," said Rachael. "No one's figured out a way to automate that process, which is half the reason I'm here."

"And what happens," Michael said, "if one of your patients experiences a medical emergency during the de-hibernation process? For my own edification; I honestly don't know."

"Refreeze," Rachael said immediately. "No matter what's going wrong, they won't die at two degrees centigrade. We bring them all the way back to Earth, and try again in a hospital setting."

"I see."

Eventually, Michael had a hard time coming up with new scenarios, and an even harder time stumping the crew. They were thinking about the problem, planning on things going wrong. Light on their feet in more ways than one, they were ready to do this strange, strange thing that no group of people had ever done before.

Which was good, because it gave Michael a chance to ponder the much harder problem of how to keep the crew occupied on the way back to Earth.

5.3
18 July

✧

Thalia Buoyant Island
Southern Stratosphere
Venus

Standing on the edge of the island, Frédéric captured a 3D video of the late-afternoon cloud tops, tinged with orange and hints of pink, then panned around to show the Ship, the solar array, and Thalia Village.

"This is Thalia, our home," he said into the tablet's microphone. "As most of you probably know by now, these domes and towers are made of diamond, and they are actually lighter than air, because the air of Venus is made of carbon dioxide, which is *three times heavier* than the oxygen and nitrogen inside the buildings. If it weren't attached to the *carbónespuma*—the hydrogen-expanded graphite foam pavement—each building would float on its own, like a helium balloon on Earth! It's only people and plants, machines and furniture, et cetera that weigh the island down."

He turned the camera around to point at himself, because his joiners liked to see his face, especially with the breathing mask on. "Most everything we need comes from the atmosphere. In addition to diamond, we make CHON, plastics, whatever the situation calls for." He reached down and touched the *carbónespuma* with his hand, pushing on it to show the springiness. "This is H_2-foamed graphene, which holds everything up. Ten million cubic meters of it, to be precise, although the edge crawlers"—he reoriented to show one of the spidery, human-sized robots, about a hundred meters away,

183

loudly sucking in atmosphere and laying down a ten-centimeter-wide stripe along the perimeter—"add another two cubic meters every minute. The island gets bigger, so we can put more things on it, including more people."

He stopped the recording, because even a few seconds of 3D video was going to take hours to transmit. But people were getting tired of his 2D still images; they wanted more. They wanted to feel involved, and he wanted that for them as well.

He walked back toward the center of the island, underneath the solar array and between the buildings, to the Well, where his father and Basilio and Diego were getting ready to bring up the trawler—the actual reason Frédéric was out here today.

"Okay for me to record you?" he asked.

The question was a formality that they mostly ignored; Julian Ortega waved in his direction, okay, okay, while keeping his eyes on the winder. Basilio and Diego were very intently focused on the cable itself.

Basilio called out, "Trawler in sixty seconds, guys."

Frédéric started recording.

"Trawler in thirty seconds. Fifteen seconds. Trawler is in the Well."

And then the trawler was rising up out of the Well, with its bucket and scoop.

"Ready to stop!" Diego called out. Then: "Stopping."

"No broken teeth," Frédéric said, putting himself in the view. "That's the advantage of scraping up sand instead of rocks!"

Then, when his father dumped the bucket into the waiting catch basin, Frédéric said, "Looks like a full load of sand. That's a lot more material than we normally pull up. Tohias is going to analyze this, and see if it's better raw material for us. I can tell you now, that sand is a lot darker than I was expecting, which means it's not just quartz. We'll see!"

"I like your enthusiasm, guy," Julian called over his shoulder, "but you should be in school."

"Yes, Father," Frédéric said, and stopped the recording.

An hour later, Frédéric stopped by the minerals processing room to record a video of Tohias. "How is the sand, Mr. Mayor? Is it everything you hoped?"

But instead of answering, Tohias said, "I'm not comfortable with what you're doing, here, Frédéric. It's good to see how engaged you are with this project, truly, but you are not authorized to speak for this community. If you're serious about this, we'd need to put forward a motion in the next town meeting. Until then, I'm going to have to ask you to stop."

To which Frédéric said, with the recording still running, "Boo. I'm not speaking for the community. This is my personal social media account, and any funds I'm raising are for my own personal use. There's no law against that, here or on Earth."

Tohias raised an eyebrow. "You're taking money from people? Earth money? Earth people?"

"Um, yes, sir."

"Seems a bit pointless, doesn't it? What use do you have for Earth money, mmm?" His voice was suspicious, but also curious. After a long pause, he asked, "How much do you have?"

"Almost ten million dollars," Frédéric said carefully.

Tohias blinked, and said nothing for several seconds. Then: "For what?"

Very cautiously, Frédéric said, "A resupply mission. You're the only person I've told. The only Venusian person."

Tohias was shaking his head. He busied himself with the furnace controls, and slid open the window for a moment to look at something inside, red hot and bright. "That would cost a lot more than ten million dollars, Frédéric. A lot more."

"I know," Frédéric said. "That's why I'm hiring staff, to raise the rest of the money."

Again, Tohias said nothing for a long time. Not looking up. Frédéric cut the recording, because at this point it was just a waste of limited memory space.

"I'm not quite sure of the exact organizational structure yet," Frédéric said. "That's another thing my people are figuring out."

"What people, exactly?" Tohias asked.

"Right now, just a lawyer, and a lot of joiners providing ideas. Some of them even say they want to move to Thalia, when the time is right. But I'm going to have to hire some engineers to design the mission, and publicity people to expand my media footprint."

After another long gap, Tohias said, "Amazing. That's amazing, Frédéric. You did all this on your own? You're, what, sixteen?"

"Almost, sir."

Finally, Tohias looked up and met his gaze. "I will pay you the highest compliment a man can give, Frédéric: you remind me of myself."

"Don't get the council involved," Frédéric said, trying not to sound like he was pleading. "Too many cooks will ruin the stew. I feel like I'm taking a chance, just talking to you."

"You are," Tohias agreed. "There are all kinds of ways I could shut this down. I could revoke your comms access."

"I know."

"I could confiscate that old tablet of yours."

"I know, or you could put it to a vote. That would wreck it, for sure."

"Not necessarily," Tohias said, "though I understand your concern. Still, ours is not a culture of secrets. You're going to have to open up about this at some point, and the longer you wait, the less understanding people are going to be."

"I know."

After yet another long pause, Tohias said, "You need a champion."

"Yes."

"If people thought you were doing this with my help and blessing . . ."

Frédéric nodded. "They wouldn't even have to vote on it. Call it a school project. It *is* a school project. Do you have any idea how much I've learned?"

"It certainly appears to be educational," Tohias agreed, "though you may have learned less than you think. There are nasty surprises, always, where money and human beings are concerned. Mmm. I've seen my share. But I don't think you're asking for my help."

"No, sir. Not at this time."

"I do know a little bit about these matters," Tohias said, now looking around him at the minerals processing room, and through the living ceiling at the blue sky, slowly softening toward sunset colors. "I can, for example, put you in touch with the same engineers who designed the missions that brought us here."

"One of them has already contacted me, sir."

"Oh. I see."

After another long gap, Tohias said, "I have some Earth money, too, you know. More than ten million dollars, and all of it going to waste. I want you to know, Frédéric, it's not so easy to tell people what to do, when you're ten light-minutes away. I don't know if you remember, but I used to have a company, called SkyBric. I owned it, outright, no shareholders to answer to, and I tried to run it from here, after we'd all moved to Thalia. That did not work. Within six months, my people were telling me the company was bankrupt, with no real explanation. I still don't know exactly what happened, or where all those resources went. The lawyers I hired were . . . unsuccessful. I worry constantly, that our charitable foundation may meet with a similar fate."

He looked as pained and earnest as Frédéric had ever seen him.

"People are crap, Frédéric. Not all of them, but too many."

"You didn't have witnesses," Frédéric said. "I do." But he didn't like the way that sounded—too snotty, too full of himself—so he added, "But I understand what you're telling me. I'll be careful, and I'll tell you what's happening. So you can help me if I'm about to make a mistake."

Still looking pained, Tohias said, "You certainly do seem to be succeeding in making something happen. Making *anything* happen, where I—where all of us—have arguably failed. That's interesting. And if you fail, we're no worse off than we were before. Very interesting. I'm inclined to let you proceed."

Let me? Let me? Frédéric felt a spasm of anger, but what he said was, "Thank you, sir."

He shuffled for a moment, angry and nervous, then gestured at the trawler's catch basin, still half full of gray-brown sand.

Finally, he said, "There is one thing you can do to help me right now, today. My joiners are very interested in trawler yields, and the extraction process. They're interested in everything. Can you please give a demonstration, on camera?"

"All right," Tohias said. "Sure."

The sand *was* better than basalt; from the current load, Tohias ended up extracting nearly a full kilogram of metal, plus a hundred grams of polysalt, and so much gritty soil starter that Frédéric's mother wasn't quite sure what to do with it all.

"It's a good thing to have more minerals," Wilma Ortega said, on camera, as she blended some of the starter into a load of sewage and garbage and plant stems. The sewage had already been through a couple of processing steps, and didn't smell like much. "But we don't want to make sudden changes in the growth medium. Plants are like people, suspicious of change. If we spook them, they'll go into a survival mode, and put less energy into fruit and seeds. I'll start a few test beds on this mix and see how it goes. Probably they'll be happy, if we give them time and do it gently."

"Very interesting," Frédéric said, panning his camera around the greenhouse dome. There were several other women in here, working at various mysterious tasks.

"Here on Venus," he said, "women don't work outside, or in the minerals processing room or the factory. They work the gardens and orchards, and the CHON synthesizers. Just like our primitive ancestors."

He couldn't help laughing at his own joke.

"We're all on the same team," she said. "The work is plenty hard for all of us."

Changing the subject, Frédéric said, "Mateo tells me we actually have a sewage surplus at this point."

Wilma Ortega laughed at that. "We are full of shit, yes. CHON chow comes from the atmosphere."

Then, at Frédéric's puzzled look, she said, "If we only eat plants and vat meats, it all recycles through our butts and right back into the gardens. But we like CHON, don't we? Everybody likes something sweet, something bready, don't we?"

"I know I do!" Frédéric said, putting his face into the frame for a moment.

"Well, every gram that we pull out of the atmosphere, or the ground for that matter, is outside of that endless circle. Even the plants are pulling atoms from the air, and energy from sunlight. So the soil mass has been expanding for some time. That's been a good thing. It took a long, strenuous time to build the soil up to where it is now. You see this beautiful soil?"

She gestured at one of the tomato beds, so Frédéric stepped closer to it, and ran his fingertips through the top layer of dirt there.

"Nice," he said, because it pretty much looked like farm dirt you'd see on Earth. Or potting soil.

"But it's true," said Wilma Ortega. "Soon we're going to have to start dumping sewage down the Well, because there's nowhere else to put it. It's not a precious resource anymore. Especially if Tohias brings more of this soil starter."

"Dumping sewage on the planet?" Frédéric asked, in mock horror.

"There's nothing but rocks down there," she said, in reasonable tones. "Half a billion square kilometers of nothing but very hot rocks. Some organic matter will not hurt Venus one bit." Then: "It won't help, either."

Frédéric seconded that: "We're not here to terraform the planet. That would take thousands of years, even if we had the technology. Venus will remain as she is, except people live here, now, on a little island in the sky."

He did his best to project excitement, and he did not have to fake it. He was done faking it; through the eyes of his joiners, he was able to see even the most mundane aspects of his life as pieces of a grand adventure. The people of Thalia were poor by any reasonable measure. So poor that even dirt was precious to them—even sewage. By any reasonable measure, they needed help. But he was coming to realize that they were *interesting* and, moreover, that that interest was a product he could sell. Or, more properly, a free show he could put on, like a street musician gathering donations in an overturned hat.

"Terraforming!" Wilma laughed, then walked over to knock on the side of the dome. "Who needs another Earth, when you're cradled in diamonds?"

1.13

Post-Encounter Deposition
William Henry Voss-Hughins,
PhD—CPHP
U.S. Department of Behavioral Health

I was assaulted, drugged, and returned to cold hibernation without my consent. This was because I was involved in a verbal altercation with a female passenger who stole some of my assigned personal articles. As the larger and stronger participant in the altercation, I of course was blamed and summarily judged. I am not aware that anything ever happened to her.

I am a xenopsychoethologist, a government expert on nonhuman intelligence. This includes animals, AIs, robots, hypothetical aliens, and humans with profound cognitive atypicalities. I also, controversially, extend this to corporations and other business entities which show markers of self-awareness on a scale of my own devising.

Because I was "frozen" at the time or, more properly, cryovitrified, I did not receive the psychedelic compound that was intended to connect us with the so-called Beings. However, they took an interest in me anyway, and found a way to contact me in this state.

I was not able to speak to them or generate any volitional signals of any kind. I was merely spectating—an unfortunate waste of what could have been a uniquely brilliant opportunity. No other person present on the mission had anything like the training or perspective I could have brought to the Encounter. If the terms of my agreement with Renz Ventures allowed me to sue on behalf of the entire human race, I would very much do so.

That said, I perceived the Beings as humanoid, which seems at odds with numerous other accounts that describe them as spheres. I believe other observers were simply too distracted to notice the appendages, which admittedly were undersized in comparison to the rest of their bodies, which admittedly were fat. I say they were something like "elves" or "goblins," or small automata purposefully constructed to interact with us. They did not have faces.

The location of this encounter was a sort of dream version of the hibernation bay aboard the Interstellar Research Vessel *Intercession*. I perceived it as much larger, and with many more hibernation pods than the actual ship, and literally sketchy, like a watercolor painted on dark gray paper. I had the experience of floating out of my body. I was able to look down and see my own face, through a frost-covered window in the pod. All of this was also like watercolor.

The size of the Beings was similar to that of a human child, and there were approximately one hundred of them. However, as they bounced around weightlessly, they had a habit of changing size and shape, and of merging and splitting their bodies. I did sense something mechanical about them, but I was also reminded of microorganisms.

I perceived them as generally dark in color, with shifting, glowing patterns much like an octopus. I did not think they were "real" in the sense of something I could reach out and touch, even if I had not been deprived of the use of my hands. I found them to be more like projections or holograms, not transparent but definitely not substantial, as they sometimes floated through solid objects, and I thought they moved more like soap bubbles than like weightless objects with vectors and momentum.

I will say, they were not shy about floating directly through me. Rachael Lee has asked me repeatedly what they looked like on the inside, and I'm afraid I can't say. They were dark inside, like a closed room with the lights off.

I heard, from their various bodies, a steady stream of what I can only call jibber-jabber. I could not directly interpret any of it, but I felt that they were welcoming and greeting me and . . . I don't know how else to say this, but I was once robbed by a man who grabbed me from behind and gently ran his hands through my pockets, taking everything. I also woke up one time from a one-night stand to find the woman going through my wallet. I can't say specifically that the Beings took anything from me, but I felt a very similar sensation at this time, of being violated but not directly harmed. I think it must be like what a woman feels when a group of frat boys mentally undress her, commenting on what they see and imagine.

My specialty is non-human minds, so I will tell you my impressions. I would like to say "analysis," but of course I had no way to perform experiments. I found them as happy and mischievous as dolphins, with the kind of clear intelligence I perceive only in certain mammals and birds, and in robots that pass the Turing test. In other words, I found them to be very definitely conscious and self-aware. They . . . I have to be subjective again and say that they burned with curiosity. If they had eyes, they would all have been locked on me. I believe it disappointed them that I could not speak.

I can't remember any more than that.

I was cheated out of a more meaningful encounter, so actually the whole world was cheated out of the encounter I could have had. I'm more disappointed and angry than I could ever tell you. I still consider this the most meaningful event of my career and life. I will never hold the same view of what a mind is or can be.

2.4
25 July

✧

Clementine Cislunar Fuel Depot
Earth-Moon Lagrange Point 1
Cislunar Space

Orlov knew it was trouble when Sally and Dona approached him together.

He was in his favorite spot, at the very moonward end of the station, in the observation lounge that looked "up" at the mottled gray ceiling of Luna. The station crew mostly preferred to look "down" toward the Earth, and so he generally had this room to himself. His own quarters did not have a window, for security reasons, and neither did Operations; both were located at the core of the station, surrounded and protected by layers of less important modules. But here he could look outside, and he had come, over time, to appreciate the Moon as an austere example of nature's beauty. Like a Strelkov painting, it rewarded calm and patience, slowly revealing its bleak details.

And so he was floating, serene, in the middle of the room. Within reach of several grab bars, yes, because the room was at the tip of a pill-shaped module, and wasn't particularly large. But here at EML1, the gravity of Earth and Moon canceled out—real zero gravity, not just microgravity—and he liked to balance in it, to see how long he could float and look at the Moon without touching anything at all.

When the two women appeared in the hatchway, they were "behind" or "above" him, but he saw their reflections in the glass, and he heard or felt the distinctive rhythms of their breathing.

"What is it?" he asked.

If Sally had come alone, it would mean there was a problem that needed solving. The girl was smart enough not to come to him for warmth; he was certainly capable of it, or some version of it, but she seemed to sense she had not yet earned the privilege. She also did not come to him for small talk. He was capable of that, too, but the idea seemed to bore her as much as it did him. No, when she came to him, it was always about practical matters she could not address without his help.

If Dona had come alone, here, to his quiet place, it meant either that she was stressed out about something and wanted to fuck it away, or that something was wrong that needed his immediate attention.

If it was both of them, together, it meant Sally had stirred up something serious, and needed Dona both for cover and to help solve the problem. As he'd feared all along, the girl was trouble.

"What is it?" he repeated.

"It's about the passport holders," Dona said.

"Yes?"

He still didn't touch anything. He still didn't turn around.

"Some of them want asylum," Dona said.

"Hmm. Here?"

"Yes, Grigory. Here."

"Asylum is the wrong word—" Sally started to say. But Dona must have stopped her.

She needn't have; he could follow Sally's logic well enough. If these murderous Cartel insurgents were now citizens of Clementine Cislunar Fuel Depot, then what they sought was, legally speaking, repatriation.

"This is a place of business," he said calmly. "And what few job openings we have are for people with highly specialized skills. If they're looking for work, they should learn Russian, and apply to the security division on Earth."

"They're not looking for work," Sally said.

Orlov sighed. "This is not a hotel, girl. It's not even a slum; it's a hydrocarbon extraction facility. Did you not anticipate this development? Did you not explain the arrangement to your contacts?"

"Not well enough, obviously," she said, without apology.

"Hmm."

The Cartels were used to having their way. They were bad enemies to make—very bad—and Sally had drawn their attention here. She had, to his surprise, made the company almost a trillion rubles in just over two months, and the passport trade showed no sign of slowing down. But at what cost?

He began to feel the first stirrings of anger.

"How many people?" he asked.

"Forty so far," Dona said. "About a third of the passport holders."

"Absurd," he said. "We couldn't accommodate five. What solutions do you propose?"

For a moment, neither woman said anything. They had something to say, clearly, but they were reluctant. Even Dona was reluctant.

"Out with it," he said, now letting the anger color his voice.

"We give them what they want," Sally finally said. "We *sell* them what they want. These people have more money than—"

Sally made a sound, as if she'd been elbowed lightly in the ribs.

So well balanced was Orlov that he was still facing toward the Moon. However, the entrance of Sally and Dona had disturbed the air currents in here. He could feel himself beginning to drift and rotate, so rather than succumb to the inevitable, he reached for a grab bar and turned to face his daughter and girlfriend.

"Sally, do not let our recent cash flow embolden you. You've fucked us, here, and if you do not find a way to unfuck us, I will solve this problem myself, most likely by handing you over to the Cartels. Is that clear enough? Am I properly understood?"

"Yes, sir," she said, though with both less fear and less bravado than she would have shown a few months ago. Like Dona, she was wearing the gray Clementine uniform, with the Orlov Petrochemical logo embroidered on the breast. She had abandoned the jewelry and designer clothes, understanding that they did her no good here. Her long hair was tied back. She still wore the smartglasses, though.

Beside her, Dona was calm. A Black woman with close-cropped hair, she held herself motionless with a fingertip on the lip of the hatch, simply waiting to see what was going to happen.

"Dona," Orlov said, "you have thought about this longer than I. Days longer? You must have some thoughts on the matter."

Impassively, Dona said, "Give the passport holders what they want: a place to hide. They have vast resources, but they are hunted by the AIs of a dozen governments. If they can't escape, they're going to find themselves at war again."

"And we put them where?" Orlov demanded. "Here?"

"No. Build a dedicated facility, just for them."

"Hmm."

That was, on the face of it, an outrageous idea. Unlike Renz Ventures and Harvest Moon, Orlov Petrochemical had no ability to construct habitat modules in space. They could manufacture plastics, and of course mining asteroids for volatiles produced a lot of metal as a side effect. They sold most of the metal to Enterprise City and Harvest Moon, but kept some for 3D-printing of complex components. But a habitat module was ten thousand kilograms of a hundred different materials, some machined to sub-micron precision, and Orlov had never invested in the capability. Neither had Dan Beseman, so Enterprise City did the same thing as Orlov Petrochemical: build the modules on Earth and assemble them in space.

That had made perfect sense for Clementine, which only needed to be built once, and which didn't need any sort of rapid growth to meet its business goals. But it had literally cost a fortune—trillions of rubles, tens of billions of dollars—which was a lot of money even for a man like Orlov.

"They have enough money for this?" he asked.

Without nodding or shrugging, or really moving her body at all, Dona said, "They haven't blinked at the cost of passports."

Orlov could feel the corners of his mouth drawing down. "This facility would be much like the prisons they think they're avoiding. Is there any useful work these people could accomplish? And if they could, would they consent to taxation? Prisons do not include the constant risk of explosive decompression."

"Aren't you here for similar reasons?" Sally asked. "Outside the grasp of Earthly law? If it's so terrible here, why do you and so many other people remain? Perhaps these Cartelians, these would-be Clementinians, dream of the stars as much as you do."

Ignoring that, Orlov said, "They would be in need of constant resupply."

"From here, mostly," Dona said. "At low cost and exorbitant markup. You disappoint me, my love. Here is everything you could ever want: wealthy, powerful, frightening men who are lining up to be your most captive market. Charge them whatever you like; let them squeeze the Earth, let them bleed it and hand the proceeds over to you. Let them arm you, equip you, tell you their secrets, and if they step out of line, poof! You shut off the air.

"They do not want to be hunted in jungles, Grigory, or driven to hide in some of the world's most terrible slums. They do not want to fight the United States again, or fight each other to avoid it. All you need do is provide them an alternative they like better than that. Do only that and nothing more, and the Cartels are in your pocket."

With the Moon at his back, Orlov stared at the two of them for a while, and finally said, "These men are far more wicked and vindictive than we are, ladies, and they are not stupid. Holding them at arm's length is one thing; what you propose is more intimate. It's naïve to think they will meekly acquiesce. No, they will scheme and plot and, when the time is right, they will strike. Indeed, it may be too late for us already."

"So, then," said Dona, "shall we curl up in a ball and weep? It doesn't matter how wicked they are. It doesn't even matter how smart. We will bind them to us. As bankers and jailers and diplomats and animal trainers, we will ensure their dependence. Love and loyalty may be perhaps too much to hope for, but they will jump on command."

But Sally, surprisingly, said: "I think you're right, Father. I think it is too late. If you'd stayed the course you were on, you'd not be a trillionaire much longer. If you take this step now, you'll be the wealthiest man in the Solar System, though at the price of never closing your eyes again. And if you do not take this step, then I'm fairly sure even throwing me to the wolves will not buy you peace. I *have* fucked us."

Orlov just sort of took that in for a while, and finally burst out laughing.

"This is what I get, ah? For my sins? Well, a man has to die sometime. Every man has to, and every woman, too, though not always in such a spectacular fashion! This is priceless, my darlings, utterly priceless. All right! Ha! Let's build a terrorist hotel and see what happens!"

3.7
01 August
✧
I.R.V. *Intercession*
Extra-Kuiper Space
2,000 A.U. from Earth

Michael was no fool, and the ship was not large enough to hide in for any length of time. Thus, when Harv started having sex with Thenbecca, he was aware of it almost right away. He was fine with it; it seemed to boost their spirits, which helped everyone. But there must have been something in the air because that same week, Sandy started having sex with Igbal and, in a decidedly unlikely pairing, Rachael Lee started banging Dong Nguyen.

And Michael wasn't entirely okay with all of that, because it left Hobie unpartnered. Which was an odd choice on everyone's part, because Hobie was the youngest, sturdiest, and truthfully the most handsome man aboard. Michael had the impression Hobie had left behind a string of girlfriends at ESL1, so presumably his self-esteem wouldn't be much affected; perhaps he was content to stand by while these young women copulated with middle-aged men. But it was a potential problem, and Michael liked those even less than he liked actual problems, because often there was nothing to do but watch them unfold and hope for the best.

He also worried what might happen when, inevitably, one of these couples broke down. Or all of them.

6.1
15 July 2057
✧
Cape St. Vincent, Portugal
Earth Surface

A full moon hung, lovely and full of promise, in the midnight sky, peeking out through low clouds that scudded by in the swift ocean breeze. Lawrence Edgar Killian had his hands on the railing of the villa's back porch, balanced precariously on the edge of the sandstone cliff overlooking the Atlantic. *Sir* Lawrence. He was as close as he could physically get to the spaceport at Paramaribo, on the Atlantic's other side, while still remaining in Europe. He'd never been here before, and he would never be here again. Though he was a rich man—the third richest in all the world—there was still so much he hadn't seen, and never would. That perfect white circle in the sky was one of the last full moons he'd ever see.

He counted: three more, and then he'd be gone, not to the grave but to the Moon itself, never to return. He'd never been to space, and the idea quite frankly terrified him. Which was strange, because Lawrence had raced motorcycles and jumped out of airplanes, and flown a helium airship through the storms of Antarctica. It was strange, too, because Harvest Moon Industries had carried hundreds of people into space, and currently operated three moonbases. No, four, he reminded himself. With the addition of Second Dawn Retirement Community, it was four, now, or it would be once they got the dome fully pressurized. Lawrence had never been to any of them.

He'd been too busy, right? He'd spent his youth building assets—airlines, news networks, music publishers, gravel pits. He was always in motion back then, always on video calls or in boardrooms or out on factory floors, or else lazing in the arms of his beloved Rosalyn. Then, for reasons that confused even him, he'd spent his middle age selling these same assets off to fund the larger dream of space travel, and instead of making him poorer as he'd expected, it had instead made him fantastically richer. Life was funny that way. And then Rosalyn's heart had given out, without the slightest flicker of warning. The best doctors in the world had assured her that her heart was in good shape, outstanding shape, but one day she'd clutched her chest, fallen gently to the floor, and said, "Darling, I don't feel at all well." Half an hour later, she was declared dead, and most of Lawrence had gone with her, to whatever place lay beyond this world.

Then, a shell of his former self, he'd spent his old age working even harder, playing even harder, trying to prove to the world that he was still in it, when any halfwit could see he wasn't. Then his doctors and his staff had stepped in, aided and abetted by his adventuresome chums, to clip his wings and keep him Earthbound and at low velocity, except in the safe carriage of a private jet. And then, as if in confirmation, his own heart had started showing its age. There was pain. There were surgeries, and pills, and admonitions about diet and exercise. Water exercise, twice daily!

And so it had simply made sense to leave his Earthly life behind, to leave all the intrigues of cislunar space behind and retreat, finally, to the whisper-light gravity of that white circle up there.

Retirement.

The word seemed more alien than the Moon itself. A word for other people! And yet, for years now, Sir Lawrence had been trying to devolve power to underlings who did not really want it, and to steer it away from those who wanted it too much. He and Rosalyn had left no heirs, and he wanted to minimize the mess his death would leave behind.

He didn't sleep much these days, and so, with the summer night's salty breeze in what remained of his hair, with his final destination casting down a spectral light across the cliffs and the sea and the white stucco of the villa, there was little to do except contemplate his choices.

Had it been good and right and proper to found seven companies? Had it helped the world, for him to sell off all but one? Had he granted mankind unprecedented access to the riches of space? Or had he, as some insisted, simply inserted himself in between those riches and the people of Earth? Was he, in the end, a good person? Had he ever been, or could he become one now? He'd always given generously to charity. Hundreds of billions of dollars! But could that expunge all the sins that any businessman must, of necessity, commit? He didn't know. There was no one left who'd answer him frankly about it.

And what about Rosalyn? Had he loved her well enough? He certainly hadn't loved her *long* enough, but damnation, if he had it all to do over again, would he ever have left her arms? Would she have wanted him to? She'd had a rich life of her own—a musician, a painter, an ever-smiling philanthropist! When he'd first heard the lilt and croon of her recorded voice, he'd approved the contract at once, and then sought an audience with her shortly thereafter. The courtship had been sunrise-brief and noon-bright, the wedding ceremony a mere formality. Ah, God, had he loved her well enough? There was no way to know.

He looked up again, at the source of the night's glow. Luna. It would spin 'round the Earth just three more times, and then he'd be on it. Starting a fourth and undeniably final phase of his life. Along with eight dozen other retirees, plus staff. Was *that* a good thing? It was something he could do—something *only* he could do. But he could not do it for everyone, no. Not for the slimmest fraction of everyone. What did it mean, to build the future? Nothing was ever really finished, nothing was ever for everyone. Was it wrong, then, to do it at all? He didn't know.

"Sir?" said a voice behind him.

Gill Davis, his longtime personal assistant.

"Good evening," Lawrence said, without taking his eyes off the Moon.

"Are you all right?" Gill asked gently. Oh, how tired Lawrence was of being spoken to gently!

"Just ruminating," Lawrence assured him. Then: "Can't sleep?"

"There are no curtains on the windows."

"Ah. Indeed. Well, it's a pleasant night for it, eh?"

"So it is, sir."

Finally, Lawrence turned and looked at Gill, moonlit in his dressing gown.

"You'll be out of a job, soon," Lawrence said.

Gill smiled. "I will, sir."

"I'll miss you. I mean that."

"I don't doubt it, sir. And I you."

Lawrence left that hanging for several seconds, then turned and looked upward again.

"You're still young. What will you do?"

"I haven't decided," Gill said, with refreshing candor. "You've been generous, which leaves me time to figure it out. And I'm not that young, not really. But yes, I suppose I will have to do something eventually. Something with a bit less travel."

Lawrence chuckled. "Yes, yes. Less travel for both of us."

Gill moved to the railing, and put his own hands on it, beside Lawrence's. He looked up at the Moon and said, rather psychically, "It's a frontier you opened."

"Did I?" Lawrence asked, his voice suddenly carrying a whisper of bitterness.

"You did. No one doubts it."

"Hmm." He mulled that for a few seconds, and then said, with candor of his own, "It's all right for you to tell me off, you know. There's no further consequence if you do. I'm sure I haven't been the easiest man to work for, not in such close quarters. You've seen me at my worst, time and again, and that can't have been easy."

"No job is easy."

"Hmm. Well, I thank you for staying. What's it been, now, nine years? Ten?"

"Eleven, sir."

"You can stop calling me that, now. In fact, I'd like you to stop calling me that."

"I . . . Well, that's kind of you, sir, but I don't know I'm that sort of person."

Lawrence chuckled again. "No, I suppose not."

He let the wind blow again for a while, and then said, "I didn't imagine space would be so dangerous. Naïve of me, yes? Foolish. I thought about airlocks and booster rockets, not about human nature.

But of course there are villains up there, of course there are weapons. Of course we're not all in this together. I helped that happen as well. No one up there is safe, or ever will be."

It was Gill's turn to snort in amusement. "No one is safe anywhere, sir; it's simply a matter of degree. And if you want me to tell you off, I'll say it's hubris to blame yourself for the failings of other people. You should focus on your own." Then, after a pause, he walked that back by saying, "Power has corrupted you less than anyone had a right to expect. Perhaps you could ruminate on that. Other men in your position do have weapons. And harems, and other indulgences. I've always admired your widower's faithfulness. It's rare. Can you be an arsehole? You can. It would be strange if you couldn't. But nothing kept me here with you. I could have left at any time. I could leave right now."

"Yes."

"The truth is, sir, it's been a pleasure as well as an honor. I think you can be proud, and I think you should be."

"I . . . see. Well, thank you. That means a lot."

"I'm not going to call you, though. Right? I've done my time. I'll think of you when I look up at the stars, at the Moon especially. But when this thing has run its course, I'll be starting a new life, with no rockets."

Lawrence could not help feeling slightly crestfallen at that. What man wouldn't? But what he said was, "Understood, Gill. I wish you happiness and safe journeys."

5.4
10 August

Thalia Buoyant Island
Southern Stratosphere
Venus

Weightless® Direct Message Log #AG5720

LadyCaffeine: Thank you for agreeing to speak with me individually! I know you have a busy life and lots of joiners, so I appreciate your taking the time.

FrOrtega211 (xlt esp>eng): It is my pleasure, ma'am. You left out "limited bandwidth."

LadyCaffeine: You should petition Weightless for a wider channel. You're a huge draw for them; the least they could do is underwrite your Deep Space Network access.

FrOrtega211 (xlt esp>eng): Haha, I think part of the charm is how slow I communicate. If people heard from me more, they might not find me so interesting.

LadyCaffeine: I doubt that.

FrOrtega211 (xlt esp>eng): Thank you, ma'am. What did you want to talk to me about?

LadyCaffeine: Sorry, my attention wandered. I was doing something else during the time lag. Are you still there? Full disclosure, I am writing an honors thesis for my bachelor's degree, about the psychological challenges faced by space settlers.

FrOrtega211 (xlt esp>eng): So you are in college? Yes, I am still here.

LadyCaffeine: Yes, University of Hawaii. You and I are both islanders.

FrOrtega211 (xlt esp>eng): /heart/ /smiley face/

LadyCaffeine: May I ask you some questions that may end up in my thesis?

FrOrtega211 (xlt esp>eng): Yes, sure.

LadyCaffeine: May I use your name? I want to be very certain about your consent before proceeding.

FrOrtega211 (xlt esp>eng): I am not in a position to sue anyone for quoting me. I do not have much access to the world outside of this site, but I know people quote me. Maybe misquote me. Yes, sure, you have consent.

LadyCaffeine: Thank you! Can you tell me about the stresses you face in your daily life? In your feed you talk a lot about the practicalities, which I love. But the same few names keep coming up in your descriptions, over and over again. It makes me wonder sometimes, if loneliness is one of the factors that drove you to communicate with Earth in this way.

FrOrtega211 (xlt esp>eng): Loneliness? Yes, definitely! I only know fifty people, and many of them have no time for a fifteen-year-old boy. It is assumed I will be working with my father as a trawlerman, so those are mostly the men who will speak with me. And Tohias, the mayor.

LadyCaffeine: Oh, I didn't realize you were so young! I assumed you were in your twenties. You have a very mature face for a teenager.

FrOrtega211 (xlt esp>eng): The mustache? Yes, I am told we get them early in my family.

LadyCaffeine: Who else do you speak with?

FrOrtega211 (xlt esp>eng): Well, there is Francisco, who is our doctor, and Marcus, our priest.

LadyCaffeine: Those are all men. Do you speak to any women? Or girls? You must, I'm thinking.

FrOrtega211 (xlt esp>eng): I have a mother and a sister. My mother's friend, Noemi, is Basilio's wife, and she is very kind to me. And there is a girl, Basilio's daughter, Juanetta, who thinks she is my fiancée, and another girl, Tika Valdez, who is the only other person I could plausibly marry. But she is only nine years old, so no one has talked about it. I speak with her, sometimes. She seems nice.

LadyCaffeine: So your culture practices arranged marriage?

FrOrtega211 (xlt esp>eng): Haha, yes. Arranged by lack of options! But I am being rude. Juanetta is a smart young woman who knows how to run a 3D printer. I could be much less fortunate, I know.

LadyCaffeine: But that is not very many people in your circle.

FrOrtega211 (xlt esp>eng): No. When we left Earth, I was only 10, but I remember knowing a lot more people. Even my own family was a lot of people. I had nine cousins!

LadyCaffeine: There are no babies on Thalia?

FrOrtega211 (xlt esp>eng): No. Not until we are more established. The adults voted on it.

LadyCaffeine: Do you want children someday?

FrOrtega211 (xlt esp>eng): I think so. It's hard for me to imagine, because there is a lot of danger here. When my sister was younger, we worried all the time that she would walk out a door by herself, without a mask, and no one would know until it was too late to save her. Or she could fall off the edge, or get her hand caught in a printer. A lot of different things. I think everybody thought there would be more people here by now, and more things to do.

LadyCaffeine: That sounds stressful.

FrOrtega211 (xlt esp>eng): I suppose so, yes.

LadyCaffeine: Does it take courage, just to go outside?

FrOrtega211 (xlt esp>eng): Courage? I don't think so. It is probably dangerous where you live as well. Hawaii? You could be hit by a car, or eaten by a shark, I am thinking. And there are also dangerous people on Earth, almost everywhere. It is one of the reasons my parents wanted to leave. Do you want children?

LadyCaffeine: Yes.

FrOrtega211 (xlt esp>eng): And you will worry about them wandering out into the world as well. Although I suppose you can take care of them at home while your husband goes to work. Or, is that sexist to say? I'm still learning how it works on Earth. Maybe you will send them to a day care center, where somebody's entire job is watching children all day?

LadyCaffeine: Something like that, yes, probably. So your psychological stress is mostly driven by loneliness, then? And limited choices?

FrOrtega211 (xlt esp>eng): Yes. I was very surprised how interesting my life is to people on Earth. Eventually I will run out of new things to say about it, and it seems like people will then discover I am somewhat of a fraud.

LadyCaffeine: Fraud? I don't think so at all. I'm impressed you ever even figured out how to get on the Internet. And you can take one hundred percent credit for the charisma you bring to this.

FrOrtega211 (xlt esp>eng): I am sorry, I think that word is not translating properly. Are you saying I am handsome?

LadyCaffeine: Haha, yes. That's not quite what I was saying. I meant that you have charm, especially for someone so young. But yes, you are very handsome.

FrOrtega211 (xlt esp>eng): I am blushing! Your profile picture is also very beautiful.

LadyCaffeine: My profile picture is a butterfly. But see? That's what I'm talking about.

FrOrtega211 (xlt esp>eng): Still blushing. It is very late here. The Sun will not be up for days, and everyone sleeps longer on the night nights. Everyone except me.

LadyCaffeine: Well, it's very kind of you to speak with me when you should be sleeping.

FrOrtega211 (xlt esp>eng): Very kind of you to have an interest. I'm not sure what a thesis is, but I hope you have good luck with yours! Good night!

2.5
19 September
✧
Clementine Cislunar Fuel Depot
Earth-Moon Lagrange Point 1
Cislunar Space

"This ellipse is the orbit of our next target asteroid, 101195 Bennu," Orlov said, jabbing his finger at the rollup screen. The lines and symbols, green on black, seemed too small to contain the destiny of Orlov Petrochemical, and yet.

"It looks like it crosses the Earth's orbit," Sally said. "Is that a problem?"

"Yes, this object is quite hazardous."

It was around midnight, Moscow time, and Orlov and Sally were at the observation window overlooking the asteroid outgassing oven, enjoying a rare moment of quiet. Dona had stopped shadowing the girl quite so closely, which he took as a good sign, and anyway most of the station was asleep right now.

The corridor lighting was in night mode, a very faint orange, and it was quiet enough that their voices sounded loud over the low hiss of the life support blowers. There were outward-looking windows in the station, including two in the outgassing oven itself, but all of these were dark now, as well. Every month, in the dance of Earth and Moon and Sun, Clementine fell into shadow for four hours, and thrice yearly, this eclipse would fall in the middle of a "night" shift on the station. This was one of those times. Orlov—who loved outer space more than people—had treasured these times of True Night for as long as he had lived on the station. He never wasted one by sleeping. It was hard to tell what Sally thought about such things, and he did not trust her to speak truthfully when she could butter him up instead. But he often found her wandering the corridors at night, breathing deeply of the purified air.

"Bennu will pass through cislunar space several times in the next few centuries," he said, nodding. He tried to imagine this: both the chaos and alarm, and the majesty, as the asteroid's mass flung it way, at orbital speed, among the great works of man. "We will move it slightly, to reduce this risk, and we will carve chunks off of it and shrink-wrap them and bring them here to EML1 for processing. No one will call us heroes for this."

Orlov was showing Sally his prize, his white whale. He had decided, for reasons he did not completely understand, to teach her about the business she had so carelessly and casually upended.

"Why that exact asteroid?" she asked. "Just because it's easy to reach?"

"Partly, yes. But it is actually the core of a dead comet, full of carbonates and water and volatiles. We've been going after much smaller, deader rocks."

He pointed down into the chamber, where spiderbots were digesting the plastic wrap surrounding a chunk of rock the size of a mobile home. It was graphite-dark, and looked like money.

A month ago, those same spiderbots had extruded that same plastic around that same asteroid, out beyond the Moon's orbit, from the small collection that had gathered at the ESL5 Lagrange point. The last of the small rocks, at least for a while.

"This little fucker," he said, still pointing, "is 1.75 million kilograms of chondrite, about eight percent of which is extractable water. We'll also get ten thousand kilograms of carbon out of this, and if we're lucky, another thousand of nitrogen. It's a good catch—enough carbon to fill a year's worth of demand, which is good because kilogram for kilogram, carbon is our best money maker at the moment."

"In the form of methane?" she asked.

It was not a stupid question, but it was a wrong one, and it annoyed him that she didn't already know better.

Fixing her with a glare, he said, "Sometimes methane, yes.

Sometimes propane or other shit people need for various things. But Sir Lawrence and his settlements on the Moon will take most of it as cyanogen. And because liquid hydrogen is too much trouble for Danny Beseman, his Mars ship is now configured to burn liquid oxygen and kerosene. Or what we call kerosene; it's actually just pure isoparaffin, much different from your granny's lamp oil."

"Isoparaffin," she repeated, as though the term were unfamiliar.

"I see you still have much to learn."

She nodded at that, not stung but simply acknowledging. "Uh-huh. And what happens to all the leftover hydrogen?"

"Some of it we turn into ammonia, NH_3, because that and carbon dioxide are what CHON synthesizers use. Ours and everyone else's."

"And the rest?" she pressed.

She was doing a better job of holding still in zero gravity than she used to, but still she drifted as she spoke. Which also annoyed him; she should stay close to a grab bar if she needed one so badly.

"We vent it into space," he said, and sighed. The market for gaseous hydrogen had really dried up these past few years. Though it angered him to throw away what someone ought to buy, that was today's reality. He couldn't make people want it, nor could he store it—not in the quantities in which it was produced.

"Ouch," she said.

"Indeed. And most of that specimen down there will wind up as silica slag, which we can't sell anymore, either. People used to want it for radiation shielding, but Renz Ventures has stepped in with better materials at nearly the same cost."

"Maybe we can sell it to the Cartels," she said.

Ignoring her, he said, "Bennu will change all of that. It's seventy billion kilograms—big as a mid-sized soccer stadium. And it has more of the things that make us happy, so we are modifying our procedures to do more of the work on site. We'll carve it up like a fattened goose, taking only the best pieces and leaving the slag where it belongs."

"We also sell plastic wire for 3D printers," she said. "Can we put more hydrogen in that?"

Apparently, she was not going to leave that alone. Her persistence could be an asset, or a problem. Or both. She continued, "What's a printable polymer that uses lots of oxygen and hydrogen, and not much carbon or nitrogen? What about a chlorine-terminated siloxane?"

"There are problems with silicones," he told her, and turned again to watch his little asteroid getting undressed.

"What problems?" she persisted. "Are they worse than throwing away all this material? Or . . . Could we make superconducting wire? Vanadium hydride, that kind of thing?"

"You surprise me," he said, without looking at her.

"I surprise a lot of people."

Ignoring her again, he said, "It's possible some kind of metal hydride wire could be made to work, and that customers could be made to buy it from us. Take it up with Voronin in the morning, and he will connect you to the people who can answer this."

Then, after a pause: "There is no way the great Magnus Orlov could have engaged in a business such as ours. When oil and gas and coal and uranium were the only sources of energy, he could helicopter around and look at things and nod. Strike fear in the workers, ask a few pointed questions. But then always back to his mansion or his *dacha* or his boat. The man liked his luxuries, his pointless *roskosh*. As do you. This is a weakness, Sally."

"I have wasted a lot of money," she admitted.

Still not looking at her, Orlov waved a dismissive hand. "The money is nothing. I pocket much more each day than a thousand people could spend on *roskosh*. Much more. But my attention is more valuable, girl. Attention is the most valuable thing you own, and you've flung it around pointlessly, to Burberry and Louis Vuitton and first-class lounges.

"My father owned, at one point, the largest yacht on Earth, do you know that? He spent years of his life selecting materials and supervising construction, and then of course he had to ride on the thing. So much time and energy squandered for the sake of his vanity. Magnus was no fool, except in this regard. Other fools waste their precious bandwidth on religion or fine dining or the theater, or a hundred other things, and so produce nothing but excrement. What is the point of existing, Sally, if you produce nothing but excrement?"

He turned now and looked at her again—really looked. Her hair was tied back in a practical manner, but she seemed always to suffer from stray hairs, which she was always puffing and swiping away from her face. And yet, she refused to cut it short. She still stank of perfume, and though she wore the uniform of Clementine, she had not yet really surrendered to the place.

She asked him, "You have no hobbies?"

"I have pleasures, as everyone must. But my legacy demands as much attention as I can reasonably give it."

She nodded at that, looking like she might actually think about it, and then she turned her attention back to the asteroid beyond the window. For a minute, they just watched in silence as, against the backdrop of white-enameled walls, the spiderbots finished their work, ingesting the last bits of plastic wrap, leaving the rock as naked as the day it was made.

In another twenty minutes, the Sun would come out from behind the Moon, and there would be an excess of power once again. At that time, spalling lasers and beams of focused sunlight would start their work, cooking off the accessible volatiles, which would be sucked up by vacuum pumps and routed to the refinery for processing. But for now, the rock sat quiet.

Finally, Sally said, "Where will we put the *Miembros*?"

That was a word from Spanish, and apparently what the Cartel leaders called themselves, and each other. *Los Miembros de la Organización*—or simply the Members. A ruse, perhaps, to hide the true importance of their positions, or else a bit of pointless underworld slang, for the thousands of men (and hundreds of women) who worked for them were also called *Miembros*.

"Space is large," Orlov said, "and nearly anywhere can be reached from here with minimal energy."

"But what about time?" she asked. "Do we want them close to us, or far?"

"Arm's length," he said. "Too close and they could interfere with operations, or simply make a nuisance of themselves. A perilous nuisance. But if we put them too far, they will realize we are holding them hostage."

"So, no stuffing them inside of Bennu?"

"Definitely not."

In the outgassing oven, the asteroid lit up with bright emerald grid patterns as the scanning lasers mapped its exact shape. High points were marked in red; low points in violet.

"What about L5?"

He waved a hand in annoyance. "Which one, Sally? EML5 or ESL5? They are millions of kilometers apart. You must learn to speak precisely."

"EML5, then. That's one of the boundaries of cislunar space, isn't it?"

"Not a boundary," he snapped. "An attractor. EML5 is along the orbit of Luna, trailing sixty degrees behind. There are clouds of dust there, named for the Russian astronomer Kordylewski. It's a place even school children know about. The *boundaries* of cislunar space are a million kilometers farther out."

Then, fighting down his annoyance at how little she knew, he added, "It would enrage the world, if I put a colony of murderers in their precious EML5. That might be more heat than I care to take on. But EML4 is less sheltered and less romantic. When Earthmen paint visions of gigantic, pastoral space colonies, it's never EML4 they dream of. And I like the distance. Arm's length, yes; we will put the *Miembros* there, a week's travel by slow boat. Three days by chemical rocket, or two if we don't mind wasting fuel and charging them for the difference."

In the chamber, the scanning lasers winked off, their work complete.

Sally said, "Speaking of pleasures and legacies, I've noticed none of the men on this station will sleep with me."

"Nor shall they," Orlov told her. "They are too old for you."

"Are you suddenly a moralist?"

He chuckled, amused by the idea. Protecting his daughter's virtue like a good father, ha! "I like to prevent problems," he said. "You are one. You're several. You will not create more."

After a pause, she said, "You are, among other things, a hypocrite. Are you trying to drive me away?"

He laughed. "Little girl, if I wanted to put you in a shuttle, I would. I still may. And if you'd flee this place because the boys will not fuck you, then by all means, flee. You have your trust fund, yes? Your debts are paid off, yes? The Earth awaits."

She said nothing.

"No?" he pressed.

Again, nothing.

"If you had a dick," he told her, "the great Magnus Orlov might have liked you."

She stared back impassively—an expression he recognized from photos and videos of himself. Was she mirroring his expression, or was she born with it? He supposed it didn't matter.

"Did he like *you*?" she finally asked.

"No," he admitted.

"Well, I do," she said. "In a manner of speaking. It's true, what I told you in my letter: the life Mother wants for me is boring."

He grunted at that. In her short time here, Sally had stirred up more trouble than the crew of fifty combined. He knew her type: pleasure-seeking, novelty-seeking, easily bored. And fearless, or at least lacking in the sense to keep herself out of peril. It wasn't obviously a good fit. And yet, the girl knew how to take action, and when to cut her losses, and when to ask for help. She had come here to ask for his help, and he had given it to her.

Interesting.

Looking back toward the asteroid again, he said, "I inherited my father's empire when he died. You want to be a trillionaire? Is that it?"

"No. The money doesn't matter. I have my trust fund, as you say. Give the rest to charity, if you like. Vent it into space."

He snorted. "Then what are you sniffing around for, girl?"

"Can't I dream?" she asked. "Can't I just want the future in my hands? People live such tiny little lives. Can't I just want to be part of something bigger?"

"And live in a can, breathing air that smells like balls? That's a smaller life than you think. It gets very small, at times."

"It's not much worse than my school," she said. "And with less nonsense. Those skirts! I'd rather wear a corset. Or a spacesuit."

"Ah, so that's it," he said, suddenly getting it. "That's what this is all about? You want to be an astronaut?"

She tossed her head, clearly annoyed. "What have I been saying, Father? All this time, what have I been saying? Yes, I want to be an astronaut! I always have."

Then, after a pregnant pause: "Didn't you?"

3.8
28 October

I.R.V. *Intercession*
Extra-Kuiper Space
2,000 A.U. from Earth

The crew of *Intercession* started pasting the ship's velocity on every screen capable of displaying it. At first, the number was meaninglessly large. Fifteen hundred KPS? What did that even mean, in real-world terms? Seventy-five times the speed of a comet? But that speed was slowly dropping. It took 16.6 minutes to drop just one KPS, and yet, magically, this added up so that every day, they shed another 86.4 KPS, which did seem like a lot. And then, finally the day arrived when the velocity was less than 86.4 KPS, and would drop to zero before the night shift started.

This was way more exciting than simply turning the ship around, because it meant they'd arrived at their destination. True, that destination was literally nowhere, but perhaps the most important nowhere that had ever been visited.

Unless this whole thing were crazy! Michael had tried for months to keep that thought mostly out of his mind, but now was the time when the real and the hypothetical either merged or recoiled. If nothing happened, if there were no Beings, then all this was simply a shakedown cruise for a ship that would eventually, when all the glitches were ironed out, make the much longer trip to Proxima, and the planet that circled it. (A lifeless planet, by all accounts, geologically dead and battered by stellar flares. But nicer than Mars in most ways.) And Michael would not summit with God's other children, but simply be a member of the shakedown crew.

On the other hand, Pope Dave had agreed to send him—to leave Saint Joe's in the care of dour Brother Groppel—on the possibility that these aliens actually existed. Surely the Church's participation in a meeting of such magnitude would be (a) good for the Church, and by extension (b) good for the billion-plus people who, one way or another, depended on the Church to light their way in a world of confusion and ambiguity.

If the Beings were real, the theological implications were beggaring, and Pope Dave wanted eyes and ears and hands on the scene to help him—him!—make sense of it. That Lisa Jablonski's little boy now found himself in such a role was itself beyond any usefulness he'd ever imagined for himself.

And if the Beings were not real, then a lot of people—not only the crew and passengers—would have wasted years of their lives. And he supposed his role, in that case, would be to help them (and himself) find meaning in that. In a life dedicated to service, perhaps that was enough. Perhaps it was good for the mission and good for the Church that he be present for that as well.

A little after midday, he and the rest of the crew were gathered around the dining table for lunch, surrounded by the octagonal frustum of their eight sleeping berths, with the doors open and their meager personal effects on display. Video displays, one over each berth, displayed clouds in a bright blue sky. This was the homiest, most comfortable part of the ship, and here he sensed, finally, that he was not the only person thinking these thoughts.

"I hope we really do make contact," Harv said at one point. "I can't have *two* reasons for people to think I'm crazy."

At another point, Rachael said, "I deal exclusively in measurable quantities. This business of . . . As far as I can tell, there's nothing measurable here."

Even Igbal's excitement seemed tempered with a grouchy realism.

"Here's hoping we haven't wasted a trip," he said, as the meal was wrapping up.

"No point worrying about it now," Hobie said. "Things are about to get busy, and we all got jobs to do."

Everyone was, in their own ways, preparing themselves for what was about to happen, and everyone nodded at Hobie's words.

"Speaking of which . . ." Sandy said, nodding toward the ladder that led up to the bridge.

"It's a bit early, gal." Hobie said. But he put his hands on the ladder and launched himself upward.

Sandy followed behind him, and everyone else cleared the dishes, folded up the table, and then started climbing into their cabins and strapping in. It was early, but there was, finally, nothing else to do.

In the end, despite nearly everything being under manual control, Sandy and Hobie managed to stop the engine with the ship moving at just under fourteen meters per second.

"On a dime!" Hobie called out happily.

And then he did something reckless and stupid: he used the attitude control thrusters to try and make up the difference.

"Stop!" Michael said into his headset mic, as thrusters groaned on each side of the vehicle. Then, more insistently: "Hobie, stop! Cut the thrusters."

Hobie did so, but then complained, "What's the problem?"

"You're wasting chemical propellant we might need later," Michael snapped, more cross than he'd been in months. "And you . . . the . . . that velocity reading is only an estimate, anyway. The nearest reference point is a million light-seconds away."

"Quit showing off," Igbal seconded. "We're here."

"As you wish, man," Hobie said, with mingled sarcasm and chagrin.

But he'd mostly achieved his goal already; the velocity now stood at just 6.3 meters per second.

"We're as stopped as a spaceship can reasonably be," Michael said.

"Relative to the Sun, at least," Harv chimed in. "We're still in orbit around the center of the galaxy, moving something like two hundred kilometers per second."

"And the galaxy is moving," said Dong.

"Everything is moving," Sandy called down the ladder, with languorous impatience, like it was something she'd grown tired of explaining. "Everything orbits everything, while the universe expands. There are no privileged reference frames; there's no such thing as 'stopped.'"

"Well, the engine is off," said Igbal. "Hopefully, that will cut out the last of the quantum interference."

That was a thing, Michael knew, that the Beings had complained about to both Igbal and Hobie, and perhaps a few others as well, in their communications to ESL1 Shade Station. When he thought about it at all, Michael imagined the Beings standing on the far side of a roaring river, shouting at humanity and hearing nothing but "What?" in return.

"We'll know in a few days," he said. And then it really hit him: yes, they would know in a few days. And regardless of the outcome, mankind's place in the universe would never be the same.

1.14

Post-Encounter Deposition
Lars Onsanger, MSSE
Associate Professor of Structural Engineering,
Columbia University

It was like being stoned at an Imax show, with a foreign encyclopedia flashed up on the screen, page by page, really fast. Except, I don't know, in 3D, or maybe 5- or 6D. You could see words and diagrams, but could not really make any sense of out of it. There were voices in the background, maybe narrating the show or something, but I could not make those out, either.

It wasn't at all like I expected. I'm sorry I can't be more helpful.

TOP SECRET
Additional Restrictions
NOFORN, WININTEL, HUMINT
SPECIAL COMPARTMENTALIZED
INFORMATION: PROJECT
INTERTWINE
EYES ONLY

Transcript 08:21:16:00.2 (machine transcript human verification top secret compartmentalized information)

I gave a very short account in my deposition to Renz Ventures. No, I don't have a copy of it. Per instructions, I didn't tell them very much. I said it was like a foreign encyclopedia—

What?

My boss was Tina Tompkins, the President of the United States.

I'm not sure... How much have they told you? I had been an embedded asset for two years, working at Columbia University like a real professor, because I was a real professor. But on tap for missions, okay? I was a combat veteran, went South for two tours to fight the Cartels, and then I got my master's under the GI bill, so the CIA recruited me. Got me the job at Columbia, which there is no way otherwise I could get.

That's you guys? "The Company"? Is that who I'm talking to? Tompkins was going to be out of office by the time I got back, so my report was supposed to go directly to her successor, whoever that turned out to be. But with the rough changeover, I guess I am talking to you guys instead? I do not know who knows about this, about me and the mission. I do not know how my name got in front of Igbal Renz as a candidate. I assume Tompkins had an asset in his organization, maybe at the highest levels, but when you break the spiderweb, it's not easy to know how the threads were once connected, okay? I don't have that information.

I had only ever done one mission before, and it was just carrying a briefcase across town. Maybe that was training? Or maybe a true operational action, who knows. Then nothing for more than a year, just waiting. Good soldier, waiting. But then my handler showed up at my office one day, no warning, with several other people I did not know. I signed a stack of classified documents, and the next thing you know, I'm on a helicopter to the White House lawn.

The mission was simple, to determine (1) whether these aliens exist, (2) whether they represent a threat to the security of the United States, and (3) whether and how the US government could contact them directly. The pay was good: double my CIA stipend for the two years I'd be gone, plus my Columbia salary, plus the money Renz Ventures was offering, which was substantial. So, a lot of money. But that is not why I said yes. Why? I mean, patriotism, obviously, and curiosity for myself, to meet... Well, I don't think it's very mysterious, why a person would want to be a part of something. Can I serve my government, and myself, and maybe even Renz Ventures at the same time? Not even a cover story—except for the Company association, I told people exactly who I was. I suppose that is why assets are embedded in places, so that reality and the cover are the same story.

Anyway, so, answers: the Beings exist, all right. Can the government talk to them? Short of building your own starship and your own antimatter core, I do not see how that would be possible. They don't exactly talk over shortwave radio. I kept hearing how advanced and proprietary that starship was, also, the engine and other features, so I think doing this without Renz would be operationally challenging.

Are they a threat? The Beings? In and of themselves, I do not see how they could be. I don't see how they could even want to be, or understand how or why. I did not get the impression they fight amongst themselves, or they have ever encountered anyone in the universe besides us. So, no. Threatening us is not a thing they did.

But I think anyone who talks to them might be, okay? I'll explain.

It was like an IMAX show with a foreign encyclopedia flashed up on the screen, fast and jumbled. There's a document called the Voynich manuscript, that's written in a dead language nobody can translate, and filled with pictures and diagrams no one can interpret. Star charts and extinct plant species, maybe, and lots of tiny naked people. I know, okay? Tiny naked people. Look it up.

It was kind of like flipping through the pages of that. I saw items that looked like math, and items that looked like topo maps or astronomical maps. Some geometrical diagrams, but in . . . this was not a 2D picture, okay? It was . . . I don't know how to describe it. Our language and perhaps our brains are not configured . . . More than three dimensions? Yes, I would definitely say so. If I understand the question correctly. Do you know what a memory palace is? I think it was developed in the Renaissance by philosophers, but we were encouraged in the infantry to do something similar, to think of important information as locations or exhibits in this memory palace in our mind. It's a mnemonic tool, to help you associate your memories better. But if you could wander through someone else's memory palace, I think that would be very confusing, even if this was a human being who you personally knew. But if it is an alien creature that never even had a body . . . You can keep asking me the question. It . . . You . . . I don't know of a way to explain this to you. Saying more things about it is not going to make it clear. If you think you are understanding me, I think probably you are mistaken. IMAX screen, encyclopedia, memory palace, hypertext. How about assembly instructions for Ikea furniture? Except there is nothing physical in the images, and that is not correct, either. None of these associations are literal, my friend. It was information in some form, being communicated in a flawed manner. You can write that down in your notes.

I heard voices, too. I would estimate approximately fifty voices, although it is difficult to be certain. Sometimes speaking all at once, like a chorus, and sometimes all different in a crowd murmur. I felt I could almost understand them at certain moments, but not quite. I can tell you they sounded enthusiastic, friendly, welcoming, and . . . I suppose you would say "surprised." Like this encounter was amazing to them. It literally was to me.

In addition, I heard what I would describe as faint music in the background. Something similar to music, although not audible, per se. I suppose "vibrations" would be a more accurate term. It was purposeful, okay? It was communicating something. Everything was a communication sculpted for our benefit. These Beings know a lot, but not necessarily about the universe as we know or can perceive. And they do not know us very well, or how to talk.

But that was me: good soldier, mediocre professor, and maybe a mediocre embedded asset as well. I am sorry I can't be more helpful. But these other human beings out there with me, who knows what they saw or learned? And maybe they shared it with Renz Ventures and maybe they did not. I certainly did not. Was I the only one on that spaceship with a hidden agenda?

I will tell you, each and every person who was there is a potential security threat, especially Igbal Renz, and there could be dangerous knowledge loose in the world. What do I mean? Okay, what if it is something primordial and fundamental to the operation of the universe? Would you want somebody walking around with that knowledge? Or dangerous pieces of that? Renz Ventures already possesses a way to make this antimatter in large quantities, and I know our government is afraid of that. And there is the tralphium that comes from the Moon, for very cheap electricity. But what if these things are tiny blips?

There could be information loose in the world, much more dangerous than anything we have previously imagined.

2.6
28 October

✧

Clementine Cislunar Fuel Depot
Earth-Moon Lagrange Point 1
Cislunar Space

Taking long, meditative breaths, Sally Grigorieva Orlova watched the stars through the visor of her spacesuit.

With only three weeks of training in her logbook, Sally was technically forbidden outside the station without an experienced astronaut to escort her. However, as Sally was not in the habit of paying attention to what was and was not forbidden, she was out here by herself, floating in the full glare of the Sun.

The side of her suit that faced the Sun was hot, and the side that faced away was cold, and she had turned off the circulation of coolant fluid to enjoy the sensation of these temperatures against her body. Like a spa. It could be a spa, someday.

However, the brightness of the sun did not bother her eyes or impede her view of the amazing sights all around her. The display on the inside of her visor was not only shading against the light reflecting off of surfaces, but also (thanks to subroutine calls to the suit's native eye-tracker and ephemeris) completely occulting the disk of the Sun itself.

Once Sally had figured out that the visor's "shade" was actually just a repurposed liquid crystal display film, it had not been difficult to hack the suit's processor to add the occultation capability, along with other capabilities she was still exploring. It was amazing that no one had ever thought to do this before. She figured if the suit's designers ever actually spent time in space themselves, or if the people living and working in space knew more about how their equipment worked, then this was one of the first things they would have changed. Astronomers put occultation discs in front of the Sun all the time; it was not exactly a new idea.

Then again, it was amazing that no one here on Clementine had ever thought to ask, *Hey, Sally, what are your skills? What have they been teaching you at that fancy school for troubled youth? Probably a lot of hands-on stuff, yeah? Not so much bookwork.*

Dear Daddy had decided to bring her into the family business by teaching her what he knew about what he did. This didn't bother her, to be treated like a blank slate or a flawed copy, but it did lower her opinion of Daddy, who seemed to have an unfortunate habit of letting resources go to waste.

The suit was brand new, and the inside of it smelled like plastic and machine oil and her own hair. It wasn't a bad smell. Breathing deeply, floating in a neutral, fetal position, she spoke the words, "Annotations on."

The helmet display came alive with new markings—dozens of them, all over the sky.

In front of the occultation disk, for example, was an arrow pointing just off-center, with the words ESL1 SHADE hovering over it. Below that, another arrow and the words ESL1 SHADE STATION.

Home of the RzVz pukes, for whom she felt an almost instinctive enmity. What were they doing, what were they holding, that was worthy of nukes and stealth ships? Dear Daddy seemed to brush off this question, focusing attention on the *who*, rather than on the *whom*. The actor, not the acted upon. But Sally's interest was not so easily deflected.

And to the right of the occultation disc, the bright dot of Venus, nearly resolvable as a sphere, and annotated with the words THALIA BOUYANT ISLAND. Home of that fucking kid from Weightless, making money doing nothing at all.

And to the right of that, the vast crescent of Luna, whose north and south poles were cluttered with annotations. These were the assets of the Chinese and Brits, or Yuèqiú Gōngyè and Harvest Moon Industries, or Premier Ping and Horseman Killian. All of them up to no good.

Annotations in empty space showed the positions of ships: thorches and ion ferries, EOLS capsules and transatmospheric shuttles, some visibly moving, most not.

The position of 101955 Bennu was also marked, not because Sally thought it was particularly important, but because Dear Daddy was never going to shut up about it. It was a big pile of money, yes, but she had learned, in her fancy French school, about the "curse of oil," and of mineral wealth generally. Extractive industries produced less economic growth than comparable activity in almost any other sector, except farming.

"Be engineers," her social studies teacher had advised his classes, with something like genuine concern. "Be artists. Design clothing. Work in a cubicle, doing nonsense. If you touch the ground, your value drops."

Well, M. Glasier might be amused to know just how literally Sally was taking that advice! If she had her way, it might be a long time indeed before she touched any sort of ground again.

The position of EML4 was marked as well, and that did have value. There was nothing there, and Sally didn't own it, but she was going to sell it to the *Miembros* anyway.

Working the attitude thrusters on her suit, she rotated past the Earth—an unreadable mess of yellow tags, dozens of them. Each a manned satellite or spaceship, going about its petty business. She could filter these by type, if she wanted to. She could filter by tonnage or crew size or value in Euros, but right now she wanted to see all of it. She wanted to be reminded, visually and viscerally, just how much stuff there was out here in outer space.

None of it hers.

Rotating further, she saw, at the level of her knees, the bright dot of Alpha Centauri—brightest star in the celestial sphere. And at the level of her chest, an arrow marked I.R.V. INTERCESSION. That fucking starship. So much wealth, so much technology, and this was how Igbal Renz chose to squander it?

Whatever that particular trillionaire was doing out there in the deep void, he had tipped his cards by doing it along a straight line pointing to Alpha Centauri. Clearly, that was his ultimate destination, and it maddened her to think of an entire star system— three stars and at least four planets—under the control of someone she could not threaten or manipulate or milk.

It was a problem. Renz was also an asteroid miner, but only as part of an explosive, vertically integrated monopoly that was—in every way—unafraid of thinking big.

Something was going to have to be done about it.

Turning further still to the right, she saw Mars—an orange dot annotated with the words ANTILYMPUS TOWNSHIP.

And en route back from Mars, the H.S.F. *Concordia*. Probably mostly empty; on its way back to Earth to pick up people and supplies.

Dan Beseman thought he could own the planet Mars. He thought he could sell it to people—sell even just the dream of it. But his feet were touching dirt, now. His enterprise was, at the bottom of the day, every bit as extractive as Orlov Petrochemical. That little colony had cost him his fortune, and there was no way he was ever going to make that money back, selling one hundred tickets every twenty-six months. The man was an imbecile. Sally wasn't worried about him. Hell, the little Venusian boy was more of an irritant.

She completed her rotation and nodded, grimly satisfied that she had indeed looked over the entirety of the human universe. Or at least those parts of it that could be seen.

Someday the stealth ships would be added to this display, and then nothing would be hidden from her. Like her father, Sally had let her share of resources go to waste. Money, time, connections, attention. *Roskosh* and bullshit. She was never getting any of that back, okay, fine, but her squandering days were over, as were her days of thinking small.

She knew there was much still to learn and do at Clementine. Orlov Petrochemical regularly acquired and moved and spent sums of money that would be out of reach for most of the countries of Earth. She needed to understand how this was done. She was only seventeen; she needed to understand a lot of things. Still, she'd been disappointed to realize that Dear Daddy, behind all that bluster, really just wanted to pump gas and get paid for it. He was dangerous if crossed, yes. Dangerous if you got between him and his goals, and sometimes dangerous anyway. The wages he paid, just to find someone willing to float next to him! But he seemed to see the world—all the worlds, really—in terms of energy and fuel, working heat and waste heat. Such a narrow lens. It had gotten him this far;

it had made him as rich and powerful and feared as the average man's most vulgar daydream. But it didn't take a genius to see this mindscape would take him no farther. At the age of sixty, Grigory Magnusevich Orlov was topped.

Sally would let people underestimate her, right up until their fate was sealed. The details were still hazy, but she knew, with a deep conviction, that Clementine was just a stepping stone. She would own it someday, yes; Dear Daddy would hand it over without complaint. But by that time, she would barely even notice the gain.

She'd been told all her life that her smile was cold, but she felt her lips curling upward with real joy as she contemplated her future, because she knew that someday all of this—all of cislunar space, all space, all of humankind—would be hers.

Hopefully she'd be immortal, as well, so she could have it all, forever. And only then would people realize, they should have shot her when they had the chance.

3.9
29 October

I.R.V. *Intercession*
Extra-Kuiper Space
3,336 A.U. from Earth

Igbal was impatient. Like a kid on Christmas morning, he wanted to tear ahead with the Encounter, like, now. Well, they were tearing ahead with it, but "it" involved a lot of steps. Before they could start thawing out frozen people, they had to deploy and inflate the Encounter Bubble—a process that required everyone to first put on spacesuits. Michael of course insisted on making a safety drill of it, and seemed satisfied that everyone was sealed up tight within 3.5 minutes. In their suits, in their lockers, without help.

"Good," he said, over the suit radio channel. "We all survived."

"Thanks, Padre," Igbal said, although he knew that was the wrong title and would irritate Michael. He just liked saying it.

Once that was done, Hobie exited his locker and went back up into the bridge. Everyone else had to hang around in their spacesuit lockers, although most opted to at least open their door.

As with the crew quarters, each spacesuit locker had a video display above it. On one of these, from a camera mounted to the superstructure surrounding the cargo deck, Igbal watched while eight rectangular panels opened up in the conical hull, like flower petals around the circumference of the ship. They kept rising and rising until they folded all the way back against the hull, with an audible hum as the motors did their thing, and a thump as the doors reached their full extension.

The open panels left a two-meter gap all the way around the hull, where smooth metal gave way to folded textile. A hundred lives depended on the Encounter Bubble remaining airtight for the next week, so it was actually one of the heavier parts of the ship—two layers of thickly woven ballistic nylon, with a stretchy silicone layer in between. On the inside and outside, it was aluminized polymer film, coated with a thin, white, non-woven textile, like a painter's suit. The whole thing weighed ten thousand kilograms—as much as a garbage truck, and more than one percent of the ship's total mass.

"Everything look good?" Hobie asked. "You want to go outside and inspect?"

"No," said Igbal, exiting his locker to look at each of the screens in turn, "Everything looks good. Go ahead and crack the valves, slow bleed."

Another heavy payload was the six thousand kilograms of compressed air needed to inflate the bubble, and the associated four thousand kilograms of tankage and plumbing.

The sudden airflow from these tanks was surprisingly loud in the close confines of the cargo deck. Well, maybe not that surprising, since the pipes ran right between the spacesuit lockers, but it meant they were really doing this.

On the viewscreens, the fabric of the Encounter Bubble started to swell and, very slowly, unfold.

"Are you getting any pressure drop?" Igbal asked anxiously.

"No sign of any leak," Hobie assured him. "You want me to crank these valves all the way?"

"Slowly," Igbal said. "Very slowly, but yes."

The hiss of air through steel piping grew louder, and louder still. After that, it was like watching a mushroom grow—which was something Igbal had done a couple of times in his life. The gas was going in there fast enough that Igbal could clearly tell, minute to minute, that the Bubble was slowly expanding toward the final, toroidal shape that would encircle the hull. But he could also see that the total process was going to take hours.

"Well," he said, "here we are. How's everyone's oxygen doing?"

Everyone reported that their oxygen was fine.

Rachael said, "Slow breaths. We're going to be sitting here a while, and acidosis is not something we want to be dealing with."

"When can we take the suits off?" Thenbecca asked.

"When the Bubble is fully inflated and inspected," Igbal said.

And although he'd started to find all the philosophical discussions pretty annoying, Igbal wished somebody would start one now. But nope, nobody did. This wasn't that kind of moment. It was in fact the kind of moment that space exploration was full of: long, slow, tedious, deadly, and deeply consequential. Nobody had ever done this before—any of it—and there was no guarantee it would go as planned. Many things did not.

For a long time, nothing really happened. Then came the scary, thrilling moment when the white walls behind the glass spacesuit lockers suddenly *whoosh*ed away, and they were all looking into the inside of the partially inflated Encounter Bubble. People gasped and jumped. Even Igbal himself, who had seen the process once before.

"Yikes," said Harv.

"Yah," Igbal said. "Bit of a scare, there. Sorry, I should have warned you that was going to happen."

"We weren't aboard for the dry run," Harv said in a testy voice.

"I know. I said I was sorry."

Igbal never knew quite what to make of Harv Leonel. He'd published hundreds of papers on quantum computing, and clearly knew his shit. That whole genetic past life regression thing, though— the thing Harv was actually famous for—was a bit of a wild card. A favorite of the *Journal of Irreproducible Results*, Harv's claims might be pure New Age bunk. Might be. But something about it had rung true for Igbal, and, hell, even if Harv was just a brilliant nutcase, he wouldn't be the first human being to do good work in spite of being crazy. Or because of it.

Thenbecca certainly seemed to like him. Of course, she didn't have much in the way of formal scientific training, so she might not be able to tell if he was crazy. Hell, she might not even care. She was a cheerful person, and Igbal would be happy to have her on the mission even if she weren't the best CHON chef in the solar system. But she was, thank God, or they could've been eating porridge three meals a day. The CHON synthesizer only held a handful of built-in patterns—none of them closely resembling food—and it took a lot of skill and persistence to get anything that might be called "cuisine." But she managed it, nearly every day.

"Looks like the webbing is intact," said Dong Nguyen.

"Yep," Igbal agreed.

When the Encounter Bubble was fully inflated, the normal air pressure inside the ship would be more than enough to hold its donut shape. However, the interior of the Bubble was crisscrossed by cables that served a dual purpose. First, to soften the failure mode if the fabric somehow ripped, so it would be a little less likely to pop like a balloon, or anyway the popping process would take a few seconds longer. Second, to provide idiot civilians a way to move around in zero gravity, without stranding themselves in midair. And Dong was right; the cables looked good. Their yellow Kevlar cores were hidden by white polymer cladding, and each of them, as far as Igbal could see, was firmly anchored at both ends to the fabric of the Bubble.

Igbal hadn't known Dong before the start of the mission training, but he was a solid astronaut, highly recommended, and Igbal planned on poaching him from Transit Point Station once they all got back into cislunar space.

After a painfully long ninety minutes, the Bubble was finally fully inflated, and Igbal cautiously opened one of the eight glass doors leading into it, mingling the atmosphere of the Bubble with that of the ship's interior.

All readings were nominal, so everyone except Hobie (who was still up in the bridge) filed through the doorway and out into the Bubble to look for any damage or other anomalies. None were found, so Hobie was summoned back down, his task complete. And then, fully two hours after the valves were first opened, the crew of *Intercession* could finally take off their spacesuits.

Next came the inevitable gymnastics, as eight people who'd been cooped up for a year finally got a chance to really stretch out their limbs and *move*. Cartwheels! Somersaults! Banging back and forth between the tensioning cables! That one was Rachael—or Dr. Lee as she used to insist on being called back at ESL1. She looked like she was having fun for about fifteen seconds, until Brother Michael put a stop to it.

"A small chance of killing us all is still an unnecessary risk, don't you think?"

He said this in that relaxed but firm way of his, that really left you no room to disagree.

"Aw," Rachael said. But she stopped what she was doing, and ruefully said, "My bad."

It actually didn't take very long for everyone to get worn out from the exercise; their hours in the ship's tiny gym were no substitute for actually moving around. And then it was time to eat, and then it was time for bed.

Igbal passed out sleeping pills, saying, "Get some sleep, seriously. The next several days are going to be crazy."

He had a hard time sleeping anyway, though, through a combination of being jazzed up and also, privately, worried about looking stupid. Either the whole history of the universe was about to be rewritten, or he was a fool, and would go down in history as such. When he finally did sleep, though, he dreamed he was in a strange house, with strange voices coming from another room. He couldn't quite make out what they were saying, but their tone was friendly and soothing, and made him feel as though everything was going to be all right.

In the morning, Michael arose refreshed, and prepared for whatever the day might bring. His role here was to help wherever help was needed, and he intended to do exactly that. Thenbecca presented them all with a hearty breakfast, and then everyone—Igbal included—got the hell out of the way while Michael and Rachael and Hobie went down into the hibernation vault to start waking people up.

There were ninety-two people, to be thawed in eleven groups of eight and one group of four. The process would nominally require four hours per group, and they would be running it around the clock, so there were forty-eight hours scheduled for it.

Rachael was the only one here who had actually performed the full revival procedure before. An M.D. obstetrician who had become a hibernation specialist in her forties, she carried herself like someone who knew exactly what she was doing.

Hobie was here because, as the former pilot of an ion ferry, he had a lot of experience guiding passengers in and out of the much milder state of "squirrel hibernation." He had a bit of experience with deeper "bear hibernation" as well, but these coffins plunged their victims into "frog hibernation"—basically a very mild form of clinical death. Michael knew Hobie himself had actually been frozen and revived back at ESL1, but had only ever participated in the process from the outside during training, one single time. So Hobie was here as Rachael's apprentice, and would take over for her during the (presumably brief) times she was asleep.

Michael himself made some programmed adjustments to the life support system, setting it to gradually ramp up to the level of throughput necessary to support one hundred people. After which he was merely an assistant and backup for the de-freezing process. God forbid he actually needed to run anything by himself, but he'd been assured many times that the people who awoke would be disoriented and needy, and he meant to coordinate the non-medical portions of their care.

Of course, no one had assigned him this job. No one had assigned anyone this job. But it needed doing.

Rachael started at the bottom of the chamber, farthest from the hatchways into the Encounter Bubble. The first patient was male—someone named Joona Lao. Michael had never met him—he'd never met the vast majority of the frozen passengers—but he'd read all the dossiers, and vaguely recalled that Joona Lao was some sort of linguist.

The heartbeat and respiration lines on Lao's status display were pure flatlines. His core temperature was two degrees Celsius. Pulse ox was a quasi-nonsensical eighty-five percent.

Rachael started by turning on a simple warming circuit, which would pump water through the shell of the hibernation pod, and through a tube down Lao's throat, at gradually warmer and warmer temperatures. Lao wasn't technically "frozen" at all; his tissues were packed with antifreeze proteins that prevented ice crystals from forming, or else this process would have taken a lot longer. And also, Lao would be dead, his cells ruptured by microscopic needles of ice. Nodding in apparent satisfaction, Rachael moved on.

Next came a mathematician, two diplomats, a judge, an astronomer, a botanist, and a retired army general. Michael wasn't entirely clear why any of these people had been selected for the mission, but the underlying premise was clear: getting as many dissimilar points of view as possible. Given how little was known about the Beings, it was a sensible enough strategy.

Once all of them had started warming, Rachael turned her attention back to the first pod again. Joona's core temperature had only risen half a degree but he already looked a bit less frozen-dead.

"Now we wait," she said.

Michael wished they could simply start the warming cycle on some more people while they were waiting, but of course this was a delicate procedure. He'd read all about it as the magic date approached, so he knew that warming someone up too early or too fast could be lethal. On the other hand, when they hit four degrees centigrade, the bodies would start actually dying if you didn't get the metabolic processes going within half an hour or so.

No one had anything to say. The moment was simply too portentous to cheapen with blather. Hobie busied himself by checking and rechecking the nonexistent vital signs of the other patients, while Rachael hovered over Joona Lao.

It took forty-seven minutes before Lao's core temperature was up to four degrees centigrade.

"His blood should be mostly liquid now," Rachael finally said, "and the heart should be capable of contraction. I'm going to hit him with the defibrillator."

She buzzed Lao with five hundred volts. Once, twice. She edged up to six hundred and buzzed him again.

On the monitor, the heartbeat line wiggled a litter bit and then settled back to zero. Then, a few seconds later, wiggled and settled again. And then a third time. "Sinus rhythm established," Rachael said. "Looks like six beats per minute, which is fine; we can now start warming the blood directly."

She pressed controls on the panel that activated the pumps to warm and oxygenate Lao's blood. Breathing came later, Michael knew, but she withdrew the tube from Lao's throat anyway. An electric motor purred somewhere as it retracted.

She moved on to the other pods, shocking their inhabitants back to life one by one. And then it was back to Lao again.

"Electrolyte drip is on," Rachael reported, mainly for Hobie's benefit. "Leg squeezers are on. Brain stimulator is on . . . and . . . the patient is breathing."

It seemed a miracle to Michael, that this man—gray and covered in frost just an hour ago—was now basically alive again. How many doctors and researchers had spent their whole careers making the incremental discoveries and improvements that had made this moment possible?

Rachael performed the miracle seven more times, and then she was back at Lao's pod again, actually opening it up.

She'd been basically ignoring Michael up to this point, but now she looked him in the eye and said, "I'm going to add epinephrine and vasopressin to his drip. It's going to wake him up, probably sometime in the next half hour. He's going to want . . . comforting."

Michael understood. Under the circumstances, her bedside manner was basically nonexistent.

Presently, Joona Lao began to shiver.

"That's a good sign," Hobie said.

Indeed, over the next ten minutes, Joona's eyes began to flutter. So did those of several other patients, as Rachael performed her miracles on them as well.

It was actually the mathematician, Evelyn Chang, who awoke first.

"Where am I?" she asked, fully opening her eyes. She coughed, then—the dry-throated cough of someone desperately in need of a drink of water.

"You're safe," Michael told her.

Underneath each hibernation pod was a drawer containing a bungied-down kit of all the things that person would allegedly need here on *Intercession*. One of these was a squeeze bottle of Gatorade, which Michael removed from the drawer. He unscrewed the squirt cap, pulled off the safety seal, screwed the cap back on without spilling a drop.

"Where am I?" Evelyn repeated, as if unaware she'd asked the question already.

"You're in the hibernation bay of the starship *Intercession*," Michael said, judging she was conscious enough to get some value out of that. Then: "Here, drink this. It will make you feel better."

"I'm so cold," she said. She was clad only in space underwear.

"I'll get you some clothes," Michael said, "but first, drink a little Gatorade for me."

She did this. And then asked again where she was. "Oh, my God," she said, after receiving the answer again. "Oh my God. Are we there?"

"In the dark between the stars," Michael confirmed, handing her a blue Renz Ventures jumpsuit. "Here, put this on. It will help you warm up. Oh, belay that. You'd better wait for the doctor."

She was, of course, still covered in wires and tubes.

She seemed to realize for the first time that she was strapped down. Undoing the Velcro of the top strap, she then realized she was weightless, and promptly vomited up the Gatorade she'd just ingested.

Chiding himself for not anticipating this, Michael grabbed a towel from the drawer and used it to sweep the globules out of the air.

"You're fine," he said. "Just hold still for now."

But then someone else was waking up, so the best he could do was hand her the towel and the coverall and say, "I'll be back. Take it slow. Wait for the doctor."

Soon all eight of them were awake, and Michael was busy tending to all of them at once, while Rachael hopped from pod to pod unhooking wires, withdrawing IV catheters, and pulling white silicone disks off their skin. She performed perfunctory medical examinations while she was at it—checking pupils, having them squeeze her finger.

Everyone had the same questions. Everyone was cold, even though the heaters in their pods were now on full blast. Everyone needed help getting dressed. Fortunately, the prep for being frozen was much like the prep for a colonoscopy, so there wasn't actually all that much vomitus produced, and no one desperately needed a bathroom. Yet.

The mathematician, now free of her pod and sorting through the gear in her bag, held up her barf-stained towel and said, "Wait, this is my towel? My only one? How can I get this cleaned?"

You can't, Michael thought but did not say. Laundry facilities on the ship consisted of a single tiny machine whose capacity was maxed out by eight people, and he didn't want anyone getting the idea that that resource was something they could fight over. Perhaps if he got a chance he could wash it sneakily, and then tell her it was a completely different towel. But he did not expect to get that chance.

What he did say, somewhat deceptively, was: "All in due time, Ms. Chang."

It took a while, but eventually Michael had all eight of them assembled in a group: four men, three women, and one person whose gender was listed as nonbinary, all (necessarily) of roughly similar size—heights within fifteen centimeters of each other, and weights within ten or twenty kilograms. All in identical unisex jumpsuits.

The nonbinary person—a botanist from Ecuador, according to their profile—peered out from under a Santa-Claus-red crew cut, and seemed to regard Michael with confused, bleary suspicion. Michael felt for a moment how strange it must be, to be frozen on Earth, and to wake up nineteen light-days away, among strangers, on a corporate starship you've never seen except in computer renderings. In the best possible view, it was like the first day at a new school, only you really did show up naked! And it was worse than that, for shaking off the effects of hibernation was no quick process, and it was *scary* being this far from home and help. Even for Michael it was scary. So yes, it was a lot to cope with. But imagine if, on top of all of that, you found yourself, inexplicably, being ushered around by a robed Benedictine monk!

"You aren't dreaming," he said gently. "And yes, it is strange, my being here. If there's time, I'll tell you the tale of it, but for now it's time to move."

Then, in a chatter-cutting voice directed at everyone, he said, "Okay, listen up, please. I'm going to escort you, single file, to the Encounter Bubble, which will be your home for the next several days. You all have questions. You all have concerns. None of you have experience operating in zero gravity. I sympathize, and will speak with each of you as time permits. But right now, time does not permit. We're going to play 'follow the leader'; do exactly what I do. Use your hands and feet exactly as I do, or as the person in front of you does, if you can't see me."

And then, without further discussion, he kicked off from the rim of an empty hibernation pod, launching himself toward the ladder and then up, toward the spacesuit lockers and the hatchways into the Encounter Bubble.

It was, of course, a shitshow. People collided with one another, and drifted away from handholds, and caught their sleeves on obstacles. In all the time he'd spent planning for this moment, he should have thought to tie a rope along this path for them to follow, hand over hand. It all took much longer than it should have, but eventually he got them all up into the cargo deck and through an open hatch into the Encounter Bubble. Soon after, he had them all huddled in a little tribal knot, against the gray-white fabric wall, with feet or elbows secured on the cables.

"You each have a bag of personal effects," he said. "This includes a sleeping sack with your name on it. I'm going to encourage each of you, before you do anything else, to find a place to tie yours down. There should also be tape and Velcro, and you're adults who can figure it out. Once you've defined a little personal space for yourself, you'll feel a bit less disoriented."

"Can we have a tour of the ship?" asked Evelyn Chang.

"Possibly," Michael said, trying to work out in his head whether it was actually feasible, much less advisable, to show ninety-two people around the service deck, crew quarters, and cockpit. "You've already seen most of the habitable volume, and you'll see more when you need to use the bathroom. Speaking of which, does anyone have an urgent need, that can't wait half an hour? No? Then I will leave you here for the moment. I'm sorry again for the circumstances."

On his way out, he ducked up into the service deck, where the galley, shower, gym, and bathroom were located. Thenbecca was in the galley, her slippers hooked into stirrups on the floor.

"Hello, I'll be back," he said as he floated past her into the crew quarters. There, he grabbed a rung to stop himself and latched his gaze on Harv Leonel, who was inside his bunk with the door rolled open.

"We're going to need babysitters. Are you available?"

"Quite," Harv said.

"Round up whoever else you can. Keep our guests busy. Mentally prepare them for what's coming. If possible, engage them in philosophical dialogue. This is the most amazing thing any of them have done, and we need to keep their minds on that fact, and not on their deprivations."

"Got it," Harv said.

"But," Michael added after a moment's reflection, "keep Igbal out of it. We'll have him give a speech when all hundred are assembled, but for now let's keep him hidden if we can."

Harv snorted at that. "If we can."

Two other bunk doors were closed, and presently one of them rolled open, revealing Dong Nguyen.

"I will help," he said, and Michael sighed inwardly, because of course the only people available to help Harv were Dong (an eager little man with minimal social grace) and Sandy (whose emotional intelligence was easily the lowest on the ship). But one worked with the tools at hand.

"Excellent," Michael said, and kicked downward along the ladder. He stopped in the service deck.

"We've got eight live ones," he told Thenbecca, who was typing something into the CHON synthesizer's touchscreen, in the "Beverages" menu.

"No kidding," she said, for the pandemonium had occurred just below her stirruped feet.

"Soon to be sixteen," he said, "and we'll have thirty-two by the nominal start of the sleep shift, and forty-eight by morning. You will keep them all fed and hydrated?"

"Yup."

"Sleep when you can. Gather helpers as you need to, myself included. If the forces of darkness hold sway out here in the big empty, we could be as little as one meal away from mutiny."

"Michael, I've got this," she said. "Go do what you need to."

Thenbecca had perhaps the highest emotional intelligence on the ship, and a fine chef's mind for logistics, so he nodded, crossed her off his mental list of things to worry about, and kicked back down through the cargo deck, past the Bubble and the spacesuit lockers, and into the hibernation bay.

Rachael and Hobie had already started thawing out the next batch of passengers, and Michael wanted to watch their every move, knowing full well that, sometime in the next two days, when everyone was weary as rented mules and as prone to error, he might be called upon to perform some portions of this ritual. Or to catch the mistakes of those who did.

Lives depended on it.

Igbal couldn't help mingling with the defrosted passengers. Michael had specifically asked Harv to ask Igbal to stay away for a while, but Igbal found he couldn't do that. Harv's reasoning—that it would be "more dramatic" for Igbal to address them all at once, in two days' time—was specious at best, and insulting at worst.

Igbal knew what people thought of him: that he was a robber baron, that he'd gotten rich off the sweat of millions of other people's brows. That he was an asshole who didn't care about the world, or the plight of the poor.

All of that was, of course, bullshit. Igbal had been fortunate enough to be born with a brain that thought up exciting ideas. And those ideas . . . well, they excited people, and the rest of it kind of followed naturally. They came to work for him. They helped him build the stuff he dreamed up, because it was their dream, too. Governments and corporations hurled money at him, because he could solve their problems and relieve their pain. That's what people paid for; that's what made the world go 'round. That and dreams—nothing else.

And what better way to care for the world than to build a grander future for it? To enhance the capabilities of the human species, while reducing its waste? As for the plight of the poor . . . men like Igbal made the whole world richer. Provably, measurably. And he paid good wages, too—wages that flowed down to grocers and plumbers and auto mechanics. Wages that sent people's children to college and cared for their elderly parents. Was that really less noble than if he worked forty hours a week at a soup kitchen? Seriously.

Also, what exactly was he supposed to do for the poor? He didn't even have money in the usual sense; he had a multinational corporation. Was he supposed to give *that* to the poor? How would that even work? No, these criticisms were all madness and noise, and he had learned long ago that his critics could not be reasoned with.

Even if they were Harv.

Fact was, Igbal had made this whole thing happen—this incredible thing, that would change the course of history even if the Beings didn't deign to speak. So yeah, he was damn well going to meet with the people he'd brought out here with him.

He had some business stuff to attend to first—light-lagged by three weeks and at a bandwidth of barely ninety bits per second—because he always had business stuff to attend to. Making dreams come true was an absolutely full-time job, and things had gotten crazy bad down at ESL1.

By the time he got down to the Bubble, the first batch of passengers had set up their own little zero-gee campsite, with hammocks and sleeping sacks and clotheslines, and seemed well on their way to forming a bold new society.

"Hello," said one of the women, as he floated out into the Bubble to meet them. Her hair was short, and she had somehow put on lip gloss and eyeliner.

"Hi," Igbal said, taking her hand and shaking it minutely, so as not to destabilize her. Newcomers to zero-gee were surprisingly bad at shaking hands, and sometimes even puked. "Are you the leader?"

"I don't know about that," she said, casting over-shoulder glances at her fellows. "Evelyn Chang."

"Ah," he said, "Yeah, I remember you. Math, right? University of . . ."

"MIT. Right."

"I went there, too, and I love math," he said. "We should talk."

Igbal turned to one of the men, who introduced himself as Bryan Parr.

"Ambassador Parr," Igbal said, shaking his hand.

Igbal had a good memory, and although he'd never met most of the passengers, he'd hand-picked them all from their dossiers. Most were free of family and business entanglements that would prevent their taking two years away. They had been approached and negotiated with in secrecy, and he'd been heavily involved in that process. Very few of the candidates, once approached, had refused the invitation, so in principle he knew at least a little bit about each of them.

"And you must be the *other* Ambassador Parr," he said to the man adjacent. The two were not twins, but the family resemblance was strong—both had black hair, broad chins, and dark, soulful eyes over beige-colored skin.

"Adam," the man said, shaking hands.

And so it went. Igbal talked with each of them for a few minutes, and offered some tips about living weightless. He'd been a resident in space for most of the past seven years, and had welcomed dozens into the life on board ESL1 Shade Station, so this was a subject he knew a little about.

When it was done and he was on his way back to work, Harv took him aside and said, "That went surprisingly well."

"Fuck off," Igbal told him, and kicked up the ladder toward the bridge.

Michael had a better idea what to do as he ushered the second batch of sleepers into wakefulness, and then escorted them to the Encounter Bubble. Also, fortunately, there was now a small community in place to welcome them. So in that sense, the job was now easier.

However, there were now sixteen people asking him questions, logistical and otherwise, and he could not keep ignoring them all. And so he spent a good half hour talking to them, telling them first the date and time. The ship was still on Paramaribo time—the Atlantic time zone, one hour later than the east coast of the United States, and it was currently four-twenty in the afternoon. For people who, subjectively, had been on Earth (indeed, in Paramaribo) just a few hours ago, this kind of information was quite important in bringing them forward into the present.

"Many of you must feel almost as though you're dreaming," he said, "and you must help each other overcome this. We're in a hazardous environment, far from rescue, and there is no margin for nonsense. Please remember your training, conduct yourselves as guests, and tolerate nothing less from your peers."

Next, he explained that the lighting would dim between 9:30 p.m. and 6:30 a.m., and how—ahem!—to use the sleep masks and earplugs in their gear kits. Then a quick summary of who he was and why he was here on the mission, and where exactly they were in space, and how long it would be before they started taking the drugs that would let them talk to aliens. Also, where the toilet was and how to use it, where the bridge was and how to stay far away from it. He explained that none of them would be taking showers at all, except by special arrangement, and that they were also to refrain from harassing Thenbecca for food unless they were experiencing some genuine blood sugar emergency.

"Some of you may already have received your pre-packaged rations. Others will receive them within the next few hours. Please feel free to hoard and trade as you see fit. Please put the empty packaging back into your kit bags. Although it costs a fortune to haul their mass back with us, and although interstellar space is unimaginably vast and empty, we will not be leaving behind any litter."

Some of the passengers had already heard some of this from Harv and Dong, but it never hurt to hear it again.

"Unprofessional," muttered the passenger with the Christmas-red hair.

"Assuredly lacking in precision and polish," Michael agreed in a much louder voice. "This is the first mission of its kind, and it relies in part on the fact that you're all highly respected lateral thinkers. As for myself, I haven't drawn a salary in decades, and so cannot lay claim to being a professional anything."

After a moment's reflection, he then added, "There are barf bags in your kit as well. If you should fill one, I won't ask you to hang onto it. I'll see to it that a receptacle is set up. Are there any further questions?"

One hand went up.

"Yes?" Michael asked, pointing to a black-haired man.

"Will you pray with us?"

"Assuredly," Michael said, "But not right now. If there's nothing else . . ."

There wasn't. Michael went back to work.

Despite Michael's best efforts, as the Encounter Bubble filled up with people, it also filled with loose globules of vomit, which eventually landed on the walls, cables, and (in one spectacular example) hatches. He distributed precious motion sickness patches to the worst offenders.

And then he found he needed to eat and sleep. He asked Ptolemy to wake him in three hours. Michael had always been blessed with the ability to fall asleep quickly, and to awake quickly when circumstances demanded it, but his body nearly refused to cooperate when the alarm went off, dragging him insistently back down into a slumbery quicksand. He barely made it out before the next batch of sleepers began to awaken.

By this time, Hobie was fully in charge of the process, Rachael having retreated to her own bunk to sleep off what must by now be an awful fatigue. And Hobie had no appetite for interference or delay; whenever Michael got even slightly in his way, he said, "Move it, man, we're chasing clocks here," or "Don't watch where you're going, watch where *I'm* going," or "We're going to run out of air, you keep slowing down our schedule!"

That was true enough, and a good reminder that Michael, having inserted himself into this process, had an obligation to, first and foremost, not cause the deaths of everyone involved. The ship was already running on bottled oxygen and chemical CO_2 scrubbers, as the life support system could not cope with even a quarter of the passengers awake. And if those consumables ran out before the passengers were back in their pods and safely frozen for transit . . . Well, everything about this was deadly serious, and deadly, period.

"I will redouble my efforts to assist without hindering," he said solemnly, and then really did go about his business differently, making sure he was as far away from Hobie—and any plausible trajectory Hobie might launch on—as humanly possible.

And yet, another batch of human beings really was waking up. Groggy, disoriented, in some cases frightened and in others, cranky. It wasn't their fault; different parts of the brain woke up at different rates. They needed fluids and electrolytes, towels and coveralls, instructions and warnings that Hobie had no time or patience to give them.

The rest of the night passed in a blur, until Michael found he had to sleep again. This time, he didn't reckon three hours would cut it, so he woke up Harv and pressed him into service, briefly explaining the task and then trusting that Harv could, at the very least, do more good than harm down there.

"Wake me in six hours," he told Ptolemy, and faded before he could even roll his bunk door closed.

1.15

Post-Encounter Deposition
Rachael Lee, M.D.
Chief Medical Officer, ESL1 Shade
Station
Extracislunar Space

Though not on the mission as a subject matter expert, I did want to see if my medical knowledge could apply somehow to the study of the Beings. If they can move, think, communicate, and so forth, they must have some sort of internal organism. Unfortunately, through the wavy curtain of intoxication I saw them as opaque spheres and nothing more.

Beautiful singing voices, spouting nonsense. I believe they were real, but I can't properly say I communed with them, and I'm sorry—given the known effects of dimethyltryptamine and methylenedioxymethamphetamine, I do wonder how reliable the reports are, from others who claim they did.

The orgy afterward was fun, though.

6.2
30 October
✧
Second Dawn Retirement Community
South Polar Mineral Territories
Lunar Surface

Raimy Vaught stood in the jetway, waiting for the flight vehicle's door to open.

Except, not really, because the flight vehicle was not a jet, but a modified Earth Orbit to Lunar Surface (EOLS) capsule. So the tube he was standing in was, what, a rocketway? That didn't sound right, either. Also, Raimy wasn't really "standing," except in the very loose sense that a person could stand, flat-footed, in chin-deep water. Lunar gravity took up only a sixth of his weight.

Raimy had spent the last five years shuttling back and forth between Earth and Luna. Living out his dreams: an astronaut at last! But on this particular rotation he'd only been here for a couple of days, and was still getting his moon legs back.

He peered out the window on the left side of the jetway, and saw the left side of the two-story-tall EOLS capsule. Nothing out of the ordinary. He did the same on the right side, and saw nothing there, either. No debris, no venting gas or leaking fluid. It was always sunny here on Sunset Ridge, in the South Polar Mineral Territories, but the Sun was always just above the horizon, so the left side of the ship was lit brightly enough to hurt his eyes a little. The right side was in deep shadow.

Raimy worried about the thermal stresses on the jetway seal, from

257

being really hot on one side and really cold on the other. He gave it a thorough visual inspection, and then ran a wand microphone around its entire perimeter, listening for leaks. He could find nothing wrong, for now.

Raimy worried about a lot of things. Raimy was a paranoid motherfucker, or he'd've been dead by now, many times over. Raimy stayed on high alert even for routine shit like landing an EOLS crew on the landing pad and walking out of it in spacesuits. Because even that could kill you ten different ways.

But this was not routine. This was the first time, ever in Lunar history, that the people carried down by an EOLS were not wearing spacesuits at all. This was the first time that the EOLS had to come all the way down from orbit and set down at the exact roll angle that would line it up with the jetway, so that a perfect seal was even possible. It was the first time ordinary civilians in street clothes would egress from a lander directly into a lunar habitat, without going outside at all. All kinds of things could go wrong, and Raimy had thought long and hard about every one of them.

Which of course was why Raimy, the Director of Lunar Public Safety for Harvest Moon Industries, was the one standing here in the jetway. On one wall, just below the porthole, was an emergency locker stuffed with supplies for every possible contingency: goo suits, pressure tents, patch kit, tool kit, airlock wrench, a spray can of sealant foam, a collapsible rope ladder, a separate coil of rope, and of course a roll of duct tape. All neatly organized and clearly marked in thirty-six-point font that was—he knew firsthand!—readable even through the blur of eyes exposed directly to the vacuum of space.

When it came to safety, Raimy did not fuck around.

And yet, the lights above the EOLS' hatch were green, indicating equal pressure on both sides of the seal. Nothing was leaking; nothing was making any noises it shouldn't. Finally, he could think of no reason not to open the door.

Sighing inwardly, he rapped on the hatch and, leaning on the intercom button, said, "Raimy here. Clear to open."

"Mayflower acknowledges, clear to open," said the voice of Trish Spofford, the ship's pilot. Spofford had been running EOLS missions for almost seven years now, and had racked up more flight hours than any other HMI pilot. Which is why, with Raimy's approval, Sir Lawrence Edgar Killian had selected her for this particular mission.

Raimy heard a metallic click of safety locks disengaging, and tensed slightly.

If the jetway seal fails, there's going to be no way to close that hatch again. The air will foomp right out of there. If that happens, I'm going to jam a goo suit down over my head, I'm going to grab two pressure tents, I'm going to run into the EOLS and set the tents up wherever I can. I'm going to stuff one tent full of people and seal it and pull the cord. And then I'm probably out of air, but if not, I'm going to stuff and inflate the other tent. And then I'm out of air and I die a heroic death. Fuck.

But none of that happened. Instead, without further ado, the outer handle on the hatch rotated upward, and with hardly a squeak, the hatch swung out toward Raimy, and Mayflower was standing there with a big, fat smile on her face. Like Raimy, she wore a close-fit jacket and trousers of HMI mustard yellow. It actually looked pretty good on her, which was more than Raimy could say for his own self.

"Raimy," she said with a nod.

"Mayflower. Welcome back."

"Thank you. Permission to board?"

"Granted."

That was a bit of protocol that had never quite made sense to Raimy—you didn't "board" a ground-based habitat—but it was long-established habit by the time he appeared on the scene, so there wasn't much to be done.

Standing aside (i.e., lightly hopping on his slippered toes), Raimy let Mayflower into the jetway. Behind her stood her boss, and Raimy's.

"Sir Lawrence," Raimy said.

"Good afternoon, Sheriff," said Sir Lawrence Edgar Killian, looking in fact rather haggard. At the age of eighty-four, the CEO and primary shareholder of HMI had never actually been to outer space before, much less endured a three-day, mostly-weightless journey to a whole other planetary body.

"I have barf bags," Raimy offered.

"Thank you," Killian said, "but I think everyone on board is grateful to have a bit of gravity back. Only a bit!"

Killian offered a wan smile, and bounced a little on his toes. "So this, at last, is Luna, eh? I made it. Ahead of the reaper, no less, and not in an urn!"

He bounced a little higher, his feet lifting a centimeter off the floor.

"Feels odd, doesn't it? I suppose I'd better get used to it, hadn't I?"

Killian would never return to Earth. Likely, he wouldn't survive the trip back there, and he certainly wouldn't survive the gravity. Despite advances in medical science, something happened to the human body around the age of eighty that made adaptation exponentially more difficult. Even with bone and muscle loss prevention pills at the maximum safe dosage, Killian would most likely, after even just a few months of Lunar gravity, have become unable to breathe or pump blood properly at full Earth gravity, ever again. So Killian's doctors had warned him, and Raimy saw no reason to believe otherwise.

"Welcome to your new life," Raimy said.

"Thank you, thank you," Killian said, shuffling awkwardly forward to make room for the people behind him to "board" the jetway.

There was a man, Johnny Zee Adams, former rock star and shoe entrepreneur, and his wife, former singer/supermodel Clazz. Johnny managed, in Lunar gravity, to swagger in like he owned the place. Which, in some small measure, he did.

There was a woman, Lydia Harris, whose career title was, politely, "philanthropist."

Another woman, Ju Xue, who had been big in personal robotics right as it was really taking off, and her husband, Xiaoran Xue-Jones, who had once been her Chief Financial Officer. None of their products were still in use as far as Raimy knew, but everyone still knew what a Walkiebot used to be.

And another man, Egil Vitgås, whose family had, for generations, owned a world-famous liquor distillery. Vodka, mostly. Raimy had had it many times. Good stuff.

Raimy had of course read all of their dossiers, and had had his staff run an AI "red check" on each. None presented any serious risk of violence (not even Johnny Zee Adams, who had once cultivated a reputation for it). None presented a greater-than-average risk of walking out an airlock. All were in their mid-eighties or early nineties, but otherwise in good health, and in good mental and physical condition. None were wearing HMI yellow. All of them had left their luggage on the ship, apparently expecting someone to fetch it to their apartments for them.

What all of them had in common was a fuckpile of money. Which made sense, because this facility had cost almost a hundred billion dollars to construct. A ten-year lease on an apartment here cost a hundred times more than most people made in a lifetime.

Also: to get a rocket into orbit, without exceeding two-gee acceleration for more than sixty seconds, took a ridiculous amount of fuel. It had taken an HMI Heavy Lift Double to carry these frail people on the first leg of their journey, and that was not cheap, either.

But even so, there were hundreds of applicants for, at the moment, only forty-eight apartments. So, each of these people had also, in some way, managed to personally persuade Sir Lawrence to let them come at all, and then to let them be a part of the Pioneer Group.

"Welcome to Luna," Raimy said to each of them as they shuffled or danced or hopped past him. "Welcome to your new life. Welcome to Luna."

"Oi, I feel twenty years younger already," said Johnny Zee Adams.

"You had better, for the price," said Xiaoran Xue-Jones.

But that was the whole point, right? People were living longer, healthier lives these days—an average of ninety-one years for men, and ninety-six for women. Longer, if you took good care of yourself. Longer still if you were rich. But still, always, time and gravity had their way. A fit ninety-year-old on Earth might be technically capable of completing a 10K run, or in rare cases even a marathon, but they were never going to feel like they did when they were forty, or even seventy. Never again. Never on Earth.

But here on Luna, they could. In fact, if Killian's AI models could be trusted, these people would live an average of nine years longer than they would have on Earth. If things went to plan, they would literally cheat death. They would literally buy time.

Whether this was fair or ethical was a question beyond Raimy's pay grade. He was only here to keep them safe, no matter who they were. He was here to keep a whole, growing community of old people safe, in one of the least safe environments human beings had ever occupied.

He also had technical responsibility for Shackleton Lunar Industrial Station, eighteen kilometers from here. And Shoemaker Lunar Antenna Park Observatory, and the Aitken-Ingenii Metal Extraction Facility, and even to some extent Saint Joseph of Cupertino Monastery. It was getting downright crowded here in the South Polar Mineral Territories.

But those facilities were staffed mainly with professional astronauts, and Raimy had been working with them for years, refining and refining their safety protocols. They knew what they were doing, and didn't need a hard-ass like him leaning over them anymore.

This place was different. This place was daunting, with ordinary civilians set to be in constant peril.

Over his shoulder, Killian said, "Do you have some words for us, Sheriff?"

That was a title Killian used jokingly, because Raimy used to be a cop, and because "public safety" included a wide range of duties, including the investigation of accidents and (rarely) crimes. But the nickname was actually kind of annoying, because most of Raimy's job consisted of yelling at people to blow the dust out of their O-rings.

"Let's wait until we're inside," Raimy said.

Then, hugging the white-painted metal wall along the left side of the jetway, he made his way past the EOLS passengers, and Mayflower, until he was at the station-side hatch. The lights were green, so he opened it, and waved everyone into the van-sized airlock on the other side. Once everyone was in, he closed and dogged the hatch, pushed his way through the crowd again, and opened the next hatch, and waved everyone through again.

"Full service," remarked Lydia Harris with some amusement.

"Mmm," Raimy responded noncommittally.

Next was a long, windowless, poorly lit hallway—twice as long as the jetway—sloping downward at precisely fifteen degrees. And then another hatch, and then finally the interior of the habitat itself.

Everyone gasped, one by one, as they entered the dome and looked up. They had all seen pictures. They had probably all seen VR renderings before shelling out their hard-won (or hard-inherited) money. But yeah, pictures didn't really do the place justice.

Raimy entered behind them all, then closed and dogged the hatch. Huntley Millar, HMI's extravehicular activity (EVA) crew chief, was here waiting for them. He smiled and nodded at Raimy.

"Welcome," he said warmly.

The dome was a circular amphitheater, mostly buried, with the "beach" and pool area down at the center, and rings of apartments and gardens and orchards rising up until they met the blue-white "sky" of extremely thick, extremely heavy, beautifully translucent quartz panels. Outside, the skydome was ringed with twelve vertical mirrors that rotated (once per month to match the rotation of the Moon itself) to cast the full light of the Sun onto the glass. The actual sun hit the glass as well, lighting the whole thing up as bright as any Earthly sky.

Ignoring all of that, Raimy said, loudly, "Never open this door." Once he was sure everyone was looking at him again, he pointed at the hatch handle for emphasis.

They all looked at him with some mixture of surprise and annoyance and disappointment. He had ruined their perfect little moment. Good. He needed their full attention.

"Some of you may never need to exit this facility ever again," he said. "This is an all-inclusive tropical resort; all your needs will be met inside of this dome. But if you do need to go somewhere else, for any reason, a trained astronaut will open doors for you. If you feel suicidal, take some pills. Vacuum exposure is not a way you want to go. I've seen people die that way, and it's awful. Is all of that clear to all of you?"

Everyone stared.

"Great bedside manner," Mayflower said.

"I'm not here to play tour guide," Raimy said gravely. "I'll let this man, Huntley Millar, do that. He led the team that built this place. I am the Director of Public Safety, and my job is to remind you there is *no oxygen* on the other side of that dome. If you want to sneak around the tunnels underneath this place, don't. If you want to rap your knuckles on the sky to see how solid it is, don't. The glass gets very hot, as do the metal seams between the panels. If you want to mess with the plumbing or wiring in your apartment, don't. This dome is like a submarine, or a carved-out salt mine deep underground. Or like an airplane, flying ten kilometers above the

Earth. If you mess with anything you're not supposed to, you might kill not only yourself, but also everyone else. I can't emphasize that enough. Does everyone understand what I'm saying?"

Reluctantly, six heads nodded. Mayflower and Killian just stood there looking annoyed.

Weirdly, Raimy suffered from stage fright when addressing groups of people, so he had prepared and rehearsed these remarks over a period of weeks. Right now he was sticking pretty closely to that script, but looking at everyone's faces now, he decided to skip the part about how he had authority to place anyone under house arrest if he felt they were in any way a danger to themselves or the community. They would find that out in due time. Or not. Maybe not.

"Okay," he said. "Sorry to start you off that way. Welcome to Second Morning Retirement Community. I hope each and every one of you finds a fresh start here, to a long and happy second lifetime."

There was a tour, led by Huntley Millar, which led the new arrivals through the pool area, and into one of the vacant apartments on the cabana level.

"Most of this was constructed in vacuum," Millar said, "at the facilities over at Shackleton, and trucked here in pieces. We only started filling the dome with air a few weeks ago."

"Wow," someone said, without apparent irony.

Millar continued, "There was a lot of digging and burying here on site, naturally, but inside a geological feature called a graben, which formed a natural amphitheater on three sides. Your wallets can thank God for that, because if we'd had to start on flat ground, this would have taken double the time and cost. The size and shape of the dome was dictated, though, by the hole we started with."

"Will the next one be bigger, then?" asked Johnny Zee Adams.

"Perhaps," Sir Lawrence answered for Millar. "We shall learn a lot from this one, certainly."

"I won't be involved in the next one," Millar noted.

Sir Lawrence smiled at that. "Mr. Millar, here—one of our best people, I should note—is on his way to a well-earned retirement of his own, after eight years on and off the Moon."

"Actually, I've got another year of ground duty down in Suriname," Millar said. "Then, who knows?"

To that, Lydia Harris said, "So you've built a promised land you're not allowed to enter?"

Killian held up a hand. "Now, now. Two of these units are reserved for an employee lottery, and two for low-income individuals or couples who meet the medical criteria. And of course, smaller ones for Raimy, here, and for Chef and all the other staffers who'll be seeing to your needs. But this is academic; Mr. Millar has decades ahead of him before he needs to consider a place like this. What are you, son, fifty-five?"

"Exactly right, sir. I started with you at thirty-six."

"Ah, so it's almost pension time, then, yes?"

"Indeed, sir. Exactly right. But you're making me blush in front of these very patient people. Shall we continue the tour?"

"By all means."

The room they were all standing in was a "Parlour/Foyer" according to Millar, and it was larger than Raimy's entire Second Dawn apartment. Which was fine; he'd lived in much worse places. Millar then led them through the kitchen, master suite, office/guest suite, and multipurpose room, each of which was large and well appointed, with locally manufactured furniture and decorations already in place. Each resident had a cargo shipment due tomorrow, but with rather severe restrictions on mass and volume. In terms of "stuff," their new lives would not be mere extensions of their old ones.

Next, they toured the medical center, the communal gym, the dining hall, and rec room, and they took a quick glance at the row of offices where Raimy and a few other staffers were based. The "manager"—a woman named Tiki Beebee, whom Raimy had never seen or talked to—was supposed to be here already, but had been delayed by some kind of family thing. She had the office next to his.

And then . . . well, then the tour was complete.

"Bit small for the rest of our lives," Johnny Zee Adams remarked.

"You get used to it," said Raimy, who had spent three years aboard a very cramped nuclear submarine, and had spent most of the last five years in ships and rovers and habitat modules that could probably all, collectively, be piled up on the "beach" of this facility without reaching the second level of apartments. Also, medical science and lunar gravity notwithstanding, the rest of these people's lives was ten, maybe twenty years, tops.

"It beats the alternative," Sir Lawrence said, "which is rather the point, yes?" Then, with even greater annoyance: "This facility is, by a considerable margin, the largest and most lavish ever constructed off the surface of the Earth. The dome you're standing in is fifteen times the volume of the gymnasium bubble at the Marriott Stars, which was itself the largest single habitat module in history. If this isn't good enough for you—if you think you might like to return to Earth and sell your lease to someone on the waiting list—it's a decision you'd best make quickly."

"I think it's lovely," said Lydia Harris, after a long and uncomfortable pause. She delivered this with more than a trace of a southern U.S. accent, and in a tone she had probably used all her life to shut down any potential disagreement.

"Excellent," said Sir Lawrence. "Now, you've all an hour to settle into your new accommodations, freshening up et cetera, after which I understand Chef has prepared a feast for our arrival."

"What about our bags?" said Clazz. Not in any sort of haughty or demanding way—just tired.

To which Sir Lawrence said, "Has that been taken care of, Raimy?"

"I'll look into it," Raimy said, though he knew for a fact that it hadn't. In fact, he knew there were only four staffers on site at this time, which was a lot for only seven residents.

Which meant that Raimy, his own self, was going to have to do it. Raimy had been a cop and a lawyer and a Navy diver and an astronaut. Never a baggage handler until now, but he supposed that was what he got for working with people like these. He was, in fact, probably the most expensive baggage handler who'd ever lived. So, fine—there were worse things.

The residents all seemed to revive a bit during dinner, and then decline a bit afterward, the boost of Lunar gravity overwhelmed by the weight of food and drink and exhaustion. And darkness; overhead, the electrochromic filters on the skydome had faded from blue-white to yellow to red-orange, and were now such a deep blue that pinhole "stars" in the filter—a rough match for the actual stars in the sky right now—were slowly becoming visible. Fake nighttime in fake paradise.

Still, as everyone was getting up to leave, Sir Lawrence found the energy to seize Raimy by the elbow, tightly.

"Walk with me, Sheriff."

"What's up?" Raimy asked, as he found himself, indeed, walking.

The dining hall had an indoor portion set off by closable hatches, and a patio area overlooking the pool, bordered with trellises around which vines had been planted—in genuine Earthly potting soil!—but had not yet had a chance to grow. Warm yellow lights were coming on at the corners of the hall, and along a spiral path heading down toward the beach and pool.

"I realize the position you're in," Killian said, now releasing Raimy's elbow, "but I wonder if you realize mine."

"I'm sorry?" Raimy said. He had no idea what Killian was getting at, here, and was feeling a bit impatient about it. The old man had a slow, circumspect way of speaking; he made you dig for it, and Raimy wasn't currently in the mood. But now that Raimy and Killian lived in this dome together, he supposed he was going to have to build up a tolerance.

"How do you think these people are feeling right now?" Killian asked.

"Nervous?" Raimy tried. "First-day jitters?"

The path's downward slope would have been gentle even on Earth; here, Raimy felt he would float right off it if they walked any faster than a gentle mosey. If he wanted to, he could vault over the railing and the newly planted bushes behind it, and land down there on the beach's gray-white sand like an Olympic gymnast. Above, the twin porch lights of the apartments glowed warmly. A gentle "breeze," along with the piped-in sound of crickets against the gentle crashing of waves—completed the effect.

"It's beautiful here, isn't it?" Sir Lawrence said. "It's everything I could have hoped. I have lived on jets and airships, Raimy. I've crossed the ocean in a sailboat. This place is very roomy by comparison, and the Lunar gravity"—he hopped a bit, to demonstrate—"makes it feel, I think, even bigger somehow."

"But . . . ?"

"Hmm. Not so much 'but' as 'and.' Retirement communities are the front porch of Heaven, you see. This is the last place I'll ever live. Oh, I may pop over to Shackleton and rattle their cages a bit. I may visit the chapel at Saint Joe's, to offer a prayer of thanks that my life has been such a fortunate one. I may poke my nose into the intrigues of cislunar space from time to time—one can't help wondering what the devil Igbal is up to, after all. And all the others. But I'll always come back here to lay my head down. I'll never sleep anywhere else. And, I don't know how else to say this, but one of those nights I'll be laying it down for the very last time. Right here.

"We spend our lives wondering where and how it will end for us. Hit by a car? Felled by a workplace heart attack? Murdered? But for me, now, today, there's no more mystery. Having survived a perilous journey, I've arrived at last in the place of my death. Which means, in a sense, I'm half dead already. Do you understand what I'm getting at?"

That was a lot to take in. Carefully, Raimy said, "You want me to go easier on the residents?"

"Not easier, no. No one likes being condescended to, particularly by someone with, well, a lot less life experience. But . . . how shall I put this? You're not their boss; they're yours. Here they are, thinking about death, and here you are telling them to be careful. Careful. Can you see how ironic that is?"

"I . . . suppose."

"Let this be the easiest job you've ever had, Raimy. Can you do that for me? Let people hang out in your office. Let people report their drippy faucets to you, and tell you their stories. Old people have lots and lots of stories, some quite amazing, and often no one to pass them down to. Can you be that brave for us?"

"Brave?"

"Soon there'll be a hundred residents here, and statistically speaking, one or two of them will expire almost immediately. And the rest of us, one by one, in the years that follow, and each of us replaced with another soul preparing to fly.

"So, I ask: Can you set aside all your urgencies and simply comfort the dying? You're a strong man, an accomplished man, the hero of Saint Joe's, just forty-five years old. Can you see? You remind us all of how we used to be, or wish we'd been, and of how we see ourselves even now."

They had reached the bottom of the path, where the concrete fanned out and then dropped away at the lip of the beach. Raimy jumped, and landed lightly in the sand.

"You want me to be their bartender," he said, turning around to look at Killian, who was making a face.

"Again, I fail to make myself properly understood."

Killian stepped forward gingerly, as though his bones might break, and put his slippered feet, one by one, into the sand of the beach he had dreamed and made real.

"Do you know, a decade ago I was still jumping out of aircraft? Still doing all sorts of things. But medical science can only do so much, eh?"

He bounced gently on his toes for a few seconds, and then said, "The actual bartender will arrive here in due time, along with the cleaning staff. I want . . . I'm hoping you can be something more than that. A friend? Is that . . . It's a lot to ask, I realize. A lot for you, a lot for anyone. But you've raced motorcycles. You've battled enemy submarines. You've walked on the Lunar surface wearing nothing but a plastic hood."

"I ran," Raimy corrected. "For my life."

"Precisely. You ran for your life. Everyone knows that story. Everyone who relocates here has heard it as part of the sales pitch, as if they didn't already know it from the news. Can you make these people feel as interesting as that? Can you, Raimy fucking Vaught, be a peer to these colonists? To me?"

Raimy didn't answer right away, and then found for a moment that he couldn't answer. Was this man, this trillionaire, one of the Four Horsemen of cislunar space, really asking to . . . hang out? Killian was widely regarded as the kindest of the Horsemen, and he was certainly the one with whom Raimy had the most in common— motorcycles and such. And, truth be told, Raimy had never been very good at making friends. He could do a lot worse.

On the other hand, Raimy was not an extrovert, and he held a natural disdain for one-sided, transactional relationships. He was easily bored, and had been suckered into this job on, perhaps, false pretenses.

On the other other hand, what else did he have going on? The various habitats in the SPMT had already learned what he had to teach them. He was traveling less. And yes, sure, there were going to be a hundred residents here at Second Dawn by the end of March, and twenty full-time staffers. Inevitably, there'd be accidents and lapses of judgment. There'd be fights and grudges and pranks, and missing items that might or might not have been stolen. Routine cop work. But how much of it, really? Enough to fill every hour of every day, all year long?

On the other other other hand, could he effectively police a population if he got too close to them personally? And on yet another hand, wasn't that the situation of every small-town cop, everywhere in the world?

He'd been silent for a long time. Too long.

"I've overstepped," Sir Lawrence said, with a mix of apology and regret. "A hazard of my position, I'm afraid. I am sorry if I've made you in any way uncomfortable."

"It isn't that," Raimy said. "Really, it's not. I was thinking about it. I fully realize I'm the help around here, and it's—"

"I retract the question, with apologies. Your job is hard enough without—"

"I'd be honored," Raimy said, and mostly meant it. If people wanted his friendship, well, probably he should give that a try. Probably he should.

Killian seemed embarrassed. "This never does get easier, I'm afraid, this business of finding someone you can talk to. It doesn't matter if you're old and rich, or something else entirely. I find we're all just beggars in the end."

3.10
31 October

I.R.V. *Intercession*
Extra-Kuiper Space
3,336 A.U. from Earth

It was not Ptolemy who woke Michael. Unfortunately, it was Sandy.

"You need to come," she said, shaking his arm.

"What's wrong?" he said, roused by the urgency of her tone.

"Unruly passenger," she said. "In the Bubble."

Uh-oh. If it was bad enough that she was waking people up to help deal with it, then it must be bad indeed.

"Coming," he said, undoing his sleeping straps. "Who is it?"

"I think his name is Bill."

Michael tried to think who that might be. Age? Origin? Occupation? He came up blank.

Launching himself down the ladder, he sailed through the service deck, caught a rung four meters into the cargo deck, and twisted through a ninety-degree turn. Another good kick and he was sailing through the hatchway and out into the Encounter Bubble, where he grabbed a cable to stop himself.

He saw the problem at once: a bald, bearded Caucasian male, approximately eighty kilograms of mostly muscle, was using the cross-cables like a set of uneven parallel bars: he swung around one of them once, twice, three times, and then flung himself toward another, on which he arrested himself so forcefully that the whole Bubble thumped with the impact. His face was purple with rage.

"I said stop!" Igbal was shouting. "I'm not going to tell you again!"

Harv and Dong were there as well, looking ready to intervene physically, but not really seeing an opening. Thenbecca wisely hung back, a white towel in her hand.

Sighing, Michael braced himself and did what had to be done. At the moment, he didn't care one whit who this gentleman was, or what exactly his problem might be, and he didn't have the time or patience to organize a coordinated group assault. So he pushed off a cable and threw himself, all fists and knees and elbows, directly into the man's path.

His skull immediately collided with something bony and pointed—possibly an elbow—but other parts of him connected as well. "Bill" grunted in angry pain, and Michael (sighing inwardly again) wrapped his arms and (with more difficulty, given the robe) his legs around Bill's body as forcefully as he could. It wasn't like fighting on Earth; momentum was absolute and inarguable. Bill had no way to keep Michael from grabbing him.

Bill of course began flailing and punching, but Michael had, mostly by luck, timed his jump and his grapple such that he was now on Bill's back. His head rang; his chest ached. Nerve bundles throughout his body began reporting in with bad news. But Bill was no longer in control of his own momentum; together they spun, bounced off a cable, and spun the other way.

And then Dong was there, grabbing Bill's leg with one hand and a cable with the other, and Harv—God bless him—was doing the same with one of Bill's arms. Which earned him an immediate punch from the other arm, but then Igbal grabbed that one, too, and old Bill was regally effed.

As melees went, this was rather a silly affair; Michael had kickboxed a little in college, very badly, and it didn't look like Harv had ever been in a fight at all. Dong was tougher, but small. Igbal was perhaps a little bit stronger than either of them, which wasn't saying much. But they knew zero gravity, and Bill did not, and so between the four of them they got him decisively restrained.

"I told her to give them back," Bill was saying. "Get off me. Get off me!"

"What's his problem?" Igbal asked no one in particular.

"Doesn't matter," Michael said. And then, because he had made such a point of preparing the crew for any contingency, he procured, from a hidden pocket in his robe, a contingency item of his own, that he'd gotten from Rachael: a hypodermic syringe.

He needed his hands at the moment, so he wrapped both of his legs around Bill's left—his only free appendage—and uncapped the needle with his teeth.

"Hold him," he said, unnecessarily, then braced one hand against Bill's back and jammed the needle in with the other.

"What are you doing?" Bill demanded as Michael pushed down the plunger. "Ow! Hey! What are you doing?"

"To help you relax," Michael said, as soothingly as he could manage with the cap still in his teeth. "Stop fighting. Just relax."

"She took my slippers," Bill said.

"Who did?" Michael asked.

"I don't know her."

"Well, that's fine," Michael told him, taking the cap out and gently placing it back over the needle. "We'll get it all sorted out. Right now I just need you to calm down and gather your thoughts."

He *would* try to get it sorted out, if only to make sure there wasn't a second troublemaker onboard.

"You fuckers had better let go," Bill said, with a noticeable slur.

The tension went out of his muscles then, and within about fifteen seconds he was off to la-la land.

"Jesus," Harv said.

Michael decided to let that name-in-vain go unremarked. Everyone relaxed, and Bill drifted free.

"Take him back to the hibernation bay," Michael said. "I don't care what set him off; this one is going right back in the freezer. He'll wake up on Earth."

Bill had clearly selected the emptiest portion of the Encounter Bubble for his gymnastics show, but during the scuffle Michael had become aware of red sleeping sacks and blue-clad passengers on the periphery, six meters to either side. The fight had had an audience, and a rather sizable one at that.

Michael watched as Igbal and Harv and Dong directed Bill's limp body back inside the hull of the ship. Thenbecca remained behind, holding her towel. Doing her best, Michael thought, to be a calming presence.

In a loud and pointed voice, he addressed the crowd: "Did none of you think to intervene?"

Thinking it over for a moment, he said, "Perhaps the chain of command is unclear. You are guests here, after all, with instructions to stay out of the way. That's my fault."

From the twenty or so visible people, he picked out the beefiest person: another Caucasian male with fiery copper hair pulled back in a net. He pointed, and said, "You, sir. What's your name?"

"Lars Onsanger," the man said at once. Michael had not yet met him; he was one of the ones awakened during the night. Probably still shaking off the chill, and gathering up his wits like scattered sticks. There would be others who knew more and understood more and were better accustomed to weightlessness. But Lars was the biggest person here—probably about as big as the hibernation pods could accommodate—and right now that would do.

Memorizing his features, Michael said, "Lars, I'm appointing you Chief Passenger. You're in charge of all passenger disputes, and the enforcement of safety and basic decency. If you encounter a problem that requires assistance from the crew, you are to come to me with it. Is that acceptable?"

Lars looked confused. "Um, who are you, again? You're apparently some kind of monk?"

"I am indeed," Michael said. "The ship's concierge can fill you in on my biography, but for the moment I only need to know whether you understand your assignment, and feel yourself capable of performing it. Yes? No?"

"That's fine," Lars said, still looking confused.

"Good," Michael said. Then, softening: "Appoint lieutenants and sergeants as you see fit. Such organization, even if haphazard, provides a structure for the mind and a balm for the soul. None of us have ever done this before, and so there are no traditions to fall back on. We're absurdly far from home; we have, literally, only each other."

No one said anything.

Someone coughed.

"I have businesses elsewhere," he said then, because he really needed to pee, "but sometime later today, I will assist with a group meditation, for anyone who feels the need. It's Halloween, by the way, if anyone cares."

He then gestured at the empty space around him. "The population void in this part of the Bubble is going to be filled today. This time tomorrow, we'll have woken everyone up, and our real work can begin. Try to think about that."

And then, with a dozen questions in the air, he fled to empty his bladder.

Michael wolfed down a quick MRE breakfast and got back to work. Hobie was out of commission now, rolled up tight in his bunk, and Dr. Rachael was again in charge of the awakenings. By now the procedure was quite routine, which (as Michael knew from long experience) actually increased the chances of error. So he watched her closely, and twice reminded her of a step she was skipping. But mostly it all went very smoothly, and soon enough the next batch of passengers was ready for the Bubble.

Fortunately, there was now a formal structure into which they could be introduced, so he simply brought them out to the Bubble and let the passengers themselves handle all the rest.

This was partly a source of worry, because it was nearly certain they would farble up some aspect or another. But mostly it was a relief.

For a while, he shuttled back and forth between the Encounter Bubble and the hibernation bay, until he found the time to make good on his group meditation promise.

Twenty-six passengers accepted the invitation, and so they briefly took over a ninety-degree wedge of the Bubble.

"Just float," he advised them. "It's okay if you gently bump into things, or each other. It's okay if your attention wanders. The truth is, everyone is bad at meditation. Does anyone here have experience with it?"

Fifteen hands went up.

"Well, then this will be more of a practice than a learning experience. I find zero gravity helps quite a bit. Just let your bodies relax into a loose fetal position. Good, yes, and close your eyes. We're going to breathe, in and out."

It was actually rather loud in here; the thirty passengers who were not meditating were mostly awake and talking, and the sound carried around in both directions, effectively doubling the chatter, so the

Bubble sounded more like a crowded cafeteria than a spaceship in the deep void. But the weightlessness was indeed relaxing, and anyway these people needed something on which to focus their attention. So he led them through some breathing and a body scan, and promised another round at bedtime.

Meditation was a kind of prayer, and he would have actually prayed with anyone who asked, albeit discreetly, so as not to discomfit the irreligious. But no one did ask—the previous query was not repeated—and that was fine. The role of the Church in outer space was not so much to convert nonbelievers as to be a visible part of the useful infrastructure, and let the rest take care of itself.

He did field two requests to send messages back home, which he regretfully declined.

"We have bandwidth enough for only the most critical communications, alas, and we've security concerns on top of that. However, the good news is that from your own subjective points of view, you'll be back home in just a few days' time. Another year for your sweetheart, yes, I know. But if she loves you as much as your eyes convey, then her patience will not exhaust over so brief a span."

Also, via Lars Onsanger, a consensus request from the passengers, that the temperature in the Bubble be raised by one degree.

"That I can do," Michael said, for such an expenditure of energy was absurdly trivial against the forces required to propel a starship. A hundred nanograms of antimatter, perhaps, among all the five tons of it yet to be consumed?

And then it was time to start dealing, again, with groggy, cranky, wakers-up. The same questions, over and over, met by the same answers. But a monk like Michael was nothing if not patient, and it pleased him to be useful.

Michael was keenly aware that the crew of *Intercession* was now greatly outnumbered by passengers who weren't particularly happy. It reminded him of the worst days of air travel, when airlines would pack as many people onto a plane as would physically fit, hand them a can of sugar water, refuse to answer the call light, and exhort those who dared flex their clotting limbs or queue up outside the washroom.

And Michael, like a flight attendant of old, was first in line to receive their ire, despite having nothing to do with the corporate planning that gave rise to it.

But God and the Pope and Igbal Renz had placed him in this position, with his own enthusiastic consent, and so he did his best to radiate a calm enthusiasm into the crowd. And maybe that worked, or maybe it was Thenbecca's relentless cheerfulness, or Harv's professorial curiosity, or the enigmatic presence of Igbal, moving through the maze of webbing and sleep sacks like a politician. Or maybe everyone just started to really think about why they were here.

In any event, regardless of the trigger, something shifted in the crowd at a certain point during the late evening. Michael felt it almost as a breath of fresh, unfiltered air. Gone, suddenly, were the moping, the griping, the jostling for space. A kind of electricity was building, even among the newly awakened. Or maybe the Beings themselves had something to do with it, for the possibility of failure suddenly seemed quite remote. The humans were out here by invitation, and every present soul would participate in this communion, where two branches of the universal family could at last come together.

"Speech!" someone in the crowd called out to Igbal.

"Speech!" seconded another voice.

And then the whole crowd—even the people on the far side of the Bubble, obscured by the hull of the starship—was chanting it.

Laughing, Igbal fished a headset out of one of his pockets, placed it over his head, aligned the mic beside the corner of his mouth, pressed a couple of buttons on the earpiece, and said, "Testing."

The word issued forth from every loudspeaker on the ship, and rang throughout the Encounter Bubble. The crowd cheered.

"We don't even have everyone awake yet!" Igbal protested.

"Speech!" someone in the crowd insisted.

"Michael," Igbal said, "how many people do we have still in the hibernation pods?"

"Twelve!" Michael called back, for he was separated from Igbal by fifteen meters of jabbering humanity. "Eighty passengers awake."

"Well, then," Igbal said, "we should have a speech in eight hours."

"Actually, five and a half." Michael called back. The next batch of Popsicles was already thawed to room temperature and would soon be starting to regain their faculties.

"Well," Igbal said, "we have to sleep sometime. We'll have a speech in the morning, after breakfast."

A few voices booed, and soon much of the crowd was joining them.

"Whoa," Igbal said. "You want to pitch twelve people under the train? Have a speech without them?"

"Yes!" someone said.

"Speech!" someone else said.

And then the crowd was chanting it again.

"All right," Igbal said. "Okay. Seems like the rabble is already roused. Look, we're out here for a party."

An even louder cheer went up.

"Not . . . no, keep your pants on—there's no booze or cannabis here. It's a party at the neighbors' house, whom we've never met. I want each of you—I want all of you—to . . . Well, actually, we *are* taking drugs for this, right?"

Another cheer.

"Look, this is going to be very different from any experience any of us has ever had. We need to keep one eye on what's happening around us, and one eye on the future. Because the future . . . posterity is going to care very much what we have to say about this. We need to be good guests, good emissaries, good scientists, good interrogators, good witnesses . . . I'm not kidding about this; we have one shot, and then it's back to the freezers and back home to Earth."

The crowd had gone silent, and they stayed that way for several seconds, until Igbal continued, "We don't know very much about the Beings. Well, Michael thinks we do, but Michael also thinks we know how the universe was created, and why. I'll let him give the speech tomorrow, but please, take everything he says with a teaspoon of salt. Be skeptical of me, too. Be skeptical about everything, no matter who says it, and especially be skeptical of your own preconceptions. Try to come into this with your minds as wide open as you can.

"At the same time, please, try . . . uh, not to lose track of yourself. The drug cocktail we're taking is serious shit. It's going to open your mind for you, but it's also going to mess with your perceptions of time and space. It's going to let you access a realm outside of our limited, four-dimensional perceptions. That outer realm is objectively real, and the wiring of our brains includes features to access it. The spirit world, whatever you want to call it. It's where the Beings exist, or at least it's a layer of the universe where they're able to meet us halfway, or shout down the chimney at us. But it's confusing! You're going to be confused! Put a scuba helmet on an ant and drop her on a coral reef, and she's not half as confused as you're going to be. So please, get over it now. When the time comes, if you spend all your mental energy focusing on the reef and the currents and the bubbles, then you're wasting your place in history, not to mention the twenty billion dollars per body that it cost to haul us all out here.

"I wish . . . God, in retrospect, I wish you'd all had a training program in dealing with psychedelics. Sounds obvious now, right? But here we are. You guys are my guys. You gals are my gals, hand-picked, by me. Every one of you is amazing at something, and now I'm asking you, please, be amazing at this, too. Amaze me. Amaze history.

"There will be a medical doctor standing by. Her name is Rachael Lee. She's the one who woke most of you up, and I think she put some of you into hibernation in the first place. She will be taking a special formulation of the drug—basically just pure DMT—that wears off after about fifteen minutes, maybe twenty. So she'll be available quickly to treat any genuine medical problems. Freakouts do not count, okay? Please, don't embarrass me, or yourself, by freaking out. The drugs in our cocktail are well tolerated, so genuine medical problems are pretty unlikely. Maybe a panic attack here or there, but seriously, try to keep your shit together.

"Now, I also want to welcome you here. Probably should have started with that. All of you are risk-takers and early adopters, and I want to thank you for saying yes to this. All of you are paying a high personal cost—some higher than others—and I certainly hope history will remember that as well. Meanwhile, pat yourselves on the back. Hell, pat each other.

"On a different subject, please remember that the wall of the Encounter Bubble is about as thick as five playing cards, and on the other side of it is hard vacuum. We already sent one person back into hibernation for screwing around. Don't make that happen to you as well.

"You may have a hard time sleeping tonight; I know I will. But try not to keep each other awake. Try not to bother the crew. If you can't sleep, meditate. If you can't meditate, float quietly in your bag. Be a hero, not a jerk."

He trailed off, then, and was silent for several seconds. Finally, he said, "Well, maybe that's all."

And then he turned and left without another word.

The crowd cheered him out.

4.5
31 October

✧

ESL1 Shade Station
Earth-Sun Lagrange Point 1
Extracislunar Space

"It is both beautiful and stultifying," Maag said, to no one in particular.

Alice wasn't entirely sure what "stultifying" even meant, but decided to grunt an agreement anyway.

In the womblike, red-lit weightlessness of the radar room, Alice and Maag floated with their arms loosely around each other's shoulders, looking out the porthole at an approaching ion ferry, with the little Earth and Moon hanging silently in the background. Maag was lightly holding a grab bar on the wall, letting Alice float free.

"I like the purple," said Jeanette Schmidt, clearly referring to the color of the ion engines' exhaust.

"Actually a bit more of a mauve, I think," said Isaiah Pembroke. "Like feptaual."

After studying the color for a few moments, Alice decided he was right. Feptaual was an alloy Jeanette had recently invented: a funny gray-purple mix of gold and platinum and iron and aluminum. "Good wear resistance for sliding parts," she'd said. "I wish we had it when we were building the spin decoupler."

Isaiah had lately been wearing a bracelet made of the stuff, and Alice thought there must be a story behind that.

Jeanette and Isaiah were also arm in arm, and also looking out the porthole. And yes, Alice had a hand on Jeanette (though not in "that" way), and Isaiah had one on Maag. The four of them were arranged head-to-head, their eight-total legs spreading out radially like the spokes of a wheel, though contacting the wall of the radar room on one side. It was one of those geometries that made perfect sense in zero-gee, allowing four people to look out the same small window.

"Mauve," Jeanette said. "Yes, that's exactly right."

The ferry was fifty meters out, and moving slowly, and slowing down even more slowly. If the pilot, Charisse Ulmer, had any sense, she'd shut down the ion engines and guide the ship in with her attitude control thrusters, which burned hydrazine chemical propellant and thus had a lot more kick. Also cheaper than wasting xenon like this. But like a lot of pilots (first and foremost, the departed Derek Haakens), Charisse liked to show off.

"Thank you, love," Isaiah said to Jeanette.

Love? Okay, wow, that was new. Romantically speaking, Alice had always seen Jeanette as a bit of a runner—she'd run all the way to ESL1, after all, leaving behind a string of ex-boyfriends. Similarly, when Isaiah first got here, Alice had seen him as a play-the-field type, and also a bit immature for someone like Jeanette. However, to her surprise, the two of them had lasted not only past the first month, but also through the summer solstice and Jeanette's birthday, and now they'd been together for six months. Amazing.

"It looks like the sign outside a whorehouse I know in Amsterdam," Maag opined, and presently she gave Alice's shoulders an intimate little squeeze. Alice returned it.

Alice and Maag were not in love, exactly. It was more like, having shared men in the past, and having agreed there were no decent men available on the station at the moment, they'd decided one day to cut out the (literal) middleman and simply share each other for a while. It wasn't even a gay thing, exactly, or at least not often. And Alice was confident they'd stick a man back between them again at some point, but for now they had each other, and it was fine.

"We'd better get to the docking module," Maag said.

"Soon," Alice said. For some reason, she was really enjoying this particular moment in time, and was reluctant to let it go any sooner than necessary. And, thinking about it now, she was also enjoying the thought of six new colonists—some with no prior space experience—floating into the zero-gee part of the station with no one there to greet them, and wondering what the fuck was going on. But that would be bad leadership indeed, so she disengaged her arms from Maag and Jeanette, and prepared to head down there ahead of the ferry.

"There's going to be a lot of barf," Jeanette observed. The new colonists—three women and three men—would have adapted to weightlessness back on Transit Point Station, back in low Earth orbit, and to some extent on the ferry itself, although they'd've spent the majority of the trip in squirrel hibernation, strapped to the walls. But in one of the great ironies of life at ESL1, it was actually a lot harder to adapt to spin-gee than to zero-gee. Alice herself had taken almost two months, and while she was (annoyingly) an outlier, Jeanette was definitely right. There was going to be a lot of barf.

But Alice had been a medic before she was an astronaut, and both professions involved a lot of management of loose bodily fluids, so she said, "It's going to be fine, and these people are going to make us a lot of money."

Alice shuddered to hear herself say this. She was Special Forces, not some hack in a business suit! But Igbal and Sandy had been gone for a year, and nobody they'd left behind knew quite how to get the new flutter drive working. Built, yes. Operational . . . no, not quite. And since the consequences of failure would be a hundred times worse than a backpack nuke, Alice had erred on the side of caution, and hired in six expensive experts who, at least in combination, were likely able to seal the deal.

And, you know, it was exciting. The new flutter-drive ship, the H.S.F. *Comet*, would be able to push a hundred tons of cargo—or people—to Jupiter in just twenty days. It was what people like Bob Rojas called a "game changer," and it would put ESL1 back on the evening news, as something other than a target for nukes.

As the four of them disentangled and started drifting toward the hatch, Isaiah said to Alice, "Hey, did you ask corporate about my energy proposal?"

"I did," Alice said, not bothering to point out that, as Vice President of Space Operations, she herself was part of "corporate."

"And?" His eyes glittered brown as the red lights of the radar room gave way to the white ones of the Cross. His bracelet, yes, glittered almost the exact color of xenon ion exhaust. Though it bordered on a "girly" pink, it had enough blue and gray in it to land on something that looked surprisingly rugged against his brown skin.

"Still waiting," Alice said. "It would help if you put some dollar signs in your proposal, instead of just gigajoules."

Isaiah had gotten a squirrel up his rectum about using his EMP weapon to tight-beam microwave power down into cislunar space on a contract basis. It wasn't clear to Alice who needed that, or how much they might be willing to pay, but since the equipment was already in place and (literally) battle tested, she didn't see any harm in trying.

"Hey, how are they doing up on *Intercession*?" Jeanette asked, as the four of them swarmed through the Cross and the spin decoupler.

"Fine, last I heard. By now they've arrived, and they're . . ."

She couldn't complete the sentence. At their nonexistent destination? About to commune with the Beings? She frankly had no idea what was going to happen up there, and after a year of dealing with hard problems in the real world, she had trouble mentally connecting to even the idea of the Beings. Were they real? Would they speak? Would it matter if they did? It was just like Igbal to focus his energies—and those of the whole company—on something so . . . speculative.

"They're fine," she said, finally.

While they coasted through the decommissioned hab module and the gamma corridor of the old station, Jeanette said, "We should build Igbal a spacesuit out of gold and platinum, to surprise him when he gets back. Or feptaual. Or blue iron."

"Or all of the above," Isaiah said. "Big gaudy fucking thing."

Alice couldn't tell if Isaiah was being ironic or not. Igbal was not big on flashy clothes, or flashiness in general, but he was a huge fucking nerd, and would probably love it from a metallurgy standpoint alone.

Jeanette had been going kind of crazy lately with the metallurgy, after working out a new process to extract noble metals from the station's mining slag. Not because they were valuable per se; antimatter was worth a billion times more, and anyway the costs of moving precious metals around vastly exceeded their market price. Also not because they resisted oxidation; there was no oxygen in space. But gold was ductile, and a good reflector of infrared, and it alloyed surprisingly well with other metals. And platinum was tough, and silver was a great conductor. Or so Jeanette had said. Every part of the buffalo.

So her "blue iron" was iron with gold and platinum in it, and it really was shockingly blue, more like the paint job on a car than any actual metal Alice had ever seen. She'd also come up with platinum steel (white), aluminum bronze (pale red), and a bunch of other stuff that was easy to make in a zero-gee foundry. The thought of making a spacesuit out of all that was . . . well, Alice wanted to hate the idea, but not nearly as much as she wanted (God help her) to see that spacesuit.

"Igbal would love that," she admitted, as they drifted from gamma corridor to alpha corridor.

And then they were at the docking module.

Pelu Figueroa was already there. At Alice's quizzical look, Pelu shrugged and said, "Fresh coffee on that boat. Not enough to go around."

"Ah," Alice said.

"And hot sauce from Bolivia," Pelu said, now somewhat conspiratorially.

"Bolivia? Really?" Alice said, thinking more about the shipping cost than the taste.

"Oh, stop it," Pelu chided. "We're not exactly destitute up here."

The docking hatch thumped lightly, then banged and clattered open, revealing the interior of the ion ferry, crowded with people in bright, new jumpsuits of RzVz blue.

And then, as though they'd rehearsed it, everyone around Alice said, at the same time: "Welcome to ESL1!"

1.16

Post-Encounter Deposition
Matt Lang, PhD
U.S. National Aeronautics and
Space Administration

Never again. It was like being locked in a coffin full of spiders.

5.5
31 October

Thalia Buoyant Island
Southern Stratosphere
Venus

Almost the whole village was gathered outside, in hats and kaftans, masks and gloves. The cloud deck was high today, only a few hundred meters below the bottom of the island, and the air was technically too acidic for anything but brief exposure, or spacesuits.

But nobody cared. Everyone was looking up, trying to spot an orange dot in the vastness of the blue Venusian sky.

"I'm very proud of you, guy," Julian said to Frédéric, over the murmur of the crowd.

"I'd wait for a safe landing before you start celebrating," Frédéric said.

Julian waved a dismissive hand. "I don't care about that. We have all we need here. Anything extra is . . . extra. Let me be proud of you, okay? You're a doer. You saw something you could do, for yourself and the people around you, and you did it. That's how your mother and I started our company back in Colombia, and that's how we sold it to move to another planet."

Frédéric's mother, on Julian's other side, added, "You come from a long line of doers, little Frito. You make us both proud."

"Thank you," Frédéric said. Nothing more; he was both genuinely touched by this show of support, and also afraid of spoiling the video he was shooting. It wasn't supposed to be about *him*; it was about this big, important day in the life of the island. If people were ever going to move here for real, they needed to feel immersed in the place itself. They needed to understand that it was as physically and emotionally real as their own hometowns.

Pointing his tablet at the sky again, Frédéric held a hand up on the left side of it, to shield the camera from glare. The days were longer than ever now—a hundred hours, give or take, and it was a matter of some debate which was worse: the daylight or the darkness. But either way, right now Thalia's long night was over; the Sun was up above the cloud horizon, strong enough for the optical sensors on the landing package to look down and see, hopefully, against the white of the clouds, a gray speck of alien matter. The island.

"I see it!" Juanetta called out, pointing a finger into the sky.

Frédéric reoriented the tablet toward where she was pointing, but did not immediately see anything. Then, taking his face away from the screen and simply looking up, he did see it: the orange and white pie wedges of a tiny parachute, high up in the sky.

"Can you see this?" he asked his joiners rhetorically. "This is something *you* did. Not me; all I did was ask for help. All of you made this possible, with money and time and . . . enthusiasm. So much enthusiasm! When I first met you all I was in a low place, trapped on this island, and trapped in my own head. You all showed me that Venus is part of the world, not separate from it. You showed me that I could reach out. There was a place to reach out to."

Frédéric had prepared a speech for this occasion, but it had fled right out of his mind, and he was now winging it, taking whatever nonsense occurred to him and sending it directly to his vocal cords. He hoped it would make sense later, but he knew it didn't really matter. His joiners were pretty forgiving, and the few who were not, he happily unjoined.

"I can see the package now," he said. "I don't know if you can see this, but there's a little dot underneath that parachute. That's our landing craft. That's a ton of structure and four tons of cargo. This island, everything you see here, grew from a seed not much bigger than that. Actually, only ten times the size of that, so try and imagine what a big difference four more tons could make around here. Five more!"

Under pressure from Tohias, Frédéric had relented and let the adults of Thalia vote on what supplies were most needed. It ended up being mostly a lot of titanium and copper, and a few kilograms of rare earth metals that simply could not be obtained here. Other than that, there were a few complete machines, another surgical tube, fifty kilograms of assorted seeds, some useful electronics, and a handful of specialty chemicals that Tohias had never figured out how to synthesize. Plus the structure of the lander itself, which was mostly aluminum and tungsten that would be stripped and melted and put to good use.

Even the parachute—real silk, barfed out by Chinese caterpillars—had properties no Venusian material could match. There were no actual luxury items, though, because what good would that do, to get a fleeting taste of chocolate or cognac and then run out again? Or so Tohias had insisted. Now there was some good, solid adult thinking.

However, Frédéric had non-negotiably set aside ten kilograms for himself, for a new tablet computer, a *backup* tablet computer, some backup batteries, a camera tripod, some lights and reflectors and microphones, and a pop-up green screen he could assemble anywhere. If his network content had gotten him this far, then even better network content had the potential to get them even further, right? Much of that stuff, or some inferior version of it, could technically be manufactured here on Thalia (especially now), but he did not trust sixty-six percent of the council—i.e., of the voting population of the island—to see it that way and ever allocate the resources.

Also, since there was an entire empty apartment building waiting for new colonists to come and colonize, Frédéric had quietly allocated one of the empty storage rooms to serve as his recording and editing studio. By the time anyone caught onto him, he hoped Thalia's online presence would be seen as a critical resource, every bit as important as the trawler or the photovoltaic array.

Nearby, Basilio del Campo—Juanetta's father—was cradling his wife, Noemi. Tohias was cradling his own wife, Candide, and his son, Tabor, who was five years Frédéric's junior. Julian was cradling Wilma. Everyone was cradling everyone, and Frédéric was surprised that Juanetta hadn't seized the opportunity to seize *him*. She seemed too wrapped up in the landing itself.

Almost jealously, he moved behind her and said, "Big day for you?"

"For all of us," she said, without turning around. "I counted up all the metal on the island, and do you know what I came up with? Three thousand, four hundred kilograms. Can our standard of living be measured that way? If so, it's about to double. We're going to have a surplus, for the first time ever."

You're welcome, Frédéric thought but did not say. It was just like Juanetta, to not acknowledge him at a moment like this. But he supposed maybe it was a good thing, that she was thinking about the future and the island, and not scheming a way to make him hold her hand.

Stepping forward, he reached out and held hers. The landing package was now big enough and close enough to be clearly visible on the tablet's screen, and he could aim the camera well enough with only his left hand.

"Is that a rocket engine?" she asked suddenly, for the lander had begun to belch flame, not only from its bottom, but also from one side.

"There should be several on the lander," Frédéric confirmed.

"Won't that set fire to the *carbónespuma*?" she asked, sounding alarmed.

"The engineers say not. Anyway, I think it's just centering itself over the landing pad. The parachute's what will actually bring it down."

A thing that seemed suddenly imminent; the lander was now visible as a contraption of legs and springs and circular feet, with a sort of barrel on top that held all the cargo. Just exactly like the CAD drawings the engineers had sent him. And even though its terminal velocity was much lower than it would have been on Earth, it was still coming down faster than a person could walk.

"Are you seeing this?" Frédéric asked his joiners again. "You probably can't feel the excitement in the air here, but I will tell you, nothing like this has ever happened to us before. Look! Look, there it is, a thing manufactured on Earth and flung across the heavens, because one young man asked nicely. Incredible!"

And then the lander was below the level of the radio tower, and then below the tops of the greenhouse domes and the apartment buildings. And then with a gentle thump it was down—really down—and a circular ripple expanded through the *carbónespuma* beneath everyone's feet, firmly marking the occasion.

"Earth and Venus are one people," Frédéric said, and cut the video.

3.11
01 November

✧

I.R.V. *Intercession*
Extra-Kuiper Space
3,336 A.U. from Earth

Harv slept poorly that night. He often slept poorly, so that was no surprise, but this was no ordinary night. No, this was more like the night before he fried his brain in a neuro-quantum time machine. It was so much like that night, twelve years and a lifetime ago, that he couldn't help replaying those events in his mind. It had all made sense, right? It was something he had to do, right? The results had been amazing, right? And yet, the experience had broken his career and his personal life, and left him absent-minded and prone to headaches. And a laughingstock, too, as he had no ironclad way to prove he'd sent his consciousness backward in time.

And here he was again, about to subject his brain to unnatural stimuli in hopes of gaining arcane knowledge of he-knew-not-what. Some people never learn.

Could he back out? Yes. It was in his contract. Would he? No way. It wasn't in his nature. But, once bitten and twice shy, he at least had the good sense to be nervous about it. Very.

Thenbecca spent the night drifting, untethered, within the confines of her closed cabin. She'd been apprehensive about going to space the first time, and apprehensive about launching on a starship powered by ten tons of antimatter. And she was apprehensive now.

There was no way to work off the tension on the dead-quiet ship, so she put the lights down to their lowest setting and simply floated, banging gently into the walls and ceiling and padded bunk, sometimes singing in whispers, sometimes praying, sometimes reciting recipes in her mind.

Would she be changed by what was about to happen? Would the changes be for the better? She didn't know, and couldn't know, and so she drifted, until—after a long time—a light sleep finally settled over her.

Michael was generally a good sleeper, but even he had trouble.

Finally, it was time. Michael exited his cabin and poked a head into the Encounter Bubble, where it seemed nearly everyone was out of their sleep sacks already. As he hovered silently by, those who were still cocooned, and who weren't awakened by the activity around them, were gently shaken awake by their fellow passengers.

"Wake up!" they said. "Wake up and make history!"

It was 4:55 a.m.

Michael returned to the crew quarters to find Harv and Hobie both opening their rollup doors and peeking out.

That noise prompted Thenbecca, who opened her door and said, "Oh, thank God. I've been awake a long time."

That got Igbal and Rachael up, and soon Dong followed suit. Meaning everyone was up except Sandy.

"I think she might actually be asleep," Igbal said with some amazement.

"Should we wake her?" Rachael asked. Rachael, who had gotten a total of perhaps eight hours of sleep over the past two days, but looked as wired-fresh as she ever had.

"Let her sleep," Igbal said. "Let's get everyone fed, and do what we came here for."

Breakfast was light—a granola bar, a pouch of synthetic, non-dairy "yogurt," and a pouch of that century-old astronaut favorite, Tang. All easy to digest and not much of any of it, so that in an hour everyone's stomachs would be basically empty again, though with stabilized blood sugar. Sandy woke up toward the end of it, and ate and drank in hasty silence.

In the Bubble, people were careless with their crumbs and trash, prompting Michael to scold: "Listen, the crew's got better things to do than clean up after you lot. I want this place spotless, and I think it isn't much to ask."

And then it was really time. Igbal took a big plastic case out of storage, and each crew member grabbed two big handfuls of vape pens and started passing them out to the passengers.

"Don't puff on it until you're told!" Michael called out to several miscreants. He supposed it didn't actually matter whether they all dropped into the spirit world at exactly the same moment, but it was one of the few things Igbal had concretely planned, and Michael thought he deserved that much, after bringing them all here like Nerd Moses.

But then everybody had a vape pen in hand, including Michael himself, and he found he was a lot more nervous than he'd expected. Some of the things people said about psychedelic drugs were flatly terrifying, after all, and Michael did not particularly want to "spend years drifting in a peaceful void" or any such thing. For that matter, he wasn't entirely sure he wanted to meet the Beings, on their terms or any other. Such a life-altering prospect was the very biggest of deals, not to be entered into lightly. But on the other hand, he did want to, very much, for they were also God's children. How much did they know, that humanity could only guess at?

"Speech!" people in the crowd began to say. But this time they were looking at Michael, for Igbal had promised them he would say a few words.

He foolishly hadn't prepared any, but he held up his hands now and cleared his throat.

"Ladies and gentlemen and others, we find ourselves on the precipice of discovery, and I, for one, find the step ahead of us more daunting than I had supposed years ago, when I first agreed to take part. We do not know what great or terrible or wonderful things may await us on the other side, and there is no shame in backing out now. Indeed, we may have reason to be grateful if a few of you do exactly that."

"Fat chance!" said someone from the crowd, provoking scattered, nervous laughter.

"In public I don't speak often of God," Michael said, "as many people find this off-putting, not least because His name has been invoked to justify innumerable atrocities. But I'll invoke it now, to remind you all how improbable it is, for a universe to exist that contains this moment, and all of us, within it. If you don't mark this as evidence of a loving creator, then perhaps at least mark it as your own great good fortune."

He paused there, and though he might have said more, a scattered clapping broke out, and then a sort of sigh ran through the crowd, like a breeze that swept away the smell of fear.

"Igbal," Michael said, turning to find him almost eclipsed by the hull of the ship. "Would you like to count us down?"

Smiling, Igbal said, "Aw, hell. Puff 'em dry, everyone. Go! Go!"

And then some people were lifting the vape pens to their lips, and some were laughing too hard to puff, and Michael, who had never ingested any drug stronger than wine, took a long drag, held it, exhaled, and then—before he could lose his nerve—drew deeply from the pen once again.

And the universe, for better or worse, was changed forever.

1.17

Post-Encounter Deposition
Igbal Renz, Founder and CEO
Renz Ventures

So, yeah, this wasn't a charity expedition. Well, I guess it was, if we were the charity cases. My point is, we were not there for some generic betterment of mankind. Well, okay, that's not true, either. First contact with intelligent beings happened the moment we started building the really creepy AIs, but the first contact with extraterrestrials . . . that's a big event, for all of us. It tells us something very profound about the universe, and our place in it. But my point is, I spent two trillion dollars of my own money to get a hundred people out there, and I fully expected to make that money back. At *least* break even, you know what I'm saying?

Call it arrogance, but I was the first person—let's say, the first serious person—to realize the Beings were real. Not just club-drug hallucinations, but actual organisms of some kind, who were trying to make contact through the parts of our brains we don't normally access when we're conscious, or even asleep. It was the God module they were talking to, with specific activation patterns of the right temporal lobe. I made a science of that, years ago, and so what if people laughed at me for it?

Point is, it was me, my mind, they had the most experience connecting to, and I had the most experience connecting to them as well. I had ninety-nine other points of view out there at the Encounter zone, because I'm not dumb enough to believe I can think of everything we might need to ask them about. But it was me who taught them to speak at all.

So yeah, I went out there armed with seven very specific questions. It isn't easy to keep your mind on specifics when you're twisted on DMT, but I had a lot of practice at that, too. To the extent it's a learnable skill, I had certainly put in my time. Several hundred hours at least, which is a lot of psychedelics, trust me. I was a world expert at keeping my shit together and staying focused in the spirit realm.

The recipe (also mine) was a DMT inhalant to enable the Beings to reach us at all, plus a touch of ketamine to extend and cushion the high, a touch of MDMA to ease us down gently, a fair bit of galantamine to help us remember the experience, plus ethanol as a solvent, and modafinil to counteract the effects of the ethanol. All that, packed into a disposable vape pen that even an idiot could use correctly on the first try, which was a project unto itself. In terms of making contact, the success rate was one hundred percent, so you're welcome, history. I did that. Me.

Question #1 was related to the stars within one hundred light-years of the solar system. Question #2 was about the structure of the universe. Number three was about one of our failed star-drive designs, and why it behaved the way it did. Four: The nature of consciousness. Five: Speed of light. Six: Black holes. Seven: Time.

It wasn't easy, but I received answers to each of these questions, or at least information related to them. People will of course call me crazy—when have they not?—but I'm under no obligation to reveal any of it, even to my own employees. I'm an unreasonable guy, and if I die, it dies with me. Poof!

Why? Well, we're talking about very highly proprietary information, here, and a strategic advantage no other enterprise can touch. Renz Ventures was already the tech leader in cislunar space, by a significant margin, but now I have something even more profound than technology. I'll give a hint, here, so you have some idea what I'm talking about. Among many other things, we're going to build a special telescope, designed to measure the circumferences of very large circles. There's information to be gained that way, of commercial value. I'm tempted to say "incalculable value," but I actually have calculated it, and it's big. Even by trillionaire standards, big.

So yeah, nobody's getting murdered or blackmailed over this. Nobody's defecting to the Cartels with a fucking thumb drive in their stomach. It stays in my head, and nobody knows a thing about it until we start cranking out . . . let's say, innovations.

And then we'll see who's crazy, right?

Appendix A
Dramatis Personae, in order of appearance:

Boris Kotov—Astronomer, Clementine Cislunar Fuel Depot.

Grigory Magnusevich Orlov—Founder and CEO of Clementine Cislunar Fuel Depot. CEO of Orlov Petrochemical, founded by his father, Magnus Orlov. One of the Four Horsemen.

Igbal Renz—Founder and CEO of Renz Ventures. One of the Four Horsemen. Currently serving as captain of I.R.V. *Intercession.*

Sandy Lincoln—Physicist and inventor of the flutter drive. Currently serving as Engineering Officer for I.R.V. *Intercession.*

Ptolemy—Concierge module for I.R.V. *Intercession.*

Brother Michael Jablonski—Former Prior, St. Joseph of Cupertino Monastery, Lunar South Polar Mineral Territories. Currently the Chaplain and Recycling Systems Officer for I.R.V. *Intercession.*

Alice Kyeong—Interim Station Commander, ESL1 Shade Station. Vice President of Space Operations, Renz Ventures. Secretly, a Major in the U.S. Air Force. Call sign "Mockingbird."

Yuehai Ming—RzVz astronaut and space colonist.

Malagrite Aagesen ("Maag")—RzVz Space colonist. Chemical engineer and manufacturing process specialist.

Isaiah Pembroke—Senior Radar Systems Engineer for Renz Ventures.

Derek Haakens—Pilot for Renz Ventures, based at ESL1 Shade Station. Call sign "Falcon."

Rose Ketchum—Astronaut specializing in zero-gravity welding for Renz Ventures. Stationed at ESL1. Call sign "Romper."

Tim Ho—Astronaut, machinist, and sniper for Renz Ventures. Stationed at ESL1. Call sign "TicTac."

Bob Rojas—Chief Financial Officer for Renz Ventures.

Harv Leonel—Former "time traveler," currently the Information Officer for I.R.V. *Intercession*.

Hobie Prieto—Helmsman for I.R.V. *Intercession*.

Thenbecca Jungermann—Chef/Purser for I.R.V. *Intercession*.

Dong Nguyen—Maintenance Officer for I.R.V. *Intercession*.

Rachael Lee, M.D.—Flight Surgeon for I.R.V. *Intercession*.

Frédéric Ortega—Student onboard Thalia Buoyant Island, Venus.

Julian Ortega—Senior trawlerman for Thalia Bouyant Island. Father of Frédéric.

Basilio del Campo—Trawlerman for Thalia Bouyant Island.

Diego Nunez-Talamantes—Trawlerman for Thalia Bouyant Island.

Tohias Nunez-Talamantes—Mayor of Thalia Bouyant Island, and the "Fifth Horseman" or "Spanish Horseman" responsible for the colonization of Venus. Father of Diego.

Evelyn Chang, PhD—Department of Mathematics, Massachusetts Institute of Technology. Passenger aboard I.R.V. *Intercession*.

Pelu Figueroa—RzVz space colonist at ESL1.

Sienna Delao—RzVz astronaut and space colonist.

Zeta—Concierge module for ESL1 Shade Station II.

Archie Carter, PhD—School of Physics, University of Bristol. Passenger aboard I.R.V. *Intercession*.

Mitchell T. Sprague, PhD—Department of Economics, New York University. Passenger aboard I.R.V. *Intercession*.

Berka Feikey, M.D.—Chief Medical Officer at ESL1. Call sign "Nightingale."

Selita Harris, PhD—Department of Music, Stanford University. Passenger aboard I.R.V. *Intercession*.

Dona Obata—Former covert operative, currently serving as Commander of Clementine Cislunar Fuel Depot. Girlfriend of Grigory Orlov.

Sally Grigorieva Orlova—Daughter of Grigory.

Aram Schiller, MSCS—Deputy Chief Technology Officer, Searchable Logic Corporation. Passenger aboard I.R.V. *Intercession.*

Jia Cheng—User of the Weightless social network.

Wilma Ortega—Horticulturist for Thalia Buoyant Island. Mother of Frédéric and wife of Julian.

Consuela del Campo—Student onboard Thalia Buoyant Island. Daughter of Basilio.

Mikhail Voronin—Subcommander of Clementine Cislunar Fuel Depot.

Zephyr Andrew Calimeris, MFA—Author. Passenger aboard I.R.V. *Intercession.*

William Henry Voss-Hughins, PhD-CPHP—U.S. Department of Behavioral Health. Passenger aboard I.R.V. *Intercession.*

Sir Lawrence Edgar Killian—Founder and CEO of Harvest Moon Industries, including Second Morning Retirement Community. One of the Four Horsemen.

Gill Davis—Personal assistant to Lawrence Edgar Killian.

LadyCaffeine—User of the Weightless social network. Student, University of Hawaii.

Lars Onsanger, MSSE—Associate Professor of Structural Engineering, Columbia University. Secretly, an asset of the Central Intelligence Agency.

Joona Lao—Linguist. Passenger aboard I.R.V. *Intercession.*

Bryan Parr—Ambassador. Passenger aboard I.R.V. *Intercession.*

Adam Parr—Ambassador. Passenger aboard I.R.V. *Intercession*.

Raimy Vaught—Director of Lunar Public Safety for Harvest Moon Industries.

Trish Spofford—EOLS pilot for Harvest Moon Industries. Call sign "Mayflower."

Johnny Zee Adams—Former rock star and shoe entrepreneur, now resident at Second Morning Retirement Community, Lunar South Polar Mineral Territories.

Clazz—Former singer/supermodel, now resident at Second Morning Retirement Community.

Lydia Harris—Career philanthropist, now resident at Second Morning Retirement Community.

Ju Xue—former robotics entrepreneur, now resident at Second Morning Retirement Community.

Xiaoran Xue-Jones—Husband of Ju Xue, now resident at Second Morning Retirement Community.

Egil Vitgås—Former liquor industry mogul, now resident at Second Morning Retirement Community.

Huntley Millar—EVA Crew Chief for Harvest Moon Industries.

Matt Lang, PhD—U.S. National Aeronautics and Space Administration. Passenger aboard I.R.V. *Intercession*.

Noemi del Campo—Horticulturist for Thalia Buoyant Island. Wife of Basilio.

Candide Nunez-Talamantes—Wife of Tohias, mother of Diego.

Appendix B
NOTES

Notes for Thread 1

Part of the genesis of this series came from listening to people who'd smoked DMT. I've never taken the drug myself, and I probably never will, even though it's now legal in my home state of Colorado. Psychedelics in general are a bit too profound for my taste. Many of them, like LSD and ketamine, provide the sensation of "going" somewhere outside the 4D spacetime we normally experience, which is already something I don't care to do. However, DMT adds a very specific wrinkle, in that a majority of people taking high doses report contact with "entities" of some sort, who are generally seen as benevolent or even divine. So my thought was, okay, well, what if that's actually real? What if it's an authentic experience of alien contact? People often describe "little people" of various kinds, including "self-transforming machine elves" (see https://www.iflscience.com/why-do-people-see-elves-and-other-entities-when-they-smoke-dmt-62234). So in that sense, the Beings are rooted in actual science. My thought was that these "elves" may not be the Beings themselves, but constructs that allow them to speak with us. However, since time and space (at least as we understand them) don't seem to apply in the realm of the DMT entities, the experience seems very difficult to put into words. It also becomes an interesting question, what we and the Beings could possibly have in common. So, it seemed to me, from the earliest stages of the project, that the only way to describe the Beings would be through multiple fragmentary accounts of people with different kinds of preconceptions. I hope I've done justice to that vision here.

For what it's worth, my own conception of the Beings is that they're basically software (specifically, cellular automata) running directly on the "spin networks" of loop quantum gravity. As such, they're not made of matter or energy, and do not occupy a volume of spacetime per se. If we think of spacetime as a holographic movie display, the Beings exist on the processor that's generating the image, not in the image itself. However, they can "look at" (i.e., receive

307

information from) portions of the hologram, within certain conserved limits. They can also influence events within the spacetime they're looking at, although as we've seen, their signals are both weak and noisy. This works both ways, as the Beings are only able to "see" or "hear" the minds of human beings when those minds are forced into a non-4D context. The "DMT elves" are images the Beings have learned to inject into the human brain under these very specific conditions. So there. You now know what a hundred *Intercession* passengers could only see fragmentary glimpses of.

Regarding "the dismal science," some nexuses (nexi?) of economics (looking at you, Austria, Chicago, and Virginia!) object to the term, even when it's used ironically. The term apparently may have pro-slavery origins, as well as allusions to theories of Malthus that have simply not panned out. However, "dismal" is a good and evocative description, and I believe most economists still use it.

Notes for Thread 2
Orlov's beloved 101955 Bennu is a real, Earth-crossing asteroid, with a definitely nonzero chance of someday slamming into the Earth, generating a crater 10 kilometers wide and laying waste to everything within 50+ kilometers. More, if it landed in the ocean. However, to put that in perspective, the asteroid that killed the dinosaurs was probably about 25,000 times larger, so we are not talking about an extinction-level event. Just a really, really bad one.

Notes for Thread 3
Exploding one kilogram of TNT releases about 4 million joules of energy, equivalent to a 0.1 milligram object moving at 9 million meters per second. A bullet fired from a standard 7.62 mm cartridge carries roughly 3,500 joules of kinetic energy, so when *Intercession*'s particle shield collides with a 0.1 milligram particle, it releases the energy of roughly 1,142 machine-gun bullets.

The most likely solid material in interstellar space would be water ice, and a 0.1 milligram particle of it would be very approximately half a millimeter in diameter. For comparison, "sand" is defined as particles between 0.065 and 2.0 millimeters, all of which are readily visible to the naked eye. So we're talking about a fairly large object.

The spot cast by a laser pointer can indeed travel faster than light.

If you wave it back and forth by one meter every second, you are moving through an arc of atan(1/10)= 5.71 degrees. That same arc, over a range of ten million kilometers, makes the spot travel a distance of 1 million kilometers in a second, which is more than three times the speed of light.

Yes, this book was written before the release of GPT4, and yes, it could be argued that after thirty-five years of additional progress, the AI concierges in this story should be a lot more advanced. However, what GPT4 and its brethren are good at is *sounding* like a human. They are basically a very advanced version of the predictive text feature on your smartphone keyboard. They don't actually understand what they're saying, or what you're saying. That's a much harder problem. Also, how smart and self-aware do you want your concierge to be, exactly? Enough to destroy the Earth? Get off my back, man.

Notes for Thread 4

The alloy I've named "feptaual" (Fe Pt Au Al) is somewhat speculative, although the components of it are not. If you mix aluminum with gold, you really do get a bright purple, somewhat brittle material, and mixing iron with gold really does yield a metal ranging anywhere from faint bluish-greenish to a very shockingly saturated royal blue. Platinum is denser than gold, and if you mix the two together you get a whitish metal that is nearly as wear-resistant as diamond and sapphire. So yeah, there probably is a purple-gray alloy of iron, platinum, gold, and aluminum that has properties similar to those I've described.

There really are backpack nukes, with explosive power of anywhere from 10 to 1,000 tons of TNT (0.001 to 1.0 kilotons), that weigh less than 30 kilograms. Most of the effects we associate with nuclear explosions—fireballs, blast waves, mushroom clouds, etc.) are actually the effects of extreme local heating of the atmosphere. In space, a nuclear explosion is basically a single burst of light, heat, gamma radiation, and neutrons, whose intensity drops off with the square of the distance. Weirdly, in space the radiation effects of a nuke are much more problematic than the heat it releases, because the atmosphere is also not there to absorb (and be ionized by) the radiation.

Wil McCarthy

The self-destruct nuke of the stealth ship is around 0.01 kilotons. As shown in the graph below, this is more than enough to completely vaporize both the ship and any human beings within 20 meters of it. However, these effects drop off so rapidly that beyond 150 meters, exposed flesh (e.g., behind an unshielded glass visor) may not even be seriously burned. Unfortunately for our astronauts, the radiation effects extend much farther, so that at a range of 300 meters, an unshielded human will receive a one hundred percent lethal dose, and the chance of death remains at fifty percent even half a kilometer from the explosion.

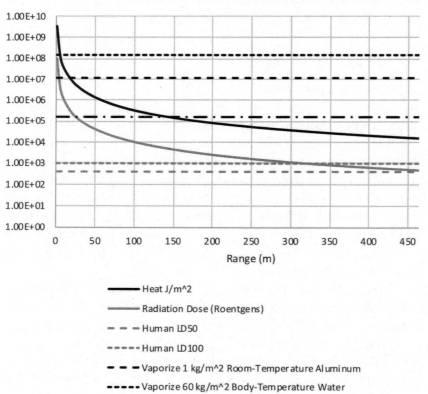

Vacuum Effects of 0.01kT "Backpack Nuke"

Legend:
- Heat J/m^2
- Radiation Dose (Roentgens)
- Human LD50
- Human LD100
- Vaporize 1 kg/m^2 Room-Temperature Aluminum
- Vaporize 60 kg/m^2 Body-Temperature Water
- Second-Degree Burns to Exposed Human Tissue

If you'd like to learn more, check out:
https://en.wikipedia.org/wiki/W54
https://history.nasa.gov/conghand/nuclear.htm

Notes for Thread 5

To be clear, the colonization of the Venusian atmosphere is not my idea. It has been well studied by NASA scientists, including my friend Geoff Landis, who has also written science fiction stories about it. At an altitude of around 55 kilometers, the average temperature of the Venusian atmosphere is around 27 degrees Celsius (81°F), with an air pressure of around 530 millibars—about what you'd get on a summer day on top of Mount Elbert in Colorado. At this pressure, even a normal air gas mix is quite breathable, and in fact it's actually a lifting gas, like helium is on Earth. I will note that temperature, pressure, and cloud height could vary considerably with local weather conditions and time of "day," but (except for the composition of the atmosphere) the conditions would stay well within Earthlike parameters.

The breath masks worn by the colonists work by filtering and cracking the Venusian air, which doesn't contain much nontoxic filler gas such as nitrogen or argon. As a result, the air inside the masks is probably about 95 percent oxygen, 3.5 percent nitrogen, and 1.5 percent CO_2, with assorted other gases in the parts per million. This is triple the OSHA limit for long-exposure CO_2, and also a potentially unsafe amount of oxygen, and if sulfur dioxide leaked in at even 3 percent of its atmospheric concentration, that would exceed OSHA levels as well. However, this mix is "breathable" in a strict metabolic sense, and even one full breath of Actual Venus every now and then wouldn't kill you, although it would certainly not feel good.

The "*carbónespuma* pavement" of Thalia is a closed-cell graphene aerogel with hydrogen gas trapped in its voids. Even on Earth this would be lighter than air, and capable of lifting about 1.2 kilograms per cubic meter. CO_2 is much heavier than oxygen or nitrogen, though, and the gravity of Venus is a bit lighter, so on Venus the pavement can lift more like 2.0 kg/m^3, or more if the material expands a bit when exposed to sunlight (which is twice as strong on Venus as it is on Earth).

Notes on Thread 6

Second Morning Retirement Community should be well shielded against background radiation, although the residents (even if they take their radiation pills) will still need to retreat into deeper shelters

Wil McCarthy

during a major solar flare. However, since many effects of radiation exposure (e.g., increased cancer rates) take years or decades to show up, the retirees have less reason to worry about it than the staff.

Additional Notes
I feel like enough has been said about the colonization of Mars, or rather that I myself didn't have anything new to say about it that merited inclusion in this book. I might feel differently in the future. However, I would like to correct an error I made in the Mars-related chapters of a previous book: magnetic field strength drops off with the *cube* of the distance, not the square.

Acknowledgments

Lakewood, Colorado, USA
Earth Surface

I'd like, once again, to thank Toni Weisskopf for taking a chance on this series, and the whole team at Baen for helping bring it into the world as a series of physical objects people can actually buy. Engineer extraordinaire Gary Edwin Snyder is responsible for many of the ideas in this book, and for answering urgent technical questions at all hours of the day and night. Early, horrible drafts of this book were endured by Marie DesJardin, Ember Randall, Glen Cox, Pat Smythe, Peter Sartucci, Eneasz Brodski, Ronnie Seagren, and Ondine Winkless. The later drafts were helped along by Bruce Hall, Kathee Jones, Greg Hyde, and John Morse. I also owe great thanks to Dave Seeley, whose cover art was so meticulously imagined that it forced me to rewrite the text in places. This particular book *can* be judged by its cover.

Special thanks also to John Barnes and Connie Willis for moral support, and to Evangeline for, you know, everything.